T0278755

PRINCE *of* FORTUNE

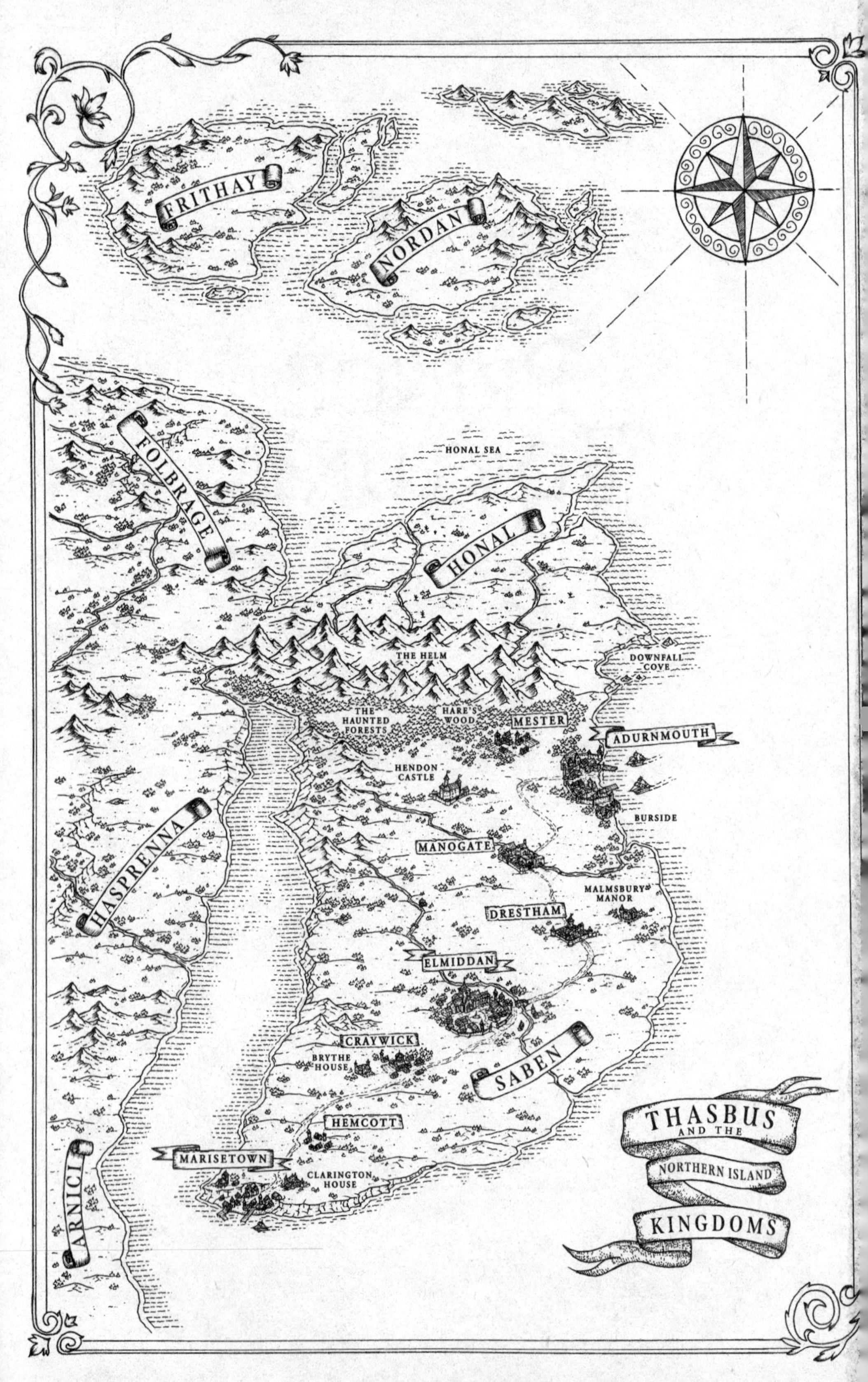
FRITHAY
NORDAN
HONAL SEA
FOLBRAGE
HONAL
THE HELM
DOWNFALL COVE
THE HAUNTED FORESTS
HARE'S WOOD
MESTER
ADURNMOUTH
HENDON CASTLE
BURSIDE
HASPRENNA
MANOGATE
MALMSBURY MANOR
DRESTHAM
ELMIDDAN
CRAYWICK
BRYTHE HOUSE
SABEN
HEMCOTT
MARISETOWN
CLARINGTON HOUSE
ARNICI
THASBUS
AND THE
NORTHERN ISLAND
KINGDOMS

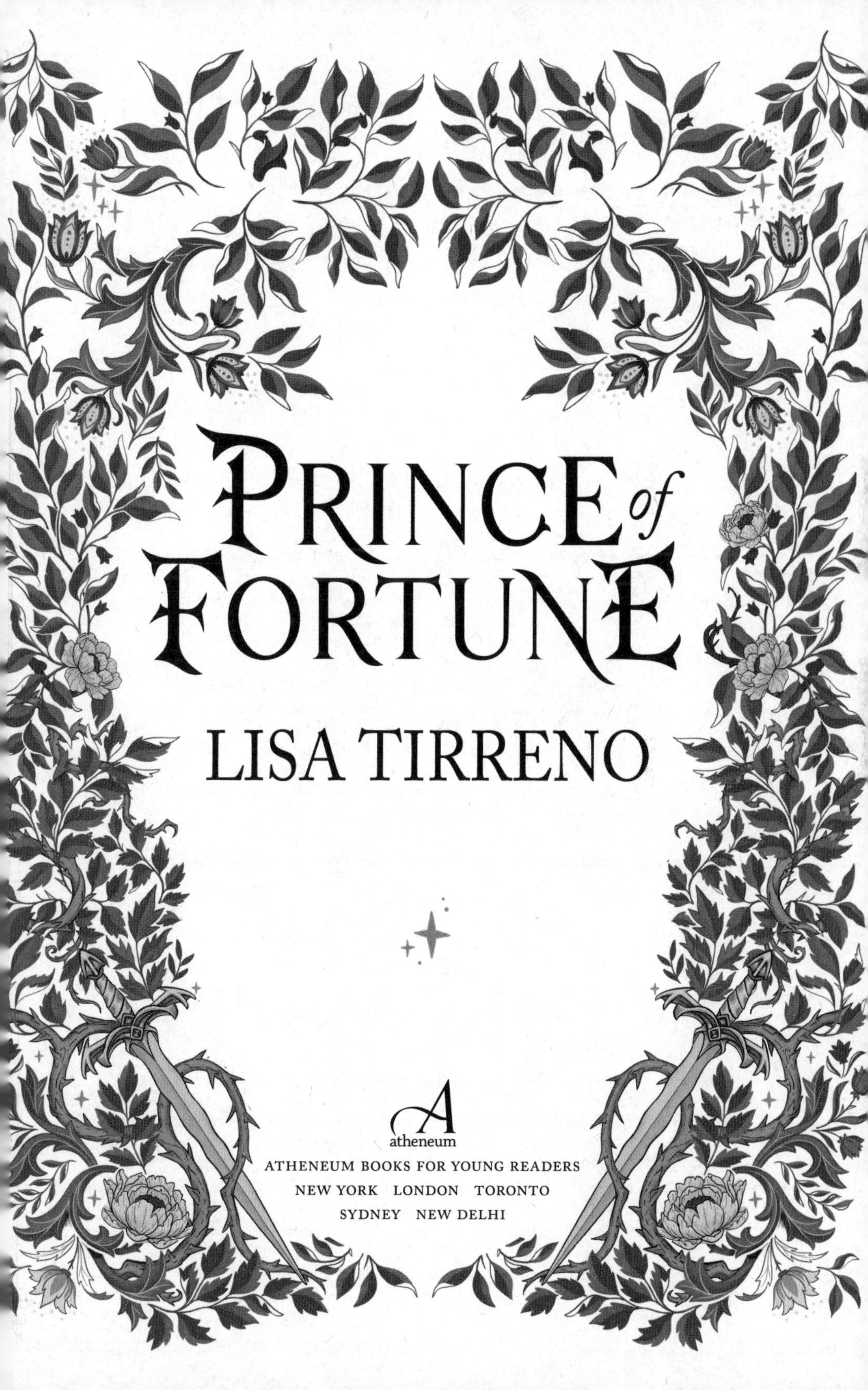

PRINCE *of* FORTUNE

LISA TIRRENO

atheneum

ATHENEUM BOOKS FOR YOUNG READERS
NEW YORK LONDON TORONTO
SYDNEY NEW DELHI

An imprint of Simon & Schuster Children's Publishing Division
1230 Avenue of the Americas, New York, New York 10020
This book is a work of fiction. Any references to historical events, real people, or real places are used fictitiously. Other names, characters, places, and events are products of the author's imagination, and any resemblance to actual events or places or persons, living or dead, is entirely coincidental.

Jacket design by Rebecca Syracuse

Simon & Schuster: Celebrating 100 Years of Publishing in 2024
For information about special discounts for bulk purchases,
please contact Simon & Schuster Special Sales at 1-866-506-1949
or business@simonandschuster.com.
The Simon & Schuster Speakers Bureau can bring authors to your live event.
For more information or to book an event, contact the Simon & Schuster Speakers Bureau
at 1-866-248-3049 or visit our website at www.simonspeakers.com.
Interior design by Lisa Vega
The text for this book was set in Adobe Caslon Pro.
Manufactured in the United States of America
First Edition
2 4 6 8 10 9 7 5 3 1
Library of Congress Cataloging-in-Publication Data
Names: Tirreno, Lisa, author.
Title: Prince of fortune / Lisa Tirreno.
Description: First edition. | New York : Atheneum Books for Young Readers, 2024. | Audience: Ages 14 up. | Summary: Shy Prince Edmund, gifted with rare magic and burdened by his nation's expectations, finds unexpected love with the Seer Lord Aubrey Ainsley, and together they must overcome war and dark sorcery to save their homeland.
Identifiers: LCCN 2024002308 | ISBN 9781665957786 (hardcover) | ISBN 9781665957809 (ebook)
Subjects: CYAC: Magic—Fiction. | Ability—Fiction. | Princes—Fiction. | LGBTQ+ people—Fiction. | Romance stories. | Fantasy. | BISAC: YOUNG ADULT FICTION / Romance / LGBTQ+ | YOUNG ADULT FICTION / Action & Adventure / General | LCGFT: Romance fiction. | Fantasy fiction.
Classification: LCC PZ7.1.T5757 Pr 2024 | DDC [Fic]—dc23
LC record available at https://lccn.loc.gov/2024002308

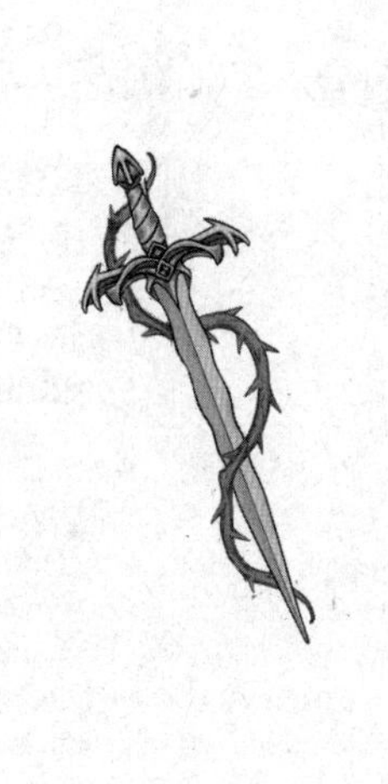

RECURRING CHARACTERS

SABEN

The Royal Family

His Majesty King Theodore

Her Highness Queen Margaret

His Highness Crown Prince Edmund, Prince of Fortune:
their son

Her Highness Princess Alicia:
their daughter

His Highness Prince Willard:
the king's older brother, a widower

Her Highness Princess Charlotte:
his only child

His Highness Prince Henri:
her betrothed

The Ainsleys and Their Circle

Lord John Ainsley:
baronet and educational reformer

Lady Mary Ainsley:
his wife, a former lieutenant in the Sabresian army

Lord John Ainsley:
their eldest son

Lord Cedric Ainsley:
their second son, a Seer

Lord Wilson Ainsley:
their third son

Lord Aubrey Ainsley:
their fourth son, a Seer

Captain Charles Mayhew (deceased):
Lady Ainsley's older brother, a Seer

Dorothea Mayhew:
Lady Ainsley's younger sister, an attorney, resides in the capital

Lady Harriet Malmsbury:
the Ainsleys' neighbor

Lord James Malmsbury (Malmy):
her great-nephew; viscount, rake, poet

Royal Staff

Sir Jenson Frenric (Sir J):
the crown prince's personal secretary

Mattheson:
the crown prince's valet

Sir Omar:
the royal surgeon

Mrs. Grant:
magical training instructor, distant cousin to the royal family

Politicians and Bureaucrats

Lord Dell:
prime minister of Saben

Mr. Young:
his secretary

Dame Edwina:
Saben's minister for foreign affairs and diplomacy

Mr. Prestan:
Saben's minister for defense

Sir Welby:
Sabresian ambassador to Nordan

The War

Commanding General Wren

Colonel Sutherton:
commanding officer at Craywick

Colonel Wyclef:
commanding officer at Manogate

Ensign Stephens:
a soldier in Aubrey's unit

Ensign Rosalie Tsung:
a soldier in Aubrey's unit

HONAL

The Pater:
an appointed leader and sorcerer

The Penitent:
an appointed leader and sorceress

The Cultivator:
an appointed leader and sorcerer

The General:
an appointed leader and sorcerer

CHAPTER 1

If Lord Aubrey Ainsley had known when he tied his cravat that the evening he was dressing for was going to change the course of his life, he probably would have picked a more complicated knot.

This is not to say that his cravat looked sloppy. His cravat had never looked sloppy in his life, and he had been even more careful than usual about his appearance tonight, since he was about to visit Talstam Palace for the first time and was just about bursting over it. But being only sixteen and the fourth son of a mere country baronet with a courtesy title, it hadn't occurred to him that his actions might affect his country's future.

"It'll be the prince's turn next, I daresay," he heard his aunt saying from the landing. They were staying in her town house for the visit. Like almost everyone in the Sabresian capital, she adored gossiping about high society. Aubrey had cracked the door of his bedchamber open in the hopes of hearing something worth listening to. "He's the oldest unmarried royal, now that his cousin Charlotte is spoken for. I still can't believe the king managed to persuade you to come to Elmiddan for this ball he's hosting for the engagement, though, John. We all know how little love you have for visiting the capital. Or anywhere."

"Yes, well." Aubrey's father, Lord John Ainsley, pitched his voice sardonically light as usual. "His letter was too pathetic. *Boo-hoo, it's going to be so boring; everybody is going to have to be on their best behavior so as not to offend those snooty Hasprennans.* I told him to just get drunk, but he said he *can't* because he's the *king*, and so all his friends had to come and save him."

His father was leaving out the best part, as far as Aubrey was concerned, because the king had asked after *him* especially. Aubrey had memorized that bit of the letter. *Surely your youngest is ready to be out in society? He and Edmund should finally meet. Do make sure to bring him, old bean. The poor lad must be sick of the countryside by now.*

The idea that the king wanted him to meet his son and had somehow known that yes, Aubrey was indeed desperate to be out in society, was very gratifying, even if Aubrey wasn't actually that fussed about meeting Prince Edmund. His brothers had all met him and reported that he barely had a word to say for himself and tended to spend half his time at events listening to the wind or wandering around touching plants. Aubrey didn't object to him touching plants—the young man was a Prince of Fortune, after all, and so that was to be expected—but Aubrey wasn't terribly interested in people who had no conversation. Princess Alicia, his sister, was supposed to be lively, but at fourteen, she was too young to be "out" and so wouldn't be at the ball. Still, Aubrey would get to visit the palace and meet people, and the royals who were there would be performing their magic, which he was looking forward to most of all.

He reached for the pomade—he thought the citrus one would be best for tonight—while Aunt Dorothea continued her chatter. "Well, now that Charlotte is strengthening ties with Hasprenna, it will be interesting to see who the parliament pushes Prince Edmund toward. Folbrage might complain if it's another Hasprennan."

"Yes, one of the papers ran a piece on that a few days ago," his mother replied, "listing possible marriage candidates from various countries, and which of them were coming. Seems a lot of pressure for the boy."

Aubrey inspected himself one last time in the looking glass. He had woken up with dark circles under his eyes because he'd had a vision-dream in the night—nothing specifically useful, just the same half-seen imagery of horses and soldiers and gunfire he often Saw: the coming war that so many Seers kept Seeing, but nobody really knew anything about yet. Aubrey's reflection reassured him that he now looked perfectly well, however, so he went out to join the adults.

"I'm ready!" he announced, and everyone smiled at him.

The room was elegant and modern, like the rest of the house. His parents were perched carefully on the edge of a silk sofa so as not to crease their finery before the night had even begun. Aunt Dorothea had not needed to worry about that, since she would not be joining them—the event was too exclusive—and so she was sprawled on a chaise longue in a dressing robe and slippers, all set for a night in.

"The prince is supposed to be very responsible," she went on. "He certainly appears very sober and serious whenever I've seen glimpses of him. You know the family best, John. What do you think?"

"Prince Edmund is not yet seventeen years old, the same as Aubrey," his father said, waving his hand at him. "Can you guess how Aubrey's life will turn out? I cannot."

"Of course I can," Aunt Dorothea said. "Aubrey will run off with a poet, and they will collaborate together in a charming old cottage in the woods with a falling-down roof, surrounded by birds and wildflowers, and pay every bill late, but nobody will even care, because they will all love him."

She winked at him.

"That seems . . . specific," Aubrey said. "But thank you, that sounds very promising."

"Yes," his brother Wilson said, coming out of the guest room he was using. "Being romantic and disreputable would sound promising to you. Try to behave yourself tonight, won't you?"

He had said "romantic" as though it were a bad thing. Aubrey looked at his brother and frowned. "Did you mean to tie your cravat like that?" he asked.

"Do fix that for him, dearest," their mother said.

Wilson huffed but submitted to Aubrey's ministrations; a mere few tweaks and tugs, but the result was still more pleasing than Wilson, despite being two years older, had managed on his own. Aubrey attempted to also fix his hair but was pushed away.

Their two eldest brothers, John and Cedric, came out just in time to see it.

"How's mine?" John asked, turning his head this way and that ostentatiously in front of Cedric.

"Better than Wilson's," Cedric said. "But that is not much of a standard, I suppose."

Wilson let out an annoyed grunt and headed down the stairs. Cedric smirked with all the confidence of someone who would not be riding in the same carriage as him and followed.

Aubrey *did* have to ride with Wilson. Being younger, the two of them went in the black family carriage with their parents, while John and Cedric got to borrow their aunt's smaller coach, which was very dashing in white and yellow and seated only two.

It was a fine autumn evening, so everyone on the roads had their carriage hoods down. That suited Aubrey. He wanted to see *everything* the capital had to show him: the street vendors, the widely paved footpaths, the floral window boxes some of the smart new town houses sported. And the *clothes.* Feathers seemed to have come into fashion for women's hats, and meanwhile nearly all the younger men walking the streets were wearing their pants so tight, Aubrey hardly knew where to look.

And then, finally—Talstam Palace. He had only seen it at a distance before on the handful of occasions he had been brought to Elmiddan. Stately and elegant, the residence had been updated by King Theodore's father and was therefore a reasonably modern building of three stories in pale stone, plus attics under a shapely gray roof, with lower wings off to each side in a pleasing symmetry. A large, tiered fountain in an older style still stood at the front, giving a feeling of history. As they got closer, however, Aubrey started thinking of beehives, since the entrance was crawling with guards and grooms and guests. The family joined the queue of carriages going up the drive and waited.

And waited some more.

Eventually, Aubrey slumped in his seat, thunking the back of his head against the wooden top for good measure.

"I'm going to *die,*" he declared. "I've waited my whole life to be out in proper society, and now the palace is *right there,* and I'm going to be a hundred years old before we get inside. Can we not get out and walk?"

"Walking is something people do in the countryside," his father said. "Along with talking *to* people rather than about them, and caring *for* their neighbors rather than just about what they're wearing. The amount of silk and jewels I can see from here—the woman in that carriage is wearing enough to pay to set up at least two new schools, and teachers besides."

"Lean over and tell her so, Father," Aubrey said. "I'm sure she'll whip it all off and hand everything over for the cause."

"She could *hear you*," Wilson hissed at this point, a little frantic. "Father, *please*."

Lord Ainsley went to say something else, but Lady Ainsley patted the back of his hand in a suppressive manner, and he subsided. Aubrey did the same to Wilson and found himself once again pushed away. He wished Cedric or John had come in this carriage. Waiting with them would have been much more fun.

He looked out to the other side instead, since something seemed to be happening there. A crowd had gathered a block or two in the distance, and soldiers from the city guard were moving toward it. He heard shouting starting up from that direction.

"I wonder what that is?" he asked, pointing.

His father glanced over. "Protestors. They often target royal events, since members of the press will be around."

"What are they protesting?" Wilson asked. He sounded outraged.

Their father gave him a look. "I can think of four recent government policies worth shouting in the streets over, just off the top of my head. We should go and *join* them."

"Or," his wife put in, "you could speak directly to all the relevant MPs at the ball, where you've been given privileged access to them. There are a few things I plan to bring up myself if I get the chance."

Her husband huffed, but Aubrey caught him smiling as he turned his face away.

When they finally got into the palace, the family could barely see where they were going for the people, each one as splendidly dressed as his father had lamented. It was all Aubrey could do not to bounce on his toes. They were announced, and then Aubrey was following his parents into the ballroom proper, which was the largest room he had ever seen. It was, in fact, so large that Aubrey found himself wondering if his family's entire house would fit inside. He ended up deciding that yes, it would; and probably Aunt Dorothea's town house besides.

He caught sight of at least half a dozen fireplaces, all carved elaborately in a different color of stone. He made a mental note to visit the ones farthest away from him, which looked large enough to walk around in and which he suspected were from an older version of the room, left over from a time in which great wild boars or sides of game would have been roasted in them whole.

The wall closest to them was dotted with paintings in scrolled frames. Aubrey recognized some of them from books or prints in his father's library. He had had no idea that the original artworks would be here—it felt a little bit like bumping into an old friend. One showed his ancestor Queen Helen in a floor-length royal blue robe and matching headdress, a sword sheathed at her hip and a feathery quill in her hand: symbology referring to her famous treaty. Farther down was a battle scene in lush oils: the final clash of the last war that Saben had fought with Honal, almost a hundred years ago. He turned to point out the paintings to his older brothers—they would be more interested in them than Wilson—but Cedric had meandered away with a pair of well-dressed young men he must have known from university; and meanwhile John was already halfway across the room with their father.

Aubrey spent a second wondering what he would do if Wilson and his mother also walked off and left him, when they were spotted by a friend of Lady Ainsley's, a Mrs. Follett, who swept the three of them into the group she was with. Aubrey bowed and nodded politely, but before he had much more than an impression of satin and sapphires, a herald-type person announced that the king and his family were very glad to welcome everyone to the ball with a display of their magical skill. Aubrey's delight must have shown, because Mrs. Follett gave him a wry look through her lorgnette.

"This is your first time, isn't it, my young lord," she said to him, and started waving the spectacles around for emphasis, "so you don't know how oddly these performances always go. The king and queen traditionally do theirs first because of precedence, but I do wonder why they don't insist on going last so the others aren't embarrassed."

Aubrey didn't really know what the woman could mean, since magic was magic and he wanted to see as much of it as he could. It would not do, however, to contradict her. He did not want his mother to decide he wasn't ready for society after all. He set his attention instead on King Theodore and Queen Margaret, who were now walking up the stairs of some sort of dais on the side of the room.

They did not wear crowns, and yet something about them looked regal; or perhaps that was just Aubrey's fancy. It was the first time he was seeing them in person rather than in the newspapers or, in the king's case, minted onto a coin. The two of them didn't resemble each other, even though they were first cousins. Aubrey started running through what he could remember of their family tree in his head. King Theodore's mother had been an Arnician princess, Aubrey recalled, which accounted for his coloring—he was all dark curls and browned olive skin, whereas Queen Margaret's creamy complexion looked like she would burn on a hot day as much as he and his own family would—but then the queen grinned over at her husband, and Aubrey stopped thinking about bloodlines.

"Oh my," his own mother said, next to him. Aubrey considered this a vast understatement.

The queen had crooked her finger, and a huge creature of flames leapt from one of the oversized fireplaces down at the end of the room and started to gambol around back and forth on the ceiling, as though searching for something. It undulated through all the shades of a roaring fire, red and orange in some parts, a yellow so pale it was almost white in others, changing constantly. Aubrey was bouncing on his toes now—he couldn't help himself—and wondering if King Theodore could also do something so strange and wonderful, when the king created a creature of his own in a great showy gesture, as though pulling from the faraway flames with a giant, invisible rope. The firebeasts started chasing each other around the ceiling, leading to a great deal of gasping from the crowd, and then they solidified a little more clearly into dragons, the symbol of the royal family.

They started looping each other, blowing flames and snapping their jaws, until one darted in to rub its cheek against the other's. Aubrey thought that one was the king's. The two creatures were blending into each other now, and then they headed for the far side of the room, settling down in one of the larger fireplaces together, embracing. People started to applaud; Aubrey joined in as enthusiastically as he dared in such a sophisticated crowd.

"Our courtship," the king joked, which made everyone clap harder, laughing.

Aubrey's heart was racing. He wished his parents had brought him to the capital years ago; he felt like the world's possibilities had been remade in front of him. He had grown up knowing that the king and queen both had strong magical gifts, giving them some control over the four elements. Seeing their abilities in person was different. This was why Theodore was the king rather than his brother, Prince Willard, who was the firstborn, but who could only manipulate water. Aubrey knew from the schoolroom that Margaret had also been considered as the next monarch, but as a niece of the previous king rather than a direct descendant, she had been considered less suitable. He wondered at that now, because they appeared—to his untrained eye, at least—to be evenly matched.

Aubrey hoped they would be running through all four elements so that he could see if they were a match in each one, but then the king and queen waved to the crowd and headed for the stairs. He was promising himself that he would quiz his father on the topic later when Mrs. Follett startled him by letting out a tutting noise.

"The young prince is hiding again," she said, motioning to a figure just visible behind a set of large potted plants that were now being carried up to the stage by an army of footmen.

The last pot was cleared out of the way, and that was when Aubrey forgot all about elemental magic, because he had just gotten a clear look at Edmund, Crown Prince of Saben.

He was well worth looking at.

Aubrey could see why his aunt had said he seemed serious. He had big, dark eyes that seemed to take in everything that was happening on the stage. His coloring met in the middle of his parents, giving him lighter brown curls than his father's and skin that, though still a rich olive, hadn't tanned so darkly as the king's. But where the king and queen had been confident and full of smiles, the prince looked tense and nervous even at this distance, his posture stiff and his hands curled. Aubrey's heart bled for him. He thought of everything that his brothers (who were clearly blind and dim-witted) had said about him: how he was socially awkward and barely spoke.

"He's shy," Aubrey said, almost a question.

Mrs. Follett nodded. "The poor young buck. Although perhaps I'd hide as well. His parents are a hard act to follow, especially when his powers are—well. He's hardly a dragon, ready to wipe out whole Honal armies for us with the wave of his hand, is he?"

Aubrey felt Wilson stiffen next to him, but then his mother said, "Blowing away enemy troops is all very well, but none of the rest of them could have done anything like, say, cleaning up that problem with the potato crops the country had two or three years ago. A lot of people would have gone hungry if His Highness hadn't intervened."

"Yes, well, I hope those pots aren't full of rotting potatoes," Mrs. Follett said, peering at them. "Last time I saw him, we were all outside in the daylight, and he made a double rainbow appear for us. That was at least *pretty*. But what's he going to do here?"

Aubrey bit his lip. He had known Prince Edmund's magic was different from the rest of the royal family's. A Prince of Fortune had some control over the weather, the crops. It was rare as well as useful; no one had borne the title in centuries. But what would that mean tonight? And how stressful must it be for that quiet young man to have to stand up and perform in front of people like Mrs. Follett? Aubrey realized he was furrowing his brow and forced his face to relax. Wrinkles.

The prince took off one of his gloves and set his hand into the first pot. Aubrey held his breath, and then there was a collective "oooh" from the crowd. The plant was growing and sending up thin flower spikes before their eyes. Aubrey, however, had almost missed seeing it. He had been focused on the prince's faraway expression, rather than the miracle he was performing.

Prince Edmund moved on to the next plant and then the next, the plants blooming more readily each time. It was like something from a dream, Aubrey thought, much quieter than the king and queen's performance but no less astonishing. They were lavender, a long-stemmed variety. Everyone started clapping politely, and Aubrey joined in. Just as he was thinking that he'd like to get a sprig for his mother, since it was her favorite plant, the herald announced that the shoots would be cut during the evening, and made available for anyone who would like a souvenir from the ball. People clapped more enthusiastically after that.

Meanwhile, the prince had bobbed his head and almost run off the stage to the stairs.

"Dozens of prophecies about what a wonderful king he's going to be," Mrs. Follett said, "and he can't even bow properly. Ah—and speaking of poor manners . . ."

The woman's tone had switched to something that was almost vicious, and Aubrey stopped trying to see where the crown prince had gone and turned his attention back to the stage.

A gray-haired older man was walking up the stairs. He did not look much like the king, but this must be his brother, Prince Willard. His eyes appeared lighter from here, his skin paler, as though he didn't see as much sun, but that wasn't the main difference between them. King Theodore had an easy, hearty energy about him that seemed to invite one to watch him, whereas Prince Willard . . . did not. As he was introduced by the herald, he wasn't even smiling, just waving in a vague, floppy sort of way at the crowd.

He took off his gloves, much as Prince Edmund had, and waved again. He had a strange mark on the back of his right hand, leading around the side and disappearing up his sleeve.

Aubrey turned to his mother, tapping his own hand in the same place. Before he could ask the question, she answered it with "Prince Willard saw action at Folbrage. We were even in one of the same battles.

That scar on his hand is from an explosive device he didn't freeze in time."

He looked back, feeling emboldened to stare since the mark was a sign of heroism. The prince was now motioning sharply at footmen in livery who were bringing up silver basins. He made a twitchy, impatient movement to dismiss them, and then Aubrey was distracted from all the ways he wasn't like King Theodore, because clouds of steam pouring up from the basins suddenly obscured him from the crowd's sight.

Everybody made interested noises. The cloud started swirling into a tighter configuration, and then it was raining down over the stage as something like hail. Prince Willard, visible again, had his arms out. He dropped them in acknowledgment as the crowd started clapping, but then he walked off the stage every bit as quickly as his nephew had.

Footmen came up to sweep the ice away.

Aubrey's confusion and disappointment must have shown in his face, because his mother bumped him with her shoulder and said, "Yes, that was a bit quick, wasn't it? It doesn't help that he gave up smiling after his wife died, but Willard never was as good with a crowd as the king and queen. Like the crown prince, he's not much of a performer."

Aubrey wanted to say something about how, actually, the two hadn't seemed remotely alike. The Prince of Fortune had looked like he needed to be reassured he had done a good job and cheered up, whereas Prince Willard had seemed oddly incongruous. He should surely have had enough experience with this sort of thing to be past the nerves that his nephew had exhibited. Aubrey kept these thoughts to himself, however, since he knew he'd sound ridiculous. He'd never met either man.

He changed the subject instead. "Over there, is that Princess Charlotte with her fiancé? Prince Henri looks much more the picture of a prince than her father."

Mrs. Follett's eyes lit up with malicious delight, and he quickly added, "Oh, I didn't mean that to be unkind—"

"No, no!" she said. "You are quite right, my lord. He does, doesn't he? He's all strong shoulders and square jawline; we can feel his presence from here. Not like Limp Wi—"

"The king wrote to John about Prince Henri," Lady Ainsley interjected. "His Majesty said Charlotte is well satisfied with the match, and that the government was very pleased, since he is one of the Hasprennan crown prince's younger sons. Look at her. She's glowing."

Aubrey looked; Princess Charlotte was in the center of the dais now, waiting more patiently than her father had for a line of servants to set up a round table and place pitchers of water on it. The princess nodded, and her assistants started pouring the water into a silver basin.

The princess looked nothing like Prince Willard. Her hair was a light brown, and her skin was reasonably fair—Aubrey thought that she must have gotten that from her mother and wondered at how little she resembled the rest of the royal family—but then suddenly her face had the same dreamy look that had come over Prince Edmund's when he had made his first plant grow. Ice started rising on the table.

The servants poured and poured the water, and a shape started to emerge as the princess moved her hands gracefully: winged creatures, like the king's and queen's, but this time there was a great eagle—Hasprenna's symbol—embracing a dragon. Aubrey watched, thinking that the sculpture wasn't just an impressive display of natural-born talent at making things freeze, the way her father's had been. It was art.

"That's beautifully rendered," he said. "She makes that seem so natural, but she must practice a lot."

"Yes, indeed," Mrs. Follett said, sounding surprised. "Clearly having this settled is good for her. I've never seen her make anything like that.

And I hear the wedding ceremony will be held in Hasprenna?"

Lady Ainsley said something in agreement that Aubrey didn't quite catch, since music started up at that point. It took Aubrey a moment or two to place the piece, because it sounded so much better performed here by professional musicians than at their neighbor's house, played by their nine-year-old daughter on an aging spinet.

"It won't be long, and we'll all be here for another of these, I'm sure," Mrs. Follett said. "The family will certainly be making plans for a match for the crown prince soon. Has the king said anything about it, Mary?"

Lady Ainsley shook her head, but before she could speak, a lady to the other side of Mrs. Follett piped up. Aubrey hadn't caught her name. "Folbrage is out of the running, of course. Anyone the right age for him is already spoken for—see, there's two of the princesses, with their husbands. But the Frithan and Arnician parties certainly look promising." She motioned with her fan toward them.

Aubrey recognized them from their fashions, the Frithans in the bright floral patterns that their textiles were famous for and the Arnicians in clashing colors, their men's breeches so short as to look very foreign to his eyes. There was a titter about thighs, but Aubrey missed the joke because he was so busy being horrified at the thought of that handsome, anxious prince marrying some stranger with his knees on display or a woman in a bright dress. Dancing started shortly afterward, however, which meant that the chatter was cut off as people went to get into position.

"Mother," Wilson hissed as they moved across the room. "Who *was* that woman?"

Lady Ainsley's body shuddered with suppressed laughter. "Mrs. Follett was my captain when I served," she said, "and she is—well, her current position is a secret, but do not be fooled by the way she talks. She would lay down her life for any member of the royal family in a heartbeat. Now, go join her daughters for the group dance, and don't forget to head to the private supper room at the first break. The king invited us especially."

She pushed Wilson in the direction of the dancers. Aubrey followed, thinking not of dancing, but of the supper and meeting the crown prince. He wanted to see that face smile.

CHAPTER 2

Edmund had been doing his best to avoid people all evening. It had been so much easier when he was younger. He remembered ducking behind his parents' legs and people just laughing. Running away or hiding under tables, that had been permissible as well.

He missed being small.

He had gotten out of the first dancing set by relying on the custom that granted a rest period to royals who had performed magic. Using their gifts did tire out some people; Edmund had always kept to himself that he was the opposite. To be fair, he had never been sure if that was because he just found it less tiring than dealing with people. It was, frankly, a relief to be allowed to ignore a room full of strangers and connect with the sky or a plant, since they were calling to him anyway, and he knew how to deal with a cloud or a lavender bush.

In an effort to acknowledge that tonight was about his cousin Charlotte, Edmund and his parents would be withdrawing for supper to a private dining area, while Prince Willard oversaw the meal in the main ballroom. Edmund was grateful, since tonight had his insides tied up in even bigger knots than usual, as people weren't focusing on Charlotte at all. A number of young nobles had agreed to attend this ball, not only from all the neighboring countries but also from places farther afield like the eastern Sunlands, and everyone knew why. There had been an article in the paper about it: COULD ONE ENGAGEMENT LEAD TO ANOTHER? Edmund's personal secretary, Sir Jenson, had put the damned piece down next to his breakfast yesterday morning, looking as though he were worried Edmund might throw the thing in the fire. He had not. Instead, he had put down his fork and pushed his plate away. He had barely been able to eat since.

Even though his parents had told the prime minister and the ambassadors and diplomats and anyone else who would listen, repeatedly, that they were not interested in negotiating Edmund's marriage until he had finished university, like Charlotte had been allowed to do, there was no getting away from the fact that he would be the next king. And not just any king. Edmund Fortuna would be one of the greatest kings Saben had ever had; it had been Seen, again and again.

Edmund wished someone would tell him how he was supposed to achieve all this greatness, because the whole thing as it stood now made him feel nothing but sick to his stomach.

While his "rest" period could get him out of dancing, it did not, however, get him out of being present at a ball, and people would still come and speak to him. Perhaps he should have danced after all, he thought desperately at one point, when he found himself cornered in one of the card rooms. He had gone in there expecting to be ignored by people focused on counting hearts and clubs or whatever it was in the game they were playing—he was terrible at cards—but had been unlucky enough to enter just as the players at one of the tables were setting up a new game. He filed it away as a lesson—he would never again try to hide in a gaming room—and struggled to work out how to get himself out of there. The longer all the polite small talk went on, the more his brain buzzed that there was a storm on its way off the coast to the south, and that the palace's kitchen garden felt a little dry after the warm day, and that the grain crops closest to them, in the fields to the east, were overtaxing their soil.

He dragged his concentration back to what the man in front of him was saying—Mr. Prestan was the minister for defense; Edmund really did need to listen—and caught the tail end of a question just in the nick of time.

"—the next few years? I believe you're planning to attend university at Craywick?"

Oh dear. Was this a dig about him putting off his military service? Edmund looked at the minister, searching for criticism in the set of his mouth or the faint rise of the brows—red, like his hair—that might suggest a query about his personal life, but the man belonged in this card room more than Edmund did. He couldn't read a thing in his face.

"Yes," Edmund said finally. "Craywick. I can do my bachelor's degree there while training at the barracks with the army cadets."

Everyone was still staring at him, and so he went on, willing his face to stop heating up. "It is, of course, why my family traditionally studies there instead of Elmsgate; and, being so central and so close to the capital, it is convenient if we are needed anywhere."

Heavens, *everyone* knew that—he was being boring and inane—this can't have been what the man had wanted him to say. He added, a little desperately, "Unless, of course, the coming war with Honal breaks out before then."

He regretted the words at once, as the man's eyes widened. He regretted them even more when he realized that the whole room had fallen silent. The only sound was a woman to his right, fumbling her cards and snatching them back up.

"Yes," Mr. Prestan said smoothly, acting for all the world as though Edmund hadn't brought up something that the government was very carefully Not Talking About. "We'll all find our plans disrupted if war breaks out, unfortunately."

Even in his mortification, Edmund found himself taken aback by this reply, since the man was responsible for the defense portfolio. Surely, if war broke out, his plans would come into effect, not be disrupted. But before Edmund could work out if saying this would be impolite, a footman arrived to request his presence in the private supper room that had been set up for the evening. Edmund took in a great, shaky breath from sheer relief.

The supper room was almost empty when he got there: just the king and queen, looking relaxed with wineglasses in their hands, and some servants setting things up. Almost immediately, however, a few families arrived whom he recognized as his parents' personal friends—nobody so important that they would be missed for an hour, or who would care all that much if he said something impolitic. He was being guided around by his mother and nodding his head at people in greeting when his father, who had been on the other side of the room, started striding toward the door.

"John!"

His father sounded so happy that Edmund almost felt like smiling too. He turned to see Lord and Lady Ainsley ushered through the door, followed by a trio of broad-shouldered, brown-haired sons: the eldest, who was handsome and charming; the funny, sarcastic one with the glasses; and the one who wanted to go into the army and had no better skills in company than Edmund did. He associated that one with awkward silences, except that he was talking now to a young man Edmund didn't know, coming in behind them. This had to be the fourth son. They had not yet met, but his father had mentioned him several times, since they would be starting university in the same year, and he had hoped that they could be friends, like he and Lord Ainsley senior had been in their time at Craywick.

Aubrey, that was his name. He was taller than his brothers: about the same height as Edmund, but slighter with it. He also resembled his mother much more than her other boys did, and Edmund had heard her called a great beauty.

He had never given that much thought before now.

"Sweetheart?"

Edmund jolted. He turned to see his own mother studying his face in concern, and he realized he had been staring at the young man. He felt his face heat up.

"Is it going to rain?" she asked.

For a moment, Edmund couldn't make sense of her question, but then understanding washed wonderfully over him: she thought he had been gazing into space, distracted by his gift. Which, to be fair, did happen.

"Yes," he said, jumping at the excuse. "Out to sea."

She made a sympathetic sort of noise and touched his chin affectionately with a gloved finger. "I know it's hard. But do try to be here and not there?"

He was trying. He did try. He nodded rather than saying that and let her guide him toward the latest arrivals. They apparently weren't quick enough for his father, though, who was looking around for him, holding his arm out to summon him over. Edmund dutifully put himself within grabbing distance and was swept into the group.

"Here's Edmund," his father said jovially, "finally able to meet the youngest of your—my goodness, John, look at those eyes! Where did he get those? Never from you."

"No, the blond hair and the blue eyes are from Mary's side; her brother Charles was the same. Aubrey just got an empty title from me, making him a lord of nothing. He's the last lord of nothing, you know."

They both looked at Aubrey then, as though expecting him to respond.

Edmund felt trapped on the young man's behalf for a second, appalled at his father—imagine meeting your king and him acting this way—but the young Lord Ainsley merely made an elaborate and somehow sarcastic sort of bow at them both, like a rake in a play admitting to everything, smirking, and their fathers laughed heartily.

"I see what else he gets from you," the king said. He looked like he was all set to go on being witty, but his friend interrupted him to demand wine at this point, and they went off.

Abruptly left to themselves, Edmund and the youngest Lord Ainsley gazed at each other for a moment in silence. Even though he knew that, as the higher-ranking one among them, he was supposed to speak first, Edmund's head went completely empty. The young man's eyes really were very blue, like the sky on a clear summer's day, and he couldn't think of anything to say but that, and he could not possibly say that. After a few more moments, the lordling seemed to take pity on him, and said, "It really is lovely to meet you, Your Highness. I can bow properly if you'd prefer? Or should we start that introduction over entirely?"

A startled laugh made its way out of Edmund's mouth. Lord Ainsley grinned in response—and Edmund had to remind himself not to just stand there staring again. He cleared his throat.

"No, I think our fathers thoroughly ruined any chance we had at a polite meeting," he said, and then couldn't resist adding, "but what was all that about you being the last lord of nothing?"

"Oh, none of us are lords *of* anything. Surely you have loads of us around here? We have no castle or fort or really any land, apart from Father's estate from the baronetcy. We're only called lord as a courtesy because my great-great-great-grandfather was King William the Fourth."

"We're cousins?" Edmund wasn't sure how he hadn't known that.

"So distant that I don't think it counts. What would it make us? Fourth cousins? Fifth? When *do* you stop counting, I wonder?"

Edmund had no idea and found himself saying so, while he followed Lord Ainsley to the supper table.

"This all looks *so amazing*. I feel like someone should draw it and put it in a storybook as a forbidden fairy banquet," Lord Ainsley said, handing him a plate. "Well, anyway, the courtesy runs out with me and my brothers. We're the last generation who are supposed to be addressed as lord, and I'm the youngest, so I'm the last. Oh my *goodness*."

Edmund, who was contemplating a platter of sliced meat, looked up in alarm.

"Yellow strawberries!" Aubrey exclaimed, holding one up for Edmund to see.

"Oh! Yes," he said. "Those are my favorites. They're from the palace gardens; I help them grow. Well, I help everything in there, but those plants are mine."

"Really? But should a prince be mucking about in the dirt like that? I know this sort of thing is your business, as it were, but I didn't think you'd be actually *tending* things. Won't you soil your regal hands, magic or no magic?"

Edmund found himself laughing again. "Not like that. I crossbred my favorite wild variety with another one to try and improve the cropping. Very little hand soiling required. They were my first experiment in botany, when I was young."

Stop talking about plants, part of his brain started urging him, pulling up memories of people's eyes glazing over as they nodded politely at him, except that Lord Ainsley wasn't doing that. His eyes were wide, his lips parted, and then he said, "Well, now I definitely need to try one!" and bit into the strawberry he was holding. He closed his eyes, letting out an appreciative noise, and Edmund had to stop himself from staring again. He quickly turned to the table and started loading his plate, almost at random, and then risked glancing back as Lord Ainsley started speaking again.

"I take it all back. Get as dirty as you like; that was the most delicious strawberry I have ever tasted. So, when you say crossbred . . ."

It turned out that the young man had some basic knowledge of the subject. Somehow or other, he ended up drawing out of Edmund that there were half a dozen varieties of strawberries in the gardens here that he had been working on, including one he had made available to farmers, that, though a traditional red—Lord Ainsley affected disappointment—was hardy and yielded very well. They led from there to his lordship asking him about the potato harvest that he'd saved two winters ago, getting them onto the risks of crop homogenization, when Edmund discovered that he'd cleared his plate.

He stared down at the pretty blue-and-white pattern without seeing it, thinking that he hadn't eaten that much in one go in days—he had been too nervous—when his mother called him over to speak to someone else. Lord Ainsley bowed politely and moved away, but Edmund found himself keeping half an eye on the young lord for the rest of the supper. It was hard not to; the conversation seemed the most animated wherever he was. At one point, he and his father made Edmund's own father laugh so hard, the king couldn't breathe and started thumping on the wall, gasping. Edmund felt such a stab of envy—he didn't even know of what—that he completely missed whatever it was that the woman in front of him was saying.

Then things got even worse, because it was time to go back to the ballroom. There would be no more hiding in card rooms; his dances for the next set had all been organized through official channels, well in advance.

First there were several of Prince Henri's very proper Hasprennan relatives. At least none of them had been on the list that had made it into the newspaper, about possible marital candidates for him. Neither were his next two partners: a widowed Frithan princess perhaps a little younger than his parents who, it occurred to him later, might very well have been scouting him for younger relatives; and then a duchess from Folbrage of around the same age who, despite not being on the newspaper's list, had still flirted outrageously, making him extremely uncomfortable.

After that, he spent what seemed like an eternity dancing with young women who *had* been on the list, while people stared at them and spoke about them and generally acted as though they were public property. Which they were. He made the same safe, practiced small talk with every one of his partners to keep himself from any more missteps like the one he had made with the minister for defense. The only partner this had proved problematic with was the Nordish princess he'd danced with next.

He had expected to find her a more relaxing partner than his previous ones, since she was married, with young children. When he had asked her how her journey over had been, however, she had launched into a lengthy complaint about how long it took to travel the usual way from Nordan to Saben, since they had to go by boat to Folbrage, travel through both Folbrage and Hasprenna, and finally ferry over from there.

"Of course, if we could simply sail directly, around Honal, that would be much easier," she had concluded, and Edmund had squinted at her, confused.

"Well," he had said finally. "Their privateers and the rough water around their country do make that impossible."

She had sniffed. "Our navy is building a fleet of larger ships, with bigger cannons on board to fend them off. The latest designs."

Edmund did not know what to say to that. He didn't see how larger cannons would help with a choppy sea. He changed the subject and did not ask any of his subsequent partners how their trip over had been.

He almost convulsed with relief when he got to the last song of the set, which he had insisted on saving for the bride-to-be. Charlotte took one look at him when he appeared at her side as the music started and gave one of her almost-silent huffs of laughter.

"It's not that bad," she said in her gentle voice. "It's a party!"

"It is a stock auction," he replied, putting out his hand for hers. "You might be off the block, but that makes me the next—the next bull to be brought to market."

He felt better, just saying the words. Like brushing off an insect that had been making his skin crawl.

"Not just any bull," she said, letting herself be led out to the dancers. "The prize bull. Just—try not to fret about it. They can't make you do anything."

Edmund knew that. But he also knew that there were a thousand ways that you could be worn down or manipulated or controlled or backed into a corner. He already did things every single day that he didn't want to do, for his duty. True, he also refused the occasional thing, since there was only so much of him to go around, but—this was different. Continuing the royal bloodline so as to pass on the magical gift—that wasn't just expected of him, it was eagerly anticipated, as were the diplomatic benefits of him making a good match. If he failed in the first of these—which he would—then the second would become even more important. Especially with war on its way.

The thought made his stomach clench, but so did the idea of letting his people down.

If I could just be enough on my own . . .

"There you both are!" a male voice said next to them. His uncle. Edmund braced himself, letting go of Charlotte's waist as they turned to face him.

"Uncle Willard," he said, as Charlotte murmured her own greeting to her father. "And my lady," he added, inclining his head at his uncle's dance partner, who was curtsying. Dame Edwina was the minister for foreign affairs and diplomacy, and her brown face under her elegant, elaborate hairstyle was pleased. She looked, in fact, like the cat that had gotten the cream—as well she might, Edmund thought, since she had surely participated in Charlotte's marital negotiations. No trace of her satisfaction was present on his uncle's face, however; he looked like he was at a funeral even more than usual. Edmund wondered if he should ask Charlotte about that. Was her father unhappy about her marriage? But then he never seemed happy about anything, so he dismissed the thought. He didn't want to upset Charlotte.

"Were you searching for us?" he asked.

"I always like watching you two dance," he said. "You look good together. It's a shame that . . . Well."

Charlotte twitched. If he had not still been holding her hand, Edmund might not have noticed.

"Oh, don't bring that up again," Dame Edwina said, her airy tone taking the sting out of the words. She tugged on Prince Willard's hand. "Come on, Your Highness, I don't think we've danced together since my debut; I'm not letting you out of it early. Your Highness, Your Highness," she added, bowing her head to Edmund, then Charlotte, and practically dragging Charlotte's father away.

Edmund turned back to his cousin, taking her waist again. He was about to ask her what on earth all that had been about, but Charlotte's face was flushed.

"Are you all right?" he asked her. "Do you need some air?"

"No, too many people are watching us," she said, quickly putting herself back into position. Then, after a moment, she added, "I'm sorry he brought that up."

Edmund led her back into the steps, but she didn't seem any more comfortable, so he felt he might as well ask.

"Brought what up, exactly? What was that about?"

She looked at him; then recognition cleared her expression. Her mouth quirked.

"Did nobody ever tell you that my father wanted us to marry?"

The room seemed to tilt. Edmund nearly tripped over his own feet. He recovered himself as best he could and asked, "Us? As in . . . to each *other*?"

"Did you never wonder why the government was so happy to wait to plan a marriage for me?"

Edmund had never given it any thought at all; he'd been too worried about his own. His collar suddenly felt too high, his cravat too tight around his throat. "They—they were giving you time to focus on university," he said, each word getting weaker under Charlotte's patient gaze.

"They were waiting for you to grow up a bit more, Edmund," she said gently. "To see if we might suit."

"But . . ." he said, and stopped. He had too many objections; he had to sort them into some kind of order. He did not say the first one: *You deserve a better husband than I would have been to you.* "We grew up together in the palace," he said instead.

That made her smile.

"Yes, my father did regret that once I told him you were like a brother to me, and so neither of us were ever going to want it. Complained very loudly that it hadn't been that way for your parents."

Edmund's mind raced. His parents had been the same age, for a start, whereas Charlotte was six years older than him; and they had not spent their whole lives together. His mother had gone away to Hasprenna to finish her schooling and then stayed for university. His father had missed her terribly and realized how he felt about her.

Not to mention the fact that his parents were both, by their natures, more likely to be inclined toward each other than Edmund would ever be to any woman, but he had not told anyone about that yet. He felt his face heating up as he wondered—had people been watching Charlotte and him together this whole time, looking for signs of—of what? Affection, beyond the familial?

"Did everyone know about this but me?" he asked.

"No, no," she said. "The bureaucracy wanted to keep it quiet so that we wouldn't look like—well, rejected goods to other prospects, or like we were scorning other countries. Your parents were never keen on the idea, if it makes you feel any better. I expect that they just didn't see the point in mentioning it to you, just like I never wanted to. I didn't actually know that no one had told you, though, so . . . I feel a bit foolish now."

Edmund felt his eyebrows draw together in worry, but Charlotte appeared to be holding in laughter.

"I'm sorry you found out this way," she said. "I thought we were just—being typically awkward and not talking about it."

They both laughed then.

"Thank you," Edmund said quietly, after a moment.

She shook her head to dismiss his words and motioned over his shoulder with a tilt of her head. Edmund turned; there Prince Henri was, dancing with the flirty duchess. Edmund felt a stir of unease for him, but no discomfort was showing on the man's perfectly symmetrical face, so perhaps he didn't mind so much.

"He's very handsome," Edmund said, since Charlotte now had a fond smile on her face that he liked seeing there, and he wanted to say something supportive.

"Mmm, I think his dance partner thinks so too. Ah well."

They spent the rest of the dance in companionable silence, and then they made their way over to the closest refreshment table, which, Edmund saw with a little twist of pleasure in his chest, Lord Aubrey Ainsley and one of his brothers were also heading toward. Edmund introduced them to his cousin, and Lord Wilson Ainsley started stuttering compliments to her on the artistry of her ice sculpture. Aubrey caught Edmund's eye and looked as though he were about to say something facetious, but they were interrupted by the herald announcing that the crown prince's lavender had all been given out.

"Oh no!" Aubrey exclaimed, and then slumped. Edmund's confusion must have shown on his face, because the young lord went on with, "I had wanted to get my mother a sprig."

“From the lavender plants?” Edmund asked. “My ones?”

“Yes, it’s her favorite,” he said. “My brothers won’t have thought to get any for her. I mean, just *look* at John,” he added, motioning to a far-off spot across the room. “He’s barely spoken to any of us; he’s busy surrounding himself with as many eligible young beauties as he can find. I daresay he hasn’t missed a dance all night. I don’t even know where Cedric disappeared to.”

Edmund glanced over, not really seeing, and then reached into his waistcoat pocket and pulled out a cutting. He held it out to Aubrey.

“I find the smell calming,” he said, to say something, since the lordling was just looking at him—but then he saw the floral spear he was holding was wilted from being in his pocket all night, the square stem bruised. “Oh—wait—” he said, and then put his other hand over it. It didn’t take much, just a second or two of focus, and then he held the thing up again. The sprig was perfect now, as though it were freshly cut. Aubrey’s whole face lit up, but then something distracted him to the side.

Edmund turned his head in time to see the wall next to them start to crack right open like a broken pane of glass. There was a great noise—a booming—and before he had made sense of any of it, Lord Ainsley had thrown himself at him.

CHAPTER 3

All the breath was forced from Edmund's body as his back hit the floor. He spent an airless second with Lord Ainsley's weight on top of him and then managed to gasp in a breath that tasted wrong and made him cough. He spent a few moments reminding his lungs how to work before realizing that whatever that booming had been, it had stopped.

No—it hadn't; it had just moved and was happening down at the other end of the ballroom now. Edmund's ears were full of ringing and shouting. He turned his head and took another few moments to comprehend what he was staring at.

There was a large piece of masonry—almost a foot wide, though not quite as high, its edges rough and uneven from the way it had been blown out of the wall—on top of Lord Ainsley's arm, pinning him in place.

"Aubrey? Aubrey!"

That was Lord Wilson Ainsley, his dark jacket covered in white dust.

He was on all fours to their left with a cut down the side of his face and his hands red with bloody scrapes, crawling toward them. He seized the chunk of brickwork on his brother and heaved it off. Aubrey cried out, a sound that went straight to Edmund's nerves, banishing his shock.

The young lord's arm didn't look right.

"Don't touch him," Edmund said to the brother, since he was showing all the signs of readying to haul Aubrey up next. "He needs a physician. Send a footman for one, quickly. The ballroom's lined with them," he added, a little sharply, since the man was just staring at him blankly.

Wilson nodded and went.

Aubrey shifted on top of him, to look into his face.

"Thank you," the lordling said, between his teeth, "for getting rid of him."

Edmund's body convulsed with something that wasn't quite laughter. "I think your arm's broken," he said. "Try not to move it. I'm going to attempt to get out from under you. Do you think you can brace yourself?"

Aubrey shifted, hissed, tried again, and Edmund wiggled himself free.

"Try not to—" he started to say, but it was no use; Aubrey had rolled onto his side, taken hold of his arm with his other hand, and sat up. A grunt of pain escaped him, his face going even paler, but then he saw Edmund observing him and smiled, of all things.

"This really does hurt quite a lot," he said in a conversational tone, like a dowager commenting on the weather, and Edmund let out another not-laugh.

"Is it just the arm? You aren't hurt anywhere else?"

"I don't think so. You?"

Edmund shook his head. They looked over to where they had been standing; there was a hole in the wall large enough for two people to walk through easily, and while dust was everywhere like a horrible sort of mist, the rubble had mostly landed in huge chunks some three or four feet farther in than where they had been standing. It took Edmund a moment to understand what that meant.

"All of that would have hit us," he said. "You've saved both our lives."

Lord Ainsley's blue eyes had closed.

"Well, you had a problem with your walls," he said, his voice sounding strained now. "Do they always explode like that?"

Edmund, who wasn't sure how the young lord was able to be flippant at a time like this, was grateful to see the royal physician making his way over to them. Sir Omar looked harried, his brown skin streaked with pale dust.

"Your Highness," he said, bowing, his Arnician accent heavier than usual with concern. "Are you hurt?"

"No, thanks to Lord Ainsley," he said, motioning to him. "Please, check him first—his arm—"

He stopped there, since the doctor had already pulled his spectacles out of his waistcoat pocket and perched them on his nose. He started making tutting noises as he felt his way up and down Aubrey's forearm.

The young lord pressed his lips together, his eyes pinching, but apart from that he didn't move. Edmund didn't want to look away from his face, but there was a commotion: Lord Wilson Ainsley back, with his parents. Edmund could see his own father coming up behind them and his secretary, Sir Jenson. Charlotte, who appeared uninjured, was helping someone else, near the wall.

"What's wrong?" Aubrey's father demanded, going straight to his son, who warded him off, holding up his right hand.

"Please don't jostle me, Father," Aubrey said. "It's just my arm."

"He's been very lucky," Sir Omar said. "It looks like a clean break in both bones. I'll need assistance to put them right, though, and my setting table." The man glanced up as the king joined them and bowed his head perfunctorily. "Your Majesty, if I could have your permission to set up an infirmary somewhere in the palace to deal with the wounded, and if you could send for my assistants and equipment? No, not you, sir," he added, as Edmund went to go with him. "I still need to check you over."

Edmund stood around feeling useless and helpless as his father left to recruit servants and organize things. Sir Jenson came over to him, looking baffled.

"Your Highness, what *happened*?"

"You didn't hear what those men were shouting, as they were carried off by guards?" It was Lady Ainsley. Edmund stared at her. He hadn't heard words, only noise. Sir Jenson shook his head, and she went on with "They sounded like one of those groups who keep protesting that Saben shouldn't passively wait for the coming war with Honal, but act to either prevent or precipitate it in some way. There were four of them, yelling slogans while being dragged away."

"What slogans?" Edmund asked.

"The ones they usually use—'Action on Honal' and 'Don't wait to protect your people.' Nothing especially creative, sir."

"But . . ." Edmund said, motioning to Aubrey. He didn't say, *They did the opposite of protecting our people.* It seemed too obvious.

Lady Ainsley seemed to understand, since she smiled a little and said, "Yes, sir, their destructive tactics are counterintuitive, but it gets their cause a lot of attention. I expect in this case, they will have been trying to demonstrate that if they could sneak into Talstam during an event and plant explosives, Honal forces could do the same."

"Explosives?" Edmund asked. "More than one?"

"There's a fountain at the front of the palace now pouring water out of its side, sir, and I believe there's a wall being held together by the force of Queen Margaret's will at the other end of the room. There could be more—I don't know."

Sir J looked stricken. "Not the Hennerly fountain?"

When no one answered him—Edmund hadn't even known the thing had a name, just that its stone fish were so grotesque, he'd been frightened of them as a child—the man went on with "It's more than two hundred years old!"

Lord Ainsley senior, who had been examining Lord Wilson Ainsley's injuries, turned at this with an incredulous expression that looked ready to spill over into shouting, but that was when Sir Omar sat back with a satisfied sound and pronounced Aubrey very well, apart from the break.

"With your permission, sir?" he said to Edmund. Edmund nodded, and the man started prodding him gently, telling him to let him know if there was any pain.

Edmund looked at Sir Jenson over the physician's shoulder. "Did you know about this? These protestors?"

His secretary looked uncomfortable. "There are always discontented people, sir, and these ones are never going to influence Lord Dell's government. You know that their policy is to wait until military matters have been Seen before making major decisions. And besides, these groups usually keep their protests to the coastal cities with military bases, like Adurnmouth and Marisetown. We haven't had anything like this in the capital before. The bureaucracy wasn't very worried about them."

Lord Ainsley senior made a huffing noise. "We're right near Marisetown," he said. "This isn't their first bombing. I expect if the government had a few more Seers in the cabinet, like it's supposed to, perhaps they could bring themselves to care more. I've got two sons who've woken up screaming for years over what they've Seen coming in this war. You'll forgive me if that doesn't sound like nothing worth worrying about to me, sir."

Sir J merely bowed in reply. Edmund was grateful; he would have expected the man to bluster defensively, as was his wont, but Lord Ainsley had a clear point. Edmund was still processing everything the lord had said—Aubrey had seemed so bright and cheerful up until his arm being smashed, not at all who one would picture waking up screaming and predicting doom—when the king returned. The surgeon stood up, having finished poking and prodding Edmund's legs.

"His Highness seems uninjured, sir, but I would like to keep him where I can see him for the next few hours, if he doesn't object. The young Lord Ainsley here will need to come with me. Where are we setting up?"

"Just one minute, now," Aubrey's father interjected. "What are you going to do to my son?"

"You can trust Sir Omar, John," the king said. "You know that the Arnicians are at the forefront of medical science; he'll take as good care of him as if Aubrey were a member of the royal family himself—"

"So he should!" Lord John Ainsley was yelling now. "This is what is wrong with this country, Theodore! Why should your family get better care than—"

"Your son saved my life," Edmund blurted out. Everybody stared at him, and he felt his face heat up but went on doggedly. "He saved both our lives. If it hadn't been for his quick action, we would both be completely broken under all that." He motioned to the pile of deconstructed wall. Everyone turned to it.

"Yes," said Sir Omar after a moment. "Very brave. Now I'm going to take my patient and mend the bit of him that did break—"

"You can't give Aubrey poppy," Lord John Ainsley interrupted, his tone still annoyed but at least no longer shouting. "He'll have a vision."

The surgeon seemed to take that in, at least. "Ah," he said. "Right. Good to know. Anything else?"

He looked down at Aubrey, who shook his head and got himself into a kneeling position and then stood up. The surgeon was saying something to the king and queen about how ice would be welcome, but Edmund had been watching Aubrey's face go from pale to ashen as he moved. He stepped closer, feeling helpless and useless.

They made their way to the makeshift infirmary, which had fewer people than Edmund had expected. There were just three other patients there, in the next room, already bandaged up by Sir Omar's assistants and presumably dosed with laudanum, dozing on the sort of bed that Edmund associated with these types of places. He had visited them after accidents in an official capacity but had never dreamed one would be set up in his own home.

He was just contemplating the matter and wondering where the palace guards had been while the explosives had been set up, when the surgeon asked him if he wouldn't mind helping Lord Ainsley. The assistant was cutting off the young man's coat, in preparation for setting his arm.

Edmund had never broken a bone or seen one set. The setting table was horrific, with leather straps and a great metal thing that the surgeon explained was for "traction." Since Aubrey could not be given poppy—if it induced a vision, he would not only be weak afterward, he might also thrash around and injure himself further—Sir Omar gave his patient brandy, which made him wince. He then produced a bottle of something new called ether, which, after enough time had passed, rendered the lordling insensible. Edmund was glad of it. Getting the bones back where they belonged was a more violent business than he had imagined. He was given the task of holding the lordling's body still while the surgeon worked, an assistant hovering and occasionally intervening. He was too gentle at first out of self-consciousness and was barked at for it. He took a firmer hold of the young man's torso with his hands, bracing it against his own to keep it from moving and thanking heaven that Aubrey was unconscious, since this would be mortifying otherwise. The lordling's dead weight was flush against him from hip to shoulder. Edmund had never held anyone this close before, outside of his own family.

Edmund still couldn't believe what had happened: that someone—several someones—had felt like they had to take such violent, extreme action to just be heard. But clearly that was the case, since he had known nothing of their concerns before they had blown up a section of his home. He was too tired to unpick if that was right or not. It was hardly as though their cause wasn't important; and he had not been raised to think that violence was never justified. He would be going into the army, after all. It was considered part of his royal duties.

"A bit to the left, Your Highness," the assistant said, making him jump. He moved Lord Ainsley in that direction, and the surgeon made an approving noise as he started straightening the limb.

Edmund couldn't watch. He turned his eyes to the ceiling and tried to think of something else. The lordling had been very impressive. Edmund's tutors had told him again and again that someone's character revealed itself in the unexpected, extreme moments of life. Lord Ainsley had not had time to think but had immediately protected, showing care as well as good judgment. Edmund could only hope that he would have done the same, but doubted it. He suspected he would have frozen in shock instead and doomed them both.

"There," Sir Omar said, startling Edmund from this train of thought. He glanced down to see the man tucking the edges of a neat knot into a fold of bandage around the splinted limb. "Nothing should shake that loose."

Edmund and the assistant moved Aubrey as gently as they could to a narrow bed in the next room. The others in there seemed to be sleeping more deeply now. Edmund found himself reluctant to leave the young lord. He had saved his life, but more than that, Edmund had liked him. He had made him laugh, in the middle of precisely the sort of occasion that had Edmund feeling like an animal performing tricks in a circus. And of course it had all ended horribly, he caught himself thinking morosely, but that wasn't fair. Especially since the one having the worst of it was Aubrey.

Edmund was just resolving that he would sleep down here with the wounded rather than leave Aubrey alone in a strange bed under a strange roof, and never mind protocols and whatever else his station dictated, when their fathers arrived, peering through the doorway. Edmund made his way over to them. Lord John Ainsley puffed out a breath, his face and posture relaxing visibly as he saw his son, whole and peaceful.

The king clapped his friend on the shoulder. "There," he said, his voice pitched low so as not to disturb the room too much. "Sir Omar says he just needs time now, and he'll be right as rain in a few months. I told you he was the best."

His lordship flicked a hand toward the room. "I assume I'm all right to take one of these other beds?"

Edmund tried to keep his face still, thanking the heavens he hadn't said anything. All his agonizing had been ridiculous, as usual; Aubrey's father would be staying with him. Of course.

Meanwhile, his own father was grinning. "Finally, you agree to sleep under the palace roof!"

"Extenuating circumstances," Lord John Ainsley said sternly, but there was the hint of a smile on his face. It fell away again as his eyes went back to his son. "It's awful, but—" He looked over at Edmund. "Don't think me cruel, Your Highness, but I did spend a moment or two there thinking that it would possibly be a good thing if the bone couldn't be set, and he'd have to lose the arm."

Edmund blinked at him, not understanding, until Lord Ainsley added, "It would mean that Aubrey could stay home, whenever this blasted war does come, you see. The army won't take a one-armed man."

"They will," Edmund's father said, "if that one arm has any magic."

This felt like an old argument. Lord Ainsley put up his hands. "It's not a competition, Theo, what I'm saying is—these are the appalling things our minds think of, with this future looming over us. I don't know why any of us are surprised that people have started setting bombs. Now—enough of this. His Highness looks dead on his feet. Make him go to bed, will you; what sort of father are you anyway?"

The king grinned again, shaking his head this time, and then the two older men were clapping each other on the arms and shoulders in farewell, and Edmund was being maneuvered out of the room by his father. He glanced back over his shoulder to see Lord Ainsley sitting down on the empty bed nearest to his son.

He leaned over and stroked the lordling's hair from his face, and Edmund felt that strange stab of envy again.

CHAPTER 4

Despite his refusal of poppy, Aubrey still had a vision-dream that night.

Eerie light flickered off the sides of a huge cavern and reflected on the surface of a dark, vast lake. Weird, rigid figures that moved too quickly were throwing things into the water, which started bubbling and writhing. Creatures rose out of it, too many to count. They moved too quickly as well. Something about them brought rocks to mind, but also puppets, except that nothing about them felt joyful.

The cavern was in a mountain that he did not recognize but, given how high the ceilings were, presumed must be part of the Helm: the mountain range between Honal and Saben, so steep and rocky that it formed a sort of physical barrier between the two countries. That was thought to be how it had gotten its name, both from the way that it curved, like a helmet, but also because it protected Saben from Honal.

Aubrey had never been far enough north to see the mountains in person, but somehow he knew, in that knowing he only had when he Saw things, that this was where it was.

It was the smell that struck him: mud and horses, but mixed with gunpowder and odd smoke, a little like incense. It didn't seem to him that mountains or lakes or caverns should smell that way. The smell made more sense, however, as his vision blurred to a battlefield, showing men and women fighting on horseback against an army that didn't seem . . . human.

Things got faster after that; blurrily, quickly, he saw Wilson and John fighting soldiers in brown uniforms. He saw himself in a red coat, calling out to other mounted soldiers to hold their position. The king and queen—they were on horses too, riding hard, their fire everywhere. Princess Charlotte, her hair blowing behind her, her expression intense. And then Prince Edmund. He was lying on some sort of military cot or camp bed, military canvas all around him, tears on his face; and Aubrey was there, wiping them away.

Aubrey might have wondered if that last part was his own dream—a real dream, rather than something prophetic—except he found out later that Cedric had Seen that part too.

They had had the same vision-dream, every detail. Right down to the smell.

Their dream had been no single battle, no mere border skirmish. It had been a full-blown war. It was not that different from other visions that he and his brother had had about the fighting that was to come, except that this time, they had seen people's faces. People that they knew.

They hadn't looked any older than they did now.

And this time there had been a word. Both of them had heard it, enunciated slowly, echoing through everything in a woman's voice.

Monium.

Aubrey was grateful when he woke up to find his father by his side. The damned visions always made him feel weak and shaky afterward, but this seemed worse than usual, what with the pain in his arm and the aftereffects of wine and whatever that stuff was that the surgeon had given him. He felt woozy and sore and miserable, but at least hadn't thrashed around and reinjured himself, which was a small mercy; and after they had gotten all the details of what he had Seen down on paper, his father even agreed that a bit of laudanum wouldn't hurt, since he was apparently going to have vision-dreams anyway. Aubrey fell back asleep shortly after that, and next thing he knew, he was blinking awake in a room full of sunshine, the heavy curtains open but his father and the other patients nowhere to be seen. Even their beds were gone, the chamber back to looking more like what it must usually be: some sort of reception or drawing room, with a rich carpet on the floor and furniture still pushed out of the way to the sides.

He had a series of impersonal visitors after that. A maid, with food. The surgeon's assistant, who warned him that the food might taste odd due to the medicines he had been given but insisted that he eat it anyway, and then instructed him on how to put on and use his sling. A footman, who showed him to a guest suite on the first floor and then helped him into fresh clothes—his own, Aubrey noted with interest, from the small trunk he had taken to his aunt's but which was now installed in the corner.

He was just concluding that he must have been invited to stay in the palace and was deciding that a broken arm was a small price to pay for that, no matter how bad he felt—and this pain wouldn't last, surely—when his father, the king, and Sir Omar all came in, arguing.

"—could not possibly weather a whole day being bumped around in a carriage, with the limb not even begun to heal—"

"—heavy-handed as usual Theodore—"

"He's not going to come to any harm in the palace, John! What do you think, that it's infested with snakes?"

Lord John Ainsley gave his old friend a very narrow look. "Yes," he said emphatically. "That is precisely what I think."

Aubrey, who had stood up when they had all come bursting in but decided that he might as well not have bothered, sank back down onto his chair.

"Aubrey!" his father said at once, going to him and kneeling at his side. "How are you feeling?"

"Fragile," Aubrey said. "Grateful. This is a lovely room—thank you so much, Your Majesty. How long will I be imposing on you?"

Please say for my whole recovery, please say for my whole recovery, please say—

"We were just negotiating that. John doesn't want you staying here at all, and is proving resistant to the idea of you remaining until your splints can be removed. What do *you* think? Since your father is famously so interested in people being free to make their own choices."

Lord John Ainsley's eyes narrowed again, but it was time for even more visitors to arrive: Prince Edmund, looking very sober in a dark green jacket, his eyebrows drawing together as he observed the room, and someone who resembled him a great deal, who had to be Princess Alicia. She had a pretty yellow frock on and a sunny smile to match.

"Have you all agreed yet, Papa?" she asked, without waiting to be introduced or acknowledged. "Is Lord Ainsley to stay with us for the rest of autumn?"

The king raised his eyebrows queryingly at Aubrey.

"I really do not feel like I could travel," Aubrey began, thinking it was an argument that would work on his father, but the man interrupted him anyway.

"His *schooling*, Theo."

"Oh, his lordship will join us, surely?" the princess said, looking to her own father, who nodded.

"My children have the finest tutors in the country, John," the king added, as though holding out a treat to a small child.

Aubrey watched his father's mouth twist from refusal into defeat, and then the corners went up wryly. Relief bloomed in Aubrey's chest as his father turned to him.

"Promise me that you won't run off with the first circus that comes too close to the palace."

Aubrey shrugged his shoulder, with its sling. "With a broken arm? As if I would sabotage my debut to the stage in such a way."

"And no falling in with artists. If I find out you're hanging on some salon wall painted as—as the fairy king or some such, half naked—"

"Father!"

"—I'll be very put out."

Aubrey risked a glance at the prince—his color was high, which suited him very well—and the princess, whose shoulders were shaking, her hand over her mouth.

"And if these fine tutors try to teach you any outdated nonsense you know to be incorrect, you make sure to put them right, you understand? I won't have you thinking you need to listen to that."

"Certainly, Father. I shall endeavor to be as disagreeable as possible, if you like."

He had meant it to be tart, but something in his arm twinged as he said it, and he couldn't stop a wince from crossing his features. The surgeon insisted that he needed rest then, and something more for the pain, and that everyone had to leave. The last thing he saw before the door closed was Prince Edmund taking one last glance back, his brows still low over his thickly lashed eyes.

Aubrey liked those eyes so, so much.

Aubrey and Princess Alicia were on a first-name basis within days.

"You saved my brother," she had said. "So I will always be indebted to you. Although—there have been all those prophecies about him, and what a wonderful king he's going to be, so I'm not sure how much danger he can actually have been in."

"Well, I expect that I was always going to save him, then," Aubrey replied. "Did you ever think of *that*?"

Her eyes widened, and then her smile. She had brought a box of sweets to his rooms that they were making their way through, cups of tea cooling on the table in front of their chairs. She popped a square of marzipan into her mouth and then said, around it, "Do you suppose that is how it works?"

Aubrey shrugged his good shoulder.

"We don't know how it works. My own vision-dreams usually leave vital information out. But since Seers' visions always come to pass . . ." Aubrey intoned it like a schoolmaster, since it was the standard line. Alicia rolled her eyes. "In some way or another, I've always considered it futile to think I can change very much in the grand scheme of things. You mustn't think me fatalistic," he added, since her cheerful face had fallen a little. "I don't mean to make it sound so bad. And, in fact—some variable must have changed the other night, for so many of us to start Seeing that war is coming soon, when things have been so vague for years."

The king had told him that almost three score visions had been reported, supporting what Aubrey and his brother had dreamed. Since there were only a few hundred Seers in the entire country, this war would clearly be a significant event, if so many of them had Seen it. The news had made a little bubble of hope that he had been keeping in his heart deflate, that perhaps what he had been Seeing for all these years would be just the one battle, horrible but quickly done and over with. It clearly wouldn't be.

And now—well. He had never actually Seen himself in uniform before. He was unsure how he felt about that and so had decided to just not think about it.

Alicia picked out another sweet—rosewater delight, this time—and chewed it thoughtfully. She seemed on the verge of saying something else, but her brother knocked on the door at that point and came in, looking handsome in a blue coat.

Something about him was different. It took Aubrey a moment to realize that it was his manner. He was usually so hesitant. He had been visiting Aubrey every day, bringing him things like books and drawing materials, and normally when he appeared at the door, he acted as though he wasn't sure that he was welcome, or if he would be intruding, which was absurd.

Now that uncertainty was gone. More than that—today the prince looked *happy.*

"Mamma wants you," he said to Alicia. "Something to do with your coming-out ball."

"The extra guards, I hope," she said, standing up. "I don't want any explosions marring *my* special night. Poor Charlotte. In her place, I should have demanded another ball to make up for it."

Prince Edmund looked so alarmed at that, Aubrey and Alicia were both laughing as she made her way out the door. The prince took her chair and put down an identical box of sweets to the almost-empty one that Alicia had left. His mouth twisted apologetically.

"We clearly raided the same pantry," he said. "We aren't . . . used to guests."

"Since your sister ate most of that first box, you won't hear me complaining, Your Highness."

"Edmund," the prince said abruptly. Aubrey paused on his way to reach for a chocolate, startled, but the young man went on with "That is—I don't want you to have to call me 'Your Highness.' You have my permission to use my name. Your mother has just written to mine, thanking her for her hospitality, and she mentioned your vision-dream and the bit that I was in. It seems that we are to be . . . close. And I also don't think you should have to keep calling someone 'sir' after you threw yourself in front of an explosion to save them, and—your vision—please, would you just call me Edmund from now on?"

The prince's color was high when he finished this speech, and Aubrey felt himself grinning. "Well, now—you will have to call me Aubrey in return. I can hardly call you Edmund while you keep calling me Lord Ainsley. The scandal!"

The prince went redder, but then said, "Aubrey. Well, you should also know that parliament voted last night to take action to prepare for the coming conflict. The War Office is setting plans in motion."

Aubrey blew all his breath out. He felt like he needed a fresh lungful to reply to that. While he knew this was a good thing—the best outcome that could be expected—it was also horrible.

He made himself keep his voice light. "Well, those protestors will be pleased, in their prison cells. Something's finally being done to ready us for whatever's on its way."

The prince pressed his lips together, looking unhappy, so Aubrey said, "Yes, I know that it is tradition to wait until details have been specifically Seen for the government to take action, but as someone who does See things, I can tell you, it was always coming. Although I wonder what precisely happened that night, to remove the vagueness? It can't have been the explosives."

"That's what Papa says—that it must be a coincidence. He says surely whatever it was, it happened in Honal. They're the ones who will start this by attacking us."

"I suppose," Aubrey said, taking his chocolate and pushing the box of sweets toward His Highness. Edmund. "It is a shame that they refuse all contact—I mean, apart from when they decide to make war on us. We could at least make better guesses, if we had relations with them. Perhaps they just voted in a bloodthirsty new leader. Perhaps one of their own Seers has Seen something. Or perhaps this is all being set off by something random."

"Like what?"

"Hmm. Like . . . a fisherman from our side of the border being rescued by one of their privateers in that storm you mentioned off the coast, on the night of the ball. They will fall in love and it will cause a mutiny on the ship, and then all their sea-force will revolt and they will decide our whole country is to blame."

Edmund let out a startled laugh. "You should write that down. Make it into a story or a play, perhaps. I'm sure it would be a runaway success."

Aubrey held his arm up. "Just as soon as Sir Omar says I can reenter the schoolroom."

It transpired that Sir Omar, however, had a prejudice against swelling and did not want Aubrey exerting his body or his mind until his arm was back down to its usual size. He did, however, clear him for little walks, which he took with the prince, who showed him the strawberry beds and all the various other gardens closest to the palace, including the greenhouses, which were of the latest style, with bigger panes of glass, and more of them. Edmund had spoken at length about how this didn't just lead to better yields on the sorts of plants that were grown in there, but also meant that he had been able to keep specimens alive from farther south that wouldn't grow in Saben under ordinary conditions. Aubrey loved seeing the rare plants, but he loved watching the way that the prince's face animated when he talked about them even more.

Most of the area outside the ballroom was closed off, due to repair works. The Hennerly fountain, being a feature at the front of the palace and visible for some distance, was being given priority.

"It's as though the bureaucracy is trying to cover over what happened as quickly as possible," Alicia said one day when she came with them and they paused to watch the stonemasons smoothing cement. "They want to go back to pretending everyone's not worried about war being imminent, even as they're increasing military recruiting and giving us twice as many guards as usual. Mamma thinks they're putting pressure on the papers to not talk about it, did I tell you? The conservative ones have written more about Edmund's dance partners at the ball, and which of them he might like to marry, than on anything that happened afterward."

"Could we not talk about that," Edmund said, and then avoided eye contact with Aubrey for a while. Aubrey tucked that away in his mind to dissect thoroughly later, since if His Highness didn't plan to get married any time soon, that left all sorts of interesting possibilities open. Especially paired with how often he caught the prince watching him.

A tiny part of his brain spoke caution. It reminded him that Prince Edmund was destined for a diplomatic match, like his cousin. It tried to tell him not to set himself up for heartbreak. And then the prince would frown or look worried about something, and Aubrey would want to make him smile, and a line from his favorite poem would cycle through his head.

And so fortune makes happy fools of men
With love, again, again
Again

He decided not to worry about it.

When Aubrey finally was cleared to join Their Highnesses in their classes, it felt too good to be true. It was a wonderful luxury to be one of only three in the class and not have to help younger students, like he did at his father's school, or constantly bite his tongue, so as to give other people a chance to talk. Academically, it transpired that he was ahead of the pair in some areas and behind in others. Edmund and Alicia had no drawing master, for instance, since neither had any inclination in that area; but Aubrey's foreign language skills were nowhere near as diverse as theirs, since he had no expectations of needing them in the way that they would. Aubrey did, however, impress their literature teacher with his knowledge of contemporary poetry, and their history professor with his thorough understanding not only of each of the three past wars with Honal, but also of the civil war that had split Honal off from Saben in the first place hundreds of years ago: part of the last war across Thasbus, before Queen Helen had negotiated peace across the entire continent.

That treaty—the Thasbian Treaty, to use its official title, even though most everyone called it Helen's Treaty—was on display in the palace, which Aubrey had not anticipated. He had stared at it—at the five-hundred-year-old signature of his ancestor Helen the First—and felt so strange and wonderful, to see this important piece of his country's story, that he had felt tears prick his eyes.

Helen Fortuna, it said, the only piece of solid evidence that scholars had that she had been a Prince of Fortune, just like Edmund, although their history professor did point out that in Old Sabresian, the meaning of the word "fortune" was complex.

"It's linked to the concept of luck but also of chance and choice. Of things that aren't choice, but destiny. Visions and prophecies are common about Princes of Fortune. This is further complicated by the fact that our culture views the powers of the royal family as a gift from the land, but the Princes of Fortune as a gift to the country, since they always change things for the better—fixing the country's fortunes at times when they have been threatened."

Aubrey, who had noticed Edmund's ears going redder and redder, changed the topic by lamenting how impossible it was to know the full etymology and historical usage of the word, with so many of the records and so on from Saben's past lost, due to them having been written in runes and therefore destroyed after the civil war. The professor had bristled at this, as though he were questioning her sources. Aubrey had not meant to offend her—he was just talking about what had happened, when Saben had made their old writing system illegal—but she had moved on in her lesson all the same, and the prince looked more comfortable, so Aubrey decided to call it a win.

No one had been sure what Aubrey should do when it came to the usual time when the prince and princess would practice their magic. Their instructor, Mrs. Grant, was some sort of second or third cousin to the royal family who nevertheless had some small capacity with water and air; enough that, combined with a history in the military, she was able to guide her pupils.

Aubrey went with them to the room where they also practiced their fencing and other fighting skills, hoping to be allowed to observe, but Mrs. Grant insisted upon including him in the lesson. She was delighted to learn that Lord Ainsley came from a family that ran with the Sight. She set Edmund and Alicia a number of challenges to keep them occupied at the other end of the room, and then focused on Aubrey, asking detailed questions regarding the extent of his history with visions.

Aubrey tried his best not to be distracted by the flames that Alicia was making. Yes, he had had the dreams since he was small. No, it did not extend to scrying or any other sort of divination. Yes, he Saw the upcoming conflict often. Yes, he planned to join the army if war broke out.

"I've Seen myself in uniform," he said. "Although I would have joined anyway. My mother's was a military family."

"And yet," Mrs. Grant asked, sounding baffled, a line forming between her brows, "you are entirely untrained at attempting to bring the visions on? Even though they are so valuable to the nation?"

"Alicia!"

Aubrey glanced over just in time to see Edmund throwing a pitcher of water over the hem of his sister's dress, which had caught fire. The prince started begging her to be more careful, while the princess staggered with laughter, looking down at her skirts.

"They're not fire," Aubrey said, motioning at her. "They're only vision-dreams. They can't be guided."

"No, but they can be given a hint that they'd be welcome. You should know how to do that, with war coming. The last thing you want to do is agree to take something in the middle of a battle without knowing how your body will react. I'm surprised your family hasn't taught you about this."

She went over to a cupboard and pulled out an apothecary case.

"Let me see," she said, extracting a clear glass bottle. "Yes, here—this is the usual Sight tincture, containing belladonna, poppy, mugwort, envisioning mushrooms, and so on."

She went to hand the thing to him.

"Thank you, but no," Aubrey said. He saw Edmund and Alicia glance over; perhaps his voice had been a little sharp, so he went on in a gentler tone with "Unless there is a medical reason, my mother has asked me and my brothers to never take anything containing poppy or envisioning mushrooms."

A careful expression crossed the woman's features, and she put the bottle away with an "as you like, my lord." She pulled out two larger bottles. "I have other options, in that case. The Angelsight tincture—a gentler version of the more usual Sight recipe, specifically excluding those two ingredients and with the addition of protective herbs such as angelica and pine. Or there is the Oracle, which is merely an infusion of bay laurel, rosemary, and sweet orange oil. If you take it before bed tonight—preferably in a tea with soporific lettuce, the palace will have some—it might bring on a vision. Or it will just help you get to sleep. Either way, it is not much stronger than anything you might eat at dinner."

Aubrey stared at the bottles. He had only ever heard of the Sight tincture before; he hadn't known that these other two existed. She did not try to hand them to him, however, but cleared her throat and added, "If your family has a history of problematic reactions to induced visions, sir, then of course, we could merely discuss the theory. And though nobody can legally be compelled to take the tinctures, you may very well feel pressure in the army to help in any way you can, and I would be remiss in my duty of care to you, as my student, however briefly, to not help you make an educated decision."

Aubrey wanted to refuse—he didn't *want* to have more visions—but he hesitated. She was respecting his boundary while still making her point, which was, he had to admit, a sensible one.

He looked over at the prince and princess. They were practicing their skills, to be ready to help their country. The least he could do was try, just this once. He felt a pang of guilt at what his mother would say and fiddled with the seam of his sling, but—if they didn't even have poppy or mushrooms in them . . .

"Thank you, Mrs. Grant. I cannot imagine that anyone could object to lettuce and rosemary. I might try that one. Was there anything you wanted me to do? Write down my experience perhaps, in the morning, as I usually would?"

"Yes, but also—make sure to note if anything seems different, in any way. Some Seers find inducing visions useless, for instance—it just shows them things that they have Seen before. Others find that they are very sensitive to them. It is worth you knowing if either is the case. Or if the Oracle doesn't work for you at all."

Aubrey took his tea after dinner, while he and Edmund and Alicia were lounging around in Alicia's sitting room. They played a silly drawing game, which Aubrey won, and then Alicia thrust a book of old stories at him and asked him to read aloud. Aubrey had to give it up not a quarter of an hour later.

"I'm sorry, Licia, I'm just so sleepy," he finally said, after trying to hide yet another yawn behind his hand. He could barely manage to make sense of the words in front of him. "I can't believe *lettuce* has done this. It's just . . . greenness. I should—"

He went to get himself up but swayed on his feet a fraction, unbalanced not just by his sudden fatigue but by his arm, still wrapped and splinted, in its sling. Edmund was up and by his side almost quicker than Aubrey could see, his hands hovering as though ready to catch him. His brows were down in that worried shape that they made, and Aubrey was gripped suddenly with the desire to rub in between them with his thumb until His Highness's face relaxed.

He should not do that.

They stared at each other for a moment, but then Alicia said, "Yes, Edmund, do help Aubrey to his room," and they both started.

It wasn't until they were halfway down the corridor that Edmund spoke.

"Can I ask why your mother doesn't want you to take any of the usual vision tinctures?"

A breath of laughter came from Aubrey's mouth. "I am starting to suspect you of being the most terrible eavesdropper," he said. Edmund's eyes went wide, so he quickly added, "I'm teasing. It's fine, it's not a secret. Mother doesn't think it's ethical to push Seers to take them. Her brother was Captain Charles Mayhew. Have you heard that name?"

The shape of Edmund's forehead moved from worried to thoughtful. "I have," he said finally. "But I don't remember where. Something to do with that border conflict between Hasprenna and Folbrage, before we were born?"

"Yes. Uncle Charles had vision-dreams too. He was at the front and no solution was in sight, so he took a lot of anything that would bring on a vision. His information ended up turning the tide of the Battle of Sitian—you know the one, it was the only battle of importance. But it took a toll on his health, and he died not long after. Highly decorated, but that didn't really make his family feel any better. My mother has always said that he must have been pressured into it. She said she saw a bit of that in the army. I heard Aunt Dorothea say once that Uncle Charles was ambitious, keen to prove himself. I don't really understand that. If he had wanted to do anything he could to help—well, I can see how you could lose yourself to *that* aim. That sounds quite romantic to me. Probably why Mother doesn't want me, especially, to go near the stuff."

Edmund made a contemplative humming noise. "Plenty of Seers take the tinctures, though. Hardly any end in tragedy. Do you not feel your mother should be showing more faith in you?"

"But it's not about me, Edmund. It's about her grief. And—it's to protect us. She doesn't want us exploited. Surely *you* can understand that."

Edmund's eyes widened again, and Aubrey worried that he'd overstepped, so he went on with "Anyway, just look at me. Look at what *lettuce* has done to me. Do you really think I should be taking anything stronger?"

They were almost at Aubrey's door now. Edmund stepped ahead to open it in a courteous sort of way and said something about opium-eating that sounded like a joke, except that Aubrey didn't quite hear it, because all his attention had been on the prince's hand, which he had put on the small of Aubrey's back to help him through the door. Warmth ran all the way up Aubrey's spine and down his arms, leaving his hands tingling.

He turned to His Highness, still standing in the doorway to his chamber. His eyes were the deepest, warmest, best shade of brown that Aubrey had ever seen, and they were focused on him like he was the only thing in the entire palace that mattered. *Ask him to kiss you,* Aubrey's sleepy brain said. *Tell him you'd take a hundred tinctures and break a thousand bones, for just one kiss.*

Aubrey murmured his thanks and closed the door before he could make a fool of himself. This was not the right time. He fumbled out of most of his clothes, deciding to just sleep in his shirt, and collapsed into his bed, wondering if this was what it felt like to be drunk.

Even though it couldn't have, the dream seemed to start the moment his head touched the pillow. There was the sensation as though he were in a river, being pulled along by the current. He was underground, or—no, not under, but *in* everything, somehow, stretched out in connection to so much that it seemed impossible. He was in Saben's ancient past and its dim future, in the earth and the sea and the sky.

And then he was in a cave.

There were people standing around in the space. Their shapes seemed strange; it took Aubrey a while to realize this was because the silhouettes of their clothing were so foreign. They appeared to be having a ceremony, wearing headgear and robes, like a ritual in an old tale, and deferring to a male figure at the edge of a lake. The longer Aubrey focused upon him, the more unsettling he was. Something seemed unwholesome or diseased about his appearance. The skin around his eyes and nose was red, his bottom lip split deeply, the cracks black with blood. His eyes were too light, somehow. Aubrey found himself thinking of a dead animal, bloated and crawling with flies.

"We have drunk of the old water," the man said, his voice echoing strangely, and Aubrey couldn't tell if it was the cavern causing the effect or not. It was as though multiple people were speaking at once, and some of them were not people at all, but birds or cats, or a storm. It was worse once the crowd reacted, the cave exploding with sound. Aubrey could not make out what any of them were saying, but the man's words seemed to have equally excited and shocked them.

He gestured to his right. Aubrey saw that there were two figures standing there that he had not noticed before, with attendants behind them, including a large man with graying hair and an upright posture, like a soldier at attention, who drew Aubrey's eye. This group was stock-still, unlike the excitable crowd. He thought the closest figure was a woman. Her face was partly concealed by a mask, or perhaps paint. Her hair seemed painted as well and forced into an unnaturally high shape. The other figure (Aubrey thought it was a man, but again he could not be certain) was extremely tall and thin. His limbs were so elongated that he seemed for a moment more like an enormous insect than a human being.

Something about them made Aubrey afraid, like he would never want their attention. He had the strange feeling that he didn't even want to be Seeing them, as though they might somehow know and come after him.

And then he saw the runes.

He tried to count them, but they were everywhere, and his fear intensified. His Sight was highlighting them; they were almost glowing, just like the water in the lake. These were the runes, then, that the Honals used in their magic, that Queen Helen had promised that Saben would never use again, even for normal writing, as part of the treaty that he had been studying only the other day.

The first man started talking again.

"It was forbidden. The First Pool, the source of all the holy waters. How dare they forbid us."

The cave erupted in cheers; the man did not quite wait for them to die down before he went on.

"They treated us like children, telling stories of how drinking from it would bring down a Prince of Fortune from behind the mountain upon us. And we say—wrong. These are not prophecies, but fairy tales. All prophecies are just tales now. The waters are stronger."

The cheering reached a crazed pitch in response; triumphant, yes, but without joy. The man held up his hand, and they calmed.

"Let the Prince of Fortune come. It was his birth that brought the quake that gave us our water back, after their queen Helen raised the mountain to take it away. You, the people, Saw it, spent years digging for it, and now your hard work and faith have paid off. The ancient source is finally rediscovered. We have it back, and we will be great again.

"Some drank too deeply or were proved unworthy. We must consider their deaths our sacrifice to the cause. Let all with the old royal blood come forth. Try your luck with the water, if you would. Because now we see. Now we know. Now the water flows in us, and all that was lost will be ours, and we will be all and see all and know all, and we will fear no prince ever again."

CHAPTER 5

Edmund felt a little foolish knocking on Aubrey's door in the morning. It was just . . . the lordling hadn't seemed like himself when Edmund had left him last night. He had looked so vulnerable—even more vulnerable than he usually looked, with his arm still in its sling—and Edmund found that he felt responsible for whatever it was that Mrs. Grant had given him to take, on top of feeling responsible for the sling in the first place.

He knew that Seers were usually groggy and weak after a vision, not to mention that Sir Omar had been concerned about him thrashing about during one and causing further damage to his arm. He just needed to know that Aubrey was well. They were friends. Surely this was a normal thing, with a friend.

Aubrey's voice sounded well enough, however, when it called out, "Come in!"

The young lord was sitting at the writing desk in the corner, waving what appeared to be a letter in the air to get the ink to dry. Edmund tried not to stare as he walked over to him. Aubrey was not yet dressed but was wearing a colorfully striped silk dressing gown belted at his waist, over his shirt. It was open at the neck, and for a moment or two, all Edmund could see was the hollow at the base of Aubrey's throat and then the sinewy lines that went up from it to either side of his jaw. The only other time he had seen Aubrey's neck bared like this was after his cravat had been removed by the surgeon's assistant. He had a sudden memory of what Aubrey's body had felt like in his arms. Guilt warred with something else, and he wrenched his eyes up to Aubrey's.

That wasn't any better. The young lord's face was pale, his striking blue eyes highlighted by dark shadows under them.

"I'm sorry if I'm disturbing you," Edmund made himself say. "I just wanted to see if you were all right."

Aubrey gave him a wan smile and wordlessly handed him the paper he was holding. It was a letter to the War Office.

"You had a vision, then," he said.

"As you'll see," Aubrey replied. "I'll need to tell Mrs. Grant. The vision did feel different. It was quite close to the present—it might even have been happening as I was Seeing it. I also . . ." Aubrey's gaze dropped to his hands. Edmund wondered if they might have been shaking.

"It made me feel unsafe," Aubrey said eventually. "There were runes everywhere. I won't volunteer to take that again, no matter how few mushrooms it has in it. My mother's right. The gift shows me what I need to know; it shouldn't be forced."

Edmund found that he wanted to put his hand out, to touch Aubrey's arm reassuringly, like he might have done with Alicia. Instead, he restricted himself to nodding and reading the letter.

When he was done, he handed the thing back to Aubrey and nodded again. Aubrey stared at him for a moment. "Do you really have nothing to say?" he burst out, his tone indignant.

"Well, I can confess that I liked your last vision better, if it helps."

"My last . . ." Aubrey laughed disbelievingly. "We were in a war tent! You were upset!"

"Yes, and you were with me, comforting me." Edmund was proud of how nonchalant he sounded, although he wondered if his face had reddened. It certainly felt warmer. "This one—words of violence spoken by a people who have decided to be our enemy—well, it is discomforting to learn that they are focusing on me, I suppose, but I would have had to stand against them either way, if they are going to bring war upon my country. I did not know that they used special water in their sorcery, did you?"

Aubrey shook his head. "It seems important. But also, they appear to think that whatever this water is, Queen Helen took it away from them. And that she created the Helm."

"That doesn't mean she did," Edmund said. "Although imagine if that were true. Imagine how strong that would have made her gift."

Aubrey made a noncommittal noise and sank his head onto his arm.

"Did you See anything else?" Edmund asked, pleased once again at how casual his voice sounded. "Anything not related to Honal that you didn't report?"

"No," Aubrey said, rolling his face over so that his voice wouldn't be muffled but still keeping his eyes closed. It drew attention to his mouth, the red of his lips paler than usual. "Nothing personal this time. What are we supposed to be studying this morning?"

It took Edmund longer than it should have to remember. "Mathematics."

Aubrey made a dismissive noise and hid his face again. "I'm going back to bed, then. Please pass on my apologies."

Aubrey didn't participate again in the classes with Mrs. Grant, apart from one lesson when she ran through the basics of meditation, when Alicia had been struggling to concentrate. He did still join them often, however, using the time to practice his drawing—he said that Edmund and Alicia were wonderful subjects—or merely watching, cheering them on and throwing out the odd helpful suggestion.

Then, in the last week of autumn, just as they were all starting to wonder when Sir Omar would consent to removing the splints, Aubrey asked Edmund a question that changed everything.

The conversation started simply enough. Edmund had been presented with a large pot from the orangery that had been deliberately neglected and now had a variety of weeds growing in it. (Edmund had been appalled; citrus hated that sort of thing.) Mrs. Grant tasked him with killing one sort of weed at a time with his power while leaving the others. He didn't find the exercise especially difficult, and he opened his eyes when he finished to see Aubrey gazing at him across the room with an odd, thoughtful sort of expression. Edmund went over to ask if anything was wrong.

"You look different," Aubrey said, "when you're doing something to a plant in a pot rather than in the ground outside. Does it feel different?"

Edmund was surprised.

"What looks different about me?"

Aubrey waved his pencil in the air, somehow conveying that he was searching for the exact words he wanted to use.

"It seems easier for you when the plant is contained. Quicker. You sort of frown, almost, for a moment or two, if you're outside."

He held up his sketchbook.

"Here you are today," Aubrey said, showing him a startlingly good likeness, as though that were a normal thing to be able to produce. "Yes, I know the mouth isn't right," Aubrey added quickly, misinterpreting his silence. "I have trouble with those. I think I start in the wrong place, but I'm not sure where else to start. Anyway, compare that with this one from the other day, when we were in the garden. This is the face you make there."

Edmund was indeed frowning in that one. He was kneeling by some flowers outside their training room, and Aubrey had made him look like he was concentrating fiercely.

It was his turn to try to find words.

"There are more distractions, with a full garden bed," he said. "It's harder to . . . find only the plant. You'd be surprised how far roots go, and other things are usually in the soil too. Dormant or germinating or dead seeds. Fungus. Mold."

Aubrey shuddered melodramatically, and Edmund laughed.

"And yet," Aubrey said, "you never look that way with the weather. Here you are, calming down that high wind we had last week."

Another sketch: he was almost smiling in this one. Edmund tried not to read anything into the number of drawings that Aubrey had done of him but instead forced himself to focus on the conversation they were having.

"The sky is . . . simpler," he said. "It's one system, with everything interlinked."

Aubrey made a conciliatory motion, which Edmund was starting to recognize as something he did when he was going to try to persuade someone of something but didn't want to seem like he was arguing. He pointed out the windows in the double doors near them, leading outside. "Those two clouds over there appear quite separate to me, so that seems a matter of perspective. What would happen if you simply decided to *think* of the soil as one system with everything connected? Would that make it easier?"

Connected. Edmund considered the plants in the training room, their growth and potential inhibited by their terra-cotta containers, and thought of the plants outside.

"Mrs. Grant," he found himself calling to her, even before he fully understood what he wanted to do. "Lord Ainsley and I are going to try an experiment in the garden."

Mrs. Grant, whose hair was falling out of its pins as she busily tried to help Alicia with something for her coming-out performance, waved them on. They headed out the glass doors.

It hadn't rained for a few days; the grass was mostly dry when Edmund knelt down on it and put his hands to the soil. It felt strong, alive. The plants here had coped well with their autumn pruning last month and were getting ready for winter dormancy. He could feel each one of them as a vague, separate hum in his mind as they spread across the map of this particular patch—but that wasn't what he was supposed to be doing.

He peered up at Aubrey.

"The sky," he said. It sounded almost like a question.

Aubrey moved one shoulder in an apologetic sort of way. "I feel a trifle absurd now that we're here, telling you your business. But surely it's worth a try. *Can* you treat all of this garden as one piece, rather than honing in on each individual plant?"

Edmund wasn't sure he could do that at all, but he nodded and closed his eyes, moving his hands into the edge of the grass where it met the garden bed. It had been trimmed recently, the cut edges still callousing over. He gave that a little nudge so that it would heal more quickly and then thought about the way that lawn was, to his mind, one thing, even though it wasn't simply the one plant at all, but the idea kept slipping away because he could feel Aubrey's eyes on him.

He opened his own, and yes, Aubrey was watching him intently. Edmund found himself thinking of the sketches that he had done. They had been . . . flattering. Was that how he looked to Aubrey's eyes?

"I think I'm making you self-conscious," Aubrey said. "Would you like me to go away?"

"No," Edmund said quickly. "But could you . . . stand next to me?"

"I'll do you one better," Aubrey said, and knelt down next to him, also facing the garden bed.

Edmund was suddenly aware of his body. His pulse had kicked up for no reason. The young lord had left a respectable amount of space between them, but somehow Edmund was conscious of every inch, and he had the preposterous notion that he could feel the heat of Aubrey's skin transmitted through the air between them. Ridiculous. Embarrassing.

Friends. They were friends—it was *wonderful* to have a friend—and with friends you weren't supposed to feel—and especially not in his situation, when his life wasn't his own. Not when one's marriage had to be sanctioned by a vote in parliament.

Edmund wrenched his concentration back to the soil under his fingers and pushed a little desperately. *The sky,* he thought, envisioning the wide expanse of it as he urged his power into the ground.

Nothing. Or rather plenty, but nothing out of the ordinary. Life. Roots and seeds, mold and fungus, like he had told Aubrey. It didn't feel disgusting. It was all in balance, comfortable and comforting. Although in truth, there was air in there too, and rainwater. Like the sky.

He focused on that and pretended it was all the one thing.

Nothing. Then—the glimmer of something. Edmund reached into that, let it fill his mind. There was a moment full of possibility. He felt a wonderful widening of reality, like he had lifted his head and discovered he'd crested a hill and the view had opened up in front of him while he had been busy watching his feet.

As quickly as it had come, though, it was gone, like a spark gone out.

He took in a great breath—he wasn't sure he'd been breathing—and opened his eyes. Aubrey was scrutinizing him, his head cocked at an inquisitive angle, his bright hair shining in the sunlight.

"Anything?"

"Yes!" Edmund said. "Except that I couldn't hold on to it."

Aubrey pursed his lips as he thought about that. It was so distracting, Edmund almost didn't hear what he said next. "Would Mrs. Grant's meditation help?"

"Uh," Edmund said. "Yes. Perhaps."

This time when he closed his eyes, he tried to think of his breathing. He focused on that and then on relaxing his muscles one section at a time, and just as he started to feel ready, the thought came that the Honals wouldn't politely give him space to meditate when he—what? When he what?

What did he intend to do against them? Nobody had ever talked to him about this, but he knew very well that his powers were of no real use in a fight. His magical instructor had him killing weeds. That wouldn't change his country's fate.

And now, instead of focusing on what he was supposed to be doing, he was fretting about the war. Which was as ridiculous as anything else he had fretted about today, since, much as with his personal life, his actions would be dictated by tradition and the bureaucracy.

He forced himself to breathe in and then out. He told himself that yes, he had worries, but they would keep. He inhaled and exhaled, made himself be aware of his body, and let it go. This was what he was for: his country. And he did love his country.

He reached for that spark, that wide, open place he'd managed to find before, and then suddenly, there it was.

It was as though every individual awareness he had had of each plant in the garden united. They were now more like a musical chord, or the humming of a beehive, in his mind. He spent a moment or two enjoying it and then found himself idly wondering if he could move his focus back any further, like twisting a spyglass to see something a greater distance away, and then he was doing that as well, but not in the way he had expected, because he didn't have to think of how he experienced the sky with his power and transplant that to how he thought of the earth. Suddenly he was feeling both of them, and not just here, but everywhere that he could feel the atmosphere. All the way out to the sea.

It overwhelmed him for just a moment. For one glorious moment, he lost himself in fields and meadows and woods and masses of seagrass. He could feel all of it growing and alive, and under everything, the ancient, unmoving rock.

He lost the connection almost immediately, but he had done it.

He opened his eyes and let out a gasping, shaky laugh.

"I did it," he said to Aubrey. "You were right."

Aubrey's grin was almost smug. "I didn't think the way that Mrs. Grant was teaching you, treating the elements as separate things, like your power worked like Alicia's, was right."

"They aren't separate," he said, and then sat back in surprise. He held up a hand, motioning to Aubrey to wait, and he tried connecting again. It was easier this time, perhaps since he knew that he could do it now. He reached for what the ground and the air had in common—the way that they felt like different configurations of the same elements and the ways they interacted—and before he had more than a glimmer of instinctual comprehension, there was an enormous crack of thunder.

His eyes flew open to see lightning coming down from the sky within a stone's throw of where they were kneeling, to hit an elm tree at the edge of the garden.

Aubrey let out a shocked sound and fell back. He and Edmund looked at each other for a moment, and then the lordling started laughing.

"Was that you?" he asked.

Edmund's face twisted into an apologetic grimace as he scrambled up and made his way over to the tree. He didn't want it to catch fire on top of everything else.

It wasn't, it turned out, as bad as all that, but the poor thing did have a split in its bark all the way from one of its main branches down to the base of its trunk. That, at least, Edmund knew how to fix. He put his hands to it, murmuring an apology and closing his eyes. When he opened them again, the seam was mostly gone, skipping years of healing and strain.

He turned to see Alicia and Mrs. Grant dashing to the tree.

"Edmund, what on earth—"

"I didn't do it on purpose!" he said. "Lord Ainsley was encouraging me to think about my gift in a different way. It . . . worked. I felt the way that the moisture in the air makes the rain clouds, how it interacts with the ground to make the lightning, and then it happened. It's all connected."

Alicia started demanding he do it again, and Mrs. Grant started reproaching her, but Edmund felt too elated to care about any of it. He looked to Lord Ainsley, who had been silent. He was gazing back at him, a small smile on his face now.

"What a wonder you are, Your Highness," he said, and the last of Edmund's uncertainty fell away.

He felt in that moment, for possibly the first time in his life, like he could do just about anything.

Sir Omar unsplinted Aubrey's arm the next day. The queen held a special outdoor luncheon to celebrate. She had only arrived home the previous night. Edmund had barely seen his mother for weeks, as his parents had been all over the countryside since the parliamentary vote to prepare for the upcoming war. They were inspecting military sites, helping with the recruitment drive. The king was still in the north, encouraging naval enlistment for the base up in Adurnmouth; the queen was heading down to the second-largest one in Marisetown in a week. Edmund would be going with her. He was dreading it, but it was nice to have his mother back in the meantime, and he was looking forward to this lunch, and to watching Lord Ainsley charm her.

He headed down with Aubrey and Alicia to the queen's garden at the allocated time. His mother and a group of attendants-in-waiting were already there—four ladies, plus Noble Florian, who preferred not to use a gendered title. Today, Florian was in feminine dress, although their hair was not pinned up but rather tied simply with a black ribbon, as some more old-fashioned gentlemen with longer hair still wore. Edmund saw Aubrey eyeing the entire effect with discreet interest.

The table was covered in platters of sandwiches, several different composed salads, an onion pie, and pitchers of lemonade. Everything was delicious. When the servants cleared it all away, they replaced it with not only a molded jelly and two kinds of cheesecake, plus platters of fruit, but also pencils and small cards. A few people started sketching the scene. Aubrey offered to draw Alicia, who posed ostentatiously with her arms in the air, holding a spray of flowers aloft and gazing up at them as though they were a marvel.

Edmund found, however, that despite the lovely food and the nice day, he could not fully relax. This was not unusual; the presence of so many people made this a social occasion, for a start, but that wasn't it. Something felt . . . strained, somewhere. It didn't feel like something as simple as a struggling garden bed, but he wandered over to his mother's flowers just in case to make sure they weren't overtaxing themselves.

He could feel the queen's eyes on him. *Please try to be here.* She never did seem to understand that he did try. He tried all the time. He pulled off his right glove and put his hand to the soil, immediately feeling calmer.

"When did you know, ma'am?" he heard Aubrey ask the queen. "That Edmund was a Prince of Fortune, I mean. Oh, I hope that isn't impertinent to ask—"

"Of course not. He was little, not yet three years old. We were in the vegetable gardens on the other side of the palace, and Edmund had made straight for some strawberries he'd spotted in the patch. It was the nurse who noticed what he was doing; the good woman fell to her knees. I thought she'd tripped, but she was pointing at the plants. They were all flowering, right before our eyes.

"Edmund saw me and held his grubby little hands up and said 'good dirt' very seriously. To this day I don't know if he was suggesting that all dirt was good, or that particular patch, but I nodded and said that yes, yes it was."

Edmund tried not to squirm. He checked to see what Aubrey was making of the concept of him as a toddling child, since it was hardly *manly*, but Aubrey was just nodding, his sketch temporarily abandoned as he gave the queen his full attention.

Alicia seemed to have noticed his idle pencil as well. "Are you finished yet, Aubrey?" she called out.

"Sorry, Licia," Aubrey said, and Edmund saw two of the ladies exchange glances, presumably at the familiarity. It annoyed him.

His mother seemed perfectly happy, however, and went on with her story as Aubrey returned to sketching.

"The parliament and the university decided we all should have known. There was an earthquake when he was born, you see, a big one; I'm sure you've been told about it, since we aren't prone to them."

Edmund felt his spine straighten. He turned to see Aubrey ready to catch his eye, as though he was remembering the same thing he was. What was it that the Honal leader had said? *The quake that gave us our water back.*

His mother didn't seem to notice. "Similar natural phenomena were recorded as accompanying the birth of every Prince of Fortune. As we've only had four of them since Queen Helen, and the last was some two hundred years ago, however, you understand how these things fall out of common knowledge. Ah!"

Edmund looked up at the exclamation and saw that Aubrey had finished his drawing. Alicia dashed over and clapped her hands, and Edmund saw why when he came closer; Aubrey had drawn her with fairy wings, the bench she was sitting on transformed into a gigantic toadstool with similarly scaled vegetation rendered with a few strokes behind her.

"That is actually quite well done," one of the ladies said. "Did you have access to a drawing master, all the way down in—where was it again, Lord Ainsley?"

Edmund felt himself go still, but Aubrey seemed oblivious to the woman's tone. Edmund had never heard her speak like that before, but then it hit him that of course he wouldn't have. Not as the crown prince.

"Oh, a tiny village called Hemcott, in Sawwick," Aubrey replied blithely. "We aren't very far from Marisetown, though."

"Oh!" she said. "The ports. All those merchants. I expect you must have . . . natural talents, then."

Edmund's face grew hot. He glanced at Alicia, whose eyes had gone wide, and then they both looked to their mother.

"Anne," the queen said, "be a dear and go and fetch me my embroidery. I believe I left it in the blue drawing room."

Something in her tone reminded Edmund that his mother could freeze things with a wave of her hand. Lady Anne curtsied and set off. When she was out of hearing, Noble Florian quietly put in, "Your embroidery bag is at your feet, ma'am."

"Thank you, dear," the queen said, "but I couldn't possibly do needlework on an afternoon like this. Let's all take a turn around the formal gardens."

"I assume you *do* have a drawing master at your school?" Alicia asked Aubrey as they set off.

"We've had several," Aubrey said. "The place confused a few of them. They didn't understand why they were teaching the local children along with me and my brothers. Those ones didn't last long."

"I did hear that Lord John Ainsley had set up a village school and was encouraging others to do the same," another lady said. "I didn't realize his sons were educated there as well, alongside—what, the children of farmers?"

"And anyone else around," Aubrey said. "That's the point. Father said he'd be paying a fortune anyway, sending us all off somewhere or getting in tutors, so the whole area might as well get his money's worth."

"He never did want to be praised for being a good man, your father," the queen said.

"He also says that he refuses to live surrounded by ignorant people."

"Yes, that also sounds like him. Given that, you'd think he'd come to Elmiddan more often. There are several educational reformers who keep on inviting him to come and speak, as I understand it. He'll barely even talk to the ones who *are* adopting his egalitarian model."

Edmund wanted to ask something, but the question kept slipping out of his mind. Something still felt off. He wondered if this had to do with the broader awareness he had managed to connect with yesterday. Even thinking of it had him scanning the clouds he could see to the north and—

There.

Was he imagining it, or was there a strange section of gray in among the blue and the white? The queen took his arm to get him moving again; he hadn't even noticed that he had stopped walking to stare at it.

"It does sound a little *radical*," another lady was saying. "I also heard a rumor that your mother herself teaches the students to fence? Surely that's not true?"

"Oh, it is," Aubrey said cheerfully. "She was an army officer, you know, before she had children. She says it helps her keep her hand in, and that we're all going to need it for the war, whenever it comes."

Edmund stopped walking again; his mother let out an exasperated noise. He pointed to the sky in response. A dark storm cloud had now formed in the section he had been watching, but something was not . . . right about it. It had condensed too quickly and was now moving toward them at a great speed, which made no sense, as the winds were not up. There was a rumble of thunder, and one of the ladies said something about going back to the palace, but Edmund still didn't move—it was not supposed to rain today, let alone storm.

"Edmund?" his mother asked.

He put his hand out toward the cloud before he had really thought about what he was doing. He could feel the storm's edges from here, and they were jagged and sharp, more like the manufactured sides of a cog than the gradual gradients of nature that he was used to. It was wrong in that sky in the way that a fishbone was wrong in one's mouth—or worse, a piece of broken glass.

It was upon them when he got to the center of it, but before it could spill into rain—somehow he knew he did not want that rain falling on his home—he . . . got rid of the thing. It had popped like a soap bubble, and all it had taken was the slightest push with his power. That wasn't right either, none of this was, but it had not been a proper storm. He was sure of that now.

"We should go back," he said.

CHAPTER 6

Edmund sent for Sir Jenson and then made for his own writing desk. He started jotting down some notes but wasn't sure which of the ministries should be informed of what had happened. There was one for farming, which also monitored weather. Perhaps that one. Sir J would know.

When his secretary arrived, however, the man seemed at a loss.

"A strange storm?" he asked, finally.

"Yes. It almost seemed unnatural. No, it *was* unnatural. I do not know how it might have behaved, but it would not have been anything . . . good. Should not someone be informed?"

The man just stared at him, seemingly stumped, for several moments.

"Which ministry is it that monitors weather patterns?" Edmund persisted pointedly. "Is it the minister for agriculture? Or is there someone at one of the universities we should tell?"

"Well, I suppose Craywick's department of atmospherical science would be interested." The man paused here, rubbing his hands together absent-mindedly, before saying, "But how could it be unnatural, sir? Are you suggesting someone other than yourself affected the weather?"

"I could never make a storm like that! It was completely out of balance with everything around it."

"Well, then, who or what are you saying did make it?"

Edmund stared at him. "I do not *know*," he said. "That is why I am asking you to tell me who we need to speak to."

Sir J ran his hands together some more, as though gathering his thoughts. "Sir," he finally said. "If someone other than yourself is able to do magic like that, I cannot help but suggest caution. It would not be wise to let information like that leak out. Would it not be better to conduct our own investigation—"

"Investigate how, Sir Jenson, without the use of the specialists and experts I am asking you to point me toward?"

Sir Jenson blinked at him for a moment and then said, "Of course, Your Highness. But may I propose that the appropriate people be sent for, rather than written to? A letter may go astray or be easily passed around, whereas a confidential conversation will always be more discreet, and given that it is only supposed to be the Prince of Fortune who can affect such things, if anybody else had made the suggestion to me, I might call it treasonous."

It was Edmund's turn to blink. "I see. Well, if you could make the arrangements as soon as possible."

The man nodded his assent, his expression worried.

The next few days were bittersweet for Aubrey. He finally had free use of both arms—he had laughed in delight when he had been able to dress properly rather than going about with his jacket unfastened and only one arm inside it—but that also meant that he would be leaving the palace.

He told himself he was being ridiculous. He would be returning in the spring for Alicia's ball, for a start, and both she and Edmund had promised to write to him in the meantime. And it would be *lovely* to go home. He had been terrified the war would start before he got to return. As wonderful as the palace was, he missed his family and his own bed, and to make it even better, John and Cedric would be back for the university winter break, and probably their friend James Malmsbury, too, whose great-aunt lived in the neighborhood. Malmy was always good fun.

He was very busily thinking about all this and refusing to examine why he felt so mopey about going, when he had an unexpected reprieve.

It was the middle of his second-last day, and he was taking luncheon with Alicia and Edmund in between lessons in a lovely parlor not far from the ballroom. They were enjoying an excellent chicken pie, flavored with rare herbs that Aubrey hadn't even known existed and served with a dressed green salad that contrasted beautifully with the richness of the pastry.

Out of nowhere, as was her wont, the princess asked him, "How would you have gotten home? If you weren't going with Edmund and Mamma on their way down to Marisetown, I mean?"

That was something else Aubrey should feel grateful about. At least he was being dropped off by Their Highnesses, on their way to their official visit to the naval base.

"I would have taken the mail coach, of course," Aubrey said, and then laughed at her astonishment.

"But that is such a shame!" she said. "All sorts of exciting things happen during mail coach rides in novels—runaway brides, dastardly rogues! Holdups by highwaymen!"

"Mostly you get squashed in with a bunch of smelly strangers," Aubrey said, "which is even less pleasant than it sounds. In fact, I expect that particular day will be even more squashy than usual, since that evening will be the Firemoon Market in Marisetown. They have it every year on the first full moon of winter. I'm not sure if Father will consent to let me out on the very first night I come back, though. Which is a shame, since I expect this one will be good. People will want to enjoy themselves before the war starts."

"I've never heard of it," Edmund said. "Is it a local festival?"

His brows were making an anxious shape. Aubrey sat on his hands and said, "Nothing so structured as that. I'm not surprised you don't know it; it's not something that you would ever be expected to go to. It's for everyone, so there'll be merchants and clerks and naval men and other people from the base, and soldiers from the gunpowder magazine, but also the local sailors and fisherfolk and farmers. There will be trinket stalls and festival food and fire-eaters and a bad puppet show. I do love a bad puppet show, don't you?"

Edmund's eyebrows were surprised now. Alicia laughed. "I'm not sure we've ever seen a bad puppet show. In fact, I don't even remember the last time we saw a good one. You should sneak out of the residence and go, Edmund, it sounds like such fun. Oooh, wear a hood over your face like a prince in a play, pretending to be a commoner."

"Oh yes, do," Aubrey said. "Commoners wear hoods over their faces in Marisetown all the time. Very common, that."

"Would . . . you come with me?" Edmund asked, and now it was Aubrey who was taken aback. Edmund started speaking more quickly than usual. "You're right: it's not at all the sort of thing we normally go to, but we should. Would your father mind if you returned a day later? You could come to Marisetown with Mamma and me, and stay with us overnight at Clarington House, and go home the next day instead?"

He sounded so anxious, Aubrey couldn't help but reach across the table and put his hand on his arm. "Of course! I would love to. And I shall just tell Father it's in pursuit of educating Saben's next king on the practices and pastimes of his subjects. He would never object to that."

The time flew past. Next thing Edmund knew, their trunks, including Aubrey's, were being strapped onto the back of the royal carriage, and they were away, down to Marisetown. There were servants with them, including his mother's lady's maid and his own valet, Mattheson, and a troop of guardsmen.

Despite the size of the procession, they made good time and reached Clarington House just as the sun started setting. It bathed the residence in a flattering light. The grounds were well tended, all rolling hills covered in picturesque sheep being herded home for the night. There was a meandering river in the distance with an old bridge Aubrey proclaimed delightful. Edmund had forgotten it was there. He found himself thinking that it was, indeed, quite pretty.

The young men spent the bare minimum of time getting settled in before they headed off into town. The queen had been perfectly happy to let Edmund go to this market, even if she seemed surprised that he wanted to. She did, however, have one stipulation. No matter how discreet he was attempting to be, Saben's crown prince could not possibly go anywhere without guardsmen, not when nobody knew when or where the Honals would launch their first attack, and especially not since the palace had been attacked by a group with roots in Marisetown.

For the sake of discretion, however, Edmund managed to argue his mother down to just two guards. And so, when the young men were set down from their deliberately plain coach a little way from the square, the escort they had to lose was small.

The full moon was bright in the clear sky, but the town square was also lit with lamps and torches, making everything flicker. While Edmund had visited Marisetown before, it was an entirely different creature like this—and so was Aubrey, who seemed part fae with his grinning face half in shadow, taking Edmund's hand in his and pulling him on to the next attraction, and the next.

Edmund hadn't had someone hold his hand like this since he was a child. It was not the same. When Aubrey let go to pay for something at a stall, the loss felt greater than it should have.

The young lord obtained for them the exotic fare of a pair of fish pies, some roasted chestnuts twisted up in paper, and two cups of negus. He also bought some chocolate-covered marzipan in a pretty box to take back for his mother and a large piece of rosewater delight for his father, who was partial to it. Edmund had no idea what his parents might like, so he bought them the same with the coin in his pocket—not something that was usually there. He considered a painted doll for his sister, but Aubrey wondered if she wouldn't prefer one of the carved shells—a specialty of the area—and so he went with that instead.

Nobody seemed to recognize him.

He hadn't realized how liberating that would feel.

"You're smiling," Aubrey said to him, and it took Edmund a moment to be able to articulate why.

"I'm a young man at a fair," he said.

They ate their food, watching the puppet show and the jugglers and the crowd, their attendants keeping a discreet distance. The boys ended up chasing each other around the market, giddy at their own bravado and tipsy on the hot wine (they had gone back for more), and then Lord Ainsley had pulled Edmund into a little hidden space he had spied in between some stalls and the back of a building.

A seat was built into the stonework here, and Aubrey flopped onto it, boasting of his fatigue as he tugged Edmund down next to him. They caught their breath and just regarded each other for a moment in the cramped space.

Then, without really thinking about what he was doing or why he shouldn't do it, Edmund did what he had been wanting to do for weeks and reached a hand out to trace the curve of Aubrey's lower lip with his thumb.

Aubrey let out a little exhalation, and his mouth twitched into a smile. Edmund came a bit more to himself at that. He whipped his hand away, blushing and stumbling through an apology for such familiarity, but Aubrey just said, "Don't be sorry. But surely there's something else that you want to do with my mouth?"

Edmund had no idea how to respond to that. It must have shown in his face, because Aubrey rolled his eyes; and then he kissed him.

It was Edmund's first. It was overwhelming. Instead of focusing on everybody else and on the wind and the earth around them, there was nothing but Aubrey's hand on his face and his warm lips on his.

He was a young man being kissed at a fair.

He didn't get a chance to become used to the sensation, however, before a trader spotted them behind the stalls and yelled at them to be off, scooping up a handful of fallen autumn leaves and throwing them at them to make their point. They ran for it, Edmund blushing, Aubrey laughing wildly, and then their guardsmen found them, apologizing sheepishly for momentarily losing them.

They walked back to the carriage. Edmund could feel his pulse in his fingers, in his stomach. Aubrey kept sneaking sideways glances at him as they went, biting his lip, like they had a secret now; and they did. Edmund felt over-aware of his body and of the distance between them. One of the guards rode inside with them, which was frustrating.

They arrived back at the residence and were informed that Her Highness had retired for the night.

"We shan't disturb her, then," Edmund said, pleased with how steady his voice sounded. "Lord Ainsley and I will withdraw to my rooms. We will ring if we need anything."

"Very good, sir."

And then they were making their way upstairs. Edmund couldn't remember where his room was; he ended up following Aubrey. When they got to the sitting room, Aubrey backed up against a nearby wall in a movement that was somehow an invitation. Edmund could not stop himself from following, and then Aubrey was smiling against his mouth and fitting against him. He fit so well against him. And this was everything that Edmund had been too afraid to want and, even as it was happening, still wasn't sure he could have.

CHAPTER 7

In the early morning—much earlier than expected; no one was yet dressed—Aubrey's father arrived himself with the Ainsleys' black carriage, their crest with its birds in fading white paint on the side, and took Aubrey away.

Edmund watched it crunch over the white gravel drive and go out the gates, and then he went up onto the rooftop, where there was a battlement-style balcony. One could see all the way to the sea from here, but Edmund had his eyes fixed on a black speck moving along the highway, away from him and back to Hemcott.

And then he saw the smoke, coming from near the alternate road, closer to Marisetown.

There wasn't that much of it, but it was oddly bright, which was why it caught his eye. There was some mist lingering there as well, but this was different. He walked along the balcony in that direction, trying to see if it was worth worrying about, and saw that it was coming from several places.

He found himself split between the urge to raise the alarm or to find out more first—what if it was just brick works or a bonfire made of the rubbish from last night's market, and he made a fool of himself. Before he consciously decided to do it, his eyes closed, and he was reaching out through the air currents to see if he could feel the source. His hands curled around the top of the low wall—nowhere near as good as sinking them into the earth, but better than nothing—and he was in the air when the shock wave hit.

An explosion.

His eyes flew open to see a plume of black smoke and, briefly, a tall lick of flame, just visible farther west, at the coast. He spent a second staring at it dumbly, wondering what could be on fire right on the water there, before he remembered where he was, why he was here.

The naval base.

"There is a fire at the port!" he shouted as he ran down the stairs. Servants, their eyes wide, started following him as he tried to get to his mother. "Prepare the horses and tell the guards—the queen and I must go, as quickly as possible."

Which corridor is it; why are these residences all so big? he thought desperately, turning corners, and then he saw a door open ahead of him and his mother's maid Dawson peer out of it. He ran toward her in relief.

"Mamma, there's been an explosion at the naval yard," he said, dashing through the door.

His mother stared at him. She was swathed in a floral brocade robe, a pretty porcelain cup in one hand, the saucer in the other. Her hair was only half dressed and was still full of curling papers.

"It was so big I could see it from the roof; there's smoke everywhere," he pressed on, desperate to be understood. "We must go now! You need to help put out the fires!"

But his mother was already shoving aside her tea and ripping pins out of her hair.

"My uniform," she said to Dawson, who went immediately to get it. "Edmund, have you—"

"The servants know. The guards are getting ready. Should I go on ahead?"

"Safer to stay together," she said, her hands now plaiting her long hair back efficiently. "Can you—make it rain on the fire, from this distance?"

Now it was his turn to stare. He hadn't even thought of that, only of letting her know. He nodded and then pelted down the corridor again, making for the main doors.

I can do this, he thought desperately. It wasn't so far, and he had been trained for this sort of emergency, even if he had had no experience in practice—at least not with a fire. Making it rain was easy, to be sure; the trick was in making these things specific. He could practically hear Mrs. Grant telling him that high winds, which usually accompanied any rain he created, would carry embers.

Control is the key, sir, she was always saying to him, as though he needed reminding, and—as he sometimes unkindly thought—as though she knew anything about it.

He ran through the doors, which were wide open now. He was certain that he could smell smoke even from here, a horrible acrid note in the cold, fresh sea air. Things that shouldn't be burning. He ducked through the guards collecting on the gravel drive and threw himself onto his knees on the patch of grass to the side, ripping his gloves off. He could feel dozens of eyes on him, but he couldn't care about that now.

No wind, only rain, he thought. *Make it safe.*

He pushed with his power, trying to focus on the place where he had felt the explosion coming from. There was so much—too many things clamoring for his attention—but then suddenly he could feel a horrible *wrong* note in among it all, like something he needed to fix. It took him a moment to realize that it felt a little like the storm that had moved toward the palace the other day that had unsettled him so much, and he felt his panic spike through his gift.

There was a rumbling noise, and he had some sense that the light was changing on the other side of his closed eyelids. He opened them.

It was too dark. No, no, no, no—he'd done exactly what he'd been afraid he would do and called a storm, complete with the sort of winds that might spread the fire everywhere. Marisetown would burn, and it was going to be all his fault because he wasn't good enough—

He felt something snap in his head as his frustration peaked, and he grabbed hold of it, turning it into power he could use to at least move the direction of the wind, so that it blew out toward the sea. If he couldn't calm down the air currents, he could at least force them that way, where any sparks they carried would have a hard time causing problems.

Take that, Mrs. Grant.

He took in a shuddery sort of breath and stood up. The rain was here as well, now, falling on him. He turned. Fewer people were watching him than he had feared—just some of the guards waiting by their horses. They all looked away quickly, except for the captain, a tall dark-skinned man named Huntley. His eyes were wide, making the whites stand out in contrast more than usual in his face.

They stared at each other for a moment, and then Edmund nodded at him. The nod he got back was different, somehow, from the man's usual professional politeness. Edmund hated the idea of his mother's captain being afraid of him, but there was nothing he could do about it now. He brushed off his knees and made for his own horse. His valet

Mattheson was standing by it, he saw now, ready to help him into his hat and greatcoat. He accepted them gratefully; it had been a cold morning, and he had made it colder. He didn't have time to brood on any of that, however, because his mother was striding out in her bicorn hat and her white coat, covered in coils of gold braid, the embroidered dragon on her shoulder.

"We go to assist at the port," she called out. "There has been an explosion. Have we had no messenger?"

"None, Your Highness," Captain Huntley said.

"Very well. Be ready for anything. Mount up."

The captain repeated the order, and then they were all away, galloping into the rain.

The town, when they got there, was bedraggled and largely empty, everyone presumably having withdrawn indoors from the rain. Edmund had given the place such a drenching in his haste and panic, some of the laneways they passed were underwater. There were trees with fallen limbs, and the odd flimsy wooden fence was down. The town square, which just last night had hosted such a beautiful event, had been drowned. He saw a coffeehouse with its colorfully striped awning torn in half, one section up on the roof. An aproned attendant was trying to get it down with a pole, to stop further damage, perhaps. Edmund felt increasingly guilty about all of it, especially since there were no signs of fire anywhere.

Until they got to the naval base.

They saw the smoke first. The queen gave the order to halt as the buildings came into sight. Edmund had been there before; the main building at the entrance formed three sides of a rectangle around the front courtyard. The stone fencing wall of the complex should have made the fourth side of the shape, blocking most of the buildings from sight, apart from what one could see through the wrought iron entrance gates, except that the gates were gone. There were, instead, twists of blackened metal lying here and there, the wall around them reduced on both sides to rubble. Their whole group could have trotted side by side through the gap.

The building to their left had had its closest corner blasted away as well, the roof collapsed and the interior on fire. Edmund would wonder later if the explosions had been timed to happen together, and if that was the shock wave that he had felt; in the moment, however, he was most distracted by the bodies. Edmund's mind slowed down like a reined-in horse and then stopped completely as he saw them.

Piles of people lay sprawled all over the scene being pelted with rain, their heads lying on the compacted dirt and the laid stones of the base's front courtyard as though they had simply collapsed in the middle of responding to what was happening. They were most of them in naval uniforms, but there were plenty in the garb of soldiers as well: too many to account for, since this was not an army base. The soldiers did not barrack here but at the gunpowder magazine they guarded, on the outskirts of the town.

Edmund raised his hands to the sky and broke the clouds up above them, stopping the rain. The queen was saying something to the captain about sending for help—firefighters, physicians—messengers, to send word for military reinforcements—but Edmund was distracted. Something felt . . . horrible here. He kept getting wafts of it, like there was a decaying animal carcass nearby, except it wasn't a smell. It was something else.

"Do you feel that?" he asked his mother. "Something . . . wrong?"

She looked at him sharply but was then distracted by the captain issuing orders to his troops to start putting out the fire.

"Stop, wait," she said, her arm going out as though to physically prevent them from going past her into the complex. "It will do no one any good if all of you pass out as well."

The captain motioned at the bodies. "They're alive?"

"I can see the closest people breathing. Let's hope the rest are." She turned to Edmund. "What do you sense?"

"I don't know," he said, dropping from his horse, "but you must sense it too, or you wouldn't have stopped the men from crossing over this boundary wall. There's something—"

He closed his eyes, trying to work out where the feeling was coming from. It was somewhere near them, to his right, so he went slowly toward it, stepping around stones, some with mortar still attached, as he went. He heard his mother behind him, telling him to wait, but—it was there, right there, on the other side of the wall.

"It can't hurt *me*," he found himself calling back to her. It felt true, although he couldn't have said how he knew.

Then there it was. A Honal rune.

It was a complicated, asymmetrical thing, as tall as a man, all sharp angles and lines, meaning who knew what. Just seeing it twisted Edmund's stomach. It was drawn in something like charcoal, in a sheltered guard's nook in the wall. What little cover there was must have saved it from the rain.

He reached up and forced himself to swipe his hand across the center. That's what you were supposed to do with runes—destroy them. Saben was still dotted with the ruins of grand buildings that had been razed to the ground in the civil war due to the runes carved into the walls.

Edmund rubbed his hand along the black marks, and revulsion overtook him for one horrific moment—but then, blessedly, it worked.

The feeling of wrongness was immediately gone, like the marks had been a vessel holding some foul liquid that had now been tipped out and washed away. He resisted the urge to scrub off the remnants; his mother should see what remained.

"I think it's safe now," he called out, and the queen made straight for him, still mounted, holding his horse's reins as well. She stared at the smudged mark.

"Captain, assign four men to stop that fire from spreading until more help can arrive," she called out, not taking her eyes from it. "Everyone else with me and His Highness. We're heading for the docks. We need to find where all that smoke is coming from."

Edmund had forgotten about the rest of the complex, which he recalled from his last visit as much larger than one would expect. He remounted his horse and followed her, heading through the courtyard. He could now see more smoke coming from somewhere closer to the water, but everything on the way—the residences, the mast house, the ropery—all seemed fine, merely dotted with prone bodies. It was eerie, the silence unsettling. He started thinking of fairy tales about castles full of people cursed to sleep for a hundred years.

The water came into view. Three ships were in the harbor. They appeared undamaged, their flags high, their sails—well, Edmund forgot what all the special words were, but they were tidily rolled away. Yet still, no crew was visible—which, he reminded himself, they wouldn't be, if they were all passed out below deck. When more of the shoreline became visible as they cleared a fence, the source of the smoke became apparent: one section of one dock was floating about in smoking pieces, but the fire was already extinguished.

More people lying everywhere. Some half dozen or so were visible floating in the water.

Captain Huntley immediately sent more of his guards to the nearest boats to rescue who they could. The set of the queen's mouth suggested she had little hope, but she followed when the man motioned that they should position themselves up on the viewing point. Edmund supposed it was as safe as anywhere; they could at least see anyone approaching them from there.

She and Edmund sat mounted, guarded by the captain and his last four men, and spent a moment looking around at the baffling scene.

"Do you sense any other runes?" she asked Edmund. He shook his head.

"I've never felt anything like that," he said. "Have you?"

She raised her eyebrows at him. "I didn't feel anything—or rather, I didn't knowingly feel anything—but you were right; I didn't want anybody going in there. Although with everyone unconscious, and an explosion, I had wondered if it was a pocket of noxious gas, like in a mining accident. Something tragic, but natural and blameless. We know who to blame now, though, with the rune there, but—this is all so strange. What do you make of it, Captain?"

Captain Huntley had been squinting at the water, watching one of his teams heave a streaming body into their boat. After a moment, he said, "It makes no sense, ma'am. If the Honals did this, where are they? And why pick such a large target, but do so little? It's as though they stopped. Like they got started in their task of blowing everything up, but then something happened."

"I made it rain," Edmund said, and then flushed so hard his face felt burned by it as his mother peered at him in confusion and then something like skepticism.

"I don't know!" he added. "Perhaps it—it washed away the rest of the runes? The captain is right: something clearly went wrong. They can't have meant to put hundreds of people to sleep, then blow up only a handful of things and disappear."

"Where *did* they go?" she asked. Edmund looked at her, and she added, "Everyone's unconscious."

It took him a few seconds to understand her meaning.

"You think they're still here?" He motioned at the bodies. "You think some of these people aren't from the base at all?"

"There were a lot of soldiers in the front courtyard, sir," the captain put in. "They're not from the base."

Edmund thought about it. "I saw smoke in another place from Clarington's roof," he said. "Further north, along the secondary road, a few miles outside of town. Could another building have come under attack there?"

The queen bit her bottom lip, thinking; and then her head flew up, even as her shoulders slumped.

"The gunpowder magazine," she said. "Perhaps the garrison there could have been made to carry the powder here and use it in the attacks."

"Made? How?"

She threw her hands in the air. "We're going to have to wait for them to wake up."

A glad cry rang out from one of the boats. It lifted Edmund's spirits for a moment—their newest rescue must be breathing—but then the captain said slowly, "So the magazine is . . . unguarded?"

Edmund looked to his mother in alarm. She narrowed her eyes in a calculating sort of way.

The captain clearly saw it too, because he said, "We don't have enough men to go and check. We shouldn't divide up further. And, ma'am, I'm sorry, but I won't deliver you to whatever could be waiting for us there."

She appeared torn—Edmund certainly felt so himself—but they were saved from having to think it over further by more cries, coming from behind them.

Everyone was waking up.

Edmund was exhausted and filthy by the time they returned to the residence late that night. After everyone had awoken, the rest of the day had been bustle and helping—official messengers and the bearing of gratitude. Edmund liked the bustle better than the gratitude, though he tried to accept it as graciously as he could.

Almost a thousand people had been affected. As many people as possible were questioned on the scene, and details were taken for the rest. No one had yet been found who could not be vouched for. Still, it was impossible to be sure that no one had fled the scene, for all that the area had been barricaded by the reinforcements when they arrived and the roads blocked off.

There were only a handful of serious injuries, all caused by the explosions, and a handful of dead, all seemingly drowned from falling into the water. None of that seemed to be by any design, but all accidental. Incidental. A by-product. Edmund wasn't sure if that were better or worse.

Through the questioning, certain details emerged often enough to form a pattern. None of the soldiers from the garrison at the gunpowder magazine remembered anything prior to going to sleep the night before, whereas the staff at the naval base mostly remembered starting to go about their business that morning, and then nothing until they had woken up. Everyone was confused and shaky.

A fair percentage remembered a mist. This would not have been considered noteworthy except that about half of those said that it had moved "strangely." A few more remembered a woman's voice saying something like "monium." None of them had ever heard the word before. Edmund remembered it from Aubrey's vision, though that didn't get them any closer to knowing what it meant.

He was cleaning himself up at a washbasin in his room when his mother knocked on his door and came in, swathed in a soft robe. It took him a moment to recognize it as the same one she had been wearing that morning when he had gone in to tell her about the fire. It felt like a hundred years ago.

"How . . ." he found himself asking. "How did they—"

He made himself take a deep breath, then another, because he could feel the temperature in the room dropping and was worried he might be altering the weather outside.

"Yes, I know," she said. "How did the Honals get into the port undetected? How did nobody see them leave? We have had ships patrolling the entire coastline and all the watchtowers on alert—we have been ready for years, waiting for what had been Seen to start to happen, no matter what that protest group thought. We were prepared. How did they get *in*?"

Edmund nodded helplessly, and his mother reached into her robe pocket and pulled out a letter. She held it up. "This was just delivered. Another set of reinforcements has arrived to protect the gunpowder magazine."

Too late, Edmund thought. Word had come around noon that the stores had been raided. Half of the powder was missing, and most of that was unaccounted for, although some had been found at the docks, clearly set up in preparation for destroying something or other, but unexploded. Abandoned.

No one knew where the rest of the powder was.

"Our official visit is canceled," she said, waving the letter in the air now. It had the War Office's green seal on it, he saw, the kind they put on important mail. "You and I are to go back to the capital first thing in the morning and await instruction."

Aubrey was sitting in his room by the window gazing out over the garden, wet from the morning's storm, and thinking dreamily about Edmund and the previous night, when he heard a commotion downstairs. He had spent his day quite comfortably. He had ridden home with his father, making him laugh with stories from the palace. The journey had taken longer than usual because of the sudden downpour, but that meant they had had more time with just the two of them—a rare thing to be savored. The entire family had luncheoned together, and then Aubrey had gone upstairs to settle back into his bedroom. The shouting was an unwelcome disruption.

It took Aubrey a moment as he walked down the stairs to recognize the voice as belonging to Alfie, one of the manservants. Aubrey had never heard him raise his voice before; he was normally entirely unflappable.

"What on earth is the matter?" he asked Cedric, who was coming out of the family library, a volume in green leather still in his hands.

"Father sent him to the village post office," Cedric said as they both moved toward the noise. "Something must have happened."

Something had certainly happened, but nobody could agree what.

Aubrey had half a mind to mount a horse and ride back to Marisetown to make sure Edmund was all right, until his mother casually mentioned that the roads might well be barricaded while the attack was investigated, and the royal visit there would surely be cut short. Which left him nothing to do but sit tight at home for more news.

Marisetown had felt so safe, only last night. It hadn't been. The Honals must have taken advantage of the celebration to sneak in. Aubrey was suddenly struck with how dangerous and irresponsible it had been to deliberately shake Edmund's guard the way that they had. The thought made him feel sick for a moment, until he reminded himself that nothing had happened to Edmund, after all. Not last night, anyway.

The family had to wait for the next morning's newspaper for more details. As soon as it arrived, Lord Ainsley started reading it aloud to the family and most of the servants in the front parlor, which was slightly too small for the task, but they were interrupted not a quarter of an hour later by the crunch of carriage wheels on the gravel of the drive. It was their neighbor, Lady Harriet Malmsbury, clinging to her great-nephew's arm. Malmy—who spent holidays with her rather than go home to his horrible father and stepmother—patted her hand soothingly until they could get her into a chair. It wasn't solely her gout, which she usually pretended didn't exist; she was clearly very upset.

The servants all fled to do things like fetch tea, since Malmy was, unlike their own master, a proper nobleman. Lord James Malmsbury was not only the Viscount Malmsbury but would also be the next Marquess of Stratingford: something that both his great-aunt and the Ainsleys were all convinced he would do a much better job of than the title's present holder, no matter what the revolting man thought.

He also tended to make the younger maids blush despite never having gone near any of them, since the handsome twenty-two-year-old had already featured multiple times in the more gossipy news sheets for scandalous affairs he was rumored to have conducted. It was, the

Ainsley brothers knew, all true—or as truc as such reports ever could be, given their prioritization of titillation over fact.

"Honals, and so close," Lady Malmsbury said shakily, by way of greeting. "They've never made it down to Sawwick before. Marisetown hasn't come under attack since the civil war."

Aubrey hadn't thought of that. He wasn't sure if it changed the way he felt about it, though. It was all quite bad enough as it was.

"It was barely attacked now," Lady Ainsley said. "Something seems to have gone wrong with their plan. That bodes well for us."

"If it even was them," Lord Ainsley put in. "No Honals were found. There's an opinion piece further into the paper wondering if this isn't just more protests."

"Involving the entire garrison at the gunpowder magazine? Who have no idea how they got to the naval yard? No, no," Lady Malmsbury started, waving her lace-trimmed handkerchief around for emphasis, "this is the start of the war, and all our precious boys will be in uniform before the end of winter!"

Aubrey's father handed the newspaper to his wife at that and excused himself.

Lady Malmsbury waited until the door was closed behind him before turning to Aubrey's mother. "John still hasn't reconciled himself to the idea, then?"

"Of course not," she replied. "He wants us to live in a world governed by logic and understanding, not violence."

"We all want that—" Lady Malmsbury started crossly, but Malmy, perched on the edge of her armchair, put his arm around her.

"It's a good thing to want," he said gently. "And would you prefer it if he weren't upset by the idea of his children going off to fight?"

His aunt deflated immediately but then perked up a little when

Cedric tapped his spectacles and said, "The army probably isn't going to take me, anyway."

"Well, that should comfort him," Lady Malmsbury said, and then, motioning with the handkerchief, "and surely Aubrey's still too young?"

Aubrey smiled apologetically. "I'll be seventeen at the end of winter, ma'am. I'll qualify then."

"You are just a *baby*," she said, "for all that you tower over me now. You know, it probably will not be so very compulsory—"

"I will not shirk, my lady," Aubrey said. "How could I stay at home safe while my brothers do their duty?"

This earned him a pat on the hand—her joints looked so swollen and sore, Aubrey thought, but resisted saying anything—but then she started and said, "Oh, wait—I nearly forgot. We did not come only to commiserate. James collected your mail when he went to the post office this morning. There are extra deliveries today because of all this. You had something with a very fancy seal on it, you know."

"Aunt Hennie!" Malmy tutted, even though he was laughing as he handed Aubrey his letter and then another two to Lady Ainsley. "You're not supposed to examine other people's *mail*."

"I was only looking," she said, unrepentant. "Don't think I don't know about that girl you've been writing to either. This one must be writing back a lot, given how often you've been going to the post office."

"Ah yes, the elusive Miss *Tsung*," Cedric said, while John laughed, Wilson blushed, and their mother pretended to be very interested in her own letters. Cedric started to say something else in a teasing way, and Aubrey took his chance to make his escape to his room to read his letter.

It was addressed in Edmund's hand, and the seal was indeed fancy, larger than the norm in a light green wax that Aubrey had never seen for sale anywhere with a stylized tree pressed into it: Saben's tree, Helen's tree. Aubrey had some notion that letters from the king, for his father, arrived with dragons pressed into them. He wondered if Edmund used this signet because he was a Prince of Fortune, or if it was the one used by the rest of the royal family. He was tempted for just a moment to cut it from the paper and keep it, but he was too keen to read what Edmund had to say, so he cracked it open, consoling himself that it would surely not be the only letter from Edmund he ever received.

My dear Aubrey,

I write this early in the morning, before Mamma and I return to Talstam. I have very little time, but I flattered myself—hoped—that you would want to know that I am unhurt after the events of yesterday. I assume the news will have reached you by now. We still don't know how the Honals did any of it without detection, which makes me more uncomfortable than anything else.

I know that you said you would write, but everything feels so bad right now, I think that I will live for your letters, as reassurances of your safety. Please send one soon.

Yours,
E

Aubrey pressed the page to his chest, torn between worry and relief. Not only was Edmund safe, but the letter also removed a smaller concern that Aubrey had had. He and Edmund had not had a chance, before he left, to discuss what had happened between them. Aubrey had planned to spend the morning professing his adoration and pressing upon his prince that he would be faithful until they were in company again in the spring, when he hoped that they could pick up where they had left off, but his father had arrived early as one of his little jokes.

It didn't matter. Clearly Edmund had understood and reciprocated his feelings, if the language he had used was anything to go by.

He sat down at his desk and pulled out some paper; nothing as fine as Edmund himself used, but it would do. He would show Edmund that he had not flattered himself by assuming Aubrey cared about his safety, and hopefully provide a bit of cheer, since that was the best that he could do from this distance. Heavens knew they'd all need it, since worse was surely to come.

CHAPTER 8

The next few months were strange for Edmund. The Honals did not attack again or invade; they would not even confirm that they had been responsible for the events in Marisetown but continued to maintain their refusal to communicate with Saben at all, repudiating all diplomatic messengers, often with force.

It left everyone on tenterhooks, able to do nothing to help other than repair the naval base as quickly as they could and continue to plan for the war to come. Military recruitment was in full force. Unlike Aubrey, who would have to sign up, Edmund would be considered in service the moment the nation was declared at war. By rights, Alicia should have been as well, but since the ball to signify her entrance to public life was already planned, it was decided that she would not be called to perform any duties until after it had been held.

The family had considered canceling the thing completely. It seemed wrong to hold a society event while everyone sat on the edges of their seats, waiting for whatever the next Honal attack would be, but they were overruled by the bureaucracy, who said they would not drop everything for the Honals' convenience and that it would be a blow to morale for it to be postponed.

Alicia was fitted for her military uniform in the same sessions that the tailor used for her ball gown. The man did a new one for Edmund as well while he was there. He left seam allowances in for both of them, so that the garments could be let out if they continued to grow. It had struck Edmund as such an odd, poignant piece of consideration, he mentioned it to Aubrey in that week's letter. He had expected something soothing in reply—the lordling's letters were usually a balm—but in this case, he received the opposite:

> *I had to smile when I saw your mention of your uniform this week, because I have news there as well: Mother took the four of us the other day to purchase our commissions at Marisetown. John, Wilson, and I are all to be lieutenants but must await our orders, which will not come until spring since, as Mother points out, there is not quite any rush yet. At least we will not have to apply for leave to go to Alicia's ball, but it does mean that we will not be going in red coats.*
>
> *Cedric is not to wear one at all. His eyesight saw him fail the army's physical inspection. This was not unexpected, but Wilson complained that it was a waste and an outrage since Cedric is the best rider and best shot of all of us, and none of us are shabby with a gun or a horse. Wilson was not wrong, but he went on for such a long time that Cedric*

ended up snapping at him that he was relieved; that he had dreaded the thought of having to kill anyone or of anyone trying to kill him. We were all quiet after that.

He and Mother left for Elmiddan the next day to visit the War Office. We have had word that they gave him an administrative role almost on the spot; and meanwhile Mother signed up at the Armed Services Support Office, which is run by an old friend of hers. I couldn't shake the idea that this had been part of her plan all along in going, but it can be hard to tell with her. Which will probably make her perfect for their work.

Edmund read this last part of the letter to his own mother when he had tea with her and Alicia that afternoon, since he wasn't sure what that department did. He had not expected her to snort with laughter before he could ask.

Alicia and Edmund stared at her.

"Oh, my dears," she said. "Aubrey could hardly be more explicit, but I can see he knows exactly what she'll be doing. The Armed Services Support Office—I didn't know that's what they were calling it."

Her children looked at her blankly. She rolled her eyes at them.

"If Lady Ainsley isn't some sort of intelligencer, I will eat this handkerchief."

She waved her embroidery at them, and Edmund was distracted for a moment with hoping very much that nobody had to eat it, because surely the unnaturally bright blue thread she was using was not safe to ingest. He then spent a second or two digesting the idea that the elegant Lady Ainsley, who taught children to fence and always seemed to know what to say, was now a government spy.

He found he could picture it readily.

Four more weeks, and they would be together, assuming war did not break out. All six Ainsleys were to visit and stay as guests at Talstam for a week. Alicia had insisted that she *required* Aubrey on hand in the lead-up to the ball, and since it would hardly do for him to stay in the palace while his parents and brothers were forced to find shelter elsewhere, she had declared that Lord Ainsley senior needed to finally reconcile his principles with his intimacy with the royal family. She said that this was all his fault anyway, since he shouldn't have had such a charming son if he hadn't wanted Alicia and Edmund to be charmed.

The king had quoted all of this verbatim when he extended the invitation. Aubrey's father had been quite rude in his reply, telling his old friend to stop hiding behind his children and suggesting where he could put his palace, but he had still accepted the invitation. The king had laughed and taken it as a victory.

Edmund was being sustained in the meantime by Aubrey's letters, which were much more pleasant than his father's. They'd been writing to each other every week the whole winter, and while the letters were mostly filled with the sorts of news that he could read out to his sister, who demanded to know what they said compared with the ones she was sent, Aubrey did include sections that Edmund had to skip over. Like the time he had written *I keep thinking of the day when you struck that tree with lightning and then healed it by placing your hands upon it. When I come back to the palace, I will make some time to visit it and tell it that I know exactly how it feels.*

There was one letter that Edmund did not think he could read to her at all. It had started with chatter about his week, but then it had gone on with:

I tried to draw you today, but Mother came in to tell me something and I smudged the thing, covering it too quickly. I feel silly about it now. It seems ridiculous to worry she might notice how intimately I memorized your features.

I want to know them better. I want to be able to draw you without using my eyes, just from touch.

This is all to say: I think of you. I think of you more and more as the day when we can be together again gets closer. I see you in the sunlight, in the rain, in the new buds on the trees.

Now I worry I have gone too far and you will think me fanciful. I have not forgotten that war is coming; my brothers and I are training every day. But we can take some moments for joy, too. Mother says that we will need them, to fortify us for what's to come. For now, my words are all I can send you, but know that my thoughts are all yours as well.

Until we are together again, I am most truly yours,
Aubrey

In the end, Edmund had pretended no letter had come that week when Alicia had asked. His skin tingled any time he thought about everything Aubrey had written. He was counting the days, but then Sir Jenson came in one morning, an odd expression on his face, and everything changed.

"There is something you should know, sir. I have received a report," Sir Jenson said, and then cleared his throat. He seemed uncomfortable. He had let Edmund have coffee and start his breakfast rather than just talking at him immediately; Edmund should have been suspicious of that. He put his piece of toast down warily.

"I wondered why I had been given it," Sir J went on, "until I realized that—" He cleared his throat again. "Sir, you must know that I would never presume to be taken into your confidence regarding your personal relationships. But in case it should be relevant, you should know that it appears your friend the youngest Lord Ainsley has been spending a great deal of time with Lord James Malmsbury, the heir of the Marquess of Stratingford."

"Yes," Edmund said, wondering what the man was getting at. "Aubrey has mentioned it in his letters. Malmsbury is visiting his aunt; she lives close by."

Sir J was nodding, but he still looked awkward. "The marquess and his son famously do not get along, partly because—well, sir, Malmsbury has a *reputation*. And he and Lord Ainsley appear to be very . . . close. He has stayed the night at Hemcott a few times over the period, and they were also witnessed bathing in a lake together. Naked."

Sir Jenson's eyes flicked down to Edmund's plate. Edmund glanced down as well to see that he had shredded his toast with his fingers. He put the crust down on top of the pile of crumbs and wiped his hands on his napkin.

"There is more, sir. Lord Ainsley was also seen just last week entering a . . . house of *ill repute* with his oldest brother, John, in Marisetown."

Edmund felt himself frowning and made his face relax.

"A . . . what sort of house?" he asked.

Sir J cleared his throat. "A meeting place for . . . men looking to meet other men, sir, for . . . casual intimacy on the premises."

Edmund's face burned hot. He hadn't even known such places existed.

He excused himself with a headache and headed back to bed.

The next weeks passed for Edmund in a haze of misery. It didn't help that several strange storms tried to erupt over the palace—they were dealt with easily enough—or that he hardly saw Alicia. She was being whisked away after breakfast each morning for dress fittings and etiquette refreshers and all sorts of other arcane mysteries to make certain that she did not disgrace herself at this ball.

When he did see her, she kept on asking him what was wrong and, when he insisted it was nothing, tried to cheer him up by reminding him how many days it was until Aubrey was to come.

Curiosity got the better of him at one point, and he went to the palace library to check the location of the Marquess of Stratingford's estate, since he couldn't remember who exactly the family was. He was too embarrassed to take the volume tracing all the noble families down to the reading area, so he flicked through it standing up by its shelf. The Stratingford seat was in Essaben, which some sensible, detached part of Edmund's brain wanted to remind him was good land for growing fruit and vegetables. The jealous part stuck on the fact that it was to the northeast of the capital: nowhere near Aubrey's family. The man's aunt had no business living where she did, he found himself thinking crossly.

He put the book back, his stomach full of rocks.

He took a deep breath and let it out slowly to try to stop the heat in his eyes from progressing into tears. He wasn't sure that he would succeed in this venture, so he turned blindly and made his way back to his room.

He was so ridiculous, he thought as he walked the palace corridors, not seeing them at all. He should not have assumed that that one night had meant more than it did. Except—they had gotten so close—and Aubrey's letters. Surely Aubrey wouldn't have written like that, said such lovely things, or . . .

Or perhaps Aubrey had been writing letters like that to Lord Malmsbury the entire time he had been at the palace.

And the worst part was that he had every right to. He didn't actually owe Edmund anything. Their acquaintance could be counted in weeks, whereas Aubrey had known Malmsbury for years and years. He had even completed his schooling with the Ainsleys after being expelled from boarding school in his final year. Aubrey had mentioned it once in passing, at the palace.

Edmund didn't know what any of this meant. Had he been thrown over? Or had Aubrey meant for that night after the market to be just another *casual intimacy*?

He made his way back to his rooms and decided that he did know one thing: he did not blame Malmsbury and he did not blame Aubrey. His upset now was his own fault. He had clearly assumed too much, been foolish and presumptive. He and Aubrey had not discussed any hopes they might have or made promises. He must have misunderstood in the wake of his own feelings, and after all, expecting anything from Aubrey under the circumstances was the utmost in selfishness. There was no future he could eventually offer the young lord. Edmund was expected to make a politically advantageous union; he could therefore give Lord Ainsley nothing more than a position as his . . . what would it be called?

Paramour.

It was the sort of word that gossips used in lowered voices. It was . . . diminishing. Aubrey deserved better. The more Edmund thought of it, the less and less he blamed his . . . his *friend* for finding company elsewhere. Wittier, brighter company, probably, with more carnal experience as well. And more freedom.

There might be a coronet in this Lord Malmsbury's future, but the burden of it was much less than a crown. A marquess stood only a few steps lower than him on paper, but it may as well have been a mountain, because his personal relationships were unlikely to affect the nation, despite how entitled people felt to gossip about them.

Edmund had no claim on Aubrey whatsoever. They would move on from this, treat that night as—as a youthful romp, not to be repeated, and perhaps once this shattering ache in every single one of his bones had passed, he could embrace the idea of friendship—unmuddied, simple friendship, something he wasn't sure they'd actually ever had—with the young lord.

He couldn't bear to open the last two letters that Aubrey sent and did not try to write himself. He had thought it would make things easier. The pain in his upper chest had not faded, however, by the time Aubrey appeared.

The family was due in time for dinner. Edmund had no appetite, but then, he hadn't expected to.

Mattheson seemed to be taking longer than usual with his cravat and his hair.

"There," his valet eventually said, standing back to view his handiwork. "You look very well, sir."

Edmund couldn't work out the man's tone. It was *something*, but that something didn't seem pitying. It occurred to him that valets in plays and novels were always gossiping with their employers; perhaps he should have taken Mattheson into his confidence, since the man had clearly noticed something was amiss. He blinked at him for a moment but couldn't even think how to start. He forced himself to take a breath; it shuddered a little.

"Thank you, Mattheson. Am I ready?"

Mattheson took a moment, and then he said, "Yes, sir."

He made himself leave the room, walk down the corridor, walk down the stairs, walk down another corridor, and then another. The door to the amber drawing room was opened for him; he could hear his father laughing, but all he could see was Aubrey. He and Alicia were talking. Then Aubrey turned and saw Edmund in the doorway, and his whole face lit up with his smile.

It was as though Edmund had been hit in the chest. He had forgotten the way Aubrey's smile made him feel. He wished that he had prepared for it. Somehow.

Aubrey seemed on the verge of crying his name out, but instead he merely walked smartly over to him and bowed. Edmund's chest hurt all the way up to his throat now. He forced in another deep breath.

"Lord Ainsley," he managed to say. "I—I trust your journey was not too fatiguing."

He'd been too formal. Aubrey blinked at him for a moment. He was wearing a deep blue tailcoat that brought out his coloring, and Edmund's heart stuttered in his chest.

"No, not at all, Your Highness," he eventually replied. "And—and you, sir, are you . . . well?"

"Yes, I am in very good health, thank you."

Mercifully, he had to greet the rest of the family at that point. That bought him a few minutes to try to compose himself—it did not work—and then Aubrey was there again in front of him, looking expectant and a little confused.

They exchanged bland pleasantries for perhaps another minute. It seemed to last forever. Aubrey's expression closed in on itself more and more until it crumpled slightly, and Edmund couldn't take it anymore.

"Excuse me," he said—or at least tried to say—and left the room. He heard Alicia call after him but ignored her. He went back up the corridor, back up the stairs. He couldn't go back to his chambers, since Mattheson might still be putting things away in the dressing area. He headed instead for one of the unused quarters farther into the palace, full of old furniture under dust covers where he had hidden sometimes as a child. He felt like a child: a silly, sheltered child who didn't know what to do in this new situation he found himself in.

He closed the door, sank onto the floor in front of it, and put his hands over his face, pressing his fingers into his eyes.

He'd had weeks to get used to the idea, to work out how to act. Seeing Aubrey shouldn't have affected him this much. He should have more control over himself than this. But he'd forgotten how beautifully shaped Aubrey's mouth was, how his eyes caught your attention when they focused on you. And he'd looked at Edmund like he was the most important thing in the world. But—no. Again, this must all be his own fancy. That wasn't how Aubrey felt.

This was all so *humiliating*. Everyone was expecting him to become this great leader, and he couldn't even cope with seeing someone he had feelings for, who didn't feel the same way. If he were better with people, they might have talked about what they were doing, and there would have been no misunderstanding in the first place. Aubrey wasn't even aware there had been one, for heaven's sake—and why should he be? Physical intimacy was common enough between young people. Given that Edmund's marriage would be a matter of international importance, what else could Aubrey have thought was happening other than—how had he put it in his letter? A moment of joy?

He would certainly know that something was wrong now, though. All Edmund had had to do was be *normal*, and he hadn't even managed a minute of polite conversation. Now he was going to have to go back down there, and what if Aubrey asked him what was wrong? What on earth could he say?

I'm a green, selfish fool, and it physically hurts to think about you with someone else. I've never hated myself more in my life.

He was just going to have to avoid private conversation with him. There was nothing else for it. This decision made, he hauled himself to his feet. If he didn't go back soon, someone was going to come looking for him.

Everyone was just getting seated when he made it into the dining room. Aubrey had thankfully been placed farther down the table, and, in even better luck, Lord Wilson Ainsley was next to him, so the conversation required was limited.

Edmund barely registered what he was eating, but he was at least able to eat. Everything was fine; nothing was wrong—remote politeness—the Ainsleys were friends of the family. Aubrey caught his eye a few times. Edmund did his best to smile. He could do this.

Except that Aubrey smiled less and less as the meal went on. By dessert, he was picking at his plate, which wasn't like him at all, and then, when it was time to withdraw, he made straight for him. Edmund braced himself.

"You promised to show me the gardens when I arrived, sir." Aubrey's eyes were a touch wide. "You wanted to show me the bulbs in flower. Is it convenient to take me now before the last of the light dies?"

An excuse, an excuse, think of an excuse—

"Certainly," Edmund said after a moment, since he never could think of ways to get out of things. "Mamma, you don't need us, do you? We are going to view the north garden."

His mother, who was engrossed in something Lady Ainsley was saying, waved them on.

As soon as they were out of the building, however, Aubrey clutched at his sleeve.

"Edmund, is something amiss?"

Aubrey's face was so open. He certainly didn't look as though he didn't care about him. Edmund had to suppress the urge to throw his arms around him and beg him to love him, or at the very least, assure him that everything that Sir J had been told was some sort of mistake. He could never have done any of that, however, so he stuttered out a polite, vague statement about everything being well.

"But," Aubrey asked, "have I done something wrong?"

Edmund shook his head, a little frantically. "It's nothing you've done, Aubrey. If anything, I should explain myself, I—I—"

"*Heaven*, what is it?"

He sounded so completely at sea that Edmund could not help but speak plainly.

"It was reported to me that—I understand that you have—that is, you and Lord James Malmsbury are—" Edmund had to clear his throat at this point, but he took a breath, and drew on every shred of royal dignity he had. "I had no right to any expectations—"

"What, is that all?" Aubrey cried out. "You were told some fairy tale about me and *Malmy Malmsbury*? That one's only interested in *skirts*, Edmund. I cannot believe someone was fool enough to think you had any competition in *him*!"

Edmund felt like he couldn't breathe.

"You—you and he are not—"

"No, of course not, Edmund! Don't tell me *this* was why you didn't reply to my last two letters?"

Edmund couldn't speak. He managed to nod, and Aubrey laughed.

"Whyever did you *believe* that, or imagine I wouldn't stay true to you, wouldn't—"

"We never discussed—"

"Well, no, but I thought I had made my feelings absolutely clear; and none of that has changed during our separation, nor have I wanted it to—"

"But there was another thing. You and your brother—that is, you were seen entering a—a—"

"Oh, the assignation house?"

Edmund could do nothing by this point but stare. Aubrey smirked and said, with his chin tilted, "John's *exact* words before he dragged me to that place were *You're such an innocent, Aubrey, so I'm taking you somewhere you can see how the job is done properly, in case the prince doesn't know what he's doing either.*"

"You told your brother—"

"Oh heavens, no, but you know siblings. He just *knew*. And he might have had a point, because I didn't even know Marisetown had a place like that. Apparently it has several! And oh, you wouldn't believe what it was like inside! There was a sitting area first, like a regular gentleman's social club, and then there were a lot of little rooms, for going off into if you met someone you liked, but also—you will never guess—a big room full of sofas where you could"—his voice dropped to a scandalized whisper—*"watch other people!"*

He took a step back to gauge the effect these words had on Edmund.

He seemed to decide Edmund's stunned silence was satisfactory and went on with "And John—John!—just strolled right on into the place!"

He impersonated the man at this point so accurately that Edmund couldn't stop the startled, nervy laugh that burst out of him. "*Oh, we're only observing today, thank you; my brother is in need of a few educative experiences*. I didn't even know 'educative' was a word, but I looked it up in Father's library when we got home, and it is. He should probably still have said 'educational,' though, don't you think?"

"I think they're both correct? The suffix would still make it an adjective, would it not?"

Aubrey put his arms around Edmund's neck at that. "I love it when you talk grammar to me," he murmured into his mouth, and what could Edmund do then but kiss him?

He made it quick, since they were still in the gardens and observable from any number of vantage points in the house, but quickish as it was, it still made the part of Edmund thaw that had gone tight and cold upon hearing Sir Jenson's report. He had some notion he was making the grass grow around them and stopped himself.

"Wait," Edmund said. "When you got home from—from somewhere like that—your first thought was to go to your father's library and look up a point of grammar?"

"Well, we were there anyway. I refused to stay in that place for more than about three minutes—everyone was *looking at us* like we were something to *eat*—and I wouldn't go into the *coupling room* at all, so when we got back to Hemcott, John insisted on showing me some *educative* books in the collection that he thought might help me instead. I'd had no idea they were in there; Father had them in with the volumes on animal husbandry, so I'd never found them. Are there books like that in the palace library? Ooooh, I bet there are! Shocking!"

"You read"—Edmund's brain was melting, and he couldn't force himself to say the word "educative"—"with *John*?"

"Oh, how horrid, no. I squirreled them away into my bedroom. Anyway, you're focusing on the wrong thing. I think you're missing the part where John knew exactly where this place was and how it all worked, which means that he *had been there before*."

Edmund blinked.

He would never be able to look Aubrey's eldest brother in the face ever again. He had a brief mental picture of John being presented at court in thirty years, having inherited his baronetcy, and of himself sitting on a throne, gray-haired, and still unable to meet his eye.

"So I asked him about it," Aubrey went on in a low, confidential sort of voice that made Edmund both want to flee and to lean in closer, "and he said it's always good to try everything once, and he'd always been curious about places like that. He said a lot of people are actively seeking out experiences they might have previously hoped would just happen at some point, because that's what the prospect of war is doing to everyone. The place was full of soldiers, you know, and naval men."

Soldiers and naval men.

It was like a bucket of ice water. The last time he'd been to Marisetown, he'd also seen plenty of soldiers and naval men. Unconscious. Edmund spent a second contemplating his people trying to fit in as much living as they could in case they were shortly to die for their country, but then he felt even worse. Was that what Aubrey's brother thought the two of them would be doing? Using each other like people did in the educational materials that were indeed in the palace library, so that at least he and Aubrey wouldn't die without having done certain things? Like ticking items off a list?

Perhaps he did. That didn't matter. What mattered was that Aubrey didn't think it. Edmund knew it was selfish—his solace over the last few weeks had been that at least he couldn't hurt Aubrey's reputation now—but he also knew that giving Aubrey up at this point was impossible, not if he'd never lost him in the first place. He had never been so miserable in his life as he had been these last few weeks.

Still, he had to say something.

"I cannot pretend," he managed, "that I'm not relieved that my faith in you was not betrayed, but I am worried that you would be better off without me. I don't want to *reduce* you, or to damage your name. You know that I am not free to marry where I—"

"What?" Aubrey's indignation bordered on outrage. "You expect me to stay away from you because of that? I've been burning to see you since we parted. *Burning.* Especially while we're all waiting for the Honals to invade. I've spent this whole time terrified something was going to happen to you. So stop this talk and kiss me, or I'll think you the cruelest, wickedest prince in all of history."

So Edmund did kiss him, but then he had to stop again, because he really did need to know. "What is your relationship with James Malmsbury, then?"

"Oh, *Edmund*. He's just a chum; we've all known him for years. I can't believe you had us spied on; it really is *too much*—"

"Spy? I did no such thing! Sir Jenson merely told me he'd had a report of—of—"

Everything that Sir J had said re-formed in his head. Edmund sank onto a handy nearby bench. "The palace guard probably did send spies after you. They must have. I've been . . . naive. I'm so sorry. That was not called for. I will speak to Sir Jenson, I promise you. Especially since . . . well, I can't conceal anything from you; I was very upset. I blamed myself for not being free and for not being explicit to you about my feelings, but for all that, it wasn't anything worth worrying about!"

Aubrey was laughing, at least, which made Edmund feel a little better.

"Honestly, you'd think intelligence agents would have better things to do right now! Ah well. At least the dullness of my existence will have proved their punishment. The visit to the assignation house is probably the most scandalous thing I've ever done, and nobody even touched me. Oh, but you haven't asked me anything about that place! The noises one could hear—"

"Aubrey, stop! You can't—" Edmund glanced around, and his voice dropped to a hiss. "This is not a fit conversation to have *in front of a flower bed*."

Aubrey's eyes lit up at this idea, but he just said, "Then take me somewhere private, please, Edmund, I want to—"

One of the under-gardeners came around with a weeding basket at this point, clearly finishing up for the day, and looked at the young men curiously. Edmund grabbed Aubrey's elbow and marched him back inside.

Aubrey's face was positively gleeful by the time they got to his quarters. "Just you wait," he said, taking off his gloves. "I hadn't thought of half the things they did in those books—"

"Now you hold on right there, Aubrey Ainsley," Edmund said with a sternness he did not feel, given how his body had reacted to Aubrey's words, and backed up several steps. "I spent the entirety of the last three weeks thinking that you'd thrown me over for a rake and possibly some arbitrary stranger; to go from that to you insisting I drop my breeches in the space of a few minutes is really just too much."

Aubrey burst out laughing and then put his hand over his mouth at whatever he saw in Edmund's face. "I'm sorry," he said, once he had gotten his mirth under control. "Keep your breeches. I won't go near them if you don't want me to. But it's been a very trying evening. We both thought we'd lost the other. Please show me that we didn't, and kiss me? I just want you in my arms."

So Edmund kissed him. And Aubrey held him in his arms. And did eventually end up showing him some of the things he had learned about.

As it turned out, they were naturals at the whole thing.

They wore themselves out so, Aubrey inadvertently fell asleep in Edmund's bed. Since Edmund had been three-quarters asleep himself, it was not as though he had complained or protested at all, or tried to wake Aubrey up and make him go sleep in his own designated room, or had even wanted him to. It did mean, however, that Aubrey was still in there when Sir Jenson came in with the maid carrying the breakfast tray, for his usual morning briefing.

Bessie, to her credit, acted as though nothing at all was amiss. Such a thing was not possible, however, for Sir Jenson. The man made a noise almost exactly like a startled chicken, which did wonders for banishing the last of Edmund's lingering languor. His eyes flew open, and he clutched the covers to himself in his panic.

Aubrey did not do that. Aubrey, to Edmund's horror, sat up, looking around in bleary-eyed confusion and making his state of undress abundantly clear. Next thing Edmund knew, Bessie had finished up at the table, and she and Sir Jenson both headed straight for the door. As soon as it closed behind them, Aubrey burst out laughing.

"Oh dear," he said. "I might just go back to my room before one of my parents tries to do the same to me and finds a pristine, unslept-in bed."

He was long gone by the time Sir Jenson came back, perhaps half an hour later. The man waited to be told to enter, this time, after knocking.

Please act like nothing happened, please act like—

"I wanted to finalize your dances for the ball, Your Highness," he said. Edmund felt a section of his spine unwinch, which had certainly never happened before whenever Sir J had uttered such a sentence. "Since only Her Highness your sister is performing the welcome, I'm afraid you will not be able to get out of dancing the first set. Here is the provisional list for you."

Edmund scanned it. His third set was free, as usual, so that his parents could foist unexpected people upon him at the last minute, and so he could speak to guests who wanted a word before they left for the evening. His dance partners for the first two sets were mostly noblewomen and members of parliament, but he spotted a few high-ranking military officers and two ambassadors. He spent a second relieved that no foreign royalty were on the list—very few had been invited, since the occasion was essentially about Alicia entering her nation's service—but then it occurred to Edmund to check quite how high-ranking some of the nobles were. He racked his brain to remember if he had met any of them before.

"Uh," he said, trying to work out how to ask it delicately. He took so long that Sir J's eyebrows began to rise, and he gave up. "Are any of these—that is—"

"I underlined the names of the . . . eligible marriage prospects, sir. I know you do not like being surprised by that sort of thing. Speaking of which—" Edmund's skin started prickling at the change in the man's tone. "I see that you and Lord Ainsley have . . . worked things out."

Edmund's eyes closed.

He inhaled once, then allowed himself enough time to let the breath out slowly.

"Yes," he said, and was surprised and pleased by how even his voice sounded. "I should probably speak to you about that."

He made himself open his eyes again. Sir Jenson didn't appear any more comfortable than he did, at least. But then Edmund realized it wasn't discomfort that he was feeling. He was angry.

"I do not know," he said, and this time his voice was less even, "why the palace saw fit to send spies after Lord Ainsley, given that he lives quietly in the country with his family and his father is a friend to the *king*, but I will not have it. A Sabresian gentleman has the right to live his own life and keep his own company; and in the case of your spy's accusations about Lord Malmsbury, apparently any gossip could have told you that the viscount has no taste for men. I can therefore only conclude that this report was submitted to merely stir up trouble between me and Lord Ainsley and"—something suddenly occurred to Edmund as he looked at Sir J's horrified face—"and perhaps between you and me as well."

Sir Jenson took a step back at this and went to speak, but Edmund cut him off.

"You certainly did not confirm the report's veracity before presenting it to me as fact. I am now in the very awkward position of having to question every piece of information that you give me, or indeed have ever given me."

"Sir, it came from the palace security service!" Sir Jenson said, his tone mortified. "I would never have dreamed it wasn't reliable or—" Here, the man shook his head. "No, I will not make excuses. Only apologies. I am very sorry, sir."

Edmund looked at his familiar face. “I think we’ve both been too credulous. I don’t know what to do about this. I want your assurances it will never happen again.”

“My eyes have been opened, sir, but I am only your secretary. I have no control over the security service. The best I can do is warn you where the information has come from next time.”

Edmund nodded, suddenly feeling very tired. “Then I think we had better mention this to the king.”

CHAPTER 9

The night of the ball arrived, fine and clear. Alicia's welcoming performance went well. Aubrey had helped her practice but still held his breath as she created a small whirlwind, which she then used to scoop up all the water from the Hennerly fountain (she had insisted upon incorporating the thing, in case someone blew it up again) before freezing it in an elaborate swirl. To melt it, she created a pretty multicolored fire using a blend of special alchemic powders Mrs. Grant had procured for her. She then struck a pose and bowed dramatically, like a street performer (Aubrey's suggestion), and the crowd's applause verged on excessive.

The dancing was opened immediately on Alicia's insistence to the planners. Aubrey did not expect to get anywhere near her or Edmund until much further into the evening, as they had a variety of duties; although Alicia had, at least, secured Aubrey for a particular partnered dance late in the night.

It was odd having to watch Alicia and Edmund from afar with the rest of the crowd, but it was fine, Aubrey thought. He never had trouble keeping himself entertained and was determined to enjoy himself while he still could. Heavens knew that the army wasn't going to be all music and punch.

Unlike the last ball, Cedric did not immediately abandon him, so he was able to dance the group dances near him and meet some of his university friends. Aubrey was deciding if he was sufficiently acquainted with one of the nearby ladies to offer her his arm for the next, which was paired, when he saw Malmy's father, the Marquess of Stratingford, also dancing.

Aubrey motioned toward him as discreetly as he could to Cedric.

His brother frowned. "I thought Malmy said he was coming tonight? Don't the two of them always try to avoid each other in society?"

Aubrey nodded. "Perhaps his father changed his mind at the last minute, and now Malmy won't have come. Have you seen him?"

They both surveyed the room while trying to keep up with the dance. About a quarter of the young people here were already in uniform, their red or blue coats easily visible. In the end it was Cedric who spotted their friend. He was standing by a refreshment table, looking every part the rogue his reputation painted him as, all black tousled hair and too-loose collar.

They headed toward him once the song had finished.

He nodded at them. Aubrey motioned to the dance floor, since apparently this was supposed to be a silent conversation. Malmy's mouth quirked.

"Yes," he said, "my father is here. He decided it would be a good opportunity to sort out some rubbish about hosting prisoners of war. Says they can work his fields while everyone else is off fighting, and then at least he'll still have grain to sell. I don't know why I'm surprised."

He tipped back the last of his punch and put down his cup emphatically.

"Yet you still decided to come?" Cedric asked.

"I was informed that I had to. He insisted that our status means that I can scrape in as a suitor for the princess, if I try hard enough. I told him I doubted she'd have me, and he tried to hit me with his stick, as though I do not have long experience getting out of its way."

He filled his cup again and then muttered, "Someone seems to have told him about Rosalie."

Something was stiff in his movements, and Aubrey wondered if some of his father's blows hadn't landed after all. He hummed sympathetically. "What will cheer you up? Cake? Cards? Dancing?"

"Yes. Come and dance with me," Malmy said, grabbing his hand. "That way nobody can complain I spent the entire night charming young ladies."

"Yes, not the entire night," Aubrey teased. He waved a farewell to Cedric over his shoulder as he let himself be pulled along and then glanced around. The dance floor was crowded, but he could see perhaps four other male couples and six female ones from here and felt satisfied that Wilson could not berate him tomorrow for drawing attention to himself. The song—it was a waltz—had already started, so they had to find a spot near the bottom of the floor. Somehow, however, Malmy maneuvered them so that they were closer to the center within minutes.

"Your prince is staring daggers at me," he said, sounding satisfied.

Aubrey peered around. "He is not," he said, jostling Malmy for the outrageous falsehood. Edmund was indeed looking over, but it was with the air of a puppy being pushed out onto a doorstep rather than one of murderous jealousy. He was dancing with an older woman Aubrey had some notion was in parliament, something to do with foreign affairs, he thought. She had huge feathers in her hair. The effect was bold yet elegant. Aubrey made a mental note to tell his mother about them.

"Well, perhaps not, but he has at least seen you in the arms of another man, even if he doesn't seem as outraged as I'd hoped. Oh, but that man does. Who is he?"

Aubrey peered around again.

"That's Edmund's personal secretary. He probably thinks I'm making fun of him, wait until you hear . . ."

Malmy laughed so hard at the idea of their romantic involvement ("I remember when you were a *toddler*, Aubrey!") that they almost danced right into another couple. They bowed their apologies.

"Oh heaven, now the king's brother is glowering at us!" Malmy said, turning Aubrey so that he could see the man. He was indeed watching them, and while he thought Malmy was exaggerating yet again, his unhappy face did have something hard about it.

"Odd," Aubrey said. "I wonder what that is about. Did you seduce his mistress or something?"

"Not that I am aware of. I'm moving us away from him. That expression looks catching. Does he even have a mistress? I barely know anything about the man, do you?"

"Only that his wife died giving birth to Charlotte's younger brother, who also passed away. It all sounded very sad. He resides in a castle in the north, did you know? I don't know why I expected that he would live here, except that the royal family is so small. I don't think that he and his brother are close. Edmund never talks about him."

Malmy looked like he was about to say something else, but the song ended then, and as he led Aubrey off the dance floor, they were immediately swamped by young ladies of Malmy's acquaintance, as well as several young men, dressed at the height of fashion, asking to be introduced to Aubrey and wanting to know if he was free to dance with them. He had to tell them he had promised it to Alicia. This did not seem to put any of them off, although they then started squabbling among themselves over which of them should be allowed to offer Aubrey their arm for the next one. They were amusing about it, although they never asked Aubrey what he would prefer, which did not seem right and was also not very flattering. It was almost a relief when a footman arrived, come to get him for the princess.

"How was I?" she asked, posing like a stage magician again.

"Marvelous. Come and waltz," Aubrey said, holding out his arm. She put her hand on it with a grin.

"I wish we could have more than one dance together," she said as the music began and they started to move. "You spoiled me in all our practice over the last few days, you know, by being so light on your feet. That last duke, I swear. Poor Charlotte's stuck with him now, over there. Oh, you should ask her to dance next! You'll be such a breath of fresh air for her. Are you free?"

Aubrey laughed.

"I don't even know. I really ought to give it to one of Malmy's friends; a good three of them asked but didn't really give me an opportunity to answer. Oh heaven, they're all standing over there, watching us—"

He nodded at them, and they all waved. Alicia contemplated them.

"That is a pack of *vultures*," she pronounced, "and I cannot possibly let you spend the rest of the night dancing with them. Edmund will weep. Charlotte," she called out, steering them both closer, and Aubrey wondered who was supposed to be leading here, "I was just telling Lord Ainsley he should ask you to dance. Are you free for the next?"

Princess Charlotte waited until they were nearer to reply rather than raise her voice as Alicia had. "No, but I am for the one after. I was scheduled for a rest period, but I would be very happy to dance with his lordship instead, if he wishes."

Aubrey bowed his head, but before he could say anything, Alicia had accepted for him and pulled him back into their proper position.

"Dancing with anyone you like during scheduled rest periods!" she said. "Why did I not think of that? Why did I refuse them?"

"You said you didn't need them. Why does *Edmund* not have those? He'd actually rest."

"He'd hide, you mean. But you know him: doesn't feel like he can ever protest, even to his own secretary, unless it's crucial, and he doesn't always consider his own comfort crucial. I wish he would."

The song ended with a flourish, which Aubrey and Alicia took to mean they should bow and curtsy to each other in an overly elaborate manner, to the titters of the dancers around them. He took her over to the refreshment table, but before he could so much as hand her a cup of punch, one of those friends of Malmy's descended—the Honorable Mr. Kaelyn—to beg to know whether or not Aubrey would dance with him. His eyes were so soulful, Aubrey took pity on the poor fellow and agreed.

It turned out that he knew John and Cedric, as well as Malmy, from university. He regaled Aubrey with funny stories of their antics in between showering him with compliments. Aubrey found himself thinking that he might even have liked it had circumstances been different. As it was, however, he put a little more room between himself and his partner—the man did seem to want to hold him a fraction too tightly for politeness—and did his best not to encourage him. This included not going out into the garden after the dance, as he suggested, "to look at the stars, you know," but before Aubrey could explain that, actually, he was due to dance with Princess Charlotte, another footman came to collect him.

"There you are!" Alicia cried, as he was deposited in front of her. "I sent someone for you after learning that your dance partner was an infamous libertine with an eye for pretty young men. Are you all right?"

"He was perfectly nice," Aubrey said, a trifle defensively. "His father's a viscount!"

Alicia snorted and said, "Come on, Charlotte's over there. Uncle looks like he's droning on at her about something. Have you been introduced to him before?"

Aubrey shook his head. He had not noticed Prince Willard there, even though he was just a few yards away. Seeing him up close for the first time, he had the sudden thought that he was glad that this man was not Edmund's father. He had none of King Theodore's good humor either in his mouth, which drooped melancholically, or his eyes, which were not the warm brown common with the rest of the family, but a cold hazel.

Those eyes ranged over them as they approached, and then the prince turned and strode away.

Aubrey glanced at Alicia and then at Charlotte. They both looked a little stunned.

"Have I . . . just been given the cut direct?" Aubrey asked.

"Oh, no," Alicia said immediately. "No, no, he probably didn't even register that we were here. His manner with people is just awful. No offense to you, Charlotte. Oh, *finally*," she added, seeing something over Aubrey's shoulder, and he turned—right into someone's chest.

Everything had been a bit much by then: alleged libertines holding him too tightly, and Alicia being domineering, and whatever had just happened with Prince Willard. So Aubrey let out an inelegant noise and would have jumped back, except that the owner of the chest wrapped his hand around his arm to steady him with a soft apology.

Relief. Edmund.

"There you are," Aubrey said.

"I just wanted to say hello," he said into his ear. "And to see if you would save the—oh, what number is it?—the fourth dance of the last set for me. I wanted it to be the first one—I was hoping to be done by then—but my father has been using me as a consolation prize for everyone he can't dance with tonight."

"Pfft," said Aubrey. "Who does he think he—"

The music started then, and Princess Charlotte was watching him, her expression amused, so he quickly said, "Yes," into Edmund's ear and took his cousin's hand to lead her out.

The fourth dance of the last set became a sort of guiding star in Edmund's mind. It got him through most of his evening. He could bear being stared at, and making small talk, and being asked euphemistic questions about his thoughts on marriage and whether he would be looking closer to home for his consort, like his father had done, or farther afield like his cousin. He could bear all of it, because Aubrey was here and he was going to dance with him.

And then the minister for defense asked him if he could just have a quick word, and Edmund was forced to send a footman to ask Aubrey if they could do the fifth dance together instead. He knew there was every chance that Aubrey would have promised it to someone else, but it was the best he could do. And now he was guiding Mr. Prestan away, down a corridor to the first room he could think of where they could be assured of some privacy: an old office that was rarely used, with just a few chairs, a desk, and empty bookshelves. The man didn't seem to mind, waiting patiently as two footmen set up candles for them and then left them to it.

"Thank you for agreeing to duck out with me, Your Highness. I did mean to find a better time than this over the last week or so, but—well, you know how hard it is."

"Of course, Mr. Prestan."

The man had a book with him for some reason. The palace librarian would have been horrified by it, Edmund thought: the corners were battered, and the leather covered in scratches. In fact, the man himself appeared a bit more worn than he had been the last time Edmund had talked to him at a ball. The minister used to be so polished and perfect; he seemed a lot more human these days.

"I considered not mentioning this to anyone at all," he was saying, "since it is a little strange, but—monium. You wrote to the War Office to make sure that they recalled that the word had appeared in visions that had been reported, after the victims at the naval base said that they had heard it spoken."

Despite his fatigue, Edmund felt intrigued now. "Yes. Nobody seemed that worried, but I also checked with the linguistics scholars at Craywick to see if it was Old Sabresian. It could mean 'my' something, but they couldn't find anything like it. Do you know what it means?"

"No, not at all, but it sounded familiar, and you were right: the War Office doesn't seem very interested, not even when I told them about this. I found it reading old folk stories to my children the other night. Look."

He opened the battered volume he was holding and handed it to Edmund.

"The Monium," the title of the story read in heavy, old-fashioned font.

"My grandmother used to tell me a similar story when I was a child,"

Mr. Prestan said, "about a sort of bad fairy that would use a magic storm to wipe everyone's memory and take over a place, and make out that their way had always been the way. The prince or princess always saves everyone in the end. Were you ever told that one?"

Edmund shook his head. He had no memory of his parents ever reading stories to their children in the nursery at bedtime, and meanwhile all the royal nurse had ever read to them was the sort of instructional, improving tale that had a very clear moral. Alicia had always rolled her eyes and then, after the woman was gone, terrified him with stories she made up herself about murderous witches and bloodthirsty pirates.

He couldn't say any of that, so instead he just said, "My grandparents are all gone."

Mr. Prestan nodded. "I doubt they would have been that well-acquainted with the old folk stories anyway, sir. I cannot help but feel that—if this is about Honal sorcery—it is good that you are the one to know about it."

Edmund was surprised, and then even more so when the minister added, "Your Highness . . . do you think you could make a storm like that?"

Edmund nearly dropped the book. "No. Absolutely not. My gift does not work that way; it works *with* the land, not against it. I would not even know how to begin."

Something in Mr. Prestan's face cleared. He nodded and then motioned with one finger to the collection of stories. "Shall I leave that with you?"

Edmund took note of the title and handed it back. "I would not deprive your children. I shall have our librarian find me a copy."

He managed to make it downstairs and by Aubrey's side just as the first bars of the fifth dance were starting. He was relieved to see that he was eating ices with Cedric and some young ladies rather than already dancing with someone else. He was even more relieved that none of the young men Aubrey had danced with earlier were anywhere in sight. And then Edmund suddenly couldn't see anyone else at all, because Aubrey had put out his hand, smiling widely.

All the relief and joy were quickly replaced, though, as they joined the dance floor and he saw how many people were watching them. He felt suddenly very conscious that this was the first time he had danced with a man in public. It was only now occurring to him that he might be revealing something about himself.

"Darling?" Aubrey murmured into his ear. "Are you all right?"

Edmund looked at Aubrey, his stiff collar skimming his jaw, his beautifully shaped mouth. His eyes dark in the candlelight and forbearing. Edmund felt calmer.

"I am now," he replied, and then turned him and brought him back in with the steps of the dance. "I am feeling my luck to have you. Especially since—how do you know the follower parts to all these dances?"

Aubrey shook his head at him. "I am the youngest of four brothers. How do you think we learned to dance?" He let himself be turned again—he really was very easy to dance with—and added, "Now, you tell me something. You did not have a coming-out ball like this to mark your entry into public life. How did you get out of it?"

Edmund could feel that he was smiling now too. "My gift manifested early. It was too valuable for the country not to start using as soon as I was able to control it. So I was in public service almost as soon as I was breeched."

He was about to add that there had been no celebration since

Charlotte's mother had just died and it would have been in poor taste, but Aubrey was already making a face, so instead he went on with "I never *minded*. I liked being taken places where I could help the crops or stop a weather pattern causing problems. It was much better than being trotted out to be stared at and made to speak to people. Tonight is exhausting. Give me a storm to calm down over this any day."

"Speaking of which: Are you all done now, for the night? The meeting you had to run off to—was that your last one?"

"Yes," Edmund said, risking holding Aubrey a little tighter. He told him about the folk story, and Aubrey's entire posture altered as he was taken over by the need to go and read every book on this subject that he could find. It made Edmund want to kiss him, so they slipped out into the garden, and Edmund found himself crowded up against the wall before he had really noticed it happening. His brain went entirely, blissfully blank. When Aubrey pulled back and said something, Edmund had to ask him to repeat it.

Aubrey sounded amused. "I said, I suppose we can't just run off upstairs? We should go back in, otherwise. Nobody's going to care about my absence, but yours—"

"No," Edmund said. "No, we should go. It's late and I find I need my bed."

CHAPTER 10

The first reports of the ball were as expected. The respectable newspapers printed factual accounts; the fashion papers printed details of the food and the clothes; the news sheets gossiped. The gossip included mention of Edmund's dance with Aubrey and speculation over the nature of their relationship, which made Edmund's palms prickle, but they mostly focused on Alicia. The whole thing distracted nicely from the upcoming war, Sir Jenson said, but still, nobody had expected for the leading news sheet to print, three days later, a half-page etching of Edmund and Aubrey dancing together.

Sir Jenson presented it wordlessly to Edmund at breakfast. At first, Edmund had thought Sir J was trying to show him a story reporting that Seers across the country had had a wave of new visions about him. Nothing specific, which was probably why he had not been officially informed, just more of the same sort of imagery they always seemed to See of his future—that he would be beloved by his people. Edmund had felt the familiar rush of blood to his face, the clenching of his stomach, and then Sir J said, "Oh, sorry, sir. Not that one," and turned the page.

There the two of them were in black ink. They had been drawn gazing intensely into each other's faces, their bodies close. Aubrey's likeness was not very accurate, the artist presumably not familiar with his features. Edmund was, however, very recognizable.

He leaned forward to read the caption; it was some guff saying how nice the paper thought it was to see their crown prince enjoying himself, and pointing to an article on page seven. Edmund turned to it.

A PRETTY PICTURE

While this paper would never wish to deflect attention from a lady during an evening in her honor, an unexpected auxiliary story has emerged from the recent ball held for Her Highness Princess Alicia that we confess has our office all aquiver.

It seems that her brother, His Highness Prince Edmund, has developed a close relationship with one Lord Aubrey Ainsley, whose father, Lord John Ainsley, is a longstanding personal friend of His Majesty King Theodore. Our readers may remember his name as the very same Lord Ainsley whose heroism kept the Prince of Fortune from injury during the attack on the palace by protestors at the last royal ball. Perhaps his lordship had a more personal reason for his actions than he has previously been given credit for.

We will not speculate on the nature of the association between Lord Ainsley and the crown prince. We

> will report, though, that reliable sources say that the pair not only danced together at the ball, as illustrated on page three, but were also witnessed withdrawing for the evening together.

Edmund sipped his coffee and, fortified, asked, "Are they saying that . . . what *are* they saying?"

"They are gossiping about you, sir."

"Yes, but they don't seem to be gossiping *maliciously* or . . . or being satirical, or making any sort of political statement. We haven't even been caricatured. Is that usual for this paper?"

Sir J squashed his lips together for a moment. Then he said, "No, it is not, sir, but this particular publication has always been favorable toward you. We need to keep an eye on this, sir. I—"

There was a knock at the door then, and Aubrey, who had been dressing, rushed in.

"Edmund!" Aubrey cried, waving the same news sheet around. "Look what—oh, you've seen it. You're very handsome. I wonder if they will sell prints of it?"

Sir Jenson's lips thinned. He excused himself from the room.

The man's lips were even thinner, three days later, when one of the racier news sheets responded to the dancing illustration with their own etching. Aubrey had left Talstam Palace by then; he and his brothers had received orders to report to the Craywick barracks for initial training, and he needed to pack and be fitted for his uniform. Edmund had already been feeling quite low that morning; when Sir J handed him the newspaper, his stomach dropped preemptively.

It dropped further when he saw the picture. It depicted himself and Aubrey in the garden, with him up against the wall, their faces just far enough apart to not risk a fine from the censor. It had been titled "A Prettier Picture."

The blood rushed so strongly to Edmund's face, he could feel it in his scalp.

"Who saw us?" he managed to ask. "How? That is a private part of the garden!"

"Yes it is, and I do not like how well it has been depicted. I will be asking the servants if they saw anyone loitering over the last few days where they should not have been."

Edmund stared up at Sir J, horrified, and then back down. Aubrey's face was barely visible—again, the artist clearly hadn't been familiar with his features—but the courtyard itself was accurate enough. Sir Jenson was right: the illustrator must have seen the location.

"You see, sir. Even when the reports are favorable, it is better not to be talked of in this fashion."

Favorable.

Edmund scanned the image caption, which made some gratuitous mention of the fineness of his own profile and the excellence of their two forms as they had been spotted entwined, only half listening to what Sir J was saying about the army being no less gossipy than the capital, and of strategies to protect his privacy.

Edmund held up the paper.

"I thought that this news sheet and the other were bitter rivals," he said. "Have you not told me before that they often take contrary viewpoints just to spite each other? And yet, this is the second paper that seems to . . . approve."

Edmund risked looking back up at Sir Jenson and felt himself go red again, as understanding moved across the man's face.

"I keep trying to tell you how the news sheets view you, sir," he said after a moment. "I don't know why you have so much trouble believing me. You read them sometimes yourself, and yet you won't see it. You're the Lucky Prince, prophesized to be a great king. You are tall and well formed, and your interactions with the public have always been fine, no matter how awkward you continue to insist that they feel. The palace informs me that the talk on the street about your relationship is kindly. Taking up with a country baronet's son has been viewed as *relatable*; now you're a young man made of flesh and blood, not—"

"A moving statue?"

"I was going to say an untouchable figure of myth who can bring down the very lightning and bless or curse the crops. Sir."

Edmund's head came back up quickly. Sir Jenson had never said anything like this before. And the man wasn't done with surprises, clearly, because he then followed up with "The trick will be managing the situation so that Lord Ainsley doesn't get put into a box marked 'paramour' in all the parliamentarians' heads rather than . . . well, until you've decided what you want to do, sir. Best to be discreet from now on."

Edmund swallowed. The man was clearly being vague in an attempt at tact, but he had managed it so well, Edmund wasn't sure what he was getting at. He couldn't possibly be suggesting that the parliament's opinion would matter because its members might let him and Aubrey—because Edmund might ask them—no, that can't have been what he meant. And Edmund was far too embarrassed to ask.

He was so distracted that all he caught of what the man said next was "—sure to provoke a reaction from more conservative quarters."

He should have listened. Sir J was right. The capital's stuffiest newspaper could ignore one popular etching, but the second was so provocative that the paper felt the need to respond. It ran a very pompous column, reminding everyone not only of the respect that ought to be due their next king, but also of the terms and intentions of the Royal Marriages Act; and then, in the next issue, several letters from readers were printed applauding the piece. Another publication included an article that pretended not to be in response to anything, but whose author was merely wondering when Edmund would start thinking about marriage; and, contrarily, another saying that given that the country was at war, everyone should have better things to think about.

A third paper published a piece that made Edmund feel the most sick of all. It alluded to "new information" regarding his presumed intentions and said that, if the crown prince did not plan to add to the royal family's bloodline, the parliament would take extra care with whichever match they ratified for him, and then included a list of high-ranking men from a variety of countries who might now be in the running for the position of his consort.

He stared at the names. He couldn't remember who any of these people were. He searched for a title that at least felt familiar and stuck on the last one: a duke from Folbrage he now placed as the youngest brother of Uncle Willard's late wife. The man had to be at least fifteen years older than him. He felt suddenly very penned in, like some sort of farm animal herded around by a smallholder who didn't think of any of his livestock as living creatures with as much right to desires and choice as they had. He remembered Charlotte calling him the country's prize bull, and a slightly miserable laugh tried to make its way out of his mouth. It didn't succeed, but he still felt better.

He put the paper down decidedly. He had no intention of marrying Charlotte's uncle. The entire thing was ridiculous, and no one could make him, like she had said.

He applied that day to be stationed at Craywick.

His request was approved within a fortnight, with the proviso that all dragons should consider themselves on standby to be moved at any time depending on what was Seen, on intelligence information, or on the needs of the government. He rolled his eyes at this, since his entire life to date had been that way. As it was, he only managed to sleep one night at Brythe House, the royal residence at Craywick, before he was called away.

There had been an attack.

It was a farming commune called Mester, up in the north. Edmund had visited it before. Its only claim to fame was that it was the closest settlement to Saben's border with Honal. Its farthest field was a cleared section of the "haunted forests" that grew at the base of the Helm.

The village was just far enough away from the port city of Adurnmouth that they had their own small local fort, complete with a garrison of soldiers who lived in the barracks. Given that the king was currently in residence at the naval base at Adurnmouth, and therefore much closer, Edmund did wonder why he had been requested.

Until he got there.

The missive had been urgent but had not specified what exactly had happened. It took him and Sir Jenson, and their guard, most of the day to get up there, riding hard and changing horses at every stop.

They tried to present themselves at the fort for instruction, but it was deserted. They worked out where the soldiers were when they rode past the most northern field, closest to the forest.

Rows and rows of bodies, all in uniform, were hoisted up on poles there. Like an army of scarecrows.

The community was still cutting them down when the party arrived.

"Could not," he asked the farmer who greeted him, after he had stared for a moment, "Adurnmouth send troops to help?"

"We sent a messenger, sir, but they've not yet returned. For now, we're it, but . . . we couldn't leave the garrison as they were. Not like that. It's just that most of us only woke up a few hours ago, you see, sir. A lot of the old and young ones are still asleep."

Asleep, Edmund thought, thinking of the naval base at Marisetown and starting to worry about what could be happening at Adurnmouth. "Why has the messenger not yet returned? When did you send them?"

"When we woke up, sir, so there hasn't been time for anyone to go there and get back yet. It is good that you have gotten here so soon."

Something wasn't right in this answer, but they had bigger problems, and Sir J was speaking to him now. Edmund missed the words, since his brain was entirely filled with what he was seeing.

"I'm sorry, Sir Jenson." Edmund pulled his eyes away from the rows of bodies, cleared his throat. "What did you say?"

"Sir, I said that you might want to speak to the head councillor; I can see her over there."

Edmund nodded and started to move toward her, but Sir J added, "And your guards are securing the site, but after that it might be best to assign them to . . . help with the bodies. I can go and assist with supplies, unless you need me to stay with you. They're going to need a lot of cloth. For wrapping."

Edmund nodded, cleared his throat again. "Yes. You go."

Sir Jenson regarded him for a moment but then nodded as well and set off. Edmund looked back but had lost sight of the commune leader now: a woman a little older than his mother whom he had met on several previous tours of northern farmland. Her name kept on slipping out of his head, while his mind tried to find hows and whats and whys, and failed.

He finally spotted her on her knees, arranging a soldier on a white sheet. She was weeping as she did it, her whole body shaking. He did not blame her.

This was not what he had expected at all.

The story was told to him several times by different people as he tried to make his way toward her. Everyone remembered going to sleep the night before and then nothing until they had all woken up. Some of them had still been in their own homes. Some of them had been on the path to the barracks. Most of them had been in the northern field, with blood all over them.

The commune had been growing wheat in that field. Edmund had visited at the end of summer. The soil had seemed good. Healthy. He had recommended more compost in a few places.

The bodies were very pale, because almost all the blood had been drained from them, their skin and clothing slashed in many places. The blood was all over the plants. It was . . . even. As though the blood had been collected and then sprayed, like liquid fertilizer.

It was a lot of bodies.

Each pole had Honal runes carved along it, saying who knew what, and each body had had a note fastened to it. The writing on these was not in runes, but in the common alphabet. They all said the same thing.

We can make the crops grow too.

By the time Edmund got to the councillor, he was exhausted from being stopped by people. From listening, from patting hands and shoulders, from nodding. From the horror of it all, and from feeling sick over whether or not this was a message to him, personally, which . . . of course it was. It must be.

He knelt down next to the woman. The body she had been working on had been taken away somewhere, and she was laying out a fresh sheet. Tears were still streaming down her face. She looked up, startled, and blinked at him for a moment before bowing her head low with a respectful greeting.

"No," he said, but didn't know what else to say after that. He thought wildly of Aubrey, of how he would act. "I'm so sorry," he said, and he put his arm around her. After a frozen second or two, she started sobbing into his shoulder.

He clung to her as she shook. He felt tears gather in his own eyes and swiped them away as best he could on the shoulders of his ridiculous white uniform jacket, covered in braid, and took a few deep breaths. He realized then that he was probably holding the woman too tightly and loosened his grip.

"We knew these soldiers," she said, pulling back slightly herself and reaching into her pocket for a handkerchief. "We drank with them at the tavern. They helped us repair that fence, right there"—she gestured with the folded square of fabric—"just a few weeks ago. This man here"—she motioned again, a bit wildly—"I never knew his name, but he had a kind face. Didn't talk much. He just used to smile and nod his head. That one . . ." She nearly fell over this time, and Edmund held her more sturdily, wanting to lend her any strength he could. She settled, took a deep breath, and said more calmly, "That was Jane. She—she had—she had these bright—bright eyes. They sparkled. And she was strung up for the birds to peck them out—"

The woman's last word turned into a wail, and Edmund held her more tightly still. They clung to each other for what could have been seconds or minutes—Edmund wasn't sure—and then finally she moved back again. She reached into another pocket and pulled out a second handkerchief. She hesitated for a fraction of a second and then blotted his face with it. He was ashamed of himself for a moment before deciding that gratitude was a better reaction. He needed to be big for these people.

"Thank you."

She nodded. "I have a son about your age, sir. I'm glad he's not here. I'm sorry you have to be. But it is good that you came, sir, since—can you tell us what to do with the field?"

Edmund looked at her in incomprehension, and she went on with "Should we burn the crop? Is it dangerous? Was this . . . Honal sorcery?"

Edmund glanced back at the site, the shadows longer now as they headed into evening. If there was any magic here, he couldn't feel it. The runes, which were being cut out with blades by the farmers or his guardsmen as each pole was pulled from the earth, didn't seem active. The site didn't have that creeping wrongness of those storms he had stopped or the rune that he had encountered at Marisetown. The very idea, however, of letting this crop continue to grow or of people eating this grain was horrifying.

And yet, burning everything did not feel right either.

"No," he heard himself saying. "Not fire. We don't need more destruction here. Once everyone can go inside, I will make it rain to wipe away what was done here. After the field dries out, I think the plants should be scythed and left to lie where they fall. Leave the field fallow for a time. We should see if . . . it can forget what happened to it after that."

She nodded, calm. He had spoken calmly himself, but as he finished, Edmund felt a wave of anger come up that he had been suppressing. Aside from the slaughter of the garrison, which revolted him so much he was struggling to keep it in his head, the damage done to this peaceful community was appalling. These were good, decent folk who shouldn't have had to see or deal with any of this—this—*spectacle.*

They had been growing good, strong plants that should have fed a great number of people. So much waste of life, and for what? For the Honals to send a message that Sabresian soldiers couldn't save themselves? That Edmund couldn't save them? All that they were learning from this was that their enemy was unnaturally cruel.

They got up and got to work. This act had been obscene, and the soldiers needed to be prepared for burial as soon as possible. There were too many of them to postpone this, but they still needed to be cleaned and wrapped, for decency. The community leaders had reluctantly decided that it would, however, have to be done in the most cursory manner, since there wasn't time for much else. Only faces and hands would be washed, and the soldiers would be buried in their ruined uniforms.

It occurred to Edmund, as he went to fetch more water, that soon there would be so many deaths that even this brief bit of respect would be a luxury. Wars led to mass graves. To bodies jumbled together in pits. It was this stray thought that had Edmund, finally, casting up the contents of his stomach in a hedge, after ignoring so many other people doing similar things since his arrival.

The messenger came back from Adurnmouth shortly after that.

Adurnmouth would not be sending help, since all the soldiers and naval personnel that had been in residence overnight were also all dead.

Not asleep. Dead.

"*All* of them?" Edmund asked, considering the pile of poles.

"Everyone that was at the base and at the powder magazine. Not . . . like this. They're just dead, sir. Fire, mostly. There were explosions. It sounded a bit like how the papers wrote about Marisetown, sir, except that everything's destroyed, sir, even the ships in the harbor."

Edmund had to steady himself at this, because Adurnmouth was much larger than Marisetown. All up, more than two thousand people would have been in that yard; not just naval men but shipwrights, rope makers, the staff at the storehouses. Everyone else who kept it going.

"The king," he blurted out. "Is he—"

"The king wasn't there," the man said. "He was called away this morning, to Manogate. Which"—he turned to the head councillor, whose name was March, Edmund recalled eventually—"do you need me to—"

Mrs. March nodded. "If you have another ride in you, George, please go there. We need help. Although it will be dark by the time you arrive. Hopefully they'll put you up in the barracks overnight. Unless they've been attacked too."

She threw up her hands, as though nothing could be known. She wasn't wrong. George nodded and went on his way. Edmund had to restrain himself and not follow him to ask for more details. He was sure he would learn them in time.

He did, however, quietly take a moment to make it rain over Adurnmouth, in case any fires were still burning. He couldn't feel any, but then, he was working at a distance. He did notice something strange, however.

He couldn't feel anything over the Helm or beyond it.

Ordinarily, he could feel the sky to quite some distance, no matter where he was. Since that day in the garden with Aubrey, in training, he had been working on being able to feel that far in the earth as well. And yet here, so near the border, he couldn't feel either.

It was absurd. Borders were only political; they were only lines drawn on pictures of places. They weren't real, physical things, and he had always been able to connect to the sky before, no matter which country it was over. It was like breathing. So much so that, while he had never been into Honal, he had a mental map of what it was like north of the border. The Helm was so high, it created all sorts of microclimates and changes to the atmosphere immediately around it. He knew the Honal side had caves, but not a thick forest, as Saben had. It had led him to assume that the soil there must be poorer, even though there were a number of rivers coming out of the mountains.

He couldn't feel any of that. There was just nothing, and when he tried to push, he felt something like a barrier. It almost reminded him of the way his mother had manipulated the air to keep up that ballroom wall at the palace when those protestors had attempted to bomb it, like the air was thicker, but instead of keeping a wall from falling down, it was somehow . . . keeping *him* out. Which was no magic he'd ever heard of and probably nonsense. He didn't even know how one would do something like that, but then, he didn't know how to make thousands of people fall asleep, either.

Edmund rubbed his hand over his face. Perhaps he was imagining it; he was very tired. Still, he and everyone else worked into the night. The community absolutely refused to leave any bodies out, both out of respect and also for practical reasons: animals lived in the forest. Every pole was now down, the runes destroyed; the focus before they retired for the night was moving the bodies, even the ones that were not ready for burial yet, into the barracks. Since Edmund was impatient to get the area cleared so that he could make it rain and wash away the evidence of the monstrous thing that had been done to this field, he worked as hard as any farm laborer, even as his muscles ached and his head swam. It was all he could do to help.

He did not understand the effect that this was having on everyone until Sir Jenson said something.

"If I might say so, sir," he said as they headed to the barracks to find somewhere to sleep, "You handled today very well. I think it meant everything to these people that their next king came and worked beside them."

"Well, they called for me," he said, and then stopped. He remembered what he had wanted to ask when he arrived. "Sir Jenson, who *did* call for me?"

Sir J looked puzzled. "What do you mean, sir?"

Edmund reached into his pocket. The messenger who had come to Brythe House had not been a local man, but a hired runner bearing a note.

He pulled the paper out, unfolded it. It had not been sealed; it had not been signed.

"I mean, we came because we received this letter first thing this morning. It takes hours to travel from here to Craywick; we thought something must have happened yesterday."

"Except everything was fine here yesterday," Sir J said slowly. His brows were contracted now. "If I may, sir?"

He put out his hand for the note; Edmund gave it to him, thinking about how surprised Mrs. March had seemed when she had seen him.

Sir Jenson inspected the note, and his brows contracted farther. "I will ask around in the morning. This could be nothing. Perhaps someone had a vision. Let's not invent problems, especially not when we're this tired. Please sleep, sir, and I will find out for you tomorrow."

Reinforcements arrived from Manogate in the morning, along with members of the press, whom Edmund was not glad to see, and the king, whom he was. Edmund had been helping to dig the grave next to the existing barracks cemetery along with a row of farmhands. His father took one look at him in his shirtsleeves with a spade in his hand and shrugged his own white jacket off. He didn't pick up a shovel, though. He put his hands into the dirt.

The king's earth powers were, in many ways, his weakest. The queen and Alicia were the same. This was fairly standard with the royal family, according to living memory, although there were old stories of some of his ancestors being able to manipulate metals or move giant boulders. Queen Helen was supposed to have been able to do all that and more; there was even one story about her being able to call up creatures from clay, like Charlotte could make sculptures of ice, but this was generally considered to be more fiction than fact, especially since they were supposed to have been able to move around and perform simple tasks for her.

The main thing that the king could do, however, was manipulate the composition of earth. Edmund could feel when it worked, since digging was suddenly easier. This would speed everything up substantially, something he was grateful for, since his hands had blistered a while ago. He saw now that they had started bleeding through his leather gloves in a couple of places. He put them behind his back when his father made his way over to him.

The king hugged him first, murmuring something in his deep voice about what a good job he was doing, and then pulled back to examine his face. Edmund tried to look as though he'd slept well.

"Sir Jenson tells me that he cannot find out who called you here," his father said. Edmund had not expected that; he expected what the king said next even less. "I, too, received a message yesterday morning, calling me away from Adurnmouth. When I got to Manogate, no one knew why I was there."

He pulled out a note; it was similar to the one that Edmund had gotten, except that his even had a red seal from the War Office on it.

Upon closer inspection, it was a little warped, as though it had been carefully peeled off one letter before being attached to this one.

"This is going to have to be investigated, since clearly someone did not want either of us in Adurnmouth yesterday morning. So the question is: What did you and your mother do, in Marisetown, that stopped their attack there?"

Edmund blinked at him. *She asked me to make it rain,* he wanted to say, but knew that was absurd. That could not have been it.

"I don't know," he said instead. "I've been trying to work it out, but I cannot think of anything."

His father nodded, taking in the hole they were digging. It was so wide, it looked like the start of a building site, like a foundation for something. Edmund did not want to think about that.

"*Was* it just like Marisetown, then?" he asked. "The attack on Adurnmouth?"

His father nodded again. "Except nothing stopped them this time. People asleep, the gunpowder stores raided, the powder used to blow up the naval base. Most of the port, too, and all the ships as well—not just the military vessels, but the merchant ones. Anything we might have requisitioned for the war."

Edmund took a moment to think about this. The merchant ships up at Adurnmouth tended to be larger than the ones down at Marisetown, since a lot of them went back and forth from the eastern Sunlands. They often had cannons as well, in case of pirates. It had never occurred to Edmund that the government might plan to use those.

The fact that the Honals had both known this and strategized to prevent it made his skin crawl. It felt a little like being robbed by a footpad who knew exactly which of one's pockets to go straight for. Not that Edmund knew what that felt like. He didn't even know what he was feeling now. He was having trouble comprehending the full scope of everything that had happened, and his father's next words proved he wasn't thinking widely enough.

"They've been very, very clever. Saben is no longer ready to launch a counterattack on Honal by ship, which would have been our first move if they had attempted to invade. The fleet has been reduced to whatever was out at sea, and Manogate had word just before I left that at least one ship was attacked by a Honal vessel overnight."

His father paused to grimace at him, and then he said it.

"The war's here."

CHAPTER 11

Edmund did not get to go back to Brythe House. Orders arrived before the day was out. He was called to Elmiddan, along with his parents, for a briefing at the War Office.

The building should have felt familiar—Edmund had visited it before—but it was draped with banners now and bustling with people in full regalia. The room they went into was entirely new to him. It was dominated by a large table in dark wood with the prime minister, Lord Dell, and his secretary, Mr. Young, already sitting at it. Mr. Prestan was there as well, and several other people he recognized, in army and navy uniforms. They all stood up when Edmund and his parents came in.

Edmund was also in his uniform. Mattheson had managed to get all the blood and mud from Mester off it somehow. It was almost identical to his parents' with its white jacket, heavy with gold braid. The gilded cords of aiguillettes came in from the right shoulder to drape across that side of the chest. The left shoulder had a large cloth badge with a dragon embroidered on it, indicating their status. The king and queen, however, were also sporting medals and other decorations from years of service that Edmund did not have.

He squared his shoulders and tried not to feel like a child in a costume trailing after them, but it turned out that he was the one everyone most seemed to want to talk to. Or at least, about.

"The Honals finally sent back word with one of our messengers," Commanding General Wren said after they had all been seated. "They have agreed to talks with one condition. The crown prince's presence has been requested specifically. They say that they will not meet without him but refused to expand on why."

His pale, ruddy face was even blotchier than usual; the prime minister's was similar. They were not looking at each other. Edmund wondered if they had been arguing before everyone came in.

"We know that they are fixated on His Highness," Lord Dell put in. "One of our Seers had a vision showing them discussing prophecies they have about this war, and how he will be important in stopping them. Perhaps they hope to prevent that by capturing him. Or worse."

"But that doesn't make sense," Mr. Prestan said. "Why bother if they know they will fail? If they have Seen—"

"They think this magic water of theirs is so strong, it can defy prophecy," Edmund said, and everybody stared at him. He felt the blood going to his face, but he went on determinedly. "That Seer you are talking about is my friend, Lord Ainsley. I spoke with him the morning after he had that vision."

"Foolishness," one of the admirals said. "Nothing can change what has been Seen. It hasn't happened in five hundred years of records."

"Five hundred years without this water of theirs," the queen put in, "if we believe that Queen Helen really did hide it from them. We don't know what things were like, last time they had it."

The man's eyes widened; Edmund felt his own do the same. He glanced around. Everyone else, including the prime minister, also looked like this thought had never occurred to them.

Wren drew himself together first. "We cannot plan around whatever nonsense the Honals wishfully think up, not without evidence. I do not care what deranged things they believe. I will continue to trust my country's Seers to See the truth."

This did not assuage Edmund's sudden worries in the slightest (how long had his mother been wondering about this? She hadn't said anything), but he was distracted by what the general said next.

"I do not think it a good idea for you to meet with the Honals either way, Your Highness. You have not been Seen doing it, after all."

It took Edmund a moment or two to understand the meaning of those words. When they had told him he had been asked for, he had assumed he would be going. He felt the blood draining from his face now, since rather than having responsibilities loaded upon him, it felt like he was, instead, being discounted. The feeling got worse as the conversation went on and it became clear that Wren was not alone: no one wanted to send him.

Indignation started growing in his mind. Why had they asked him to come here today if he wasn't going to be allowed to be useful, to do something? Were they really going to keep to the old convention that every move a royal dragon made had to have been Seen first? Was he to have no choice and no say in where he was sent and what he did in this war?

Worst of all, Saben needed these talks. They still had no idea what the Honals actually wanted, what their goals were.

"It has been Seen that I will live to be king," Edmund said, trying to sound reasonable. "So presumably if I go, I will be all right."

Lord Dell was shaking his head. "We cannot presume that at all. You could be kidnapped, and we would have to risk people to rescue you. They could do terrible things to you. You could be maimed, tortured. They used blinding powder in the last war—"

"He would not be going alone," the queen said. "They would have a hard time doing any of that with a hundred guards in between them and him."

"With respect, I disagree, ma'am. They had no hard time attacking our naval bases, and we still don't even know—"

The argument went around in circles until the king pointed out that this was getting them nowhere and asked the table to move on to something else.

"Hasprenna, Folbrage, and Arnici have all committed to sending troops in principle," Mr. Prestan said. "They were all very quick to say that they will fulfill their responsibilities under the Thasbian Treaty. All three also implied in tactful, couched terms that they would be very willing to discuss going above and beyond their responsibilities, should"—his eyes flicked over to Edmund, who felt his face flare hot again, even though he did not understand yet—"diplomatic circumstances prove it worth their while."

"That is something worth considering," Lord Dell said. "The crown prince and the princess are to marry at some point, and of course the parliament wants to see them making worthy political matches."

Edmund could not believe what he was hearing. This could not be the real reason why they had asked him to come today, this—

"Our children are not for sale," the queen said. Her voice was wintry, but it made relief burst in Edmund's chest like spring blossom on a tree. "I don't care how many more troops or ships it gets us, His Majesty and I have made very clear that Edmund and Alicia will choose for themselves when they are older. That is not conditional on peacetime."

"Of course not, of course not." Lord Dell's expression was surprised and saddened, as though nobody had suggested anything of the sort. "But of course, you know, your own grandmother—"

"Was married as part of a wartime arrangement," the king finished. "I'm sure *you* also know that that marriage was disastrous. No, Lord Dell."

"I did not mean to distract us," Mr. Prestan put in. "This sort of conversation should be held with Dame Edwina present, either way. If I could get us back to the numbers . . ."

Edmund stopped listening at that point, because the air pressure in the room was changing with his mood and he needed to calm his breathing. He didn't think he missed anything; the conversation was going in circles. Any time a decision needed to be made that didn't suit the prime minister, Edmund noticed, the man kept on coming down on the side of inaction. As though him being thwarted was something that needed to be taken into account, and not the good of the country.

He asked his parents about it when they broke for a recess at midday. They were taking a turn around the courtyard at the rear of the building to stretch their legs.

"He's always been like that," his father said, pitching it low so they would not be heard. "His nickname is Lord Deliberation in the house. Takes his time, takes the cautious road. If he can wait something out, that's always his preference. Sometimes it's for the best, and people's enthusiasm for things cools, or a better solution presents itself. But sometimes it causes a great deal of division, because delaying has not been appropriate and more damage is done in the meantime; or it has just worn people down, and that's not a good way to get along."

Edmund's disappointment must have shown in his face, because his mother took his arm. "The generals will argue harder with him when the army is engaged. I was surprised that the admiralty—"

She stopped to look back at the building. Lord Dell's secretary, Mr. Young, was making for them at a quick pace. His handsome, dark-skinned face was pulled into worried lines.

Edmund and his parents moved forward to meet the man halfway.

"The morning mail has arrived," he said. "His Highness has been Seen meeting with the Honals."

Several more reports came in from Seers to the War Office over the next few days. The meeting would indeed be a trap, just as the generals had feared, but it would fail. Either way, Edmund had been Seen going, and so he was approved to go.

He wondered what they would have decided, if he had been Seen being blinded and kidnapped and everything else they had suggested.

He had trouble eating and sleeping in the days before he headed north. He told himself being afraid wouldn't help, and that he couldn't ruin anything too badly; their party had been Seen emerging from the meeting safe and sound, after all, although that was increasingly seeming to him like a very unambitious goal. He lay awake trying to think of what the Sabresian party could say or offer to try to get the Honals to back down—reach some common ground—while also knowing that nothing they said would stop them from going to war, since it *had been Seen*. He was starting to hate those words. They were being used in ways that he did not find helpful.

He was also slightly worried about what crossing the border would mean for him. The barrier that he had sensed, as though the Honals had put up a shield to keep him out, was still there; he had not imagined it.

If anything, it felt stronger than before, as though the mountains really were a helm, but not protecting Saben from Honal. Protecting Honal from him.

It was a cold day, and the wintry sky looked like a frozen lake. The location for the meeting was traditional: a rocky beach that the Honals called Downfall Cove, mere yards into their side of the border. It was one of the only easy places for delegations from the two countries to meet, since the mountains petered out before the shore. It was the same place where the Honals had surrendered in the last war, and every war before that.

Their leaders had said they didn't care who came to the meeting, as long as Edmund did. In the end, the War Office had decided to send Edmund along with Lord Dell, Dame Edwina, Mr. Prestan, and an entourage of assistants that included Sir Jenson and Mr. Young. They also sent a military guard, whose captain would be carrying a horn, ready to call for the infantry troops who would be standing by on Saben's side of the border, just in case. It had not, after all, been Seen exactly how Saben would defeat whatever trap the Honals planned to spring.

They approached on foot, as had been agreed, and as they got closer to the border, Edmund's awareness of a barrier somehow set over the Helm got stronger and stronger. As they came within feet of the border, it started to feel like nothing short of a brick wall.

No one else with any magic was with the party, but still Edmund asked, "Can—can anyone feel that?"

He was met with blank stares.

"I cannot feel the sky over Honal," he explained. "I can't feel the earth past the border. I—I think there must be sorcery here."

Nobody appeared to know how to react to that. Edmund cursed

himself internally for speaking up and motioned that they should all proceed. After all, there was nothing to actually see.

He half expected, when he reached the space, to not be able to walk into Honal at all. Instead, between steps, the feeling dropped upon him of being in a very small chamber, or a cupboard, even: the walls too close and the air insufficient. He experienced a moment of disorientation and stopped walking entirely, because it was not just discomfiting; it was as though he were suddenly blind or deaf. Things that he was used to experiencing, that let him orient himself in the world, were missing. But it was even odder than all that because he could still feel Saben behind him.

He tried to reach back to his country with his power. It felt like he was digging a tunnel or cutting a channel out of . . . whatever this was. Once he managed it, everything was easier, and he focused on widening the space around him so that he did not feel so uncomfortable. This got harder and harder the farther into Honal he went, and as the beach came into view, he decided that the area he had now—perhaps the size of a large room—would have to do.

The strand was not picturesque. The sea here was as turbulent as all the waters around Honal, the gray waves crashing into enormous boulders. There were some forty or so guards in brown uniforms a little way down and, to their left, on some scrubby grass a small way inland, a dirty white marquee.

Edmund almost missed a step when he saw the party standing there in front of it: three men and a woman, all his parents' age or perhaps a little older, plus a younger woman standing a little behind the rest. He had been half expecting them to wear robes or some other outlandish garments, but they were in their own country's version of military dress uniforms. Dull greens and browns dominated in contrast to the reds and blues Saben tended to use.

The Honals were all watching him closely. They were frowning. He couldn't make sense of their expressions. Eventually he worked out that it was frustration and disappointment on their features. Had they thought he wouldn't be able to cross into their country?

Should he have pretended that he couldn't?

Just as this thought occurred to Edmund, the older woman made a noise of disgust. She turned to the younger woman behind her, pulled her hand back, and slapped her hard in the face. The cracking sound it made was so loud, it was audible over the crash of the waves.

The Sabresians stopped dead.

The two women turned back to face them almost in unison. The Sabresians and the Honals stared at each other for a moment, and then, as though nothing had happened, one of the Honal leaders—the shortest man—stepped forward and gestured toward the marquee.

"This way," he said, his accent unfamiliar. Without waiting for any reply, he made for it himself.

The Sabresian party exchanged glances.

We need these talks, Edmund told himself, and picked up his feet. Everyone else followed his lead, and within moments, they had made themselves walk into the tent.

The younger woman closed the flap behind them, and then the two parties stood on either side of the bare space, lit only by what sunlight could make its way through the white cloth. There were no seats or refreshments; nothing. The whole thing was, Edmund realized with growing horror, socially awkward on top of everything else.

Mr. Young, whom they had agreed would be the facilitator on Saben's side, stepped forward and introduced them. He sounded stiff and wary. Edmund did not blame him.

The Honals said nothing but merely nodded at each new name.

Once Mr. Young had finished, the young woman stepped forward, her slapped cheek still red, and motioned at the man who had led them to the marquee.

"Our head of state," she said, her accent as peculiar to Edmund's ears as the man's had been. "The Pater."

He looked . . . strange. His face was oddly pouchy, and his pale eyes contrasted horribly with the reddened skin around them, but it was his lips that Edmund's gaze kept being drawn to. They were so dry, they had deep cracks in them. Edmund thought they must hurt. He wondered if they used no salves in Honal, nothing that could heal this, until the man picked idly at the side of his mouth and it started bleeding. Edmund's skin crawled.

"The Penitent," the young woman said next, making some sort of ritualistic gesture toward the other woman—the one who had slapped her. Edmund risked a glance over to Sir Jenson to see what he made of her title. He looked appalled.

The Penitent's face was painted as though she were going to appear on the stage, except the colors were less vibrant than those used by an actor. What little of her hair Edmund could see under her brown bicorn hat curled out in rigid coils. There was something girlish about the entire effect, but also something false and off-putting.

"The Cultivator," the young woman said next. The man was painfully thin, with limbs that seemed overlong. His posture was stooped, and what bare few wisps of hair he had were colorless. His expression was blank in a way that Edmund found more and more unnerving. Afterward, he was not able to recall what the man's face had actually looked like.

"Oh, and my General," the Penitent added, motioning to the last man as though his introduction was an afterthought. He was almost as tall as the Cultivator, but all similarity between the two men ended there, as the General showed none of the human frailties that the other man did. He had thick hair, graying but still dark, and his spine was rigidly straight, his shoulders and chest broad. His appearance was not as peculiar as the others, and yet he still frightened Edmund just as much, because he seemed made to go out on a battlefield and strike down anyone who stood in his way.

No title was offered for the younger woman at all. She moved to stand by the door in an oddly servile stance, as though keeping out of the way.

Silence fell. It was like a presence in the tent with them.

"May we not know your names?" Mr. Young finally asked.

The Honals smirked at each other. The Pater was the one who answered.

"Our leaders renounce their names for the title they have been given," he said, while the others nodded behind him. "A sense of self is selfish in a leader. Leaders lead, not follow, in our country. We are strong, and we will be strong."

Edmund didn't know what this was supposed to mean. He peered around at his own people as discreetly as he could to see that they were all doing the same, except for Sir Jenson, who was continuing to stare at the Honals, horror now written across his face. It was the Penitent who finally broke the silence.

"Did you come here for our terms, to accept your surrender?"

Her voice was nasal. Even though she had said the words mildly, somehow they were also malicious and sneering. The Sabresian party all exchanged looks again.

Mr. Prestan said, "Surrender?"

"Yes, is that not the word? Sometimes you use words differently to us. You have changed the meaning of so many things over the years."

Edmund wondered again what they were supposed to understand from that but was brought back to the point by the prime minister snapping, "Why would we surrender to you?"

The Pater raised his eyebrows, as though the question had been impertinent.

"You choose your leaders—your king—based on who has the most magic, yes? I think you can see that that is us. You cannot even work out how we destroyed your port, how we are defeating your navy. This is what we can do now that we have the old water back."

"You—you want to reunite us? Rule Saben?"

"We will rule Thasbus. It was how we ruled Thasbus before—before your Helen hid the water from us. It is how we will rule again. We will undo her foul work, and we will all be one people and one place again as far as the land stretches. As nature intended."

"As nature intended," the rest of the Honals repeated together, like a chorus in an old play.

Edmund was still trying to process what they had said, because this version of their history was nonsense. Queen Helen had ordered a lot of records destroyed, certainly, since they had been in runes, but with help from other countries, Saben had been able to patch together a picture of their pre-treaty history. While Honal and Saben had certainly been one country, the entirety of Thasbus had never been one empire. The Honals couldn't really believe that.

"You imagine you used to rule the entire continent?" Edmund asked. "Your line?"

"Our line is your line," the Penitent said, the malice in her voice more obvious now. "You and the rest of the royal family—you all come from us. Helen was one of us. Most of you can only do parlor tricks with water and fire after all that breeding with those pretenders from the mainland, but Princes of Fortune, they will keep on cropping up. Her legacy."

All five of the Honals locked their eyes onto Edmund at this. He had to resist the urge to take a step backward.

"Blood will out," the Pater said. "And you're stronger than we thought, I will admit. We keep on underestimating you. You shouldn't have been able to cross past the Helm. We're going to have to double our efforts, to stop you from being a danger to us all."

Words. It was just words—

"Nonsense," Dame Edwina said. She was breathing heavily, but she looked every bit as scornful as the Penitent. "How dare you try to vilify our royal family with your ravings, how dare you try and destroy our trust in the crown prince—"

The Pater's voice did not change, merely rose to a higher volume as he said, "None of you have any understanding of what he is capable of—"

"He is destined to be our next king. It has been Seen," the prime minister said, scorn making his voice both rich and brittle. "Whatever ridiculous plan you have will fail. How do you imagine you will rule *us*, let alone the entire continent? You cannot have enough soldiers to take it. You have never once won a war against us. This is *madness*."

The Penitent smiled. Like her voice, there was something nasty about the smile, even though it seemed mild. "Is it? Why don't you come and see."

She motioned to the woman who had been standing silently by the General all this time. She secured the tent flap open, and the Honals filed out.

The Sabresian party all exchanged more glances.

"I suppose we should follow them," Dame Edwina said. Everyone looked to Edmund; protocol dictated that he should exit first, since the guard was already outside.

He stepped through the opening in the tent wall but recoiled back inside.

The air outside felt horribly, crawlingly *wrong.*

"Everyone stay here. Do not go out," he said, before stepping through again and yanking the tent flap closed behind him as quickly as he could. He heard protests, Sir J's voice the loudest, but he wasn't listening to what was being said; he was listening to the wind. One of those peculiar storm clouds was starting up, right on top of them. Edmund blinked, and the sky was suddenly as gray as the boulders on the beach.

The Pater was moving his arms strangely, and it hit Edmund that he was seeing the man create the cloud. It felt nothing like the way Edmund called a storm. Part of him wanted to watch, but there was a bigger threat. The Penitent was doing something that was making his gift scream inside his head. He turned to see that she was walking—almost dancing—in a stilted, measured way, and had summoned a fog, not from the sea but from the forest to their west. She stepped toward the Sabresian guards, pulling it with her. They were eyeing her warily but maintaining their position.

"Mon y ume," she said in a shrill voice that rang like a fire bell over the whole cove.

Monium, Edmund thought in a panic, but then the Penitent smiled horribly and called out, "These soldiers are ours now."

Edmund looked at the Sabresian guards. They had stopped watching her in that careful way. They were now gazing ahead, their expressions completely blank.

She did something with her hands, and they came to attention all at once. Then the front line pulled out their bayonets in one swift, fluid movement like a row of puppets all on the same string.

Every feeling in Edmund revolted in horror. These were Saben's soldiers; Sabresian men and women. They were supposed to be free. They were supposed to have a choice.

Edmund was frozen in place, but then, out of the corner of his eye, he saw the Pater moving his arms toward the storm cloud he had created, with what appeared to be the same gesture his own mother and father and sister used when they meant to move the air.

Edmund acted without thinking. He dropped down. The stones were sharp under his knees, but the ground underneath felt just like home. That was disorientating but also helpful, and so he *pushed*. The space he had created around himself expanded, filling the whole beach and finally the sky.

There was an almighty crack above their heads as the storm that the Pater was conjuring suddenly became not his, but Edmund's own. Lightning flashed over the water, and the storm's jagged edges and manufactured feel suddenly became organic and balanced—a normal storm rather than a wrong, *wrong* sorcerous weapon. Edmund accelerated the wind so that it drove the fog swiftly away from the beach and back to wherever it had come from, through the trees behind them. A stray misty tendril blew toward him, and he felt a moment of pure panic.

This was why the Honals had wanted him here. They had wanted to capture him, to make him their instrument. He froze for one horrified moment as the full ramifications unfurled in his mind.

If they had pulled it off, they would not have been breaking any prophecies. He could have reigned perfectly well as their mindless creature.

I will not be theirs, he thought, and then all at once the wind roared, and lightning struck down on the beach. It hit the Pater, who screamed, his arms still raised like lightning rods. Edmund lifted his head in time to watch him fall, smoking, twitching.

Edmund stayed kneeling on the stones, frozen. He did not even know if he had made that happen, or if the storm had done it on its own.

He realized, even as he thought it, that he was splitting hairs.

The Penitent let out a screaming wail, and Edmund looked over to her and to the soldiers behind her. They still had that awful blankness about them, like they were awaiting instruction.

Rain, he thought, wild ideas of cleansing and purification swirling in his head, of it somehow helping in Marisetown. Before he had consciously formed a plan, the storm cloud above them condensed. The drops of water started hitting the ground like stones.

It was only moments before the Sabresian soldiers all slumped down onto the rocks like marionettes with their strings cut, their weapons falling from their hands.

Thank you, thank you, Edmund's heart cried out to the rain—but then he started at movement to his other side. It was the troop of Honal soldiers, who had been motionless thus far.

Edmund spent a moment cursing himself, as he hadn't paid them the smallest bit of attention. Any one of them could have shot him at any time, and still could; but instead of so much as aiming their guns at him, the Honal soldiers were also falling to the ground.

Edmund fell onto his side, understanding making way for horror, but then he had more pressing worries. The Penitent started running straight for him, her face twisted.

She was unnaturally fast, not so much moving quickly as covering too much ground with each pace that she took. His eyes struggled to make sense of it. More sorcery that he did not understand.

A shot rang out from the tent behind him.

The woman dropped to a crouch, still many yards away, her eyes on something behind Edmund now. He turned to see the tent opening parted. Through it, he could see Sir Jenson efficiently reloading a handsome engraved pistol.

"May we come out and help yet, sir?" the man called out over the storm, not taking his eyes off the Penitent.

Edmund waved them out. He was glad to be able to take his attention off the Penitent, who started backing toward her companions. He focused on the clouds above them as he pushed the storm out to sea. The rain eased. He heard some murmur of calling for the reinforcements. Mr. Prestan moved over to their fallen soldiers and blew out a signal into the captain's horn.

The Honal leaders looked up sharply. Edmund kept his eyes on them as he rose, brushing sand off himself. The Penitent was making some motion to the others, and then the General hefted the Pater's body over his shoulder like a manservant with a sack of potatoes and turned away with the unnamed woman.

The wind was dying down. Edmund had a horrible sense of anticipation as he saw the Penitent turn back to them, but he couldn't have been more surprised by what she said.

"So much for your talk of a truce," she called out, the others behind her already walking away from them and from their own fallen soldiers. "There will be retribution for this, you mark my—"

"You brought all this violence to *us*," Edmund found himself yelling back indignantly over the shocked outcries behind him. "It doesn't have to be this way. It never had to be this way; we could have gotten along in peace—"

"So proper and correct," the Cultivator sneered. "Say what you really think for once. You want to destroy us and our way of life, and yet you speak words of tolerance. You are just like us, except that you are wrong, and we will show it to you."

And then, with another display of that unnatural speed, they disappeared into the trees and out of sight.

CHAPTER 12

Aubrey read about what happened in the papers, which called the meeting a decisive blow to Honal's leadership. The Honal guardsmen that had just been left there, collapsed on the beach, were taken as prisoners. The Prince of Fortune was hailed as a hero. Aubrey knew that Edmund would not have felt like one. Not if he'd killed a man.

He couldn't wait until Edmund came back. Craywick was not what Aubrey had expected.

He had spent years picturing himself moving to the town, but that had been to student lodgings, not officers' quarters in the training barracks. He had also never imagined that he would arrive to find that people already knew his name.

It was discomfiting and a little lonely.

Except when it wasn't lonely. Aubrey found that worse. He had taken to avoiding a particular groom who had a habit of standing too close and giving him lingering glances under his eyelashes; and now, as he walked through the officers' mess hall for breakfast, he altered his route slightly to avoid going past Ensign Worthing's table. The man had suggested several times that Aubrey shouldn't have to "do without" while his "special friend" was away meeting with the Honals and never seemed to take refusal seriously. Aubrey now did his best to simply stay out of the man's way.

Ah well. He had wanted to be out in society. This was part of it. He just needed to get through this, and perhaps things would be better once Edmund was back, or when Aubrey was actually posted somewhere. This was all so transient, with new recruits coming and going all the time. People would probably be friendlier, or at least better behaved, once they knew they'd be in each other's company for a while. Or perhaps everyone would start gossiping about Malmy instead. He'd be coming through here soon on his way north. His latest love affair had ended, and he had written a scandalous, broken-hearted poem about it that had been published "anonymously" in a recent magazine. Aubrey could see the thing being read out at another table. He avoided going past that one too.

People would find something else to talk about soon enough. Aubrey wasn't going to let it worry him.

"Your face doesn't help," Wilson said abruptly as he sat down next to him.

He and John were sitting at a long wooden table and eating porridge. Everyone was eating porridge. Again.

"I doubt *your* face has ever helped with anything in the entire course of your life," Aubrey replied, purely on principle. He smiled at the servant who came to pour tea into his copper mug, damping down how much he missed the feel of a fine porcelain cup in his hands. He waited until the boy was gone before adding, "What in particular are you talking about?"

Wilson started shoveling porridge into his mouth like his spoon needed to be put through its paces, instead of answering. John, who had been eyeing them both, moved his gaze to the wider room as though it could tell him what had provoked his brother's elliptical statement.

"Wils," he said. "Did you do that?"

Aubrey glanced over. Two other lieutenants were making their way to the far end of the table. One had a black eye, and the other, who was limping, had bruising on the lower part of their face and a swollen lip. They were openly glaring in their direction. Aubrey looked back at Wilson. Apart from a split on his knuckles that Aubrey had initially put down to their regular training, he wasn't visibly injured.

"I did," Wilson bit out. "If they don't want people to take offense, they shouldn't say offensive things."

"They said something offensive . . . about my face?"

Wilson didn't answer. Aubrey stared pointedly at their eldest brother, since he always seemed to know everything. John quirked an eyebrow.

"I expect they said something about it being obvious what the crown prince found to like in it, except using less flattering language than that. I've heard that a few times myself, but I find using my *words* helps. I thanked the last one for the compliment, for instance, and he went off blushing. They're usually more bark than bite. Not even bark. People are curious, and they don't really know what to do with that curiosity."

He motioned with one elegant, efficient finger to the bruised lieutenants and addressed Wilson again. "Are you going to be reprimanded for that?"

Wilson gave a tense twitch of his head. "I told the captain who came to break it up that they had insulted my family's honor. She said it looked like they'd been punished enough and told them to keep two-against-one for the Honals. That was it."

"Well, that was lax. Although you aren't the only one ready to burst around here."

John wasn't wrong. Fights broke out every couple of days, so Aubrey refused to feel bad that people were apparently using him as an excuse to have some of them. The feeling in the entire base was one of skittish anxiety, like a nervy young horse not yet used to being in saddle, and it only got worse as the weeks passed. The Honals seemed to be focusing on wiping out the last of Saben's navy just now, leaving the army training in a state of planlessness that was clearly wearing on the nerves of some recruits more than others. It was a shame everyone was so keen, Aubrey thought, since even he could see that these troops weren't ready. The soldiers all seemed to feel the need to rush, since attack could be coming any day now, but it wasn't doing them any favors.

Aubrey was starting to understand how privileged he was, to have walked into this place able to shoot and fence and ride well. Even just being the youngest of four brothers had given him the advantage of familiarity with facing multiple opponents and some basic wrestling, and helping the younger students at his father's school had given him experience at things like demonstration and correction. It was clear how new some or all of these skills were to others.

The fact that some of the recruits were turning up drunk to training did not help. John said that it was their way of dealing with the stress. The captains didn't seem that worried about it. But Aubrey was convinced that it was worsening the other main problem the camp had: training accidents, which were a lot more common than he had expected.

Every day he watched people thrown from their mounts or cut on their own blades. A few new recruits were sent home after losing fingers or, in one dramatic case, a hand. Worse were the injuries people accidentally inflicted on others. People had trouble forgiving themselves for those. One young private deserted, three weeks in, after accidentally shooting the woman next to him in the leg. She also ended up being sent home, since it had had to be amputated.

Aubrey had hoped all this would prove educational—have everyone concentrating more during their training—but it did the opposite. Morale got lower and lower. And then Colonel Sutherton had stood up at breakfast one morning with two announcements. He had a quavery voice that seemed to belong to a man twenty years older, which had led to speculation over his age and whether or not he merely *looked* to be in his fifties. The whole hall fell silent.

"Honal soldiers," he said, "have been spotted disembarking from ships in five separate locations along the northern coast."

The hall exploded with sound again. He held up a hand, and it mostly died down.

"You are not ready. There has been a shocking lack of discipline here, which we hoped would resolve itself as you all got a bit less green. It has not. We will be allocating new training groups and cracking down on poor behavior. Alcohol rations will be halved. I suggest that those of you who don't want to be punished like children stop acting like them."

Aubrey tried not to bristle at this, since none of *his* troopers had been involved in any drunkenness or unauthorized violence. He glanced over at John, who twitched his eyebrows superciliously, as though reminding Aubrey to rise above it. He tried to catch Wilson's eye too, but Wils had that enraptured expression he got when listening to senior officers and could not be distracted. Aubrey reminded himself that Wilson had planned to go into the military anyway, and wondered what in his personality made his crankiest brother more prone to admiring authority than any of the rest of them. They'd all had the same childhood after all.

"This will be especially important because of the other piece of news I have for you all," Colonel Sutherton went on. "His Highness Prince Edmund will be moving into the royal residence in Craywick and will be training with us for the next few months."

The hall erupted with noise again. This time it was Aubrey's turn to refuse to let anyone catch his eye, even though he felt the weight of their attention. He had known Edmund was on his way, of course, since he had written to Aubrey about it. He was therefore able to keep his face neutral. He was just wondering if his lack of reaction was reaction enough for people to read into, when the colonel snapped, "Quiet!"

He sounded much less quavery now. "This is precisely the sort of thing I'm talking about. I will not see these walls embarrassed by poor behavior in front of a royal dragon. I expect you to all be at least *presentable* by the time His Highness arrives next week. You will be assigned your new groups this morning."

The morning proved a combination of flattery and punishment for all three Ainsley brothers. When they went out to the training yard—a space no more attractive than any of the rest of the barracks, but at least spacious enough for its purpose—they were each of them informed by their respective captains that their units included some of the best performing men and women present. This would have been very gratifying if it hadn't meant that their charges were therefore to be removed and split up among the other teams, in the hopes that it would more quickly get everyone else up to the mark.

Aubrey at least got to keep his ensigns, something he considered a small mercy when he saw his new recruits. They were all men and looked like some of the scruffiest the station had to offer. He called them to attention and discovered they could barely make a straight line.

"This won't do," he said immediately. He sent three of them back inside to polish their boots—only two of them needed to, but the third was leering at him, so he thought it would be good for the man—and another to shave again. He had the rest of them performing drills almost well by the time those four returned. He motioned them to join the others in the way that, at home, he used to deal with cheeky little children in the schoolroom, making it clear that only good behavior would earn attention. He then worked them all so hard, they'd hopefully be too worn out to cause trouble later.

"He wasn't what I expected," he overheard the leery fellow mutter after he had let them go up for the noon meal. His friend just nodded tiredly.

Aubrey felt like whistling.

When Edmund arrived back at Brythe House, he wished desperately that he could just send a note over to Aubrey and have him come. Annoyingly, he could have, since he theoretically outranked the colonel in charge, but he didn't quite have the nerve to throw his weight around like that. It was a shame, since he frankly did feel very much like he needed Aubrey.

The last few days had been horrible. The reports he had seen indicated that Honal was not so much invading the northern coast as brutalizing it. Their soldiers did not seem to tire—probably a side effect of the Monium fog, as it was being called—and showed no mercy. Edmund had been looking forward to getting back to Craywick, not only to see Aubrey but also to get on with the day-to-day parts of being a soldier rather than trying to participate in the politics of the war, like he had to in the capital. Now that he was here, however, he felt a stone forming in his stomach. He and Aubrey would both have to be soldiers first, at these barracks. Aubrey was going to have to salute him, for instance, which was ridiculous. But then, he supposed that a lot of people were doing things they wouldn't normally do these days.

So, instead of requisitioning lieutenants who had more important things to be doing than coddling princes, Edmund tidied himself up and asked for his horse and his guard to be readied. It would not do to be late.

The full company were formed up in the parade ground when he got to the base. Everything seemed well kept, the recruits all neat and tidy. He spotted Aubrey right away and felt a bittersweet pang that he was so near but so far. He looked for his brothers and found them as well, but then he had to stop surveying the scene and pay attention to the colonel in charge, who was greeting him in a thin, reedy voice.

The soldiers were put through their paces, which mostly involved moving their guns around while they were shouted at. Edmund knew that it was traditional to honor him, so he kept himself perfectly still, trying to give them the respect of his full attention, performing every bit as much as they were. Pomp and ceremony.

Then two things happened.

One of the low-ranking infantry soldiers in the group closest to him seemed to trip, bumping into two of his fellows. All three fell. Everyone else kept going valiantly, so Edmund tried to ignore the kerfuffle—except the first fellow started to laugh. Edmund let his eyes cut over.

He was sitting in the dirt, his hat knocked off his head. He wasn't even trying to get back up. It took Edmund a moment to realize that the man was intoxicated.

The two soldiers he had knocked over tried to get him up and were slapped away. Edmund, who had had it drilled into him to pretend this sort of thing wasn't happening, tried to ignore it. He focused his eyes on the far side of the yard, but then the man called out, loud enough to carry over the noise, "What does it matter? We all know what the prince is here for, and it isn't us!"

The words were bad enough, but the way he said them made it much, much worse. Edmund's face heated up so fast, his skin prickled. A young woman in a lieutenant's uniform stepped in at that point, her face as red as Edmund expected his own was. She barked something at the two soldiers already trying to manage their drunk comrade, then strode toward the nearest building. They heaved up their brother in arms and frog-marched him after her. The door slamming behind them was barely audible over the noise of the rest of the company, still running through their maneuvers.

The scene had not even taken a full minute, but Edmund felt like something had shifted in the ground here. He risked a peek at Colonel Sutherton, still next to him by the gates. His mouth was turned down in displeasure, but Edmund was distracted again by the sight of a rider coming toward the barracks at a gallop. They looked like a military messenger.

He forced himself to focus on the yard again. There was more shouting, and everyone turned to him and saluted. He saluted back, thanking the stars that this was over, and then all the soldiers started to march out. He turned back again to see that there was indeed a military messenger coming in the gate behind them, which meant that he would not have to think of a way to ask the colonel what on earth his soldiers were doing drunk before noon, and why no one had noticed the state of the man before he had had the opportunity to disgrace himself.

The messenger went straight to the colonel and handed him a letter from his satchel and then surprised Edmund by handing him one as well. He cracked it open immediately, since the green seal indicated important mail from the War Office, rather than the usual everyday red.

> *Your Highness*
>
> *New reports are coming in detailing a magical creature that the Honal army is traveling with. Please be advised that all royal dragons are to consider themselves on standby to be deployed to the northern coast, depending on new information.*

It was signed by one of the generals. Edmund turned it over to see if there was anything else. There was not. He stared at it, wondering what the point was of telling people they might be deployed when they were waiting to be deployed anyway, and heard the colonel let out an acknowledging sort of grunt next to him. He looked over. Sutherton lifted his head up from his own letter in response and made a motion with his hand that seemed to dismiss the entire parade ground.

"If you would, sir, let us speak in my office."

Edmund nodded and followed him.

The office was similar to other military offices he'd visited: a handsome desk, a nice carpet over the hardwood floor. Another table, under the window, with a map of Saben. There were weapons on the wall and letters with cracked green seals in a pile on the desk with a rock on top as a paperweight. Edmund did not ask about the rock. He sat down to wait while the colonel closed the door in a firm sort of way.

"First of all, sir," the man said in his oddly threadbare voice, "I must apologize for that display. The man will be reprimanded. Some of these new recruits are taking longer to get up to the mark, and—to be frank—so are some of the officers, which is making things worse. I will be recommending some of them be moved into administrative roles."

Sutherton rubbed his face with his hand and then said, "Permission to speak freely, sir."

"Please." Edmund had allowed too much feeling to come out in his voice, but it seemed to go down well with the colonel, who let out a huff of laughter.

"Sir, our system of selling commissions is outdated. It was outdated when my father bought me mine. It made sense when high-born children were trained in the arts of war as part of their education, and nobles handed over funds as well as soldiers, as a way of contributing to the country's defense. Now, however, it means that those who could afford commissions bought them, so I've got a lot of rich merchants' children who have never held a sword and would be better off managing supplies—who would be *good* at that—and a lot of young people with noble connections who are used to their weapons being for sport or decoration."

He made a jerky movement then and looked at Edmund guiltily, which was baffling, until he added, "I do not speak of the Ainsley brothers, though, sir. Their mother clearly did right by them. I served under their grandfather, you know. Colonel Mayhew taught me everything I know. But your friend, Lieutenant Aubrey Ainsley. As you saw, some of the recruits have found his presence . . . a distraction. Well, they are searching for one. All this waiting hasn't been easy for any of us."

"What if," Edmund said slowly, since his mind had blanked while all the blood in it went to his face instead, "I gave you permission to redistribute some of the officers you're not finding up to the task?

You would normally need a general to sign off on that sort of thing, wouldn't you?"

Sutherton's expression looked so relieved, it hurt Edmund's head. This was a dignified military man who had spent his life in service to his country; it was ridiculous that Edmund should be his superior in rank.

"I would not have asked, sir, but yes, that would help enormously." He held up the letter he had just received. "Although, it seems that we are going to see movement no matter what. This begs that we send on anyone who we think is ready to be posted at particular sites in the north. I might send on the three Ainsley brothers and some of the troopers they've been training with. I assume that will not influence your decision to stay in Craywick?"

Another twist in the conversation that left Edmund stuck for a response. The man didn't even know him, and yet he thought Aubrey must mean so little to Edmund that it was irrelevant whether or not he was here. That was as untrue as the drunk man's suggestions that Edmund didn't care about his duty and was only here for Aubrey.

In the end, Edmund just held up his own letter.

"I've been told to expect orders to head north myself," he said. "Something about a magical creature that the Honals have. Does your letter say anything about that?"

The man's startled look answered his question. Somehow that made the rock in Edmund's stomach feel even bigger—as big as the one on the desk—something that wasn't helped by the fact that he didn't even manage to swap words with Aubrey as the day went on. They both had duties, and there were eyes on them everywhere.

When he made his way back to Brythe House, he found Sir J waiting for him with a stack of mail. He handed the man the War Office's note in exchange. Sir J made an annoyed tutting sort of noise.

"It's almost as though they are being obscure on purpose," he said. "Or do you suppose they just don't know yet what this creature is?"

"That is what I thought, yes. But Colonel Sutherton told me that he's been asked to send whoever he thinks is ready up there as well." He swallowed and tried to keep his voice steady. "Lord Ainsley is going to be sent, because he's performed so well here. I wanted to talk to you about—about what I can do, regarding where he goes."

"You want to exert your influence to keep Lord Ainsley in safer posts?"

Edmund swallowed again. "It sounds awful when you say it like that. I mostly just—is there no way I can keep us together?"

Sir Jenson examined him for a moment. "I expect wherever you are stationed, sir, isn't going to be safe, if the War Office wants you fighting sorcerous unknown *things*. I confess myself surprised by their request, since as far as you have told me, you have not been Seen doing that. Or have you? Not that I expect Your Highness to share every—"

Edmund put his hand up. "I've shown you every letter that I have had on the subject."

Sir Jenson nodded, looking relieved and then thoughtful. "You could request Lord Ainsley to join your personal guard, but he's been Seen fighting in the cavalry, sir, in a lieutenant's red coat like he was wearing today. That will be in his military record. The army will therefore want him in one. But mostly, requesting him in such a way is going to call attention to what you're doing. If the newspapers hadn't reported on your relationship, it would be a different thing, sir, but, as things stand, it could be damaging to his lordship's reputation."

Edmund did not say that Aubrey's reputation was clearly already suffering—something he felt horrible about—since Sir Jenson was still speaking. "I did tell you, sir, that this would have to be managed carefully. Have you asked Lord Ainsley himself what he thinks?"

Edmund blinked.

"I shall ask him tomorrow."

CHAPTER 13

Edmund arrived at the barracks the next morning to chaos.

His guards formed up around him, since they'd identified something was amiss before he had. He had thought two units were sparring, on the far side of the parade ground, before he heard the shouts of "Get the captain!" and "Get his brothers!" and he realized: this was not training. This was Lord Wilson Ainsley wrestling on the ground with someone, landing punches where he could, and a crowd of soldiers standing around them, yelling. Even as he watched, a female soldier tried to step in to intervene, and another one shoved her backward. A third one then pushed that one, and she fell to the ground.

This was going to end in a brawl. Edmund needed to stop it but spent a moment doubting that he would be listened to, which would be humiliating beyond belief. He was just stepping forward anyway when the man under Wilson got his arm free enough to punch the lordling full in the face, dislodging him.

A peal of thunder rang out as lightning hit the highest part of the barracks building—a decorative chimney—on the other side of the field.

Edmund was as surprised as the soldiers were, who all stood frozen for a moment.

Best pretend that was deliberate.

"Stand down and follow," he said to his own guard, and started walking toward the group, trying to think of something to say. Before he'd even opened his mouth, however, the soldiers were all a blur of movement. A few of them (whom he did not, in hindsight, blame) ran for it, including the lieutenant Wilson had been fighting. The rest, including Wilson, quickly lined up, for all the world as though he had called them to attention. Edmund was worried, just for a moment, that they were going to salute, but then the captain arrived.

She looked around, taking in the scene.

Blood started dripping from Wilson's nose.

The captain did lead a salute, then, to Edmund. He forced himself to salute back and tried to make the rest of his way over calmly. His guards had fallen into formation next to and behind him. They were starting to wear on his nerves as much as the saluting.

"Report, Lieutenant." The captain's voice echoed around the parade ground as Aubrey's brother hesitated, his eyes flicking to Edmund for a moment. Edmund's stomach sank. Then it sank further as a young man behind Wilson said, "Ainsley didn't start it, Captain!"

The captain was louder this time. "Did I address you, trooper?"

Before the trooper could react, Edmund saw Wilson move out of his perfect attention posture for just long enough to reach back with one hand and touch the side of the young man's leg, behind him.

The soldier relaxed perceptibly and rapped out, "No, ma'am. Apologies, ma'am."

Edmund should excuse himself. His presence was surely making everything worse, but he felt rooted to the spot, worried that he needed to—to bear witness or lend the captain his authority or . . . *something*.

She flicked an impatient look back at Wilson, but before she had to repeat her question, he said, "It was the same issue as last time, Captain."

His eyes flicked to Edmund again, and Edmund knew, with a feeling like a hole opening in his chest, what the fight must have been about. It was then confirmed by the woman's next words.

"Your family honor seems to need a lot of defending, Lieutenant," she said, and then Edmund did excuse himself, because he couldn't be here, not with Wilson being berated for fighting people over his brother's reputation. Because of him.

He strode away blindly, leading his guard farther into the barracks complex, his mind racing.

Being with Edmund was hurting Aubrey.

Edmund had worried this would happen, from the start. That since he was not able to offer Aubrey a sanctioned position by his side, their relationship would be treated as the butt of jokes and bawdy gossip. That it would be seen as less, which would make it less. He just hadn't expected it to be so soon.

This wasn't fair.

Did none of these people have anything better to worry about? They were at war, for heaven's sake. These men and women were all about to be sent to fight for their lives, for their country's freedom. But then, that was the problem, wasn't it? The colonel had said they were all searching for a distraction.

They should find something else, he thought, since this was his *life*.

"Edmund?"

It was Aubrey, trotting over on his horse. Edmund had not paid any attention to where he was going, but he had marched through to the training yard behind the main building. Some part of his brain must have done it deliberately, since this was where Aubrey would be.

He felt the eyes of his guard on him, of Aubrey's unit. Everyone seemed to be watching them, including the horses, the buildings, and the grass.

"Can we speak a moment?" he asked.

He must have looked as upset as he felt, because Aubrey nodded immediately, despite clearly being in the middle of a training exercise.

"The ensigns have the command," Aubrey called out over his shoulder to his men as he dismounted. A groom came over to take his reins.

"There's a garden a little way down the hill that will probably be empty," Aubrey said, peering into Edmund's face. Edmund wondered what he saw there. "Or if you want proper privacy you might need to commandeer a meeting room."

Privacy.

"Let's do that," Edmund said, and let Aubrey lead the way.

The room felt as familiar as the colonel's had, even though Edmund had never been there before in his life. Uncomfortable chairs, a nondescript table, a lot of space for people to stand at attention. It did not, now that Edmund was here, feel like the place to have this sort of conversation at all. He wished he'd picked the garden, although at least this way, his guards were all on the other side of a closed door. He'd insisted that they stay outside.

"Are you all right?" Aubrey asked, taking off his hat and tossing it onto the table. He fluffed up his curls in that so-familiar gesture, and Edmund had a sudden pain in his chest because he—

He should never touch that hair again. Or anything of Aubrey's. He knew now what he had to do. What he had known he should do this whole time.

"People are being unkind," he said. "To you, about us. We should . . . stop."

Aubrey looked at him. Eventually he said, "Stop what, darling?"

"Our association. It's hurting you. We shouldn't—" He had to close his eyes. "I—this is my fault."

He opened his eyes again to see Aubrey watching him intently.

They stared at each other for one moment, two, three. A clock was ticking somewhere—the mantelshelf, probably. He didn't glance over at it. He could only see Aubrey's blue, blue eyes, cycling through different emotions as they searched his face.

"I am assuming," Aubrey said eventually, "you don't mean to make it sound like you are trying to break things off between us."

Edmund closed his eyes. He was such a fool. He was a fool, and his heart was breaking, and he didn't know how to do this.

After a moment, Aubrey went on in a louder voice. "You cannot be doing that, since you have just gone and gotten yourself stationed here so that we could be together."

"I'll have myself moved again. They're wanting me to go north anyway—"

"Edmund, stop. Why are you talking like this? This cannot just be over that drunkard making a spectacle of himself yesterday."

"No, it's—your brother Wilson is being reprimanded right now by his captain for fighting. A brawl was about to break out between his and another fellow's units. He shouldn't have to endure insult, and neither should you. You didn't tell me this was happening!"

Aubrey's mouth, usually so generous, pressed into a thin line at this.

"Well, forgive me if I don't begin our every meeting with a recitation of all the ridiculous things my brothers have most recently done! And are you really going to berate *me* for not discussing things with you when you seem to have decided *for me* that the best thing *for me* was to throw me over?"

"This is my fault, and my responsibility—"

"Oh no you don't. Don't you dare play the—the feudal overlord at me. It is one thing for strangers to disrespect me behind my back, but quite another for you to do it to my face. If you want to show that you think of me as your equal, then you will start in this room, with *me*. If you have a concern about our relationship—*our* relationship, not just *yours*—then that is something we should talk about *together*."

Aubrey's voice was raised by the end of this; Edmund found himself almost shouting in response. "What is there to say? Do you really expect me to just not care that being with me is damaging your standing?"

Aubrey stared at him. "We are at *war*. I do not *care* about people gossiping about me. Thousands of people have already died, Edmund, you do understand that? I'm not going to be here, safe, forever, riding my horse in circles and shooting at targets. I might very well get a bayonet to the stomach in my first battle. You're worrying about the wrong things."

Edmund was frozen for a moment in horror, and then the words blurted out. "They're never going to let us get married."

Aubrey stared at him, his eyes narrowing again, like he was trying to work out the steps Edmund had taken to make that the next rational thing to say.

"What?" he finally asked. The anger had drained from his tone, leaving it flat.

"If we were married," Edmund tried to explain, "you could be properly stationed with me, and you'd be safer. As it is, I'm hurting you. Sir J said to be careful for— He said that if you got labeled as a paramour, then the parliament would never let—"

"What else was I ever going to be labeled as?" Aubrey's voice was matter-of-fact now. "An obvious choice as your consort? You do remember that I'm a lord of precisely *nothing*, yes?"

"I don't care about that! You make me feel—" Edmund had to stop here and swipe his cuff over his eyes. He took a deep breath. "You make me feel like I could do it. I could do it, be this great king, if you were with me. You. Not some stranger whose country told them to marry me. *You*."

Aubrey studied him for another moment or two and then made a tutting noise. "Oh for heaven's sake, come here," he said, reaching for Edmund. Edmund went into his arms.

"I *am* with you," Aubrey said, running one hand up and down his back, like he was soothing a child. "I'm right here. I'm here, for as long as you want me. We don't need to be married for that."

"No, you don't understand," Edmund said. "Sir J said—he made it sound like there might be a chance, but we'd have to do it right."

Aubrey's hand along his back stilled. He pulled away to peer into Edmund's face.

"Sir *Jenson* said that? You talked to him about it?"

Edmund nodded.

"Goodness, you must be serious about this," Aubrey said, and Edmund pulled him in again, because he was going to tear up.

"What do we do?" he asked into Aubrey's shoulder, which was itchy with braid. He wished it wasn't there. Damn the bloody Honals. "I can't—I can't know that people are being awful to you on top of everything else. I just can't."

"If I tell you to just not think about it, that won't work, will it?"

A choked sort of chuckle came out of Edmund's mouth. "I don't know how *you* do that. I certainly can't."

"I know, darling. Well, you said Sir J had some ideas. Shall we ask him? Come up with a plan all together?"

Edmund let himself hold Aubrey tighter. "Yes."

"All right, then. I have the whole of tomorrow afternoon and evening free, for leisure. If anyone wanted to invite me to see Brythe House, I am sure we could fit in speaking to him."

Edmund's laugh was less choked sounding, this time.

"I think that can be arranged."

Brythe House was generally only used by members of the royal family while they attended university, so it was an informal residence. It still had a full score of bedroom suites for some reason, which Aubrey had found highly entertaining.

The building was about three hundred years old, built to replace a previous version that had burned down. Most of the interiors had been updated, however, by Edmund's grandfather during his "modernization" spree, so they were ornate, with a lot of cream and gold.

"I love it," Aubrey announced. "You should have a masked ball here whenever you finally get to go to university. Everyone can dress up like their grandparents in their youth, with big powdered wigs."

"If I get my way, you'll be here with me," Edmund said. "So—you organize that."

Aubrey felt himself blush. Actually blush.

It was enough for Aubrey to have Edmund for the time being. More than enough—a grand adventure. Romantic. The lovers of kings ended up in the history books, which was a little overwhelming but nothing Aubrey didn't think he was worthy of. He did not necessarily consider himself worthy of being the consort of a king.

That said, though, he couldn't be worse than some of the consorts the country had had. His own great-great-great-grandmother, Queen Sofia, had reportedly spent most of King William's reign drunk. If he could just avoid that, they'd already be ahead. If they were going to compare him to the present queen, they might be in trouble.

He hadn't thought seriously enough about this, he knew, but then a wiser young man wouldn't have seen a worried frown on the face of a magical prince and let it sway his heart. Love had been Aubrey's goal, not *forever*. He still thought it was a good goal—the best goal—but it perhaps should not have been the only one he had cared about.

Frankly, the whole thing had seemed so big and so out of his hands, he hadn't thought it worth worrying over. It had been wrong of him not to think about how worried Edmund got about everything, but then, he knew that he himself had been refusing to think about it for the same reasons. He hadn't wanted to imagine this issue driving them apart. He still didn't, but it seemed unlikely that the parliament was going to let him and Edmund marry. His father had not reformed the country yet, after all, and social class was still the first thing that mattered in Saben. In the face of Edmund's determination, however, he found himself having some small hope. If there was anything that Aubrey could do to give them a better chance at the future Edmund wanted for them, he was doing it. And so, here he was in a cream-and-gold sitting room at Brythe House waiting for Sir Jenson to come and tell them how to get everyone to think of Aubrey as a suitable suitor, rather than "the prince's pretty little friend" (he had informed the captain who had called him that that, actually, he was a full inch *taller* than His Highness, thank you very much).

Sir J arrived looking harried. Aubrey had never seen the pompous fellow so out of sorts, and he couldn't stop himself from asking whether or not he was well.

"Yes, indeed, your lordship," he said, bowing. "I have just had some . . . complicated news, that it is good that you are here to hear. But first, the matter at hand. Tell me yourself, sir, what has been happening at the barracks."

Aubrey described what had been going on as briefly as he could, aware of Edmund going tense next to him.

"Really, I do need to put this into context, though," he said. "Fights break out all the time over all sorts of things. I think if it wasn't me, they would find something else to bait Wilson with."

"Well, that is part of what I wanted to tell you both. I heard from the king's secretary today. New orders are going to be coming through, cracking down on discipline at all the training facilities. This is not the only one full of young people ready to snap. But there was something else as well, sir. Have you—how can I put this—been paid any amorous attention, by one Ensign Worthing?"

Aubrey let out a surprised huff of laughter. "I have, in fact. I turned the fellow down," he added for Edmund's benefit, since he had gone from tense to marmoreal, next to him.

Edmund blinked at him a few times like he was remembering how to move again, and then he turned to Sir J, his eyebrows like thunderclouds. "I can't believe this. After all that nonsense about Lord Malmsbury, the palace security service is still trying to catch Aubrey at—"

"That is not why I bring it up, sir. After that . . . mistake regarding Lord Malmsbury, and you and I went to speak to your father, the king's own intelligence service has been keeping me updated on a variety of things on your behalf. They have just now let me know that this Worthing fellow is being paid to try and lure Lord Ainsley away from you. He is going to be detained this very day, so they can try and work out what on earth is going on."

Aubrey and Edmund looked at each other. Edmund's shock was probably echoed on his own face, Aubrey thought, and then he found himself saying, "The groom. There was a groom, as well, Sir Jenson, did they say anything about that?"

Edmund was staring at him, so Aubrey added, "I didn't go to bed with him, either!"

Sir Jenson cleared his throat. "There was indeed a note about one of the grooms, sir, since it is one of the other grooms who is in the employ of the king's intelligence service. I probably shouldn't have told you that, actually, but—regardless, she made a note to say that he just seemed to genuinely like you, and she couldn't find any evidence that he was working for anyone he shouldn't have been."

"Unlike her," Aubrey said, his mind reeling. He found himself laughing again, though he couldn't have said why.

"I think you must agree that she's working exactly where she should be. And as amusing as it is that people are being paid to try to seduce you, what else might these people try to organize? Your food to be poisoned? You to be shot?"

Aubrey stared at him, and Sir J added pointedly, "I think you said accidents were common, in these barracks?"

"Yes, thank you, Sir Jenson," Edmund said, back to looking like he was carved in stone. "I think we see the implications. What do we do about it?"

Sir Jenson tapped his fingers against his leg. "With regards to the first problem—with making it clear to the barracks at large that his lordship is a serious suitor—I think you are underestimating how much good it will do for the soldiers to simply see the two of you interacting with each other. I do not think it is overstating matters to say that this situation is purely due to no one having seen what the two of you are like together, sir. All they have had to go on are those blasted newspaper etchings and the fact that Lord Ainsley is an attractive young man."

Edmund swallowed before asking, "What do you mean? What are we like together?"

Sir J paused and then said, "Like you fit. Although, sirs, you are going to have to be careful. No getting caught against garden walls. Instead, Your Highness, if you can very publicly be seen treating his lordship with respect, that would do more good than I think you understand. Invite him to eat with you at the high table in the officers' hall, things like that."

Aubrey felt his face heating up again. That would be a very high honor and would set him apart even more, but then, he supposed he needed to give up on the idea that he wouldn't always be set apart now.

"Won't the colonel mind?" he asked.

Edmund shook his head. "Colonel Sutherton told me already that he served under your grandfather, and praised what a wonderful job your mother did training you and your brothers. But he also said he's about to recommend you all as ready for assignment. What do we do about that, Sir Jenson? Are you sure I can't ask for Aubrey to stay with me?"

Sir Jenson shook his head. "Not without something official. He's already being called your—forgive me, sirs, but—your bed warmer. If you were engaged, it would be different."

Something must have shown in Edmund's face, because the man quickly added, "Before you ask, I have thought about that, too, and I don't think you should make your request to the parliament yet, Your Highness. You're too young. They will use that as an excuse to dismiss it, and after it has been dismissed once, dismissing it again will seem easy. I don't think interfering with Lord Ainsley's posts will help your cause. It is not my recommendation. I'm sorry. You should, however, both feel free to meet up when you are on leave, and do so publicly with other members of your families as well, if you can, showing that you feel no need to hide your relationship. The papers will report on that, which will get the public used to the idea."

He sat back and rubbed his hand over his face. It was a very human gesture; Aubrey had never seen Sir J like this. It warmed him to the man.

"The problem," the baronet went on, sitting up again, "is that this plan may cause whoever is plotting against you to double their efforts. We will try and find out who paid this Worthing fellow. This may be nothing—a trick from the papers, perhaps—or it may be something very serious indeed."

"And—what?" Edmund said, sounding furious, surprising Aubrey yet again. "Aubrey's just supposed to go about life in the army, risking life and limb while his fellows are offered bribes to betray him? How's he supposed to sleep at night with that risk hanging over him?"

"Darling," Aubrey said. "I'm not going to go about thinking that way. I'm not going to assume everyone's about to stick a knife in my back."

Edmund stared at him. "How can you be so trusting when we've just *heard*—"

"That lieutenant and his friend who keep on teasing Wilson into punching them—nobody's paying *them*. People are going to be jealous, and any of them might do something about it. It's unfortunate, but that's not something I can plan for. So unless you're going to lock me in your bedchamber, which Sir J has just explained will most definitely ruin your plans to marry me, I think trusting your father's spies to intervene before anything can happen to me is the best way forward.

I'm going to focus on not getting stabbed in the front by Honals, and let them worry about my back."

Edmund seemed to want to say more, but before he could, Aubrey asked Sir Jenson the thing he had wanted clarified from the start. "Do you really think the parliament will let us marry?"

Sir J looked torn, as though he were weighing up what to say, but then he said, "Yes, I do, sir."

Aubrey couldn't stop himself. *"Why?"*

Edmund's brows contracted indignantly, and Aubrey patted his leg again. "I am not being self-deprecating, my love. There is simply no precedent for—"

"There is no precedent for the prince, my lord."

Aubrey and Edmund both sat up straighter at that. Sir J very carefully focused only on Aubrey when he said, "His Highness is the most prophesied monarch since . . . well, I assume Queen Helen was probably Seen a lot, but we don't have those records anymore. He is clearly going to do *something* that wins the entire nation's gratitude, and I would not be surprised if it were during this war. It seems logical. He has already killed the Honals' leader in the most heroic circumstances possible—"

Edmund, clearly not able to take any of this, interrupted with, "The prime minister—"

"The prime minister is afraid of you."

Sir Jenson had spoken quite calmly, but the words still fell like a lead weight in the room. Aubrey felt Edmund's hand reaching for him; he grabbed onto it.

"Sir, you brought lightning down on his Honal counterpart while he cowered behind me, unable to do anything. *He* depends on his party and the public's favor for power. And the public already love their prince. I think that if you are firm in your purpose, after whatever it is that you're going to do, he would let you marry a tinker, never mind a respectable young man descended from kings and generals. He might even prefer that to a foreign prince, since it won't—I am sorry, my lord, but—it won't make your position any stronger."

Aubrey waved his hand in a casual sort of way to show that he took no offense, but then he thought of Edmund saying that he felt like he could be great, if he had Aubrey next to him; of the two of them in the palace garden, while Edmund worked out how the earth was like the sky for the first time and made lightning. *You just watch me make him stronger,* some part of his brain thought, startling the rest.

"I could be wrong," Sir J said. "It will still need to be done right. Lord Dell cares very much for the look of things. I . . . think this would be easier for you if you were more like your father. At seventeen, he commanded rooms. He declared that things would be so, and they were. He would not have worried about this, and he barely had two prophesies about himself to rub together at your age. Your sister is more like him. I do not know where your self-doubt comes from, sir, but I am sorry if I have ever contributed to it."

Edmund shifted; Aubrey saw that he was swiping at his eyes. Aubrey gripped his hand tighter.

"Well, all right, then," Aubrey said. "That does give us a general way of going forward. I had best not sleep here overnight, for instance."

He scrunched up his face at Edmund, who managed to quirk his mouth a little in return. Sir Jenson cleared his throat.

"Yes, exactly. Well, then, I shall leave you both to it."

Edmund nodded. "Yes, and thank you, Sir Jenson. I . . . thank you."

Sir Jenson nodded and left.

Aubrey did go back to his quarters that night. He ignored the whispers around him over the next few days and smiled as they got more and more respectful as the weeks went by. Sir Jenson had been right; the barracks did indeed calm down after seeing the way that he and Edmund were together, and the way that the colonel was perfectly happy to have Aubrey at the head table.

But as it was, they did not get long to enjoy this new reality, because their postings came through. Aubrey was to join a garrison to the north, and Edmund was strongly recommended to get himself back to the capital, where the Prince of Fortune could be seen alive and well by the most people. It was left to him to represent the royal family in the palace, because everyone else was being sent closer to the border: even Prince Willard, who had said that his fighting days were over and so would instead be doing support work. Aubrey wondered if that meant spying, like his mother.

He rode over to Brythe House on the morning he was to set off. He had something he needed to give to Edmund. He was a little self-conscious about it, since—and it felt absurd to even think this, since Edmund wanted to *marry* him—but this was something significant in the south, and he wasn't sure that Edmund was going to understand.

The guards let him through the gate and then the door, and Edmund led him upstairs.

He wrapped his arms around Aubrey as soon as the door was closed.

"Don't you dare take a bayonet to the stomach in your first battle," he said, his voice muffled in the crook of Aubrey's neck and shoulder. Aubrey snorted.

"Not now that I need to live and cause trouble for the prime minister. Who would want to miss out on that?"

He pulled back.

"How long do we have?" Edmund asked.

"Not long. My captain only let me go at all because . . . well, because of what I'm here for."

Aubrey extracted himself—it took effort, since he wanted to plant himself in Edmund's side, not leave him—and opened his satchel. He pulled out a plain shirt, carefully folded into a bundle. He must have hesitated too long, because Edmund said, "Aubrey?"

"I needed to give you this before I set off. It's . . . an old-fashioned southern tradition, I'm sure you won't have ever even heard of it, but when sweethearts are called to arms, they trade a piece of clothing. It's usually a shirt. The idea is that they will keep it for the other, to return safely to them afterward. It's for luck."

Edmund took the garment from him with both hands. It was an ordinary linen shirt, just like any number he and Aubrey both had, but he seemed to understand its significance, because he pressed it to the center of his chest.

"Do I wear it?" he asked.

Aubrey nodded. "Just as if it were one of your own. Although one marks it, you see, so that one doesn't get it confused—"

He was showing Edmund a bird that he had stitched onto one of the tails—the Ainsley bird, just like on his family's coat of arms—when there was a discreet cough behind them. It was Mattheson, looking satisfied about something. Aubrey could not even begin to guess what, until he noticed the man had a bundle of cloth in his hands. It had been folded such that a tree sewn in green thread, very similar to Edmund's signet and about the same size, was visible.

"I prepared this earlier for you, sir," he said, his face back under control, and Aubrey laughed.

"I'm from the south originally as well," Mattheson added softly, handing the shirt to Edmund so that he could put it into Aubrey's outstretched hands.

Not long after that, Aubrey left.

ONE YEAR LATER

CHAPTER 14

My darling Mother,

I am not sure how interesting this letter will be. I am so fatigued, I can barely stay sitting upright; however, it has been a shocking interval since my last to you, so I swore to myself I would write tonight.

I wrote to Father last week in the hope of providing some comfort after learning that the village school buildings are to be taken over and used as officers' quarters for the local training troops. I had his reply by this morning's post. He did not seem to need cheering after all, but declared that he has set up the front parlor as a schoolroom for whatever children are left, and that any teachers who choose to stay will be put up within our guest rooms; and if none do, he will teach the children himself. I will reply with teasing remarks about his language skills, at the very least, being unsuited to such a task as soon as I can beat my exhausted brain into coming up with an amusing way to word it.

I confess that I was hit with such a wave of homesickness when I read of his plans, and such a wish that I were there with him to help; but I know I am helping where I am. You would not believe the improvement wrought in my unit, even since my last letter, let alone in the months since they were put in my care. Stephens, in particular, seems a natural now as he helps lead the unit, even if he'd rather be kneading dough at home in his family's bakery. That was, as you'll recall, not at all the case back in autumn when he arrived.

Aubrey stopped there and wondered if he should strike out his last few sentences. Discussing training didn't seem advisable given that the Honals were attacking mail coaches. It was, he could begrudgingly admit, a good tactic; disrupting communication caused all sorts of problems and damaged morale. They all wished Saben could return the favor, but it had proven impossible.

He read over his letter and decided that he was being overly cautious, especially since the Honals were mostly destroying the coaches rather than stealing the contents, so it hardly mattered. But every letter he wrote these days felt like an exercise in holding himself back. There was so much Aubrey wanted to ask and say. Sometimes it wasn't even that it was risky to write the information down; some things were risky to admit to *oneself.* Putting the feelings into words, sitting there in ink, made them real.

He wanted to say it was heartbreaking to go through towns and see walls and fences that were usually only there to manage livestock now topped with metal pikes and wooden spikes, and in rural areas, to see farm equipment pulled by the farmers themselves because their horses had been needed for the war effort.

He wanted to say that despite how terrifying the sorcerous creatures that the Honals sent were, the times he had had to fight their human soldiers had been infinitely worse.

He wanted to say he was worried that he was leaving pieces of himself behind on every field that he fought on.

Some things he did write down. He had found committing certain incidents to paper—turning them into a narrative that he had to explain—stopped them going around and around in his head. But he did not want to add to the strain on his mother, or any of his other correspondents, by communicating these large or small pains. He had started keeping a journal. It helped, especially if he illustrated the stories, but it was not the same as sharing them with a breathing person and having them take on some of the weight.

He dipped his pen in his ink and tried again.

> *I am grateful every day for the trouble you took to make sure that we were all so well trained. Please hug Cedric for me. I have not seen John or Wilson, although they're not posted far away. I have seen A, since her unit came through here a few days ago, but I have not seen E, though I heard from him via this morning's post. I miss him terribly but remind myself that we are all doing our part and this is not forever.*
>
> *My fondest love,*
> *A*

Aubrey was not satisfied with the quality of the letter, nor with its length, but it would have to do, because he was smudging half of his words in his tired state. He folded the thing up and sent it off to be read and sealed and posted.

He had a surprise at breakfast the next day: new soldiers—desperately needed—arrived at the garrison as they all sat down to eat. Once everyone was fed, Aubrey's superior officer, Captain Walsh, called him to take five young men and women into his unit.

He was still trying to remember why the name of one Ensign Rosalie Tsung sounded familiar when they were handed over. He tried not to stare as she smiled at him in greeting. She was a pretty woman in perhaps her midtwenties, with black hair and pale skin. She had the dark eyes that he associated with ancestry from the eastern Sunlands. Something about her air seemed self-conscious, which only strengthened his feeling that he ought to know who she was.

"Welcome to Manogate's garrison," he said, pulling his attention back to the full group. "Have any of you been stationed to protect a city before?"

One young man nodded, and Aubrey motioned that he should speak.

"Yes, sir, Drestham, sir. But it was not walled. Is it not odd for us all to be outside Manogate's walls? Why do they not just close the gates?"

His fellows were staring at him, but Aubrey felt his own smile widen.

"I asked the same thing when I arrived. There are three reasons. This city is the region's center for the postal service, which means almost constant traffic in and out. Secondly, munitions are manufactured here, and they are also sent out multiple times a day at random intervals. The fuss of the gate opening to alert the enemy of the next lot of things they might like to blow up or steal is exactly what we don't want."

He had been walking as he spoke. He took them past the laundry. The whole area reeked of the strong army-issue soap they were given, with just a hint of the lavender that the laundresses used to try to moderate the smell. He liked that. It made him think of his mother, who had always strewn lavender in all the linen chests and closets at home.

He led them all just outside the complex and closer to the town. He stopped and pointed; the huge chimneys were visible from this angle. All five soldiers were nodding now, standing in the weak, tentative early spring sunshine.

"And the third thing, sir?" This was from a young woman who was taller than Aubrey by at least a head. She looked strong as an ox. He liked her already; she clearly paid attention.

"And thirdly," Aubrey said, "the monsters the Honals send don't care about walls. They either just climb them or knock through them, eventually. As a long-term strategy, we are a better defense. The Honals have hit us again and again with waves of creatures, but they haven't—"

"To arms! Strawmen come!"

Aubrey felt the resigned sigh try to come out of his mouth and suppressed it. It had only been three days since the last attack. His arms were still tight from that fight, and he hadn't finished his spiel to the new troops, who had all looked instinctively to their left, where the cry had come from, rather than to him for permission to go and arm themselves.

Instead of snapping at them to follow orders, however, Aubrey asked, "Have any of you faced strawmen before?"

Every one of them shook their heads, and his stomach considered sinking. "What about the clay automatons?"

More headshakes.

Damn.

"Go and arm yourselves, and then—Ensign Stephens!" he called out, seeing his unofficial second-in-command coming toward them. "Please give our new friends a few minutes' brief on fighting the straw creatures. Then onto the horses and straight to me—take up position with them at the rear."

A capable "yes, sir" followed this command. Aubrey clapped the man's shoulder in thanks and went to get ready himself.

His horse seemed nervous this morning, but his unit appeared steady, at least. They had lined up in the place that had been left for them, as usual; even with the new troops, it was too much space. They had lost so many soldiers since this started.

Now was not the time to think about that.

He did not have long to brood, however, because the strawmen came into view.

They were like something out of a storybook illustration of a haunted field. Horrible mockeries of human beings with eyes burned onto their sackcloth faces and mouths occasionally stitched in (these appeared to be merely ornamental, which Aubrey found irritating). Their clothing was a mixture of items with some Sabresian military garments thrown in, as if to taunt as well as horrify. But it was the arms that you had to watch out for, as these were their primary weapons; hard wooden clubs that tended to start from the "elbow." Sometimes these had rocks lashed to them so as to better bash their victims, or sharp things like steel knives, which they would slash and stab with. The fact that the creatures knew the difference—understood what they were holding—had featured in Aubrey's nightmares.

They did not belong in those calm, empty pastures, which had been cleared so that cavalry could ride out and deal with anything before it came near Manogate. Nobody had known at the time that "anything" meant these abominations, but the strategy suited just the same.

The creatures were visible enough now that someone screamed—one of the new soldiers, probably. Aubrey had gotten used to them, but the way they moved did play with the mind. The bonelessness of their gait was completely at odds with their synchronized advance. They shuffled with a horrifying determination, moving far more quickly than their shambling steps should have allowed. Edmund had only faced them a few times, but he had said that it reminded him of the way the Honal leaders had moved at Downfall Cove, each step seeming to cover more ground than it should have, as though their magic moved the air and the earth out of their way.

"Steady," Aubrey said, seeing a few mounts shying, picking up on their riders' fear. "Breathe. We know what to do. Stop them getting past us to the city; disable their leader as soon as they are identified."

This last was not always an easy task. He looked around; he could see the soldiers in the watchtowers scanning with their spyglasses and scopes, trying to find the sorcerer controlling them. Nobody seemed to have spotted them yet.

Stephens and the new soldiers arrived and lined up behind the rest of his unit. Aubrey nodded at them.

The creatures were close enough now that the order rang out for the archers to start loosing their flaming arrows. Saben had not expected to use archers in this war, but needs must. As usual, the strawmen that caught fire seemed not to notice; they just kept on moving until they crumbled. The damp field that these ones traveled through now was in little danger of catching ablaze, but the archers could not risk firing upon the creatures after they got too close to the waiting troops.

Aubrey watched them, far off as they still were. The creatures seemed quicker today, scuttling on their blunt, footless legs like startled spiders across the field. The order rang out much sooner than usual: "Archers, cease fire!"

"Steady!" Aubrey called out again, as he saw several horses shifting, including his own, nervy for the order to charge. Or perhaps the creatures were upon them already. Aubrey squinted, trying to see through the smoke.

Then his mount reared to the left, and that was all that saved him, for he had been facing the wrong direction. Two soldiers behind him—Stephens and the tall woman whose name he had not learned yet—had been dashed to the ground. Aubrey had an impression of blood spraying and a horse twisting on the mud, screaming.

Aubrey pulled back enough to get a shot and discharged his rifle into the strawman's chest.

Bang.

The entirety of its top half flew off, landing several feet away. The legs just fell over, as usual, as though whatever it was that animated the creatures existed above the waist. Aubrey knew from experience that he had a small window of time before the top half worked out how to start moving on its own, so he took the opportunity to check his surroundings: horror and uproar and turmoil in the clearing smoke, but no immediate danger. He reloaded his gun and dropped off his horse to check on Stephens and the tall woman, but they were as dead as Aubrey had feared. He untwisted a strap that was hindering Stephens's mare from standing; she let out an urgent noise and reared up, running away before all her feet were even under her again. The other horse was nowhere to be seen.

He turned around to finish off the top half of the creature that had attacked them and saw that its shirttail had a fish embroidered on it in a vivid green thread.

It was wearing a Sabresian soldier's sweetheart shirt, probably from one of the fishing villages to the very south.

Aubrey felt a sick pain in his stomach, and then the thing started to wake up. The process was disconcerting, to say the least. Its stolen shirt started twitching horribly like a family of rats moving around in a bag of grain, and then its head flicked, too fast, in Aubrey's direction. Its blank, black eyes seemed to lock right onto him.

Aubrey had been terrified the first few times this had happened. Now he knew he had a few more moments before it regained full mobility, so he put his boot to its squirming chest and pulled the horrible thing's arms off, as he had done countless times before.

He remounted his horse, searching for the next threat.

There were none ahead of him; the creatures had gotten through their lines. The enemy got closer to the city every time.

We need more reinforcements, he thought, and then: *Where is their damned sorcerer, and why has nobody killed them yet?*

He finally spotted his own troop in a melee to his left. He rode toward it, shooting clubs off monsters wherever he could. One of the creatures he attacked made to follow him, raising its one remaining arm; Aubrey turned to shoot it and found himself thumped right off his horse by a hard blow from behind, his feet ripping out of the stirrups as he went up and then down.

All the air was knocked out of him as he landed.

There was a confusion of pain and a sudden retraction of his sight and hearing. They were replaced by a roar of fear and worry for his mare, whose black legs he could just see through the spots in his vision, dancing out of the way of the creature that had attacked him. He had lost one horse already.

His lungs suddenly decided to cooperate then, and he gasped in a breath. It hurt, but it at least brought back the sounds of battle and the full color of his surroundings. Including the large mottled brown rock that was coming down quite quickly toward his face.

He rolled out of the way just in time. There was a fresh wave of pain—Aubrey wasn't sure from where—but he hadn't had his face bashed in, which he considered an advantage. His movement, however, brought the second creature near him into better view. It was unusually large, more than twice the size of a man, and with two great pieces of sharp granite where its hands should have been.

Aubrey was hurt and disarmed, lying at its feet like an offering. The creature lifted those deadly hands in one smooth, relentless arc preparing to strike.

Oh damn, Aubrey thought.

It had been months since he had frozen in battle. Later he couldn't say if he *had* actually frozen, or if the moment had just felt longer than it was.

And then a sword came from nowhere, striking diagonally up the creature, cutting through its left arm and then getting stuck in its "neck."

"Bollocks," Aubrey heard a female voice growl as its owner yanked the sword once, twice, and then out.

It was Ensign Tsung, still on her horse.

"They have a pole running up them, like a normal scarecrow," Aubrey called out to her, rolling over to find a good angle for getting up without wrenching his side.

"I've never made a scarecrow," she called back. She was rewarded for the admission by a knock from the creature with its remaining arm. It was a glancing blow due to a combination of the monster being rendered lopsided and her own skill at dodging, but she still let out an "oof" as she struggled to stay on her mount.

Aubrey barely saw all this, as his head was now swimming from the pain. He stopped trying to rise and took a few shallow breaths to clear his vision. He pulled out his right pistol and shot off the creature's other arm. But then he saw something. He wasn't sure he would have seen it if he hadn't been on the ground.

There was another strawman standing nearby, partly concealed by the low limbs of a willow tree. This one wasn't fighting. And it was wearing boots.

The ensign had wheeled her horse around to help Aubrey up. He grabbed at her proffered hand urgently. "Is your rifle loaded?" She nodded her head. "The creature to our left, by the tree. Aim for the torso. Quickly."

She took that in for a moment, then brought her rifle up, took careful aim and fired—just as the first strawman reared up between them, its huge chunk of brown rock raised to strike.

The blow never fell. Instead, the thing swayed like a drunkard. It didn't collapse, though, until the "strawman" by the tree dropped to their knees, clutching at their stomach as red spread over their shirt.

"Puppeteer!" Aubrey yelled out, before doubling over coughing, grabbing his side. His vision started dimming again.

The next little while was a bit of a blur. He saw soldiers walk over to the fallen sorcerer and pull the sackcloth off their face. It was a woman. She grinned a haunting, bloodied grin even as someone put a pistol to her head. He dimly heard cries of victory. He wondered how badly he was injured.

Ensign Tsung and another of the new recruits helped him back to the barracks infirmary. The ward was full of noise and blood. It wasn't his first time there. He sat himself down on a cot and sent his troops back to the battlefield to help clear up the fallen strawmen. These would be piled up and burned with the sorcerer's body: standard procedure to make sure all the Honal runes were destroyed.

A nurse eventually came. She pronounced Aubrey to be in shock. He was draped in blankets and given a cup of over-sugared tea he couldn't drink without wincing in pain. He nearly dropped it twice. He waited as other soldiers with more pressing injuries were taken care of. So much of war was waiting, he thought vaguely. He had no idea how much time had passed—he had a notion that he'd either slept or passed out for some of it—before a different nurse started pulling his clothing away and tutting at his sides, which had blossomed with bruising.

"You've broken at least three of these ribs," she said in a strong northern accent. Aubrey spent a nonsensical second thinking about the nurse's phrasing—she made it sound like he'd managed to break those bones all by himself, and he wondered if the soldier two beds down from him, who was screaming as her shoulder was put back into its socket, was also supposed to have dislocated her own joint—and next thing he knew, another cup was at his lips.

He only noticed the bitterness as he swallowed. His voice was resigned when he asked, "Did you just give me laudanum?"

The nurse stared at him for a moment and then yanked a list of names out of her apron pocket. He saw his own at the top, under *A*. The brown ink looked like a bloodstain.

"My lord—I only arrived this morning—I've never served with Seers—"

"I'll need paper and a pencil left within reach."

He dozed off while the nurses were bandaging him up; the last thing he heard them say was something about poultices for his contusions.

It felt like the vision started before he even tipped over into sleep.

He Saw battles and monsters. All his visions since the war had begun started like this; nothing worth reporting to the War Office, since there were no particulars, just chaos and gunfire and noise. But then everything came into sharper focus.

He saw himself from overhead, like a bird circling above. He was in something like a cave, fighting using his dress sword, but he wasn't in uniform. Something was wrong with his movements, and Aubrey wondered if the version of himself that he was seeing was injured.

It was hard to tell, but his opponent appeared to be an older man wearing a Honal military uniform. Aubrey couldn't work out the color of his hair in the dim light. He went to slash at Aubrey's neck with some sort of long, curving knife; future-Aubrey stepped back clumsily just in time. His adversary stepped forward to thrust the knife into his stomach at this, and then future-Aubrey took a precise step to the side, out of the way, before slicing his sword across the other figure's midriff and then twisting and swiping it back across his opponent's throat. The man thrust forward with the knife, and then—there was water.

Aubrey was swimming—no, he was being carried along in a fearsome current. His vision had been terrifying up to this point, and he should still be afraid—there was no fighting water—but somehow his fear was gone. It was . . . wondrous. The water was cradling him. Purifying him. Getting him to where he needed to go.

It was forgiving him for everything he had done and everything that he was still to do.

CHAPTER 15

Edmund hated briefings. He wasn't sure why people were still insisting that he come to them, since all he ever did was ask the generals the same two questions: *What is being done to cut the Honals off from their magical water source? What is being done to target their sorcerers?*

There never seemed to be an answer.

Certainly, invading Honal had proved harder than anyone had expected. The haunted forests that covered most of the border between the two countries, in front of the Helm, had always been unpleasant and forbidding, but now they were impenetrable. A boundary of thorn bushes had sprung up, seemingly overnight, after Edmund's first and only meeting with the Honal leadership. The briars grew back almost instantly if cut down or burned, leaving no time for anyone to make it through, and the barbed thorns weren't just sharp; anyone who so much as pricked themselves on them fell ill. Some had died.

It was infuriating to be thwarted by plants. And yet nobody would let Edmund go near them. They barely let Edmund do anything. He had to represent the royal family in the capital and sit in on meeting after meeting with generals who moved pieces around on a map like the war was a table game and lives were not at stake; or if they were, they were the lives and livelihoods of "civilians," as though most of their soldiers had not been civilians before they had put on their uniforms.

He was rarely allowed to fight, since he had not been Seen doing so, and the government had said they would not do anything that might risk his capture. So, while his parents and his little sister, and Charlotte—who was now *expecting*—and several second cousins who had smaller gifts over one or two elements were out there being Sabresian dragons, Edmund wore the badge but was kept away from the enemy.

He was occasionally moved around. He stopped every one of the Honals' storms that he sensed; he had not missed any, as far as anyone knew. He also made it rain anywhere that Honal soldiers were known to be, in the hopes that they would all just fall over. Sometimes they did. Those ones were sent to work at prisoner-of-war camps, tending fields, where they proved disturbingly docile. No one was sure if this was because they were grateful to be away from Honal, or if the Monium fog had made them permanently pliable.

He mostly did what he had done before: helped the crops grow and calmed any weather that might cause problems. That was as valuable to his country as it had always been—even more so now, since food supplies were of extra importance in wartime—but it hardly helped that most of the laborers were off fighting. It was partly why the captured soldiers were always sent to farmland.

Edmund had not failed to notice that more of the poorer classes had enlisted in Saben's military. He couldn't stop thinking about Colonel

Sutherton telling him that the purchasing of commissions was outdated because why *was* it possible to buy oneself a better military position or better weaponry or a better-fitting uniform? It wasn't fair. Those things shouldn't be luxuries. But the generals disliked him bringing that up as much as they disliked him demanding to know why no one had tried to cut the Honals off from their magical water.

He simply could not understand why so many of Saben's resources were being focused on the defensive. They waited until the Honals sent monsters, and then their army fought them off, taking huge losses. This did not seem the way to end a war, to Edmund. If Honal could not make the monsters in the first place, the blasted war would be over. Everyone could go home.

He tried asking his questions in different ways. *Do we not have spies? Assassins? Can a small force not sneak in and use explosives to collapse the entrance to that cave of theirs?*

We are trying a variety of strategies, the generals said, refusing to disclose what any of them were and acting as though he should trust them. He did not trust them. He suspected that the generals liked the war. It made them important.

Edmund didn't want them to be important. He didn't want anyone to be important. He wanted everyone to be safe. This was especially on his mind this morning, as he had had word that Aubrey had been injured. Edmund's immediate urge had been to jump on his horse and go to him, generals and orders be damned, but Sir J had reminded him that his behavior had to be beyond reproach and to think of the long game.

Edmund was starting to hate the long game.

"We've had intelligence," Commanding General Wren was saying, his tone as dry as if he were discussing something entirely unurgent, "that the Honals are using new, creative ways of hiding the sorcerers controlling their creatures."

"So we'll need to organize more recruits?" General Evans asked.

"Don't kill all our troops off before their time," another said. "Our soldiers are clever and brave. They can rise to this challenge."

"They're falling, at present," Wren said baldly, and started reciting the latest numbers: equipment loss, munitions, troop movements. The number of dead and injured civilians. The number of dead and injured soldiers.

The numbers were increasingly high. And Aubrey was one of today's numbers, numbers that weren't numbers, but people with hopes and dreams and loved ones. Wren continued in his dispassionate presentation, as though none of that mattered, and Edmund couldn't stand it anymore.

"Thousands of Sabresians are being killed every week," he interrupted. "*Thousands*. And every week all we do in this room is work out ways to keep this up. How can none of you be interested in *ending* this?"

"The Honals declared war on *us*." General Evans sounded as bored as ever, which made Edmund want to throw things. "What are we supposed to do? Surrender? We'd be no safer that way."

"There has to be some other approach," Edmund said. "How can our only option be accepting that they hate us and want us dead? That has been our way for centuries, and this just keeps happening. Why has there been no plan to stop this cycle?"

"Because, sir, we cannot control how those people choose to see us!" This was from General Howe, who usually stayed silent during these meetings, but whom Edmund could now see was every bit as angry as he was. "Because not *wanting* to fight has never shielded anyone from a blow in the history of mankind."

"Sir, we will win this war," General Wren said in what was clearly supposed to be a reassuring tone. "You know that we will. It has been Seen. *You* are the next king of Saben, not one of them."

"That is no reason for complacency," Edmund said. "Irreparable damage is being done. How can there be *nothing* to speed up our victory? Have our Seers not Seen anything to give us some idea of, at the very least, how long this might take?"

"No, Your Highness," someone's assistant answered. "All our latest reports from the War Office indicate that the Seers are all still Seeing the same things. Clearly, variables are in play that might change the shape of this war, and things are not set in stone. We should take comfort in that, sir. We have a chance to do this in the best possible way."

They all looked at Edmund; in the end he nodded defeatedly, since there was nothing else he could say, and the meeting adjourned.

He very much doubted that everything was being done in the best possible way.

Edmund had not been back at the palace for more than a quarter of an hour before he heard a commotion outside: horses and at least one carriage. He had been the only royal in residence for almost two months. It was the longest he had ever stayed alone in Talstam in his life, so he was especially pleased to see his cousin Charlotte when he went outside.

She was accompanied by her husband, who she had been able to request as part of her military entourage. Edmund tried not to mind, even though he still badly wished that he could do the same with Aubrey.

Almost six months ago, he had written to the prime minister, to formally request that the parliament consider Aubrey as his consort. It had been Edmund's eighteenth-birthday present to himself.

Sir J reminded him regularly that now it was done, they must both observe every protocol and procedure to the letter, to give the ministers no excuse to reject the bid. Which was fine, except that Lord Dell barely seemed to have noticed that his crown prince had asked him for something, let alone how respectably he was behaving. Edmund had written several times to ask for an update and tried to speak to the man about it in person. He had received a lot of boring waffle every time in reply about the many demands on parliament these days and been given the strong impression that Lord Dell thought him even asking the question was in poor taste.

Charlotte had nothing to do with any of that. Edmund put Lord Dell out of his mind and forced himself to smile and shake Prince Henri's hand. It wasn't the man's fault he was an unimpeachable choice for a princess to marry.

"Was I supposed to be expecting you?" he asked Charlotte, as she hugged him around her swelling stomach. He felt, suddenly, how long it had been since he had been touched affectionately by anyone and forced himself to let go of her before he made it awkward.

"Not really; I did send a messenger, but you look like you're just arrived yourself. No, we were on our way down to Marisetown so that Henri could welcome the latest batch of Hasprennan troops, but our party was attacked on the highway an hour to the north. Actual Honal soldiers, that close to the capital! There weren't many of them, and it didn't take long to overpower them, but several of the guard were injured, and I decided it was a sign that we should stop for the night. I hope that's all right?"

It was more than all right. They all ate dinner together, and then Henri left Edmund and Charlotte to catch up.

"I saw Alicia last week," Charlotte said. "She visited me unexpectedly at Drestham. The Honals mustn't have known she was there; they made the mistake of trying to send in strawmen, and every one of them was on fire before they'd gotten anywhere near us. Should we be worried about the enthusiasm she brings to battle?"

Edmund choked on the biscuit he'd just bitten into. His cousin regarded him, amused, as he took a sip of water.

"I'll take that as a no. It was mostly a jest. She is a wonderful dragon."

"I wish she didn't have to be," Edmund said, and Charlotte nodded, but then she surprised him again.

"Do you envy them? Your parents and Alicia, being able to do that?"

Edmund put his glass down carefully.

"I just meant that I did," she said quickly. "Not in a bad, jealous sort of way. I'm sorry, I was only hoping that you might understand. We're both wearing a fire-breathing creature on our uniforms when neither one of us can actually handle fire. It never felt . . . odd before. But you know my father won't have dragons up anywhere in Hendon Castle? The staff have to cover them when he's in residence. I think I now understand why."

Edmund had not known. He had never been to his uncle's castle. The whole thing made him feel wrong-footed.

"But," he said slowly, trying to work out his objection. "They're in our coat of arms. They're the family's emblem."

Charlotte tilted her head in a gesture that didn't quite become a shrug. "I never used to think about it, but now I see how he might resent it. Not that *I* do," she quickly added. "I think I'm saying this all wrong. I just . . . always felt like he was disappointed in me and in himself for only passing on his limited gift to me."

"But it's a miracle to have anything at all—"

"I know that, I do, but . . . you should have seen Alicia, Edmund. She was like something from an old story."

"So are you," Edmund said firmly. "And I am sorry if your father has ever made you feel deficient or disappointing. All *I* keep hearing is how wonderful you are at washing away the monsters they keep sending to Drestham, and how safe that city is since you are there."

"Thank you," Charlotte said. "And up until her arrival, I would have said I was doing a perfectly respectable job. I was . . . finally being useful. Well, for something other than my marriage, of course." Her hand had fallen onto her midsection; she moved it to the dragon on her arm. "But I do feel a little like a fraud wearing this. Or like a runner-up."

Edmund put his hand over hers, over the badge. They sat together like that in silence, the only sound coming from the dining room's fire as it burned down in the grate.

He wanted to tell his cousin that she had value, that she would have had value even without any magic, but they both knew that wasn't how their country saw it at all, so he didn't say that. He also did not say that at least she was allowed to fight, or that at least she was being valued for what she actually was. He didn't say any of it, because it would be absurd. The pressure and frustration and sadness she was feeling had the same root cause as his own did. They were different, and their country did not see them as people at all, but as symbols.

"I know a little of what you mean," Edmund said finally.

CHAPTER 16

Aubrey was sent to an officers' rest home to heal his ribs. He did not remember arriving, as he had developed a fever during the bone-rattling cart ride there and been delirious for days. When he came back to himself, it was to discover that his hair had been shorn off practically to his scalp. He didn't care—it was just one more thing that had happened to him, and his hair, at least, would grow back—but he also felt his eyes prick with tears as he inspected himself in the looking glass that the nurse brought him.

Someone else seemed to be looking back at him. He wiped their eyes.

The first day he felt strong enough to move, however, his usual curiosity got the better of him. Where were they? Whose estate was this? Might he see more of the building?

He was smiled at indulgently by the staff in response and put in a chair in a warm, pleasant parlor. An avuncular nurse handed him some books and said that company was on its way. He was pleased but surprised when it arrived.

"Ensign Tsung!" he said, and then motioned to her arm, which was in a sling. "Oh dear. Has Manogate been attacked again already?"

"Not that I know of, sir," she said. "I was injured during the same battle you were but did not notice until the next morning. My right clavicle is broken; probably the work of the very large strawman that we battled together."

Aubrey clicked his tongue. "He was nasty, wasn't he. Well, at least now we will have a chance to get to know each other off the battlefield."

She was silent for a moment and then glanced around, as if to ascertain that they were really alone, before taking a deep breath and saying, "I am not sure if you know who I am, Lieutenant Ainsley, and are being tactful, or if you really have never heard my name spoken, which is not very gratifying to my vanity."

Aubrey blinked at her and then smiled in relief.

"You have my apologies," he said. "I did indeed recognize your name upon our introduction but have not been able to place it. I am glad you have brought it up. Current circumstances have not done a great deal to help my manners."

"Nor mine," she said. "But we have something else in common: a friend. Or at least . . . he was my friend at one time. I hope that he is, still."

Aubrey blinked for a moment, and then the memories came to him.

Malmy's Miss Tsung, he thought in wonder. What a funny little miracle, that they should meet in such awful circumstances. It must have shown on his face, because she sat back with a small smile.

"I understand Lord Malmsbury is stationed to the southeast of us at the present time," she said.

"Yes," Aubrey said carefully, not sure whether she wanted to hear news of her former lover or not. "I would have you know that he always spoke of you as the finest of women, and I see that he did not exaggerate. I hope that you will not hold it against me that I am his friend. How things went with the two of you . . . that is your own business."

She nodded, and they spoke of less personal topics after that; then she took up a volume of poetry, and he saw to his correspondence. He had a small stack of it to tackle; the nurse had laughed and said they'd never had so much mail for one patient. He was grateful to see none had been opened, since two were from Edmund. He replied to his father's letter, asking him to pass on the news that he was awake and on the mend to the rest of the family, since writing for too long hurt his side, and then got down to penning a condolence letter to Ensign Stephens's family. The need to do it had been running around in his brain for days.

He then composed a brief missive to Malmy letting him know that one Ensign Tsung had been put under his command and was now stuck recuperating with him.

They all fell into an easy sort of rhythm at the home. The nurses were kind and diligent; the food was better than at the barracks, though it ran to the kind of nourishing thing that invalids could digest easily. Coddled eggs. Calf's-foot jelly. Arrowroot pudding. Beef tea. He was allowed more regular fare once his ribs started to mend, for which he was grateful.

There were three types of patients here, Aubrey noted: the kind racked with guilt for being somewhere safe, healing, while their fellows continued to risk life and limb; the kind who were very grateful over the same thing; and the kind who did not think about it. Aubrey, who was by now very used to squashing down his feelings into a box, to be inspected at some later time when they wouldn't endanger him, was in the last group.

The patients played a lot of cards and read out loud anything they could get their hands on: poetry and novels, but also any funny or interesting bits that weren't too private from their own correspondence. By the end of a few weeks, Aubrey felt like he knew Rosalie's sisters personally. They seemed, from their letters, clever and funny in the same way that she was, all biting wit and pragmatism. Aubrey could see how this woman had had Malmy all up in knots. They were on first-name terms within a week.

Aubrey was especially grateful for her friendship a few weeks later. The rest home was graced with a high-profile visitor, and he didn't know what he would have done without someone to talk to afterward.

Somehow or other, Aubrey had never been introduced to Prince Willard. After that strange instance at Alicia's ball when the man had turned around and walked off rather than meet him no further opportunity had come up. He therefore felt mildly apprehensive to discover that His Highness was coming to the home. The prince's visit was a surprise; the staff only had an hour's notice. Everyone who was up and about was wheeled or herded into the nicest, sunniest parlor. Aubrey was sitting next to Rosalie with a blanket over his lap, along with some dozen other patients, when His Highness arrived.

The impressions Aubrey had formed seeing Prince Willard from afar all came back as the prince walked among the wounded soldiers. Even doing this compassionate work, the man seemed awkward and melancholic. Why the bureaucracy had sent him, Aubrey had no idea, since spreading cheer was clearly not a natural task for him. Some of the sunlight seemed to dim in the room around him, as everyone's smiles took on a slightly fixed air. Aubrey berated himself for not being more ready to give the man the benefit of the doubt. Perhaps he was just reserved, like Princess Charlotte. She was his daughter, after all.

Then he heard the man speak.

"Yes, yes, very good," Prince Willard was saying to a lieutenant near the door, who had two splinted legs. "Gotten yourself badly injured there, haven't you?"

He seemed to be aiming for jocularity. He didn't quite pull it off. The man attempted to reply, but the prince spoke over him to say that he'd better hurry up with his healing, and then he went on to the next person.

Not like Charlotte at all, then.

Aubrey and Rosalie glanced at each other. When the man made his way to them, he raised his eyebrows.

"And this is Lieutenant . . . that is, Lord Ainsley, sir," the nurse said. They never did know how to manage his title. Aubrey didn't blame them.

"Ainsley," Prince Willard said slowly. "I've seen you before, haven't I? I didn't know you were here. Aren't you one of the ones with the Sight?"

"Yes, Your Highness," Aubrey replied after a moment. He refused to display anything but perfect manners.

"Yes, yes. Hopefully you'll See more, especially while you're here and have nothing more profitable to do. Tinctures, and all that. It's in your blood. Charles Mayhew was your uncle, wasn't he? I served with him. There was a great man. A real patriot who knew how to serve his country, who knew that sacrifices are necessary. He was there when I got this."

The prince pulled off his right glove, revealing the scar across the back of his hand. Now Aubrey was so close, he could see that there were ashy-looking streaks in it, turning some of the white scar tissue black. He'd never seen anything like it.

The prince held up his hand so that the whole room could see the mark. "I know what it's like to be in your place, healing, believe me."

Nobody said anything for a moment, and then one of the women in the room, whose eyes were bandaged due to being hit by Honal blinding powder, asked the patient next to her what was happening.

The prince pulled his glove back on.

"Now, who's this girl here, next to you, Ainsley? I'd heard that your family were all charmers, but this is the prettiest soldier I've ever seen!"

Rosalie froze, but before Aubrey could think of something to say to smooth things over, a voice cried out to their left. "Oh, Your Highness, don't be fooled—she's got her eye on bigger fish than our lordling, there!"

Rosalie's entire face reddened. News of her affair with Malmy had come out around the home, then. Aubrey leapt in, hoping to divert the conversation back to more appropriate ground. "This is Ensign Tsung, sir. She fought valiantly in the battle that saw us both injured. Strawmen, sir."

"Tsung, I don't know anyone of that name," Prince Willard said. "What of your family?"

"Merchants, sir, in Essaben."

He motioned to her face with a finger. Aubrey had to stop himself from flinching at the rudeness of it. "One of the Sunland companies there?"

"Yes, sir."

He tutted.

"A pity, then, if you're carrying on with someone above you. Crossing social classes threatens the social fabric. It leads to ruination and unhappiness." His eyes flitted over to Aubrey at that, and then he said, "Well, I'll leave you all to your recovery," and, without bothering to speak to the rest of the room, he made for the door. A startled nurse opened it for him and followed him out.

Aubrey and Rosalie regarded each other for a moment.

"What a complete *arse*," she said, and Aubrey burst out laughing.

"Still not as bad as James's father," she added. Aubrey took a moment to remember that James was Malmy, but Rosalie had continued with "Although what was that about your uncle?"

"My mother's brother was a war hero who ended up destroying himself chasing visions for military intelligence," Aubrey said, too baffled and sore to bother dressing up the history, especially for the stalwart Miss Tsung. "It sounded as though Prince Willard would like me to go the same way. Although who knows what he really meant. It didn't much seem like he had any idea how offensive he was being, did he?"

"Yes! What was he even doing here? My sisters say that famous performers have been doing rounds to visit the wounded: people like Julia Huppert. We could have had someone like that instead of His Royal Rude-Face, who would have done better to stick to freezing Honal troops!"

Aubrey shook his head, laughing again. "He's not active in this war. He sustained some injury in the last conflict. Apart from his hand, I mean. Something to do with . . . his feet?"

"Well, he was certainly capable of walking out of that door quickly enough!"

They laughed until they both winced from their injuries, and then the gentleman to their left tried to make a witticism at them about their presumed shared taste for the uppermost echelons of society, and they found it was time to take a very long, slow turn about the park, stopping for many rest breaks.

They came back to the news that Prince Willard had been captured by Honal soldiers a mere four miles away, as he traveled to the army barracks to the west of them.

Several letters arrived for Aubrey the day after that: one from his mother expressing her gratitude for Aubrey's reassurances that he was recuperating well, and a promise that she would visit; one from Wilson demanding news; and one from Malmy, anguished that Aubrey was able to spend time with Rosalie when he himself had been banished from intimacy with her. He had also included a poem he was working on and a request for Aubrey's opinion of it. Aubrey thought the words were dead on the page due to Malmy trying too hard to write impressively about something that was obviously still a raw emotional wound, but he could never say that. Instead he hinted that Malmy might do better to just write honestly and from the heart, using his own voice and feelings.

Aubrey would find out later that Malmy never got his reply. The Honals had stepped up their attacks on not only the mail carriages, but on the roads more generally.

"The main highway not far from here has been blown up," one of the nurses said one day, running into the building. "The one they think Prince Willard was taken on. I saw the crater myself; it was more than a yard deep in the center and reached all the way across. Buried explosive device, they said. A supply cart set it off. I told them to bring the wounded here until the medics get here."

When the wounded arrived, they were in no state to answer questions, but it seemed the rumors that the Honals had been manufacturing more and more explosives were proven right. The medics that came to collect the patients said that buried devices were going off all over the country, and while they were more indiscriminate than the Honals' previous attacks on mail coaches, the results were the same: very little communications were getting through, and now supplies were a problem as well.

Systems were put in place to test roads before they were driven over. Official government mail was sent in triplicate. One particular mail carriage, however, posed a quandary, as the first newspaper to get through to Aubrey in a full week reported:

> Only half of the contents were destroyed, and what is left was only partly damaged by fire. While the outsides were scorched, including the delivery addresses, the words inside remain partly or fully legible. Under normal circumstances, the postal service would destroy undeliverable mail, but nobody would call these normal circumstances, especially considering that that particular coach included primarily personal correspondence from a variety of military sites.
>
> Given that the letters might be the last words that those soldiers ever sent out to their families, this newspaper has organized to print a few each week in the hopes that they might make it to the right eyes. They will not be edited, in case quirks of spelling or grammar might point to their writers, although we will print nothing that breaks the law. The letters will remain at the newspaper's offices; should anyone wish to claim one, they can petition the editor.
>
> It is our honor to print them, and we thank the postal service and the relevant parliamentary commit-

tee for agreeing to our proposal. These are the voices of our nation's soldiers, deserving to be heard. We hope that this exercise will bolster the country.

The letters proved incredibly popular. They were regularly read out at the officers' rest home and sparked a lot of discussion. One letter fragment, however, caused particular interest:

mustn't upset yourself worrying about me, although I must say—and I don't know if it is the same for you, darling, as your experience with this struggle will be so different from my own—I find that the nights are the worst.

I try to keep my spirits up by bringing you to mind, thinking of your smell, of the feel and taste of your skin on my tongue. I imagine tracing my thumb along your lips, the shell of your ear, the arch of your eyebrow. Sometimes I look down in surprise when I wake, wondering why there is no trace of you visible on my skin, and I think that it must have sunk down inside me; that your name is etched onto my bones, that the colors of you are painted over my soul.

No—not painted—nothing so quick, and nothing that can be removed or covered over so easily. You are embroidered there, not just with the art and skill that a painter possesses, but also with the care and the meticulousness of an artisan, steady and true. You are knotted there tightly in such a way as to make unpicking or ejection impossible; the surface would be damaged, would not be the same should such a thing be attempted, and I have no regrets other than I cannot see it with my own eyes, but can only feel its presence as surely as I see my hands, my arms, my legs. Even they are not so mundane now, as these are the hands that have caressed you, the arms that have held you, the legs that have tangled with yours and walked with yours and run to meet you.

I do not know if I will make it home, or, should I be so lucky, if I will be the same man. It pains me to know that your circumstances are similar. When we were younger, I don't think we ever could have imagined the situations we face now. Compared to all this violence and pain, I find myself considering even the worst hardships that you picture for our future as the most minor of inconveniences, now. I even look forward to them as part of my life with you, in any way we can manage to be together, and

The page ended there. Except that "ended" was not the right word, because (despite some complaints from more conservative quarters, who did not think this letter should have made it past the censors) this missive proved so popular that the paper was forced to reprint that edition to keep up with demand and then sought permission from the government, and was granted it, to print the fragment on its own as a pamphlet. It was quoted in multiple places as a reminder of what the nation's soldiers were risking, and sacrificing, for the populace. *The war cannot last much longer, surely,* one letter to the editor read. *Not with such brave, passionate soldiers.*

Aubrey was asked to read the thing aloud multiple times in the parlor at the rest home. He was so good at reading aloud, after all. He had happily read poetry, fairy tales, and entire novels to the group, which usually started with only other wounded officers but would sometimes swell to include whatever medical staff could be spared from their duties and some servants as well. When presented with this pamphlet, however, he always claimed to have a headache or a sore throat. One particular night when this happened, one Lieutenant Aiden knocked on his door later.

"Lord Ainsley," he said, taking a step into the room. "I wanted to see if your throat is feeling any better. I have something that's just the thing," he added, producing a bottle of whiskey from behind his back. "It's also good for passing the time," he added with a smile, "in case you might want some company."

"Oh, what a kind offering," Aubrey said. "My throat is better, but I am much too fatigued tonight for drinking. Perhaps another night. I really am quite set for bed."

"Well, I could . . . help you with that, too. If you liked."

He had tilted his head. Aubrey took in its angle and felt his expression harden. "Oh. So that's what this is," he said, and when the man didn't even have the decency to seem remotely disheartened, Aubrey put his hand on his hip and added, "You aren't the first they've sent, you know. What did they offer you?"

Now Aiden looked thrown. "Offer me?"

"Yes, to try and get me to betray Edmund. Was it money? A position? I am shocked that faction is still at it. Right now there are more important things to focus on than the crown prince's romantic life—"

"What? No—no one *paid* me; I just thought I'd try my luck. Everyone knows that you're—that is, I thought—you'd be up for it."

His voice was feeble by the end of this astonishing sentence.

Aubrey's tone, by comparison, was flat as a blade. "You thought I'd be *up for it.*"

Aiden was staring at him now, clearly trying to work out where he had gone wrong. He started stuttering something that sounded like an apology, but Aubrey cut him off.

"Oh for heaven's sake. Get out."

The man got out, swiftly.

CHAPTER 17

The interruptions with the post meant that Edmund hadn't received a letter from Aubrey in weeks. Not hearing from him for so long had given Edmund the permanent feeling in the back of his mind that he had left something in another room. He started fixating itchily on the problems with the mail service. When Sir Jenson informed him that he had seen Lord Ainsley's name on a transportation list for the next week, which meant that he would be rejoining his garrison, Edmund decided it was a sign.

"How long will it take to ride to his rest home?"

Sir J blinked at him. "I thought that you had decided not to risk visiting his lordship?"

Edmund squinted a bit at this interpretation of the conversations he and Sir Jenson had had on the subject. "Did you?" he asked, and the man huffed.

When Edmund arrived, he was pleased to see that the home was much less grim than others he had visited. The residence belonged to some baroness who had moved to her Elmiddan town house for the duration of the war while she worked in the War Office.

The garden leading up to the entry was full of color, all wildflowers and lavenders and roses. It was homey and busy and full of fat bees. Edmund loved it, loved the idea of Aubrey being here among all this beauty and life.

"What a pleasant place to recuperate," he said to the woman who had welcomed him. He hadn't caught her title but had some notion that she was something like the head physician.

"Yes, we find cheery surroundings to be beneficial for healing," she replied in a pleased tone. "The officers have free rein of the grounds and are welcome to tend the flower beds if they like, which is also good for the health, sir, as I'm sure you know. And this garden provides lovely views from the parlor," she added, motioning to the window.

Edmund looked, his brain half on the plants—but then he saw the flash of a familiar grin through the window, a hand waving. He took a step toward the building before turning to excuse himself, but the doctor was already saying, "Please feel free to go in now, sir, if you would like to see," with a smile in her voice.

He bowed, and then before he could have thought it possible, he was through the front door and Aubrey was flying to him.

Aubrey's hair, he thought, staring at it, and then, *I must be careful of his ribs,* but Aubrey had launched himself onto Edmund, right there in the hall where anyone who happened to be about could see them, including the maid, who took Edmund's hat wordlessly with the brisk air of someone refusing to see anything. Edmund told his own reddening face that it didn't matter; Aubrey would smooth it over. Everyone loved Aubrey. And here he was, solid and real and alive and whole in his arms. The Honal monsters hadn't done anything he couldn't heal from, and his hair would grow back. He shifted to bury his head in the crook of Aubrey's neck, and Aubrey flinched.

Edmund pulled back. "I didn't hurt you?"

"Never," Aubrey said, "but you will have to be gentle with me."

And then Edmund found himself being pulled down the corridor toward, he assumed, Aubrey's bedchamber.

Different instincts warred within him—this was not discreet, this was not even *polite*—and yet somehow none of that seemed important, since he had Aubrey's hand in his. His heart started beating in great throbs so strong that they disrupted his vision. He didn't manage to say anything before Aubrey was pulling him into a little room and closing the door behind them. He had a brief impression of military canvas everywhere—it must be being used to protect the house's wallpaper and the furniture—and two narrow beds.

"Help me with this," Aubrey was saying as he started pushing them together.

"Your roommate—"

"Went back to his battalion yesterday," Aubrey said, finishing up with the beds and shrugging out of his dressing robe.

"But—your reputation—the *door*—"

Aubrey gave him a look and moved a privacy screen of even more military canvas between the door and the bed. He then waved his hand sardonically over the panels as though he had unveiled a fine new painting. Edmund, who had undermined his own protests by not only helping to move the beds together but also loosening several of his own garments, decided to stop arguing, especially since Aubrey's collar was now open, exposing the glory of his throat, bare and beautiful and made of contours Edmund wanted very much to put his mouth to. So he did.

They held each other tightly afterward, Aubrey sprawled on top of him, and Edmund felt like, finally, something had gone right.

He gazed at Aubrey's face. It was different without the mass of blond curls framing it. To be fair, Edmund had thought Aubrey looked different every single time they had managed to see each other during this war. They were both at an age when a gap of three or four months did bring physical change. Aubrey's face had certainly lost some of its softness, and his body, as well. His shoulders were strong with muscle now, his arms corded with it.

Edmund knew some people found men more attractive this way, but it was the scars that Aubrey had also acquired over the last year that Edmund kept on finding his eyes drawn to. He had a map of violence and pain on his flesh. The marks on his arms were mostly small, but there was a nasty one, some three inches long, that had needed stitches. Edmund remembered reading Aubrey's letter telling him about that battle; he had felt so sick afterward, he had barely been able to eat for days.

There was something similar on one of Aubrey's thighs, but almost twice the length. Aubrey's letter about that one, warning him that he was back in the barracks hospital wing, never arrived; Edmund had found out through his habit of poring over the lists of injured soldiers.

Edmund had written to the prime minister two days later, seeking permission to marry.

Aubrey's hair being cut was a different kind of change. It made him look older, more serious; but it also highlighted how beautiful he was. There was no escaping the lines of his jaw and his nose, the curves of his lips.

Edmund loved him so much, his chest hurt with it.

He dropped a kiss onto Aubrey's forehead, and Aubrey wiggled higher up the bed to put his mouth within reach. Edmund kissed him there, too. But then he had to stop.

"You know," he said, shifting so the seam of the two beds wasn't digging into him so much, "This is not precisely comfortable."

Aubrey's entire body heaved as he laughed; then he winced.

"Are your ribs still causing problems?" Edmund asked. His worry must have been plain on his face, because Aubrey was almost apologetic when he said, "I don't think they're quite done healing, but they are much better than they were. Really, I am ready to get back to the garrison. Just a few twinges."

Edmund looked at him. "Are you sure?"

"Yes," Aubrey said firmly. "And if you had gotten my letters you would know how ready I am to get out of here. I feel like an old man in this place."

Edmund shifted again, this time to reach into his coat. "Speaking of your letters, I don't know if you've seen, and it seems . . . *conceited* to ask . . ."

He pulled out a pamphlet copy of the passionate half letter that the papers had published—the "embroidered love letter," it was being called—and Aubrey laughed again.

"Oh yes," Aubrey said. "Yes, that was for you. So nice that everybody else liked it. I can hardly go and claim it, though, given the circumstances, can I?"

Edmund pulled him back onto his chest, taking care to only put his arms over his shoulders. "I wish you could," he murmured. "It sounded so much like you, and I was so proud when it occurred to me that these words might be for me and that everybody had seen them."

"I'll write to the newspaper tomorrow, then," Aubrey suggested, his eyebrows raised.

"Better not. Last thing anybody wants right now is a reminder that any of their—their royal weapons are human."

"Edmund! Don't ever call yourself something like that again."

Edmund held his gaze for a moment. Then he said, "It's what I'm for, Aubrey. Even without the war, I am not one of Saben's subjects, but its object, to be used in its service. You know this."

Edmund wasn't aware that he had started crying until Aubrey wiped the tears from his face. He tried to regain control and found himself gasping for air. Aubrey sat up and held Edmund's head to his chest, murmuring comfort. He focused on Aubrey's heartbeat as he calmed down and tried to commit this moment to memory: not comfortable, but undoubtedly warm and loving and *alive*.

"I miss you so much," he said. "My parents get to be together. Charlotte and Henri get to be together."

"Well, I do hate to break it to you, darling, but we aren't married."

Edmund cleared his throat. "No, but I was quite upset about you being injured. I really do want to get you away from that city. It's one of the most frequently attacked sites, did you know? And I know that it's not fair to other people who don't have the connections to move them to safer locations, but you've been there for so long, and I don't think that's fair either. So I wrote to the prime minister again about you, demanding an answer this time. Mamma helped me write the letter when she came."

"About me?" Aubrey sat up a bit more, letting go of Edmund so that they could look at each other. "About *marrying* me?"

Edmund nodded, sitting up more as well. "I know we are . . . a little young, but Sir Jenson says that if I am resolute, the man might listen. That was all right, wasn't it?"

Aubrey took another few seconds to think about this, sitting back properly now. Then he crossed his arms and lifted his chin. "You know that you have never actually *asked* me?"

Edmund's whole body twitched, he was so startled. "I have!"

"You have not."

Edmund blinked at him. Then he shifted himself out of the camp bed and dropped onto one knee, facing Aubrey squarely.

"Oh good heavens, get up."

"No. Not until you've said yes. Aubrey—Lord Ainsley, will you promise to be my husband? Assuming that the parliament—no, forget the parliament. I love you. I'll always love you. I think I was in love with you within minutes of our first meeting. Marry me. Please."

Aubrey was laughing. Edmund didn't want to risk getting up yet, just in case, but then Aubrey was hugging him, which was surely a good sign.

"Of course I would marry you, ridiculous boy. Even if the parliament says no, you know I'm not going anywhere. You're stuck with me."

Edmund tightened his arms, which had drifted up around Aubrey's waist seemingly on their own, and buried his face in Aubrey's shoulder. "Please stay stuck." Edmund felt tears prick his eyes again as he said it, and he pressed his face farther into the join of Aubrey's neck. He had some vague idea that his knees were hurting—this carpet really wasn't very deep—but then Aubrey was tipping his face up to kiss him, and he figured he could get up now.

They made it back out of the room eventually. They weren't sure how much longer they would have been granted privacy, and in any case, Edmund wanted to see the garden. Aubrey was acquainting him with the beehives in a secluded clearing far from the house, when a surprise guest joined them.

It was Lady Ainsley.

"My lady!" Edmund said, bowing his head and surreptitiously trying to shoo away the five or six bees congregating around his person. Bees always seemed interested in him. "Of course you also wanted to see Aubrey before he went back to his garrison."

"Naturally, Your Highness," she said, curtsying gracefully, "but to be perfectly frank, it is you that I am here for. The Support Office has been trying to find a discreet way to send someone to you for some weeks. When I learned that you were here, I could not miss this chance."

Aubrey's mouth dropped open. "And what? I'm the cat's leftovers, am I?"

Lady Ainsley gave the tiniest of snorts and took his hand.

"Never, dearest," she said to her son. "And what I have to say affects you as well, as you will hear, and it must not go beyond the three of us, so we cannot risk speaking of it in the house. This part of the garden seems quite private. How likely are we to be interrupted out here, do you think, Aubrey?"

"I've never seen anyone else out here. I only come out here myself because the bee-skeps remind me of the ones Father keeps at home."

"Good," she said, and motioned to the nearby wooden table, which was presumably used for honey extraction, and its bench. "By your leave, sir?"

Edmund motioned his assent, cringing internally that Aubrey's mother could not simply sit down in his presence. He was considering saying something about it, until she said, "I have some news of Prince Willard."

Her expression was sitting on her face in a strange, careful way. That could not mean anything good. He and Aubrey sat down.

"If the Honals have killed him, you should feel free to say so plainly," Edmund heard himself say.

He did not know how he would feel, if that were the case. He and his uncle had never been close. Though Charlotte had lived in the palace in Elmiddan with them for periods when they were young, so that they could share schooling, Prince Willard had usually stayed in Hendon Castle.

Edmund waved away a few more bees that seemed determined to land on his arm and wondered what reaction Lady Ainsley expected from him.

Her mouth had thinned. "No, sir. At least, we assume not, since there is reason to believe that he went with them of his own free will."

"He was coerced into it, you mean?" Aubrey asked.

"No, dearest, I do not. Apparently, my superiors at the Support Office have been monitoring Prince Willard for some time. They have evidence that His Highness has been communicating secretly with the Honal leaders for more than a year. Since before the war started."

Edmund heard buzzing around his head and waved distractedly. "Communicating?" he asked. "About what?"

Her shoulders straightened. Edmund recognized the gesture; Aubrey's did the same when he was steeling himself.

"This will not be easy for you to hear, sir, but the Honals appear to have approached your uncle to alert him of their intentions to attack Saben, and to seek him out as an ally. They promised him a position in the new empire they are hoping to create, as well as access to their magical water, which they said would enhance his gifts, making him . . ." She paused, her face falling into a slight grimace. "Well, making him more powerful than you or your parents."

Edmund's voice didn't sound like his own when he asked, "And how did he respond?"

"He never agreed to anything, although he also never turned them down. At one point he does seem to have bargained with them to assure his daughter's safety, because we have a letter in which they promise to leave her out of their plans."

"So she did not know anything about any of this?" Aubrey asked, and Lady Ainsley said something about how she was entirely free from suspicion, which should have been a relief, but Edmund's chest still felt like it was hollowing out.

"He bargained for Charlotte?" he found himself asking. "But not for any of the rest of the family?"

"Nor for any of the rest of the country, either. He does not appear to have ever tried to persuade them not to attack us. He instead informed them that their plan to target the ports first was sound and alluded to the idea that he would quite like to be put on his brother's throne, even as a sort of vassal king."

Aubrey voiced the stray hope that had just occurred to Edmund. "Is there no chance that he was merely . . . toying with them?" He made a face at how weak the words sounded. "You know, finding out what he could?"

Lady Ainsley reached over and patted her son on the hand. "Oh, dearest. He never contacted the War Office or any other government department to inform them that they had made contact, or to warn them that the attacks at the naval bases were imminent."

She looked back at Edmund. "If he is ever recovered from the Honals, a warrant will be issued for his arrest, for treason."

Edmund's breathing was coming fast and shallow. He could feel sweat starting to prickle his face. He raised a hand to wipe it away and saw there was a bee investigating his glove. He shook it off and barely heard Aubrey as he continued to ask questions.

"Why has it not been issued yet? Why is this all so hush-hush? The newspapers keep berating the government for not doing more to recover the man!"

"Because it would be a blow to morale at a time when we can scarcely weather it, and a scandal for the royal family, who—aside from Prince Willard, who claimed injury and refused to put on his uniform—are all doing their best to defend their country." She flashed a grim smile at Edmund. "It would be awful for the nation to lose faith in them right now. Also, we know that half of the Honal sorcerers who drank from that pool of theirs died. If—I'm sorry, sir—but if it does kill the prince, then there is no reason for everyone to know what he did. We can all just blame the Honals for it, and it won't even be unjustified."

"Who else knows about this?" Edmund asked, hearing the bewilderment in his own voice. "Have the king and queen been informed?"

"Support officers met with them this week, yes."

Other support officers. The idea that there were whole teams of Lady Ainsleys hit Edmund suddenly, and he spent a moment frozen, but then he remembered what he had actually wanted to know.

"Why did I need to be told?"

"Partly because you needed to be aware of the risk to yourself, and partly because of the other things His Highness was doing. Specifically, with a covert group within Saben itself. It counts participants from several noble families and some of our richest merchants, with the design of exerting political power."

Edmund flicked a glance over at Aubrey, who looked as confused as he was.

"Political power?" he repeated.

"You must understand, sir, that this was a private thing, not overseen by elected officials or subject to public scrutiny. Luckily, they didn't achieve much, but they were behind an attempt a year or so ago to make you believe that Aubrey had taken up with our family friend Lord James Malmsbury—yes, I know about that"—she broke off at an exclamation from her son—"and they also bribed a fellow officer at the training camp at Craywick to try to seduce Aubrey, near the start of the war."

"Ensign Worthing!" Aubrey said. "Oh thank goodness, Mother, I'm so glad we don't have to worry about that business anymore. I mean, it's quite embarrassing to have *you* know about it, but still."

"Yes, although we have just learned that they switched to putting attractive young men in the way of Prince Edmund instead."

Edmund felt himself frown. "They what?"

Lady Ainsley cleared her throat.

"Yes, sir, it appears that at least two handsome, blond junior officers were assigned to your company when you were last in the field. Several servants were placed in Talstam. There was even someone in your personal guard. You reportedly defeated all of their efforts to get close to you by simply failing to notice their attentions. I assume that is correct, and you really didn't notice?"

"No!"

Lady Ainsley cleared her throat again. "Yes, well, the guardsman was so annoyed by your obliviousness to his charms, he deserted his post. He's due to be reprimanded as soon as the military can find him, but the Support Office did intercept a letter from him, saying Aubrey must be some sort of fae spirit who's bewitched you."

"Oh, I say," Edmund said, while Aubrey snorted with laughter next to him.

"While that particular project was clearly . . . ill-advised, we are still trying to discover all of their operations, and I should tell you that some were darker than merely trying to split the two of you up. Aubrey's garrison . . . well. It never seemed right to me that a munitions-producing city expected to come under sustained attack would refuse to close its gates.

"And Aubrey appears to have been stationed there on purpose, along with several other . . . inconvenient young people. There is an ensign here, right now, I understand, who it appears that Malmy's father was concerned about. Several disgraced younger sons and daughters of noble families, who I regret to say will never be going home. Union leaders. A prominent social reformer who has also been killed. I hope you will not think me interfering, but I have been trying to get you transferred for months. All of my attempts at string-pulling have thus far been ignored, which adds to my unease. I am not happy about you going back there in a few days."

"Wait, wait—" Edmund needed this clarified; he needed to get this new information to stick in his head. It kept on wanting to slide away. "Prince Willard and—and some other people in high-ranking positions—they deliberately put the soldiers at Manogate at risk? They have put an entire *city* at risk by insisting on the gates never being closed?"

"We are still searching for solid proof, but yes, sir, I believe so."

"Aubrey is being put in harm's way because of his association with me. Because my uncle—what? Resents me that much?"

Lady Ainsley looked at him for a long moment. Finally, she said, "Several government groups have been concerned for a number of years that Prince Willard saw being passed over as king as . . . an indignity. In any other Thasbian country, including his Folbran wife's, he would automatically have been the heir to the throne as the eldest, but Saben is not like that. Willard did not have full elemental powers and his younger brother did; the parliament did not even consider him. Your case was even more clear-cut. You were very young when your gift manifested, and, as a Prince of Fortune, the parliament declared you Saben's next monarch immediately. I expect you don't even remember it."

Edmund shook his head.

"Well, it all happened right after Prince Willard's wife died trying to birth their second child. And then you and Aubrey started your relationship just as his daughter Charlotte was leaving him to marry a Hasprennan prince."

"*Leaving* him?"

"Yes, he uses that phrase in a letter we have a copy of. He appeared to struggle with the idea of her getting married, of someone else 'coming first' in his daughter's affections. He—he had hopes before that, that you would marry her, sir, did you know?"

He closed his eyes in mortification as Aubrey gave a noise of surprise.

"I only found out after her engagement," he managed to mumble, and then added defensively, "Nobody even told me!" since Aubrey had his hand over his mouth now to stifle his laughter.

"Well, it seemed to bring everything back, since his daughter would now not be queen—"

"She didn't want me!"

"—and though he was still proud that she made an appropriate match, we think that it all got twisted up in his head, because that was something he decided that you weren't interested in: the right sort of marriage."

Edmund put his hand up in a mute request for Lady Ainsley to pause in her story, breathing deeply. Anger had spiked through his body, and he didn't want to cause a storm; he could feel that the wind was up already.

He felt like a door was being opened into a place where he didn't know his father's brother at all, like every memory he had of him was busy being rewritten in his mind, colored with all this new information.

Before, he had seen the man as distant, grieving, bad at social situations. Now he was judgmental and actively hostile. He had seemed uninterested in children; now he had specifically resented his nephew, had been jealous of him. Edmund felt tainted by association merely being related to someone so small, who thought of the world so selfishly.

He breathed in and out. He looked down at a buzzing noise; there was a bee climbing the mountains that were the knuckles of his right hand, which had curled into a fist. He uncurled it, and the bee flew away to investigate the air near Aubrey instead. Aubrey reached down to the grass beneath their feet and picked a flower absent-mindedly. He used it to lure the insect to the table instead.

Edmund motioned to Lady Ainsley that she should proceed.

"The Support Office is going to recommend a full inquiry," she said. "The information regarding Prince Willard's association with the Honals' previous leaders will be held back, but military operations are being manipulated to pursue personal agendas. It is not just Aubrey's garrison, you understand. And while your uncle may never be seen again, this group he helped form has many other members, and they are still—"

"Figure approaching," Aubrey rapped out, and Edmund's head snapped up and around, even as Aubrey let out a little laugh and said, "I mean . . . there's someone coming."

"Stand down, Lieutenant," his mother said, her eyes twinkling.

It was a servant letting them know that dinner would be served shortly, and that they were invited to join the head physician; but Edmund was distracted for the entire meal. Everything he had been told that afternoon swam around in his head, looping and twisting along with the efficient, soldierly way that Aubrey had informed them of the footman's approach.

They had to stop this war, he thought. Because Aubrey wasn't the only one behaving out of character. The whole country was doing that, and it wasn't fair. Especially if powerful people were exploiting the situation for their own benefit.

Edmund had to sleep alone that night. Keeping up appearances and all that. The discreet maid had shown him to what looked like the finest bedchamber the place had: possibly the baroness's own chamber. He would rather have slept on Aubrey's narrow soldier's bed. It didn't matter, he thought, as he tried to settle; they would get to spend the entirety of the next day together, and the morning after that.

Except that a messenger came before the sun had even risen with an urgent letter, and he was gone before Aubrey woke up.

CHAPTER 18

Edmund dashed down an apology for Aubrey before he left, explaining that he'd been called to come and assist immediately with some sort of diplomatic disaster involving a delegation sent from Nordan:

> *They arrived at Marisetown to find nobody waiting to greet them. Their own ambassador here didn't even know they were coming. To top it off, two of their king's grandchildren—the twin prince and princess—are in the party. Point to the Honals: they must have hoped for exactly something like this when they started blowing up our mail coaches.*
>
> *I've no idea why it has to be me that goes. If they've come to discuss terms for giving us aid in the war, then someone more diplomatic, like Mamma, would be better, especially after such a muddle.*

I love you, and I'm so sorry and annoyed that I'm going to miss your last few days before you rejoin your garrison. I'll work out a way to see you next time you have leave. I love you. I must go.

Mattheson had some basic Nordish and so was able to help Edmund practice in the coach as they rode down to the embassy in Marisetown. They changed horses at every opportunity, only stopping to sleep, trying to get there as soon as possible. When they got to Clarington House the next day, Edmund had planned to tidy up and change his clothes as quickly as possible before heading straight to the embassy; except there was a note saying they had to wait for the minister for foreign affairs. No one could tell Edmund how long that was likely to take.

Mattheson turned silently to Edmund for instructions.

"You and the rest of our party should take the opportunity to rest and eat, then," he said, suddenly exhausted. "I'm going to bed."

Edmund didn't feel much better after napping, though some hot coffee and some cold roast beef and potatoes perked him up a little. By the time he was done eating some sort of warm citrus cake, he felt almost human and was therefore able to receive with equanimity the message that they were ready for him at the embassy. Except that when he got there, they were apparently not ready for him at all.

He was taken into an antechamber, which resonated with the sounds of shouting, coming from the next room: a room that he was informed contained the Nordish ambassador to Saben, the Sabresian ambassador to Nordan, and the minister for foreign affairs. He could not make out what they were saying, but the diplomatic clerk who had greeted him looked mortified, as did the rest of the assistants and staff standing around.

He could see them all asking each other with their eyes, *Do we take him in? But what about the shouting?*

"Why don't I go and introduce myself to the prince and princess, and someone can come and tell me when things have calmed down a bit?" Edmund asked.

The eyes around him all turned very relieved.

He and his retinue—just Mattheson and four guardsmen—were taken to a reception room farther into the building, decorated in the Nordish style with a lot of white and accents in blues and greens. All the furniture was painted, which he was not used to; he could practically hear Aubrey in his ear saying that this was because Saben had a history of preferring more natural finishes, showcasing the inherent beauty of the wood.

Everyone in the room rose, in a nervous sort of way. Edmund assumed they had fled the shouting as well.

There were introductions. Apart from both having hair of a light brown color, the twins were not very much alike. Prince Patrik was slightly shorter than Princess Ana; Edmund had an idea that this was normal, given their age. The prince also had a large port-wine stain on his forehead that he seemed to have arranged his hair over to hide. Edmund would not have even noticed, except that the boy kept on smoothing it in place as they all stood there. He found himself wondering if it were cultural, as people in Saben didn't tend to bother worrying about that sort of thing, or if it was just his own self-consciousness. Edmund tried to give him a reassuring smile and was stared at blankly in return.

None of them had met before. The twins seemed very young to have been sent into a foreign country at war without their parents; their entourage seemed to consist of lords- and ladies-in-waiting, all in powdered wigs, which had largely gone out of fashion in Saben. They had a guard as well, of course, although it seemed strange that so many of them were here in the room with them. They all looked to be men of the same height, and their uniforms were quite dashing, with white trousers and a coat in a sort of mid blue, with yellow-and-white trim.

Edmund scrounged around in his brain for some small talk. They could hardly converse about the guardsmen being attractive. What had he been interested in at twelve? Grafting fruit trees, mostly, and a romance he had borrowed from the palace library and kept hidden under his bed for weeks, because it was the first one he had found with two male protagonists. He had read the love scene so many times, the book started to fall open to that page.

Not the best topics of conversation.

Eventually he went with "I do hope that your journey was tolerable. How were the winds?"

They just stared at him. Perhaps his accent was so bad they hadn't understood him.

"The winds to . . . fill the sails? Did I use the right word? It has been a while since I have practiced your language; if I had known you were coming today, I would have made sure to brush up on my vocabulary—"

"The journey was fine, thank you," the princess said.

"I am glad to hear it. I believe the trip takes about three weeks, going via the continent?"

The children nodded and stared at him some more.

Finally, one of the ladies took pity on them all. "Their Highnesses were indeed cooped up for many weeks. Perhaps we could all take a walk in the garden? It is fine out."

"And you can make sure it stays fine out," the princess said. Edmund couldn't make out her tone. He searched her face and wasn't sure if he saw fear there. He found himself thinking of Sir Jenson describing him as an untouchable figure from a story who could bring down the storm or curse the crops.

He made himself smile. "As you say."

They walked out in silence for a while with Mattheson as his own attendant and one of the wigged ladies walking next to him, then two of the embassy footmen and four guards behind. With so many witnesses, Edmund found himself wishing, not for the first time, that he was better at the art of general conversation. What would Aubrey talk to the children about? He'd probably start by complimenting their clothes, Edmund thought, and glanced over to see what they were wearing. The prince's ensemble was a more colorful version of the sort of thing Edmund himself usually wore, really, whereas the princess was wearing a dress in what he assumed was a more Nordish style, with a lower waist than what Sabresian ladies usually preferred. It was also a bit low-cut in the front for a girl so young, he thought. He had some notion that Alicia hadn't worn anything like that until quite recently.

He could hardly talk about that, either, and was just starting to panic when he noticed the embroidery on her gloves. He motioned to them.

"That stitching is nicely done," he said. "Are those grapevines?"

She nodded.

"Do you like grapes?"

The prince answered this time. "They're our favorite. They do not grow well where we live, so they are a treat."

Edmund motioned to their right. "Can we go this way?" he asked. "There's something you might like to see."

He had sensed the plants so was not surprised when they came into view. There was a pergola in the next section of the gardens with grapevines growing all over the roof to provide shade in the summer. A table and chairs sat invitingly inside. He took off his gloves and put his hands to the vines. There were two varieties, but being so early in the spring, neither would normally have been ready to fruit yet. He picked the one that felt the closest and pushed, closing his eyes. He opened them again when he heard his guests gasp.

"A magic trick for you," he said. Mattheson motioned for one of the servants who had been following them to cut down some of the fruit.

The prince and princess murmured their thanks, then ate some grapes politely. They did not look, to Edmund, like children who had been given one of their favorite foods, and his sense of unease deepened. When a clerk approached them to say that the ambassadors and Dame Edwina were ready now, it was all he could do not to slump with relief at the idea of heading back inside. They made their way back to the path.

"Dame Edwina is our minister for foreign affairs and diplomacy, you know," he said, wincing inside at how feeble a conversational offering it was.

"Yes, we know," the prince said. "We were told to wait for her, that negotiations regarding our country's proposal could not proceed without her."

"Your proposal?"

It took Edmund a moment or two to realize that the children had fallen out of step with him. He stopped and turned to see them unmoving, staring at him.

They exchanged a glance, and then the princess asked in Sabresian, "You . . . do not know what we are here for?"

Edmund shook his head. "I'm sorry," he said, relieved to be back to his own tongue. "No one has told me anything."

"Do not be sorry. You walked with us in the garden and—the grapevines—you did all that to be kind?"

Edmund shifted his weight back a little. "Oh dear. You're worrying me now. Why should I not have been kind? You're not here to tell us you're siding with Honal, are you?"

He'd meant it as a joke. Again, it was the princess who replied. "No. The opposite. Our country has sent us here as part of marriage negotiations. They will send soldiers and supplies to help you in your war in exchange for your hand. To me."

It was a bumpy ride from the officers' rest home to Manogate, a day later. At least Rosalie was with him, Aubrey thought, and so he had someone to both complain to and to keep his spirits up for. They cracked jokes and traded stories with the other soldiers until the garrison came into sight.

"It's not exactly an attractive building, is it," Rosalie said, gesturing at the barracks looming over the hill.

Aubrey could not disagree. It was, in fact, extraordinarily ugly, made of gray stone and surrounded by bare yards and defensive pikes. They could see movement even at this distance: soldiers performing drills.

"I find it helps to never look at it or think about it," he said. "It is what it is, and we just have to get through this. It's not forever."

They reported to Captain Walsh, who told them to go and drop off their packs, freshen up, and then join everyone else for dinner. When they got to the hall, however, a friend of Aubrey's sitting at the colonel's table—an infantry captain who had been at university with Cedric—started beckoning at him wildly, so he let himself be waylaid.

The newspapers appeared to have just arrived; his friend had one in front of him, as did Colonel Wyclef, who was saying something about the Nordans lending military aid.

That must, Aubrey thought, *have been the meeting Edmund was called away to.*

His friend thrust the newspaper at him. He read the headline.

NORDAN TO SEND TROOPS IN EXCHANGE FOR
PRINCE OF FORTUNE'S HAND

"It's not exactly a disinterested offer," the colonel was saying, "but I won't pretend not to think *any* help could only be a good thing for us. We're being slaughtered, and every other nation in Helen's Treaty can only send so many people, you know. The Nordans have been complaining for years about the Honals attacking their ships, and they have those new cannons—"

Aubrey stared at the paper. He saw the words "Princess Ana" and handed it back to his friend without looking at him. He only managed to find his table because Rosalie was already sitting there. She said something, but his ears were full of buzzing, like he was still in front of the beehives at the rest home.

He had tried not to think about this sort of possibility. He had deliberately refused to contemplate it, airily telling himself it would be irrational to allow himself to worry or become upset over something that might never happen. Would probably never happen, since Edmund was so set against a political marriage.

But it was happening now.

Rosalie put a plate in front of him and a fork in his hand. The food made clammy, tasteless lumps in his mouth. He forced himself to swallow, even though it stuck in his throat. He had some notion that people were staring at him, but he really wasn't sure. Perhaps he was unknowingly making a scene, or perhaps they had already heard. He excused himself and went to his room in a daze.

So. Those cold Nordans would not send assistance without receiving something in return, and that something was Edmund. And his fine, noble Edmund—his Edmund, *his* Edmund—he would want to save his people no matter the sacrifice to himself.

Edmund had said more than once that he would not be forced into marriage, that he would never marry someone who was not of his own choosing, but neither of them could ever have foreseen this, Aubrey thought; and then a mirthless laugh came out of his mouth, because he himself could very well have foreseen this. He just hadn't.

Either way, this was it. He could not share Edmund with a Nordish princess. The thought was ridiculous.

And it wasn't only Edmund he would be losing. The entire royal family . . . all that easy intimacy would be over with. It would have to be. He felt a whole new pang when he thought of Alicia. She would become somebody else's sister-in-law now.

He pulled out the note Edmund had left him the previous morning when he had been called to meet the Nordish delegation.

I love you. I must go.

Aubrey couldn't breathe. His throat was closing over.

And then someone was hugging him. He registered after a moment or two that it was Rosalie. He then registered that it was probably a bad sign that he hadn't even heard her come in, but didn't really have any emotions to spare to worry over it, as he put an arm around her for balance. He felt wetness on his neck.

"Oh dear," he said, pulling back and getting out his handkerchief for her. She waved it away and pulled out her own. "You aren't crying for me, are you? Or are you in love with Edmund as well? That really would be awkward."

She let out a surprised, wet-sounding laugh, and then said, "I wouldn't dare be. You'd be far too hard to compete with."

"Yes, that's what I hear; the Nordans have had to throw in a well-supplied army. Who knew my charms were so formidable?"

"Will he— No, never mind. Everything I want to say seems overfamiliar."

"I'll forgive you, I'm sure."

She contemplated him for a moment but shook her head. Then she asked, "Shall I hate him for you?"

Aubrey stared. "Edmund, you mean?"

"Yes. Did he make you promises, or . . ."

Several memories competed in Aubrey's head at this. He blinked to clear them, and fresh tears fell onto his face.

"He's to be our next king," he said, using the handkerchief on himself. "And I'm the fourth son of a baronet. So, no. I do not require you to hate him." He folded the cloth in half. "Thank you, though."

"I understand some of what you are going through. I . . . don't hate James, either."

Now it was his turn to pick through his words. "I was under the impression that you were the one that broke that off."

She made a sound that could have been laughter but wasn't.

"Oh dear. I did, didn't I? I wanted to keep him, you see," she said, and was suddenly reformed in Aubrey's mind. "And even if I had thought he felt the same way, which I did not, it would not have been possible. That blasted bastard marquess would never have allowed his heir to marry the second daughter of middling merchants."

"He told you about his father, did he?"

"He didn't have to. I've met the man many times. My mother has business dealings with him. So I knew from the start it wouldn't work."

Aubrey wasn't sure if she was telling him all this to distract him or because she needed to share it, but he found himself leaning in to listen when she went on. "I tried to ignore James at first. But he was so . . . and then I thought, you only live once. A few months of unexpected happiness, and he will replace me, and I would have a story to tell my grandchildren. But I turned out to be terrible at having a fleeting romance."

She let out another not-laugh. "It was actually *you* that convinced me that I couldn't let it go on, you know. James told me he'd danced with you at Princess Alicia's ball—the one dance he danced that night—and then there you were in the paper, revealed as the prince's sweetheart. I had spent so long not thinking about the Viscount Malmsbury's actual position, letting him be James in my head instead of the next Marquess of Stratingford. I felt how much I had been lying to myself. His future was going to be intimacy with all the upper classes of society, and I did not belong there except to sell them things.

"I had planned it all out in my head, in case I was the one who had to end it. I can at least be proud that I did everything in the most correct fashion. I sent back his letters and asked for mine in return, all that sort of thing, like in a novel. But I am guessing you are not the sort of person to plan for the end of a love affair. Oh heavens," she added, because Aubrey had dropped his head as new tears came so quickly, his body shuddered. "I didn't mean to upset you."

"No," he said, taking a deep breath and deciding that they could take Edmund's letters away from him when he was *dead*, "I did not plan."

She smiled at him in a watery, fragile sort of way, and his heart broke a bit more. He put his arm around her, and his breathing eased, even though his ribs were hurting.

Rosalie stayed with him until the last possible moment before she had to leave for her own bed. Aubrey barely slept—how could he?—and spent the next few days following orders blindly and miserably. He did drills on muscle memory alone. He ate the tedious food without registering its taste, although perhaps this was a mercy. He got out of bed each morning, grateful that at least the night was over.

"I don't mean to come over all big-sisterly on you, especially since you're my superior officer, but you look like the walking dead," Rosalie said on their fourth evening back, "and I don't blame you, but if we were attacked now, you would probably die. Can I *please* fetch you something from the surgeon to help you sleep?"

Aubrey nodded dully, thinking that being unconscious sounded quite appealing by that point, before remembering that whatever it was would probably give him a vision. That thought held even more appeal. At least that would make Aubrey useful. He found himself thinking bitterly of the time Edmund had said he was worried that their association would reduce Aubrey. Now was the first time he had actually felt reduced.

Edmund had not even written. Or rather, no letter had arrived. Perhaps he had written. Surely he would have written. He must know that Aubrey had heard, that *everyone* had heard. Aubrey supposed he should feel humiliated and discarded, but mostly he felt like he had no idea how to stop loving his prince, even now that it hurt more than having his ribs broken; and that for Edmund it would have to be even worse, since Edmund was the one being forced to marry someone he didn't even know.

"Don't hate Edmund," he said to Rosalie when she reappeared with the bottle.

The lettuce tincture seemed fouler than the last time he'd taken one—at the palace, he remembered with a pang. Well, then, that was little wonder, he thought, since surely they had used the sweetest leaves nurtured by Edmund himself, while this stuff was probably made using whatever the army surgeons' assistants could find growing by the roadside.

He didn't think to ask if anything else was in it.

CHAPTER 19

He woke half the company when the vision came.

The approaching army was truly horrifying: automatons, but different from the clay ones Aubrey had seen before. Instead of mud, they were mostly made of dirty sand and driftwood, and sometimes there was a rock or large stone here and there. Aubrey was not sure if their placement was deliberate, or if these had merely come up with the rest of them as the army rose from the sea; a three-hour walk from Manogate, and yet they still stank like a beach covered in rotting things after a storm, trailing seaweed and broken shells the whole way and flattening everything in their path.

They were armed similarly to the strawmen that Aubrey had faced so many times, with rocks and sharp objects, but also chunks of ice. In fact, the creatures seemed to be held together with ice, which Aubrey had not seen the Honals use before.

There were so many of them.

Aubrey knew somehow, in the dream, that these were not controlled by one sorcerer. Instead, the vision showed him that five of the creatures were more finely wrought and much more humanlike in appearance, in the middle of the army. Unlike the featureless lumps the rest had as "heads," these had approximations of faces and wore Sabresian military uniforms, the striped signifiers of rank torn off, a rune painted on the left shoulder instead.

Three of these leaders possessed a human appendage: an eye, a hand, a section of scalp. The last two, trailing at the rear, looked to be simply splashed with blood, which left a gruesome trail of red-tinged water behind them.

Who had been mutilated for those . . . parts?

And where was the rest of their body?

It was just as well that Aubrey's horrified bellows woke so many people, however, for it meant that they were able to wake the other half, and everyone could arm themselves in time for the creatures' arrival. They were less than an hour away, by Aubrey's reckoning. Explosives were laid down along the path that he had seen them take.

He and the rest of the cavalry rode out, but this time his unit did not take up their usual position.

"You're to aim for the five leaders, since you know what they look like, and avoid engaging with the rest," Colonel Wyclef had told him when he went to report on what was coming, "and . . . what do you think? Aim for the runes on their shoulders and any human components you can see?"

"Yes, sir," Aubrey had replied. "Although . . . sir, I do not even know if we need to eliminate all five of them to deactivate the army. Perhaps each individual controls a different section."

"That would be convenient."

"Or perhaps they all have to be killed at the same time. Or perhaps they will just keep going until we find their sorcerer, who is missing an eye and a bit of scalp and a hand, and could be back in Honal. We just don't know, sir."

Colonel Wyclef had rubbed his hand over his face. "Well, we'll only find out by trying," he'd said, and clapped Aubrey on the back. "You've saved lives already tonight, Lieutenant. We would have been slaughtered in our beds otherwise."

Aubrey kept those words in mind when he rode out in front of his unit. He wished this damned battalion of monsters had at least had the courtesy to attack *after* he was recovered from his vision. He felt weak and sick, his body only staying on his horse through a combination of muscle memory and vanity. His mother's words, about how he and all sorts of other "inconvenient" people had been sent deliberately to this site and endangered on purpose, ran through his head.

His colonel seemed so . . . fatherly. He surely couldn't know about this scheme. Could he?

Perhaps Aubrey shouldn't worry about it. Now that Edmund was to marry Princess Ana, his mother's attempts to get him transferred might succeed, since he wouldn't still be considered a threat. Or perhaps he would always be one.

The call went out. "Enemy sighted!"

And then: "Approaching fast!"

Aubrey saw them all too soon: dark shapes, things that shouldn't have been able to move. He found panic building in his mind and the familiar urge to flee, as though from a landslide or a rockfall. He tamped the feelings down.

Then the mines went off and the burning arrows were loosed, and everything was chaos. Rubble seemed to fly in all places, and sand and smoke filled the air. Soldiers and horses were screaming or making other awful noises. Aubrey kept on having to stop himself from launching into the fray; they were to let the creatures go past them and move through the first large gap they saw near the center of the army, where he thought the five leaders were.

Except that there were no gaps. Aubrey looked for some other way in, cursing how unhelpful visions could be, but was distracted by the way the creatures behaved. He had not noticed it in his dream, but their approach was not like that of the strawmen or the other automatons he had seen. These were moving in groups of five, each group targeting one Sabresian soldier at a time, simply ignoring his or her fellows as they fought to defend their comrade, and then moving on to the next one. It seemed like a very thorough, systematic way to slaughter an army, rather than the chaotic nature of the monsters the Honals had sent before.

What had changed? He looked at the creatures, really looked at them now, but all he saw was driftwood and sand and—

Ice.

He had a sudden memory of the first time he had seen Prince Willard: pulling up water as steam and then freezing it all in an instant.

Prince Willard, who had now joined the Honals.

Aubrey physically recoiled. His horse moved backward in sympathy. Had the prince helped make this monstrous army that was systematically slaughtering his own country's soldiers?

"Yes," Rosalie called over from his left, misinterpreting Aubrey's movement, "that way isn't going to work. What if we ride further down? Do you remember which way you approached them in the vision?"

Aubrey shook his head and closed his eyes, trying to block out the noise around him and bring the dream back to his mind's eye; but all it gave him was an image of Edmund's uncle bumbling like an oaf through the officers' rest home.

They needed to work out how to stop this army, but right now Aubrey could barely work out anything. And the creatures were moving so fast.

He stopped trying to remember what the vision had looked like and started trying to reach for the smell of it, a trick Edmund's tutor Mrs. Grant had recommended in her meditation class, in what felt like another life. Except that all the scents he could remember—mud, horses, smoke, and the rotting seaweed smell of the creatures themselves—were all around him anyway, so it wasn't helping. He pulled the collar of his jacket up over his nose and mouth to try to block them out, closing his eyes, and knew immediately what was missing. Lavender and soap.

"The laundry, on the side entry to the barracks," he said to Rosalie, his eyes flying open. "They're there. They're already nearly at the city!"

He turned his horse, and his path was immediately blocked by one of the creatures.

Where there was one, there were five. He looked around and sure enough, there they were, trying to surround him. Within seconds, Rosalie had both her pistols out and shot the one ahead of him. Before waiting for that to have an effect—it didn't—she pulled out her sword and started slashing at the one closest to her, trying to stop it fencing him in; but he didn't even have enough room now to turn his mare.

Aubrey pulled out both of his own pistols and shot the biggest one in its ice "neck," all the while cursing himself for *closing his eyes* on the outskirts of a *battle*, but the bullets did nothing but chip off some of the frozen water. He was wondering what the creatures would do if he simply leapt from his horse, vaulted over them and ran, when the largest one raised its clublike arm. It had an enormous chunk of ice upon it, and he felt a phantom ache in his side.

Not again.

He pulled out his sword, wondering if the steel would just break when he tried to block the blow with it—and then all five of the creatures fell into a heap of sand and rocks and driftwood, their ice suddenly melted water.

Aubrey let out a shaky, relieved exclamation just as he heard a triumphant noise behind him.

"The left shoulder of the central figure!" Rosalie bellowed out. "A slice with a blade across the left shoulder will disrupt the magic! There must be a rune there!"

Rosalie's advice was suddenly being shouted out around the battle, and sand and rocks and lumps of wood were flying everywhere now. He wheeled his horse in the opposite direction and motioned to his unit to follow him. They had to get back to the barracks.

They arrived at the laundry in time to see an infantry captain—the very same friend of Aubrey's who had given him the newspaper when he had gotten back to camp—trying to lead his unit through a row of creatures standing like a wall. They were large, and Aubrey couldn't see past them, but he knew in his bones that the five leaders were behind them. The creatures were standing at attention, blocking the way completely and ignoring the soldiers in front of them as though they were not there.

They were about fifty yards away, so Aubrey did not hear the news get to the captain on how to stop the creatures, but he saw the man turn to listen to someone, look relieved, and pull out a knife, slashing into the shoulder of the largest creature in front of him.

He had picked correctly; five of the sand creatures fell apart, revealing another row of them behind briefly, until the five to the left and the five to the right of the captain sprang to life and charged, bashing at him. The soldiers with him started slashing at shoulders with their knives, but even more of the guard were activating now.

Rosalie made to urge her horse on faster to help them.

"No, Ensign." The words cost Aubrey something as they came out. "Our orders are to stop the five leaders. We need to see how those guards react."

He guided his unit to halt for some cover behind the nearest structure, one of the timber watchtowers. Above them, they could hear the gunmen inside it firing shots into the fight. Aubrey took the opportunity to reload his own pistols as he tried to think. His hands were trembling.

One of his ensigns asked, "Can anyone work out why the sharpshooters have had no luck targeting the five leaders from up there?"

"Look at the angle," someone else said. "The creatures guarding them are so tall, they're blocking the shot."

"If only we had grenadiers up there, they could have thrown explosives down onto them."

"Our camp was allocated mine-makers instead," Aubrey said absent-mindedly, because he'd noticed something too. "Look. The sharpshooters must have seen how everyone has been destroying the creatures. They've started aiming for the shoulders of the guard."

The creatures were now going down rapidly in fives, and this time their fellows couldn't immediately start bashing their attackers. Ten guards peeled away and made for the tower—and for Aubrey and his team—but the sharpshooters reduced them to sand almost immediately. Aubrey saw the way the opening would appear before it happened, because this was the angle he had seen in his vision.

"Shooting formation," he called out, pulling out his rifle. "We are going to have to trust the tower will give us cover. Fire at any one of the five leaders the moment you see clear shots, because they won't be open long. Aim for the human body parts or the left shoulders. Fire when ready."

As he finished speaking, he saw the moment—a mere sliver of time—when he had a chance at that horrible bit of human scalp. He braced himself and pulled the trigger.

He missed. But then not half a moment later, someone to his left let out a cry of triumph.

"Well done!" Aubrey cried, watching one of the blood-soaked leaders crumble and fall. The remaining four were blocked from sight again by the huge sand creatures almost immediately, although Aubrey fancied that they were moving more slowly now. This was not much comfort, however; two more groups headed toward them, and this time their "faces" were set not at the tower, but at them.

"Stay resolved!" Aubrey called out as he reloaded his rifle. "We are being covered by the tower. Continue focusing on the four remaining leaders."

Even as he said it, one lot of the automatons coming toward them was brought down by a sharpshooter, as well as two more groups around the remaining leaders, creating a larger gap than before. Aubrey's unit could now see the four remaining creatures clearly, and be seen in return.

Each one of the creatures flicked their sand-and-wood faces with precision in Aubrey's direction. The one with a human hand raised its arm and pointed right at him. It was horrifying, nightmarish, and Aubrey's entire torso shuddered—and then froze, because Aubrey could see the hand clearly now, down to the burn scar covering the back and leading around the side.

That was Prince Willard's hand. Or it had been.

Then someone to Aubrey's left shot the hand off, and the creature exploded in a spray of dirty sand and ice turning to water.

The second blood-soaked creature went down a moment later. Aubrey made himself concentrate.

"We're nearly there!" he called out. "Hold the formation!"

They held, even when every last one of the guards that were left came to life and turned in their direction. Dozens of blank faces focused their way. Aubrey considered issuing the order to retreat . . . except the creatures were moving very, very slowly now.

That was reassuring for perhaps one heartbeat, maybe two. And then Aubrey realized that these slow creatures were not preparing to attack. They were getting out of the way of the two remaining leaders.

These were not moving slowly.

"Hold!" Aubrey yelled, since the horses were shying. And then it was Aubrey's own horse shifting, in response to some movement Aubrey had made, because he could now see the color of the eye lodged into the sand creature's head, and his stomach contracted, feeling like it was full of poison.

The iris was the same cold, light hazel that he had so recently encountered, when that eye had still been in Edmund's uncle's face.

It hit him properly then: the dreadful confirmation of who exactly had been carved up to animate this army had his head reeling, his vision blurring, because the Honals were disgusting, they were *disgusting.* Using people in this way was repulsive and sickening; that had been Prince Willard's eye, that had been his *eye*—

Then a bullet went straight into it, and whatever was left was presumably falling onto the ground with the rest of the creature, lost in a pile of sand. The last leader collapsed at almost the same moment, shot by someone in the tower. Triumphant, relieved whooping started up, and the sudden sounds of the entire remaining enemy army falling to pieces, rocks and lumps of wood thudding onto the mud.

It was over.

Aubrey felt nauseated. Someone slapped him on the back, and he worried he might be sick, but the sting from his ribs at the jostle was enough to distract him. Relieved laughter rang out all around him, and the cry of "Victory!" went out over the camp.

"I am so proud of you all," he said, between deep breaths, clinging to his reins. He hoped that he didn't sound as sick and hollow as he felt.

The battle was over, but as usual, that was not the end of it. Wet piles of sand and rocks were everywhere, for a start, but that could wait; what was more pressing was that a quick head count revealed that more than a quarter of the battalion had been lost and another quarter injured.

Aubrey told his unit to take care of their horses and then go to help dig the grave; it would be the largest one yet. He then went to talk to the colonel in his office.

The man was dictating dispatches to be sent to the War Office at first light—not far off now—detailing the battle and how the creatures had been defeated, in case of similar attack elsewhere, and outlining the garrison's urgent need for medical aid and reinforcements.

Aubrey felt very awkward interrupting, but the colonel motioned for his scribe to stop writing immediately. "I hear your unit outdid themselves, Ainsley. Well done. Did you need something?"

Aubrey explained his theory about Prince Willard as efficiently as he could.

"I think that's how they were able to use the ice, sir, to bind the creatures. The eye I saw . . . it was the same pale hazel His Highness has—*had*. And that was definitely his hand with that scar on the back. I needed you to know, sir."

"You're sure?" the colonel said, staring at him in dismay, but then added, "Oh no, of course, you'd be familiar with the royal family."

Aubrey went very still, trying to work out the implication behind the words. Had they sounded pitying? To his humiliation, tears started to build in Aubrey's eyes. He risked glancing sideways at the man's secretary, still present; she was tidying the desk and focusing on everything but himself and the colonel. Aubrey straightened his spine, lifting his chin up defiantly, but then Colonel Wyclef shook his head and said, "I had already commended you for a decoration, Lieutenant, but I am going to do so again after tonight."

Aubrey stared, since none of this followed. The man seemed to see that he wasn't making sense to him and went on with "Even without your vision-dream, it was your ensign who discovered the trick with the rune on the left shoulder, yes? And your unit that worked so well together with the tower shooters to take out those five monsters. Whatever might be happening in your—your personal life—your leadership is making a real difference here, son. I will pass everything that you did on, and hopefully it will help other sites. Now get to bed, Ainsley. You look exhausted."

Aubrey tried to follow orders, but when he lay down in his bed, he couldn't sleep. He watched the gray light come around the window drapes as it got stronger and stronger and finally became recognizable as the dawn. The colonel's kind words had been unexpected. They tied themselves into knots in his head as the sun rose.

Eventually he got up and went to his writing table. There was something he had been trying not to do for weeks, but after the last few days, he decided that enough was enough. He pulled out a letter he had been working on the previous evening and added a postscript:

> *Malmy—write to her. Things are awful enough without needless heartbreak as well.*

CHAPTER 20

Captain Walsh had been killed in the attack, and so Aubrey and his unit were handed over to a new captain the next afternoon. Captain Trestall was a black-haired man some ten years or so Aubrey's senior, full of praise for his new team's actions during the previous night's battle. All Aubrey could think about were the shots he had missed, how he hadn't known what to do, how his hands had shaken. He should have been better. All those weeks of recuperating must have weakened his skills, he thought. He trudged into the eating hall feeling like a useless fraud.

Rosalie flopped a copy of the paper in front of him as he picked at his dinner.

"Six other sites were attacked by sand creatures, but they didn't print many details. Did you want to see?"

Aubrey shook his aching head.

"There isn't anything in there about . . . Nordan."

Aubrey raised his eyes long enough to smile at Rosalie weakly. He shook his head again, putting his fork down. Everything tasted odd as well as bland today.

Wait, he thought.

"Rosalie," he asked. "What did you fetch for me last night, to help me sleep?"

She blinked at him. "A lettuce tincture from the surgeon."

"No, it wasn't. Did you give me poppy?"

"Of course not! I've just spent weeks watching you refuse it at the home! I asked the surgeon for lettuce, for sleep. I specifically said it was for you, and that it could therefore *not* have poppy."

He looked at her—at her straightforward face—and nodded.

"Would you mind doing the same thing for me again tonight?" he asked carefully. "And could you ask for a second one for yourself?"

She nodded, her expression turning indignant as she took his meaning. Indignation gave way to outrage at bedtime, however, when she tasted the contents of both the vials she had been given—labeled with their names—and confirmed that they were indeed different.

"Should we tell the colonel?" she asked, her tone dubious. She was generally suspicious of authority figures: one of the many qualities Aubrey admired about her.

"The colonel may very well have given them the orders to do it," he replied slowly, thinking with a wrench about the conversations he had had with the man over the last day. "He may have been following orders himself, to make sure Seers are dosed at any opportunity."

Rosalie's face went stony. "Can you send these to your mother? Did you not say she works at the War Office? This is against the law!"

"Mmm. I might have to keep them until I can see her in person. I can hardly send them by the post—too risky."

Rosalie insisted on staying with Aubrey until the last possible minute that night, even though neither actually imagined someone was going to come and shove tinctures down his throat. Heavens knew what she would have done, Aubrey thought, if he'd also told her that they had both been deliberately placed here in the hopes that they might be killed.

Aubrey still hadn't decided how to deal with that, now that he was back. His mother had said not to tell anyone, but just to make sure not to put himself in any vulnerable positions. He had quietly determined that he would keep an eye out for bad leadership decisions and any other ways the soldiers here were being sabotaged. He had been too distracted over the last few days to do any such thing, but he resolved, as he locked the little bottles away in his trunk, to focus on that goal instead of thinking about anything to do with foreign countries or Edmund getting married.

More details were released over the next few days regarding the other sites attacked by the new automatons. It looked like Aubrey's garrison, despite its heavy losses, had fared quite well, comparatively. There were other camps, closer to the Helm, that had been all but wiped out. Troops across the country were being rearranged because there had been so many deaths.

When reinforcements arrived at Manogate, Aubrey was both dismayed and delighted to find that they included Wilson's company. Two hours passed before they actually got to greet each other, and that was over luncheon. Aubrey was not even done hugging his brother before Wilson asked, "Have you heard about Malmy?"

Aubrey pulled back, his lips suddenly numb. His dread must have shown in his face, because Wilson quickly went on with "No, he's fine—I'm sorry—it's his father. And his half brother. They're dead."

"His—what? What happened?"

Wilson produced a news clipping. "I only know from this," Wilson said. "We had the morning papers before we left our camp, but it doesn't seem like yours have arrived yet. Here."

MARQUESS OF STRATINGFORD AND SON KILLED IN SAND CREATURE ATTACKS

It is with the deepest sympathy for the family that this paper reports the death of Gordon Malmsbury, the ninth Marquess of Stratingford. His lordship was killed along with his fourteen-year-old son Walter and several servants at the Stratingford estate on what is being called "the night of red sand" due to the amount of bloodshed it saw. Lord Stratingford is believed to have taken his son and several servants out to investigate the noise of the approaching Honal army as it made its way from the coast past Malmsbury Manor to its ultimate destination of Drestham.

The marquessate's heir, James Malmsbury, has been serving as a lieutenant with the Second Battalion. It is expected that his lordship will take leave, however, to attend to the legal and practical matters that now fall to him. The vast Stratingford estate supports the war effort in multiple ways, including the running of a prisoner-of-war camp.

Aubrey put the clipping down on the table.

"That's all very sad," he said.

"The marquess was an utter bastard," Wilson said.

"Yes, but he still didn't deserve to go like that. And poor Walter. Do you remember that one time we got to see him? Such a little thing, sucking his thumb on his mother's lap in the coach the only year she ever came to pick Malmy up. And now he's gone. The whole thing is awful."

"I wonder what Malmy will do about her? His stepmother, I mean. There's no love lost there. I hope he throws her out."

"No," Aubrey said automatically. "That would mean cutting out his half sisters as well. He won't do that. Especially not while they're all in mourning."

Wilson studied him for a moment.

"You're always so good, Aubrey," he said.

Aubrey's eyes widened in surprise and then narrowed with suspicion, because he was unclear on whether his brother had meant that to be complimentary or not, but then Wilson asked abruptly, "Has the prince written to you?"

"Just don't, Wils. Oh, but if you want to get angry, listen to this," he said, and then told him about the tinctures he had been given.

"Are there Seers with you?" he asked Wilson's shocked face. "Someone should warn them. Would they listen to you? Do you know any of them?"

Wilson seemed torn. "Are you sure? Sure that it was on purpose?"

"Yes," Aubrey said, annoyed by the question. He tried to make himself remember that Wilson loved rules and authority, that he had wanted to go into the military since they were small. It would be hard for him to accept how far from perfect it was. The thought just annoyed Aubrey even more, however, given that this was his own brother, and after all this time at war, Aubrey would have hoped his eyes had been opened to a few things.

So he added, "Perhaps I shouldn't even mind, since it helped. I ought to go ask for it again. What good am I to anyone if I won't do everything necessary to help my country?"

"Don't you—" Wilson said, but then to Aubrey's surprise, stopped himself. He took a deep breath and looked at Aubrey for a moment—a long, level look—and then said, "Do you remember the ball for Princess Charlotte's engagement?"

"Do I remember the night I met Edmund? Are you attempting to be humorous for once, Wilson?"

Wilson huffed. "I meant, do you remember the *specifics* of it? Do you remember that after the explosion, he wouldn't leave your side? He insisted that the doctor inspect you first and hovered around you like he was afraid you'd vanish. It was like he already knew, and you'd barely spoken to him for five minutes."

"I did also break my arm saving him heroically from an explosion," Aubrey said. "Don't forget that bit."

His brother huffed again. "What I'm getting at is—he's yours, Aubrey. The entire barracks at Craywick knew it, even if they weren't sure as to his intentions toward you. But, you know, before this . . . Nordish business . . . half of my company seemed to think you two were as good as engaged? Only the other day, I had an ensign I'd never spoken to before come up to me as saucy as anything and say, 'Isn't your brother going to be the next queen of Saben?'"

"Oh no. You didn't hit her, did you?"

"No, you and John would have been very proud of me. I just told her that I didn't think 'queen' was the correct term. She said that from the papers, you seemed pretty enough. I told her I didn't think she was your type, if that was what she was after."

"Oh very nice! Did she hit you after that?"

"No, she just said blonds weren't *her* type and left."

Aubrey looked at him. "So . . . she sought you out, told you saucily that non-blonds were her type, and . . . left."

Wilson stared blankly.

"You're not blond, Wilson," he elaborated.

Wilson stared at him some more.

"I expect that this ensign was *flirting with you*," Aubrey said very slowly, and Wilson's face erupted in red splotches, his eyes huge. Aubrey laughed. "Who was she? Was her pedigree not fancy enough to tempt you into following her to ask what else she didn't like in a man?"

Wilson blustered for a moment or two and then said, "This is irrelevant. We aren't talking about *me*. I am trying to remind you that Prince Edmund loves you, no matter what happens with the Nordans—"

"No, no, this is much better for cheering me up. Tell me what other women you've obliviously insulted as they tried to make romantic overtures to you. Will you introduce me to them? I think John was wrong, and *you're* the innocent of the family. Or did he take you on a trip to an assignation house as well?"

"A *what*?"

The night continued on much like this, and Aubrey laughed more than he had in days. He felt much better when he lay down in bed that night, until his brain reminded him that Wilson hadn't quite been barking up the right tree. Aubrey didn't need reassuring that Edmund loved him; he knew he did. But Edmund was the country's next king.

He should have faced reality earlier, planned for their eventual parting, been more like Rosalie. He had been selfish to imagine he could keep such an important man to himself. This really was always how it had been going to end, no matter what romantic fantasy they'd let themselves believe. They were going to be separated, and he needed to accept that fact.

He could do that.

But not with grace.

And so the next day, when Colonel Wyclef approached him for a special undertaking, Aubrey was in exactly the right frame of mind to accept.

"I won't lie to you, my boy," the colonel said. "This is strictly volunteer only. It will be dangerous. In the reshuffling, we've all been called upon to send our most suitable people for a special force near the border. You could make a real difference. If, however, you don't feel up for it—"

"Ready for duty, sir. What's the mission?"

CHAPTER 21

Wilson was outraged to learn that Aubrey was being reposted. "What? Two of us were finally in the same battalion—I asked for the Third especially—and now they're *moving* you?"

"Oh please," Aubrey said. "You won't be lonely. Try not to put *all* the ladies off, won't you? Perhaps don't speak too much." And then, at his face: "I'll ask Rosalie to take care of you. Do not bring up Malmy, though, whatever you do."

Aubrey set off before daylight the next morning with two others from the camp: an infantry private he had never spoken to, who had to be given a horse, and a Lieutenant Burney, whom he knew well enough to swap words with. They rode north all day and stopped not at the local barracks but at a private hunting lodge that smelled of must and possibly also of rats. The entrance hall was all dark timber and antlers. A servant showed him through to the main room, which was also all dark timber and antlers. Another ten soldiers were already there, and a surprise in the shape of their leader.

Aubrey stood there, dumbfounded. "John?"

His eldest brother smirked and then came forward to hug him. Aubrey met him halfway. He hadn't seen John in perhaps half a year. He felt his eyes prickling a little but didn't want to cry, since he wasn't sad. He channeled the feelings into holding John tighter instead.

"I really do feel like the colonel might have mentioned that my own brother was in charge of the hush-hush assignment he was sending me on."

"He wouldn't have known, I expect. Hush-hush and all that," John said, guiding him away from the others and through to a smaller room. It was paneled in the same dark wood as everywhere else but mercifully free of antlers; otherwise they might have poked their eyes out. "Mother says hello. I've been working with her a bit."

"And now my own mother! I only saw her a few weeks ago!" Aubrey said. At John's raised eyebrow, he added, "Yes I know, hush-hush."

John closed the door behind them. "Speaking of hush-hush, are you all right? After all this business with Prince Edmund and the Nordans?"

John sounded *casual* of all things, his usual drawl unchanged. Aubrey suddenly felt trapped in this small room.

"The crown prince will do his duty," Aubrey hedged, wondering what John was getting at, since he must know how Aubrey felt; but John looked at him in surprise.

"What? I thought he called our ambassador a disgusting old pimp and told the Nordans he wasn't for sale!"

Aubrey felt even more pinned to the spot. "He what?"

John's eyes narrowed. "Have you not heard from him?"

"No! Explain immediately!"

"I was told that he froze the place with icy winds, shouted at the officials, and then offered the princess sanctuary if she didn't want to go back to parents who would hand her over to a grown man. Did you know they specified in the contract that the marital consummation could be delayed until she was older, but had to occur before she was seventeen? The whole thing was very badly done, not at all the way we do things here, and the prince made his displeasure well known. The minister for foreign affairs was there too, and she's supposed to have yelled at the ambassador as well."

Aubrey allowed himself a moment to stare. He felt it was warranted. Then he said, "I refuse to believe Edmund used the word 'pimp.'"

"Well"—his brother waved a graceful hand—"I'm paraphrasing. Have you not seen today's paper?"

"I've been riding all day to get *here*!"

John pulled a page of newsprint out of an inside pocket and then, ignoring Aubrey's outstretched hand, started reading out loud with what Aubrey considered unnecessary relish:

UNEXPECTED SETBACK FOR BRAZEN NORDISH OFFER

Nordan's offer to supply Saben with supplies and troops in exchange for the hand of Crown Prince Edmund being given to their princess Ana—which has been damned by multiple quarters as an attempt to manipulate the fact that we are at war for Nordan's own gain—has been thwarted by the existence of a prior claim.

"His Highness requested that the parliament consider Lord Aubrey Ainsley as a consort for him several months ago," the prime minister, Lord Dell, said to

> assembled members of the press this morning.
>
> "Given that we have had more pressing decisions to make of late, we have not yet come to a decision, but this means that we are unable to consider Nordan's offer, because—as specified in our Royal Marriages Act—the members may only evaluate one proposed partner per royal family member at any given time."

He paused to see Aubrey's reaction to these words. Aubrey closed his mouth and squinted at the paper.

"That can't be a rule," he declared. "They've just made that up."

John gave him a look and continued:

> The news was met by the assembled press with a delight that reached fever pitch when Lord Dell went on to say that the parliament was furthermore not predisposed to consider favorably any negotiations with any nation only interested in offering assistance in exchange for a place on Saben's throne.

He put the paper down, pretending to ignore Aubrey's hand sneaking out to claim it. "It was a very neat solution. There is speculation that the queen intervened. She was in the capital at the time, and everyone says she was fuming; she destroyed at least three antique rugs by accidentally causing fires to leap out of their grates."

"How do you know all of this?" Aubrey demanded. "Is the royal family constantly surrounded by *spies*?"

John rolled his eyes.

"You know they are," he said. "Now, is it true? Was the prime minister only saying it as a convenient way to save face in the wake of Prince Edmund's refusal, or *did* he officially petition for you?"

Aubrey raised his chin and produced his best wounded-but-still-dignified expression. "He did, thank you very much."

"Mother didn't seem to know. You didn't tell her?"

Aubrey blinked at him. "I didn't tell anyone. It seemed easier that way, in case we were denied. I thought we would be, and at least . . . nobody would know. But that's done with now, isn't it?"

Aubrey moved his eyes to the wood paneling. Finding nothing to distract him there, he started to inspect the threadbare carpet on the floor instead. John put a hand on his shoulder.

"You," he said, "were never interested in taking easy paths. Come, let's join the others. Discuss the plan for tomorrow."

The plan for tomorrow was outrageous.

It was rather thrilling, really.

John's calm explanation of it to the assembled ragtag was met with a shocked silence that lasted, Aubrey thought, an impressive amount of time. Finally, a too-young-looking private cleared her throat and said, "The Hare's Wood? We have to go through one of the haunted forests?"

"That's right." John's smile was languid, as though challenging them to admit they were afraid. "Then we use a bridge that has been built over a sparse section of the Honals' poisonous thorn bushes, and we climb a small way—it's not steep—to get to a crevice in the Helm. There's a smuggler's path straight through to Honal from there."

"It's suicide," she said flatly. She turned to the rest of the group. "Have any of you been trained in this sort of thing? Because I haven't."

"Almost all," John said delicately, "of Saben's specially trained soldiers, who would normally be sent on this sort of mission, have either disappeared or been killed. New ones are being recruited and trained. In the meantime, you were all recommended as quick thinkers, good fighters, good shots. Survivors who can work well in a group. I think we can do this."

He unrolled a map and weighed three of the corners down with various things from the table: a tankard, a flask, a wooden bowl of apples. The fourth corner curled, but that didn't seem to bother John.

"Scouts were sent in three weeks ago via the route we are taking," he said, running his finger along the thick paper, "to see if they could find the caves containing the Honals' magic water, which are supposed to be near there. They did not return."

Aubrey removed one of the apples from the bowl and put it down on the corner of the map that had been curling up. His brother gave him the briefest of looks from under his eyebrows. A pale, wiry, red-headed woman who had arrived late, not in uniform, said, "In that case, would not another route be better? There's one about ten miles west of here."

Everyone else stared at her.

"Former smuggler," she added, shrugging.

"What did you smuggle?" Aubrey asked immediately.

"Oh, all sorts. Spirits, oil, Sabresian books—"

"Books?"

"Stop," John said. "Don't distract him with books. Yes, Miss Fletcher, we know that there are other routes in; we have used several of them. Don't think you're the first smuggler we've had. This group's task is to see if anything went wrong with this route," he said, pointing to the map for emphasis. "We must find out if this path is still safe to use and see if we can work out what happened to our missing predecessors. Which brings us all to your first order: if we are ambushed, attacked with magic, or anything else, do not stand and fight. You turn tail and run, and go straight to one of the regrouping points to report what happened. Do not stay to help anyone else. The mission takes precedence."

Aubrey peered around; no one else seemed as disturbed as he was by this command. They were all nodding grimly. He returned his gaze to his brother to find him looking straight at him.

"No heroics," John said pointedly.

Aubrey put his hands up in surrender. "Whatever you say," he said.

John's mouth thinned, but he continued.

"We leave the horses with the servants in the wood. We travel on foot through the mountain all day. We sleep in the caves here"—he pointed to a spot on the map, and then a second one—"and then travel the route they were to take—a twenty-mile walk—the next day, leaving before dawn. I will be sending pairs back at certain points to report that we made it to particular locations."

John read out the names of those who were to report back; Aubrey's was not among them. He was to stay with John to the end, along with Fletcher the smuggler and another fellow.

"If the last of us make it to this point without finding anything"—John pointed to another spot on the map—"then we are authorized to complete the original mission, which was to see if that is the location of the Honals' magical pool. If at any point we find our missing spies, we are only to attempt rescue if an easy opportunity presents itself. Let me be clear: Saben has spent this entire war losing soldiers to missions like these and so now, information is our *only* goal. We are a small team for that reason: so we can sneak into Honal and then sneak out again. We see what's there. We bring the knowledge home. A team tailored to deal with whatever we find can then act on that knowledge.

No heroics," John repeated, this time addressing everyone.

They all nodded, glancing at each other.

"I assume we aren't going like this?" Aubrey asked, plucking at the gold braid on his jacket.

John smiled.

"I have plain fustian and woolen clothes for the group. If anyone happens to see us, they should assume we are simple Honal workers. Try not to speak and give the game away with your accents. Take your pistols and knives, but no rifles. Conceal them well."

"Can I keep my sword?" Aubrey asked. "I"—*am supposed to kill a man with it*—"had a vision of myself with it; I've been making sure to always have it with me."

"I don't think it works like that," an ash-haired lieutenant said in what Aubrey considered an unnecessarily patronizing tone.

"Actually, it works exactly like that," Private Smith said. "I'm a Seer as well. And one man with a sword will not look out of place in a party of this size. Sir," she added, nodding at John.

"Quite right," he said. "Now, to bed everyone; we'll be up early to discuss the finer details."

Aubrey slept well that night and woke up feeling more refreshed than he had all week. His ribs weren't even aching. He stared at the cobwebbed ceiling above him and pictured Edmund telling the ambassador to Nordan that he would not be accepting his deal. Edmund could be so forceful when he was angry. Aubrey got up, grinning.

He enjoyed the ride north; he had never been so close to the border. He finally saw a proper moor, covered in patches of wildflowers and purple heather, and found himself wanting to spout poetry but wasn't sure the present company would appreciate it. This was a serious mission after all.

"Call it no wasteland," an unexpected, soft voice said somewhere behind Aubrey. It was that young private whose name Aubrey still didn't know. "For it brings forth a bounty, still. No timber it yields, no feast for the belly, but harvests its worth to the eye, for the mind."

"And its gentle slopes," Aubrey called back, "provide gentleness to the soul in kind."

Fletcher, the smuggler, started up a dirty limerick then, and everybody laughed. Aubrey was glad that the mood felt lighter as they rode into the Hare's Wood.

At least for a while.

The light dimmed rapidly due to a combination of the shadow cast by the Helm and the leafy canopy of the forest. Aubrey looked around; the trunks of the neighboring trees were so twisted, they should not have been able to grow so tall, and yet they seemed to go up forever. There was a smell of damp and trampled mulch and of mushrooms, which made Aubrey's skin prickle. A green hue tinged everything, making their surroundings seem even more goblinish and strange.

They rode on. Occasionally someone would point to a long-ruined hut covered in spiderwebs and vines. Aubrey could not imagine any human voluntarily living here. Everywhere there were the sounds of owls and other birds and some small creatures moving in the trees and the undergrowth, rustling unpredictably. Their chittering seemed all around them.

The acoustics, Aubrey thought. *It is only the echoes of the forest.*

Nobody was talking. Something kept on catching at John's attention, to their right. He motioned that they should all quicken their pace. Aubrey thought he saw the flash of red eyes everywhere now that they were moving faster. The sounds of their horses' breath and the jangling of gear all seemed so loud that the Honals would surely hear them coming all the way on the other side of the mountain. A mist started at some point, which made visibility even worse. Sparc, ghostly tendrils quickly became great pockets of the stuff, which the eerie light tinged yellow, like old paper.

It took Aubrey a while to notice that there was something wrong, since everything had seemed wrong for hours. He would remind himself later that he could hardly see and that nobody had been speaking. But when a bird swooped over John and he did not react, Aubrey called out to him.

He received no response.

"John?" Aubrey called again. "Are you asleep?"

His brother remained silent.

Aubrey looked around behind him. The group had fallen more or less into single or double file, as the terrain was so uneven; as he shifted to better see the others, all he saw were blank faces and empty eyes.

The mist. Was it the mist? Was this the Monium fog? He was about to turn around again, afraid of being noticed by the bewitched sleepwalkers he found himself among, except that the other Seer, Private Smith, caught his eye.

She shook her head tightly at him.

He nonchalantly moved to face ahead again, his stomach unclenching the smallest amount in relief, because he was not alone. He let his horse fall back a little. The three soldiers in between Smith and himself went past without sparing him a glance. He pulled in next to her.

"Do we continue to play along and see where this takes us," he murmured, staring straight ahead as if they were not speaking, "or should we attempt an escape?"

She nodded, a single twitch he caught out of the corner of his eye. "We know now what happened to the other team. We should both go back."

He risked a glance at the woman. Her face was gray, and her grip was so tight on her reins that it looked painful. It was a stark contrast to the others; their hands were almost slack.

"You go." Aubrey had to force the words out, since he very much wanted to go as well. "I will follow once I have a fuller story to tell."

She held his eyes for a moment. "No heroics," she said.

He couldn't help the huff of laughter that came out of him.

"No heroics," he replied.

She seemed to believe him, if the shaky breath she let out was anything to go by. She gave him a tiny nod and then pulled her horse slowly to the side and back, just as he had, to get to her. He kept his gaze ahead, but in another minute or so, Aubrey was sure he heard her galloping away. He glanced around, but no one else had reacted to her departure.

Miss Fletcher was now behind him. Last night, the woman had been confident to the point of cockiness, her movements broad and her voice sharp. Now her face was as vacant as that of a strawman, and the effect disturbed and alarmed something deep in Aubrey's own consciousness. The urge came strongly upon him to turn his horse around and follow the other Seer after all, but he repressed that instinct. He was a soldier, and he had a job to do. Private Smith could report that they had encountered the fog before they were even through the forest; discovering where everyone went afterward would mean a much faster rescue.

Assuming that they were not gunned down the moment they all got there.

Aubrey was surprised to see the group make its way through the gap in the poisonous thorn bushes as planned, although they did not leave the horses with the servants since the servants had been enchanted as well and were therefore climbing up into the crevice along with the rest.

Their mounts were simply left wherever they happened to be standing when their riders disembarked. Aubrey copied the behavior, hoping his horse would be here when he came back.

If he came back.

He climbed up to the crevice behind everyone else.

Aubrey's calves started aching after a few hours, then his feet. At one point they had to scramble up a tricky incline that seemed to go on forever; at another, the way through was so narrow that it was barely more than a crack. He squeezed himself through, grateful for the rough cloth he was wearing, the hardy boots, the thick gloves. Worse was to come; there was a long stretch where the rocky path was wet, streaked with a stinking yellow-brown slime. They went on and on, continually catching themselves as they slipped, and Aubrey resented the defilement of his footwear as much as the smell.

When they all came out the other side, Aubrey allowed himself one relieved breath, then two; and then a little thrill passed through him.

He was in *Honal.*

He'd never been outside Saben. Whenever he had pictured himself leaving the country, it had been in a civilized manner involving luggage and guides and papers dutifully handed to officials with seals, not . . . sneaking into an enemy state. He felt the adventure of what he was doing, just as he felt its danger.

Aubrey took a moment to beat the dust off himself and slide the sides of his shoes along the grass to remove any traces of the unpleasantness he had walked through. Nobody else on the team had done even that much. They continued to walk without a care for Aubrey's boots or their own, in single file, toward a larger patch of the mist to their right.

This was the first deviation from the original plan. At this point, they had been supposed to find a cave to camp in overnight. Aubrey pulled out his canteen and took a long draft, considering his options. He could follow them and see where they ended up. Or he could stick to his orders: rest and then head east to the spot they were meant to investigate. If he were to adhere to the plan's intention completely, however, he should go no farther at all but head back and report that they had all made it through the crevice, that the crevice was not the problem.

Except . . . that was his brother, leading the mindless march.

Aubrey packed his canteen away and joined the line of Sabresians now heading east. He didn't plan to lose them in the fog.

CHAPTER 22

Three hours later, they were still walking, but uphill now. Aubrey's mind was screaming at him to stop. Not because he was scared, and not because he was exhausted and his ribs hurt and his feet hurt and his legs hurt—even though all those things were true—but because the sun was setting.

He should find somewhere to sleep, go back through the crevice into Saben, and report to the rendezvous point. It would be the responsible thing. It would be the logical thing, even. Stumbling around in the dark would be ridiculous.

He kept on walking. He couldn't leave his team here, magicked, heading toward heaven knew what, although the irony was not lost on him of them all being forced to march in the same direction that they had planned to go in voluntarily.

Eventually, though, everyone stopped on their own. Aubrey surveyed the landscape. The cliffs of the Helm to the right and scrubby trees to the left, just as there had been for hours and hours. He couldn't see anything that could have triggered the group to stop walking—but then he saw movement ahead of him: soldiers, at least four of them, in brown uniforms. He spent a half second calculating if he could pass as a mindless drone and then ducked behind a ridge in the rock face, just wide enough to hide a man.

"Oh look. Saben has sent us more recruits," a voice said dryly. It sounded like a woman of about his mother's age. "I wonder where these ones came from?"

"I stopped caring how they get through months ago," a second female voice said. "Let's just get them to the General. Is this all of them? We had stragglers last time."

The General.

Aubrey was struck with three certainties in that moment: he absolutely did not want to go with these women, especially if they were going to see one of the Honal leaders; he had no faith that he would be able to help anyone on his own; and he now had a solid piece of information on top of what Private Smith would have reported. It would be useful for the military to know that his enchanted fellows had walked in the direction of the coast, been taken possession of by Honal soldiers after some ten miles, and then handed to the General. He could bring that intelligence home with his conscience clear, especially since there was nothing he would be able to accomplish here by himself, other than perhaps be caught. Going back was the right choice, even with his own brother in the group—a brother who had, in fact, made him promise not to try any heroics and insisted that knowledge was all that they were supposed to gain from this mission. He had outright ordered them all to head back at the first sign of trouble.

As Aubrey inched his head around to get a peek at the Honal soldiers who were taking possession of his comrades in arms so as to confirm that there were four of them, he was certain of one more thing: he could not leave.

He whipped his head back out of sight and pressed his forehead against the rock, screwing his eyes closed, screwing up his whole face. He wanted to scream. He couldn't think his way out of this; he was too tired and afraid and conflicted, and his ribs hurt.

What would Edmund do?

Edmund . . . would use his gift for his country. *It's what I'm for,* he had said. But if Edmund had been here, he could have just made it rain and freed everyone from the enchantment they were under. Aubrey couldn't do that. The Sight couldn't help in an emergency, unless one had Seen—

Aubrey opened his eyes and stared at the cliff face that he had flattened himself against. He pulled back and examined it properly.

He knew this mountain. He recognized the color of the rock. He hadn't made the connection before, since he had had better things to worry about than the details of the geography, but . . . he *had* Seen it. The fight he was going to have with the man with the curved knife—that was going to happen here somewhere, in a cave of this exact stone. It couldn't be a coincidence.

He closed his eyes again and made his breathing slow. What else had he Seen in that vision?

Long shadows, just as though the sun were setting. The ground they had been fighting on had been pale, rocky, and sandy.

He looked down to his feet. Pale, rocky, sandy. If this wasn't the general area, it was certainly close. And now he was starting to have that feeling he got sometimes, like déjà vu, when he was living something that he had already dreamed.

He thought he'd Seen that vision so that he would know to prepare for that fight—when to dodge and how to strike—but what if he had Seen it to help him now? So that he would know what to do in this horrible, confusing moment?

The thought gave him comfort, which made him feel braver—he needed to go and fight this man, he *could* go and fight, he knew what to do—but then the thought came to him: What if the Honals really could overcome what had been Seen with their magic water? What if Honal Seers had Seen their fight as well? What if the Honals really did know how to change the future?

"Hail!" Aubrey jumped. It was a new voice, a man this time. "Fresh meat?"

"Yes, General, sir," the first woman said, sounding somehow like she was standing at attention.

"Good, good. Take them through to the cavern; we'll carve them up, and the Penitent can get on with her ritual. Off you go."

Carve them up.

Aubrey had a sudden vision of Prince Willard's hand falling into a pile of sand, shot off an automaton's body.

He heard movement and risked another peek around the rock; his fellows were walking on with the soldiers, and the General—because that was him, Aubrey was sure of it, all gray hair and upright posture, just like in his vision of the leaders in the cave—was turning around in his brown uniform and walking into what must have been a gap in the rock face.

Through to a cave, perhaps.

More to the point, he had a strange knife sheath at his belt, drawing Aubrey's gaze like the bull's-eye on a target.

Aubrey racked his brain for the details of the fight he was supposed to have with the man with the curved blade. He realized now that his opponent's hair hadn't been colorless, a missing detail; it had been gray. And the uniform was right. It could have been the General. It must have been.

Well, then, Aubrey thought, straightening up. He didn't care if this Honal believed his water could defy prophecy; Aubrey had a vision to make happen. A sorcerer to deal with. A sorcerer who had just ordered that his brother be chopped into pieces.

Aubrey drew his sword and made himself walk out of his safe little nook and through the gap he could see just a few yards ahead.

He went into the cave with that feeling of déjà vu increasing and watched as the General—one of the most important Honal leaders, a man responsible for countless deaths—turned at the sound of his approach and started at the sight of him. He saw him take in his sword, which Aubrey was holding out in a defensive position.

Aubrey swallowed.

"You have my friends, sir," he said.

"Ha!" the man said, eyeing him up and down now. "Hello, young man. Resistant to the mist, eh?"

He walked toward Aubrey. Aubrey resisted the urge to step backward, but that was a mistake. Somehow, between blinks, the man was right next to him, uncomfortably close. He had gotten past Aubrey's blade like it wasn't even there, leaned forward, and *sniffed* him. Aubrey recoiled.

"You're one of their Seers." The man's voice was wrong too; it echoed in a way that didn't seem to have anything to do with the rock's acoustics. "You're— No, wait. *Wait.*"

He moved again, but this time Aubrey was ready for it. He danced away before he could get too close.

"Not just any Seer," the man breathed, his tone completely different now, his eyes wide. "I know you. Our own Seers have Seen *you*. You make that kingling believe in himself, you give him hope. You are his vision of a happy future."

The hateful tone of the words, combined with the way he kept on looking Aubrey up and down, made Aubrey's skin crawl; and then the man made it worse by saying, "Oh, I am going to be so pleased to have killed you. It will destroy the Prince of Fortune. It will change everything."

He unsheathed his knife in a sharp pull and then moved in that unnerving way again, too quickly. It was all that Aubrey could do to get away from his strike; and then again, again. He nearly lost his sword parrying the next blow and had another wave of déjà vu before comprehending that his brain wasn't reminding him of a vision. The horrible way that the man moved was like the *strawmen*, his limbs not quite going where they should.

He blocked the sorcerer's next move, the next after that, and went to attack, feeling an unexpected wash of gratitude that he had not been transferred out of Manogate. He had fought so many monsters there. This was just one more.

He struck out.

He wasn't quick enough. The General twisted, and Aubrey's sword missed his neck, his torso, glancing instead off his arm.

The man peered at the slice through his jacket sleeve in surprise.

"More fight in you than I expected," he said. "Wonderful. Brave. But you're no match for anyone who's taken the waters. So, here, Seer. Better use your inner eye."

His arm moved, and then Aubrey's eyes were burning.

Blinding powder. The man had used one of their blinding powders.

Aubrey hadn't even seen him throw it, and now he couldn't see anything. His stinging eyes wouldn't open. He stumbled back, panicking, rubbing at his face. Where was his opponent? He could be anywhere, and Aubrey couldn't see him—

You have seen this fight, Aubrey told himself desperately. *You've seen it, you've Seen it.*

He understood now what had been wrong with his movements in his vision. He hadn't been injured. He had been blind.

He swiped his face on his arm, attempting to clear as much of the stuff as he could, trying not to panic or to think about how the blinding could be permanent. He needed to listen for where the General was. He should get him to speak again.

What had he said? Something about his inner eye?

"I'm not that sort of Seer," he called out. His eyes watered like he was weeping, and he was grateful—anything to flush them out. "I dream."

"Time to sleep, then."

The voice had come right near his left ear. Aubrey spun away just in time, hearing the swipe of the blade and feeling the air move with it. There was a stinging near his jaw, as though he had cut himself shaving.

The man had been aiming for his throat.

Aubrey's breath hitched, and he clamped his lips shut, stepping to the side to try to keep some distance between them.

"Careful," the General chided from behind him. "Your face needs to be recognizable so they can identify you."

Before Aubrey could turn, a blow landed on his side, and he went stumbling, letting out a grunt of pain. The panic was buzzing in his head now, making it hard to think. That last hit had landed, right on his weak side, and how could he beat this man with rebroken ribs?

You have Seen this fight, some distant part of his mind tried to remind him, and then he heard the sorcerer's feet moving closer again. He pulled up his weapon instinctively and felt it block the man's knife—and the déjà vu feeling locked into place.

He had Seen this fight.

What did I do next?

He let his body go where his mind had already taken him. He stepped forward but then to the right, swiping his sword up in that same direction. It encountered something that felt horrifyingly meaty, sliced through it. He then whirled his weapon over his head to bring it back down to his left. There was resistance for half a moment, as if his sword threatened to stick in a bone, but he had used enough force, enough speed. The blade was sharp enough.

He remembered just in time that this wasn't over. In the vision, he had cut the man's throat open, and then the man had lifted his knife—

Aubrey threw himself to the side to get out of range. He smacked right into the cave wall and let out another noise, not only of fear but from the pain in his ribs, and he heard a wet, gurgling sound several feet away.

There was a thump like a body dropping. The clatter of a fallen blade.

Oh.

Oh *heaven*.

He had done it. He had survived this fight. He had killed the General. He had killed one of the Honal leaders.

He stumbled sideways several steps, holding his sword out ready, just in case, and then tripped on something. He landed on his rear, making a very undignified sort of whimpering sound, and dropped his own sword.

He snatched it back up, listening, but the body was silent. And the man hadn't managed to stab him on his way down.

Aubrey patted himself, just in case. No wound that he could find, just the cut to his face, the ache in his side. His stinging eyes. He gave himself a moment to work out what he needed to do next, but he couldn't think over the buzzing in his head.

He hadn't killed a human being in this entire war. He had only faced flesh-and-blood soldiers a handful of times. He had fought them and injured them, and one particular Honal man with piercing green eyes might no longer have a left arm thanks to him, but that was it. Until now.

Aubrey's insides were suddenly full of needles. There was a ringing sound in his ears. He managed to turn in time before the contents of his stomach erupted out of him. They landed onto the unseen ground by his side with a noise he barely heard.

He took a deep breath and another one, reaching into his pocket with a trembling hand for his handkerchief. After he wiped his mouth, the thought rose vaguely in his mind, like an object appearing out of mist, that he should rinse out his eyes, which, now that he thought of it, were still hurting quite a lot.

He most certainly would not be able to make it back to Saben blind.

He groped around for the water canteen attached to his pack. It was perhaps three-quarters empty, his shaking hands making what was left slosh around. He opened it and tipped the contents over one eye and then the other.

The pain lessened, but he still couldn't see.

He emphatically did not think about how he might never again read another poem, never study another painting, never look into Edmund's beautiful warm eyes again. He just wiped his eyes and tried again.

This time, there was some improvement. He could see dark and light shapes: blurry, but most certainly there. He let out a shuddery, relieved huff of breath. More water, that was all he needed. Surely there would be a river somewhere. He remembered seeing a lot of them marked on John's map. He turned his head this way and that, listening, not so much expecting to hear a stream but hoping for it, and his heart leapt when he worked out that some of the rushing sound he could hear was actually water moving somewhere farther into the cave, and—

The déjà vu feeling was back.

Water.

He made himself breathe again, in and out. Well, then. He might fulfill both parts of his vision in the one day. And this one would be much nicer than the one he had just experienced; the water had been lovely in his dream. He just had to try not to drown, that was all. Easy.

He packed his canteen away and put on his pack. He groped around for his sword and used his soiled handkerchief to clean the blade as best he could before sheathing it, trying not to cut himself.

He got to his feet and made it three steps forward before tripping on something and falling, landing hard on his elbow. Sharp pain shot all the way down to his hand.

He rolled over into a sitting position, rubbing his arm.

Gritting his teeth, he detached his scabbard from his sword belt and tapped the sheath experimentally in front of him as a sort of makeshift cane. It would have to do. He set off more carefully this time and headed in the general direction of the path leading farther into the mountain that he had seen before his sight had been taken. Running his sword along the wall helped him find the way quickly enough.

He had no idea how much time passed—it did not feel like very long—as he walked toward the sound, but he did know that he was moving uphill, back into the Helm. The rushing noise was getting louder.

The rock wall next to him gave way, and he had the sensation that he was moving into a larger space. The air was fresh with the spray of the water he could hear—he must be close—and then he saw a warm, indistinct burst of light ahead like a lantern or torch lit against the fading sunlight. There was a tricky bit of terrain that seemed all rocks under his feet, and the next thing he knew, he slipped and fell again. One foot plunged into something wet.

He dropped his sword as he knelt down and pulled off his gloves. He reached out with his hands—he had some notion they were trembling again—and they splashed into a shock of cold.

He scooped up the water with both hands and flushed his eyes out as best he could, repeating the action again and again. It was helping; the light was taking on color and shape. Finally he leaned back, opening his eyes as wide as he could, pouring the water over them.

He wiped his face with his hands, clearing the frigid water away, and raised his eyes, and—he could see the sky. This new part of the complex he found himself in must have had a cave-in at some point, because that was not rock he was seeing—that was a glimpse through, showing him all the shades of a beautiful twilight, purple and pink streaking across a backdrop of dark blue. He could have written a poem about it. A whole volume.

His eyes still stung, but he could have wept with relief. He looked down; he could see the shape of his hands in front of him. He could see the body of water he had nearly fallen into, foaming and white, moving fast toward a waterfall some fifteen feet wide to his left. On his right was a high, pale cliff with a fissure in it that was gushing water into the pool. There was foliage growing all around the split in the rock; and on the far side, there was a woman, watching him.

He started, badly.

"Hello," she said. "You can see me now, can you?"

He was about to reply, but the words died in his mouth, because he recognized her just as he had the General. She had very red hair and rouged lips and cheeks, making the stiff robes she was wearing seem even stranger. This was—oh, what was her title, it was something odd—the Humble. No—the Penitent, that was it.

Aubrey didn't think she looked very sorry for anything.

"The old water," she added, "is known to have healing properties. But there are often side effects."

She stared at him, her gaze unnerving and expectant.

"This water?" he said, since she seemed to be waiting for something. His heart was thumping like it was trying to get out of his chest.

"Sometimes it takes a while," she said, shrugging, and turned back to what she must have been doing before Aubrey stumbled in and interrupted her. There was an old-looking table made of some roughly hewn gray stone behind her. The right side of it was covered in an assortment of bottles and jars in different shapes and sizes—a lot of them in the sort of dark tinted glass that was used to protect volatile or sensitive contents from light—as well as feathers and candles. There was incense burning somewhere in all that; Aubrey recognized the smell of that now as well, from his visions. The rest of the tabletop was covered with dolls made of straw and clay and driftwood. With his blurred sight, they could almost have been the sort that were sold at festivals in Saben, except those closest to him seemed to be marked with runes in an unsettling brown shade.

"Tell me, Sabresian," the Penitent went on, and Aubrey's heart pounded. "What are you doing in the Mountain?"

She said it like that was its name: the Mountain. Aubrey didn't know what the Honals called the Helm, if they had a different name for it.

"I was following the sound of water," Aubrey said, wondering what he should do now. This was one of the most important Honal leaders; he would do his country a favor if he slit her throat right now. There was, however, no possible way that he could attack an unarmed middle-aged woman in the middle of polite conversation.

She watched him as he picked up his sword. She certainly did not appear concerned at finding herself alone with an armed man from the wrong side of the border.

"What a good listener you must be," she said mildly. "But there is only one entrance to this cave, and it was guarded. No one should have been able to come through except my general. Did he blind you? Did you kill him?"

She was speaking in the same steady voice she had used for the entire conversation, but then she started picking up her dolls and casting them into the water. They changed color as they hit the surface and started moving around in ways that did not seem to have anything to do with the current. It was mesmerizing. Perhaps the water *had* done something to Aubrey, because he knew he should leave, but he also wanted to know what she was doing. One of the figurines turned over in the water, revealing a face with burned-in eyes and a stitched mouth, and Aubrey jumped back.

This must have been how the strawmen and automatons were manufactured.

"Yes," she said, as though he had spoken his thoughts. "I'm creating soldiers for us; there will be a large-scale attack tonight on your country. If you have killed my general, I will be able to make an even stronger army with his remains, another day. Perhaps I should thank you."

"Why do you send so many?" Aubrey asked. He had been wondering for months, and the words just came out. "You send them to slaughter us, and yet you have made no attempt to invade."

"The slaughter is the point," she said. "You are all sacrifices. Your deaths sink into the soil, and once we kill enough of you, we will be able to make such a storm, no one will be able to stop it. We do not need to invade Saben. We will be welcomed across it and then onto the continent, as its leaders."

Aubrey's mind raced. Edmund had told him the story about the Monium. Not the fog—the magical creatures that took over a place with a storm that made you forget that they had not always been in charge. Aubrey had gone and looked the folktale up.

A story. It was just a story.

"Prince Edmund stops your storms," he said.

"The Prince of Fortune stops nothing," the Penitent said, sweeping the last of the figures up in her arms. Her voice had turned shrill and nasal. "He *delays* our plans. And meanwhile I stop *him*. I protect the Mountain. He will never find our water, no matter how much he wants to take it from us."

She dumped the dolls into the pool in a gesture that was almost childish. "But now what to do with you? The water should have affected you by now, but it hasn't."

She turned and pulled something else off the table: a curved knife, much like the General's, but with markings visible on the blade. Runes. They seemed to glow, like he was Seeing them with the Sight.

"Guards!" she shouted in a voice that frightened him more than the knife. Something in the word rang out in the air, like the Pater's speech had in Aubrey's vision: like a thousand voices at once. He was so affected by it vibrating through him that when she went to stab him in the side, he almost let her.

He dodged out of the way just in time, unsheathing his sword, and had to dodge again when she went to slash at him. He swung at her; now it was her turn to move out of the way.

"How dare you raise a hand to me!" she shrieked at him, looking deranged in her fury as she struck toward him again.

"You tried to stab me!" Aubrey cried, dodging again, wondering how long it would take her guards to get there, how he would get away before that. "You send monsters to kill us, you want to put yourselves on our throne—"

"What else were we to do?"

"Anything! You could have chosen *anything* else!"

His sword made contact, but it had merely skimmed her side, cutting into her huge robes. He went to pull it out, but she clamped her arm around it and turned, trapping the blade in an effort to disarm him.

Clever, he thought, though he moved with her and did not lose his sword; but then he saw the water behind her and had a wild, clever idea himself.

Because the déjà vu feeling was back, and something about the water was calling him now. Just like a dream.

And then the dream felt a lot more urgent, because six guards in brown Honal uniforms arrived at the scene, running up the same path Aubrey himself had used to get up here. They so distracted him, he didn't even feel it when the Penitent finally did stab him.

He glanced down, and there her blade was, deep in his side. It should have hurt, but he was focused.

He let go of his sword. He heard it clatter to the ground as he grabbed her instead, not with military finesse but in the same way that he would tackle his brothers when they were children. He put his arms around her and hurtled them both into the water, like they were two more magic dolls.

The water was much deeper than Aubrey had imagined, the current stronger. It pulled them apart and yanked them over the edge of the waterfall within moments. He could hear the Penitent screaming, and he looked over and pulled in a terrified, horrified breath, because the skin of her face was blistering and bubbling, as though she had fallen into boiling acid rather than the cool liquid Aubrey was in.

He had an impression of her face melting like a candle, and then they landed in the deep, deep pool underneath, and he lost sight of her, his eyes closing.

CHAPTER 23

Edmund peered out of his tent flap. Something was different this morning.

He and his entourage were back up north, having rejoined his regiment the previous evening. Now he had woken to some change in the atmosphere. It felt freer, like a weight had lifted.

He stepped outside, trying to reach toward whatever it was, and saw Mattheson coming his way.

"Do you feel that?" Edmund asked him, waving at the sky. "An . . . improvement in the air?"

"I'm afraid not, sir. But you might need to wait before you investigate. There's a message."

Edmund let him lead the way to the communications tent.

"Your Highness," the messenger said, bowing. He handed him a letter, the seal visible with his sister's usual purple wax, the dragon pressed into it smaller than the signet their father used. "This is from Her Highness Princess Alicia, ahead of her arrival here in a few days."

"Thank you."

"There is more, sir. I heard news on the way here that I am to pass on to your company." The man grimaced. "It isn't good. There was another large-scale attack overnight. The Third and Fifth Battalions have been almost entirely wiped out."

Edmund was suddenly cold all over. His body had processed the words before his mind had.

"The Third Battalion. At Manogate." Edmund's voice didn't sound like his own. "Any word of Captain Trestall's company?"

A line appeared in between the man's eyebrows. "I wasn't told anything about specific companies or survivors, sir. More information is on the way."

Edmund couldn't speak. He nodded and made his way blindly back to his tent.

He cannot be dead, he thought. *He cannot. We have not fulfilled his vision. Aubrey Saw us together, after we first met, in a war tent—*

He felt the memory like a blow to his chest. The rest home. They had been lying together, and Edmund had started to tear up. Aubrey had comforted him. They had been in a camp bed, the walls covered with military canvas.

He stared at the walls around him. They were the same material.

Aubrey had not Seen a tent in that dream.

Which meant they had fulfilled the vision that Edmund had been counting on as a promise of Aubrey's safety. And now Aubrey's entire battalion had been wiped out, in the posting he had been given in the hopes that he would be killed. Because of Edmund.

He became dimly aware that it was raining. There was a storm on its way. Time had passed. People had come, wanting to talk to him. Mattheson had sent them all away. Edmund could not bring himself to feel grateful.

He came out at dinnertime at Mattheson's persuading. He ate whatever it was that they gave him, and then someone handed him a status report, listing the soldiers from the Third Battalion. His eyes scanned down under the letter *A*. Deceased, deceased, deceased, deceased, and then:

Lt. Ainsley, missing.

Missing.

Edmund knew what that meant in this war.

He didn't sleep much that night, and he did not leave his tent the next day. He did not weep; he didn't seem able to. His eyes were wet, to be sure, and occasionally they spilled over with single tears that ran down his cheeks, but mostly he just felt a crushing pain in his chest and throat and a general numbness everywhere else.

If he had just been able to request Aubrey be stationed with him. If he'd insisted on the parliament approving their marriage plans. If he had asked, after Aubrey's latest injury, that the army discharge him.

Or if he'd been able to focus his lightning properly on the beach at Downfall Cove and killed not only the Pater, but all the Honal leaders. Perhaps the war would have ended then, before it had properly begun. This was all his fault.

Alicia arrived the next day. He had not slept well. She wrapped her arms around him and asked for news of the Third Battalion. Edmund shook his head, and she held him tighter. After a long moment, she spoke again.

"Papa's been injured," she said quietly in his ear.

—

"It's being kept quiet for now," his sister was saying. "The wound is . . . bad. The prime minister has requested that you come back to the capital."

Badly wounded. Impossible. It was not possible that his strong, hearty father could be doing so everyday a thing as dying. Edmund's ears were ringing, and he had a feeling like the earth was trying to pull him under, because he could not be king, not now, not like this.

I don't want to leave this tent, he didn't say. He looked around and saw Aubrey's sweetheart shirt on the top of his pile of clothes, the embroidered bird just visible in a fold.

Had Aubrey been wearing his own shirt when—

"Lord Dell says that the crown prince needs to be seen in Elmiddan, safe and well," Alicia was saying now, "since Papa's injury has come so quickly after what happened with Uncle Willard. Edmund, are you listening?"

Edmund sat back and examined his little sister.

She had circles under her eyes, darker than he had ever seen before. She was travel stained, and her hair was pulled back efficiently with none of the curls around her face that she liked. Leather gloves were on her hands instead of pretty pastel ones.

His father had been dangerously wounded, and Aubrey might be dead.

So many people were dead.

Edmund didn't want any of this.

He was angry. He had been angry for a very long time, and now that he had opened that door, he wasn't sure if anger was even the word for what he was feeling. But something was still new and free in the air, and with a rush of comprehension that almost left him giddy, he knew what it was.

He could feel the Helm again. Whatever that barrier had been, it was gone. And more, he could feel into Honal somehow, even though he had never been able to reach that far before. Air and earth, and below all that, there was something.

He reached down into the rock.

Booming, cracking noises outside. Flashing lights so bright they could see them through the tent. He took off his absurd white jacket with its dragon, then his shirt. He pulled Aubrey's on instead, and then put his greatcoat on top, to protect against the rain.

He left his weapons—he wouldn't need them—and moved toward the exit. Alicia drew away from him, her eyes wide. Something was wrong in her expression.

"I heard you, Alicia," he said, and went outside. He motioned for his horse, because he was too distracted for words.

The mountain was calling to him.

He closed his eyes and answered, pushing his power out. He could feel the layers of rock, pushed up over time, its cracks and its weak points, its invitation. And its water.

At last.

His horse blew out a breath near him, and he opened his eyes again. His sister was staring at him, as was a groom. He wasn't sure how long they had been there, but he let the man help him mount.

"I need to do something," he said to Alicia. "Don't follow me. I'll be back soon," he added, since she looked like she wanted to argue with him. It was a lie; he had no idea how long this would take, but Edmund couldn't risk her being anywhere near him.

He turned his horse north and started riding.

He didn't need to get all the way to the mountain. In fact, that would have been a terrible idea. He just needed to be close enough for his purpose, and far enough away from anyone that he might hurt.

He didn't know how long he rode for; perhaps an hour. When he stopped his horse, he was in between two open fields with the beginnings of a forest to his right. It was around noon, but the sky was dark as soot from the storm he'd raised.

Edmund dropped to the ground. The mare turned her head to him, and he patted her neck. He should send her away, but he couldn't bear to.

"Good girl," he said, resting his head against her neck for a moment, her coat slick with the rain that was still falling. She flicked her ears at him, and he made himself walk away toward the trees. Feeling the way that their roots sank down, he took a deep breath and let it out, let his power out, and there it was: the soil under the roots, and under that, the rock.

He could feel everything.

The earth did not reach for him, for it had always known him. It had recognized him at his birth. An earthquake.

He inhaled slowly and then pushed.

Everything shook.

It was startling how disorienting it was for the ground to *yield*, and even more so to know that you were the one responsible for its movement, but Edmund didn't fall; he just dropped to his knees. He needed to focus his gift, so he did what he always did: pulled off his gloves and sank his fingers into the soil.

And that was when people started shouting and shooting at him.

He dropped flat to the ground.

Enemy troops, human ones.

An unbelieving laugh burst out of his mouth.

I won't need my guns, he thought viciously at himself. *I'll just leave them at camp, because I'm the all-powerful Prince of Fortune.* He set the grass in front of him to grow higher, for better cover, and scooted backward. Honal soldiers, perhaps two dozen, were coming out of the forest and shooting at the place where he'd been. He couldn't hear what they were yelling over all the rain and wind.

Edmund made a wrenching movement with his hands, and all the tree roots under the soldiers' feet started growing rapidly toward the surface of the earth. He wouldn't normally do such a thing—the poor trees—and as it was, the trick wasn't nearly enough to stop them. The soldiers yelled in alarm and tripped over, to be sure, but of course they just got back up again. He tried to call lightning, but it was impossible, as ever, to direct; one bolt hit a tree to their left instead, and another went astray somewhere behind him.

I'm the only one of us not made for battle, he thought, dropping his forehead onto his fists with the usual flush of shame, and then a series of bullets landed just shy of him, emphasizing this point.

"Please just *stop*," he called out, but they probably couldn't hear him over the rain any more than he could them. He pushed and created a calm place in the storm around them.

"Stop shooting," he called out. "It doesn't have to *be* this way. We were living our lives in peace; *you* are the ones who brought this to our door. Just *stop.* What could be worth all this?"

There was silence. It seemed uncertain, or perhaps it was him that was uncertain, but then one of the soldiers called something out. Edmund could not make out the words, but their intonation was unmistakable. It was a battle cry. The shooting started up again, closer to him now.

He could have shouted with frustration, because he needed to do this, but these soldiers—these ordinary soldiers—were going to capture him. He saw what would happen. Lord Dell and all those generals who hadn't wanted to deploy him near the border had been right. This one unit was going to take him, and Saben would fall, and then Honal would conquer the rest of the continent, twisting everything. So many people would be hurt. He was going to fail when he should have been able to stop this, stop it all, and—

—and then there was a new noise coming from the south: the beat of hooves. He risked lifting his head up enough to look.

Alicia was riding hard toward him, with about twenty soldiers. She pulled up her horse in between him and the trees, and her guard spread out in front of her. They were given the order to shoot and to advance.

Edmund stood up. "I told you not to come with me!"

"Yes, that was working wonderfully for you," she yelled over the noise of the guns and the rain, motioning at her troop to proceed.

"I won't go back!" Edmund shouted, part of him wishing she would make him. "I need to do this!"

"Get on with it, then," Alicia yelled, and turned away from him. She raised her arms and, with one efficient movement, turned all the rain that was falling immediately on top of her into ice. Another twist of her hands and the shards were blowing toward the enemy soldiers like a barrage of bullets.

She shouldn't be here, he thought in something like panic. *She shouldn't see this.* But he forced himself to listen to her. He made himself drop back to his knees and close his eyes, blocking out the guns and the noise.

There.

There.

It was so easy. It felt like breathing properly after realizing you hadn't taken anything but shallow breaths for a while. The ground shook again—but no. He had to be more careful this time; his deserted field was not empty now.

He reached out with his gift.

There was a rift in the rock underneath the Helm. He felt it, all its intricacies. Its caverns and crevices, the system of waterways under and over and through the mountain. He reached out, and there they were, the magic pools that the Honals used. He could feel the springs they welled up from, deeper than any human could go. That water should never have sprung up. That water should stay deep and belong to the land, not to humans who couldn't know of its power without wanting to exploit it.

He stretched out and down with his gift, focusing it on where it needed to go, and he pulled. He pulled from within himself, and it was an unleashing like nothing he had ever considered possible; energy inside himself that he had not even realized could be released. He pulled until it was also a pushing, and the entire world helped him, because it was all connected to him.

He was home.

Everything was shaking again, but not too badly. He knew that he had done what he needed to do, just as he knew when he had soothed a storm or gotten a wind just right for perfect sailing. He had set the right things in motion.

That water was going back where it came from.

A series of great cracking noises started up in the distance, satisfying in the same way that it was to watch a flower bloom after asking it to.

The noises were loud.

Edmund felt something inside him want to make more noise. It would be effortless. Everything was all right there, waiting. He could bring down the whole Helm, cover Honal in rock, shake it to pieces. Even the shaking under him felt right; he was in everything, and everything was linked to him. He could feel the way the rock went down under the sea, how his earthquake was affecting the floor underneath. He could feel the way the Helm reached into Folbrage and Hasprenna, under that river that the two countries had gone to war over, which had moved and taken their border with it.

It all seemed so ridiculous now. Borders were irrelevant. Politics was irrelevant. His body was irrelevant. Some part of him registered alarm at this, but everything was so far away. He should let it go.

But then he saw a flash of blue eyes. He knew those eyes, and right now they were like a glimmer of bright sky between clouds after a storm. Then, somehow, through Aubrey's eyes, Edmund saw a woman in a dress of that same blue.

She was smiling kindly at him, and suddenly he was not a mountain. He was a man.

He took an almighty breath, as though coming up from water.

"Edmund!" Alicia was screaming, above him. He opened his eyes.

His face hurt.

"Did you *slap* me?" he asked. It was strange to have a voice, to hear it, to have it sound so normal.

Alicia made an incoherent noise that could have been relief or outrage or any number of other emotions, and then she flung herself on top of his chest so hard she made him cough.

"You weren't breathing," he heard her say, the words muffled into his shirt.

He couldn't tell if she was crying or if it was the storm wetting her face. The inconvenience of all this rain and noise came to him in a rush. He hugged his sister and got them both up slowly, relearning how to stand up in his body. He raised one hand to stop the downpour.

And then someone shot him.

CHAPTER 24

Aubrey was floating. Or at least, he thought he was floating. He seemed to be having a vision. Perhaps.

There were two women: one in red, the other in blue. It felt like he was looking at a very old painting or an illustration in a manuscript come to life, as they wore headdresses and layers upon layers of heavily embroidered fabrics. The one in blue was gazing into a basin of water, and it dawned on Aubrey that she must be scrying.

"I'm not going to manage it all," the woman said, wrenching her gaze away from the bowl. Her expression was so raw, Aubrey felt like he should avert his eyes. "I can't see a way to win them over or to get rid of them, not in a way I can live with. They just won't *listen*. They'll still be there, pricking away at everything, hurting people."

"Helen, darling, please," the other woman was saying, coming over and taking her hands. "The treaty will hold up; you know it will. And you've done so much."

"But not enough. There will never be another with all of the gifts, or gifts so strong. And yet I've failed—"

"Shhh, now," her companion said, pulling the woman in blue to her. Their arms went around each other. "Don't talk like that. Their hatefulness is not your fault. You succeeded in changing everything. You've broken their grip over Thasbus. If you cannot See how you can do all of it, then you have to trust that the work will be finished by others. Why don't you try to See that, instead?"

Queen Helen—it had to be her, Aubrey thought, and marveled—calmed a little at that and pulled away to face the bowl again. She peered back into the water, and then suddenly, somehow, her eyes locked straight onto Aubrey's. But she also seemed to be seeing right through him.

"Oh, look at *you*," she said, and her face broke into a smile.

Oh heavens, Aubrey thought. *Is she Seeing me in return?*

He had never heard of such a thing, ever, and yet he suddenly knew to his core that that was exactly what was happening.

"You're one of mine—my line." Her voice was full of wonder. "Just *look* at you. Everything you could accomplish, you and him. Oh, but—you're in the water. Do not take that into yourself. Spit it out now. You still have so much to do."

Aubrey was suddenly awake, his body heaving out water. He rolled to his side instinctively, and his hands slipped on stones and sand. He was lying on the bank of a river, soaked to the skin. The landscape was completely different from where he had been, the rocky, sandy soil having made way at some point to trees and waving grass. The birds were acting strangely too, flying around in circles, calling to each other; or perhaps they always did that in Honal. He looked around for the Helm, to orient himself. It took him longer than expected because it was so far away now.

He let himself absorb it all. He had gone into the Honals' magic water. It had taken him farther than he'd expected.

Everything felt shaky, and it took him a few moments to realize the sensation was coming from outside himself. It took him even longer to understand it was an earthquake. He'd never been in one.

It was completely disorienting. It was as though the earth's reliable solidity had always been a lie waiting to be uncovered, and instead there was a gargantuan, unhappy creature trembling beneath him. The grass was waving in odd patterns, and the rocks in the riverbank were vibrating. He couldn't really focus on them, though. He should be frightened, like the birds. He certainly couldn't think, but it wasn't panic that he felt. An exquisite humility came over him: a feeling of nothing but awe, compelled as he was into only being present in his tiny body in this moment, by a force so much larger than him.

Then the shaking stopped.

He lay there on the dirty, rocky riverbank for a moment, still, and then he started to laugh. A nervous response, probably. He surveyed the landscape to see how it had been affected and noticed something happening to the stream that had carried him here. The water had been flowing away from the mountain, and yet now it was draining in the other direction, back toward the Helm. The Helm itself . . . was *crumbling*. At least parts of it. The sound was so loud, he could hear the cracking from this distance. As he watched, a massive landslide started up with huge boulders falling down one of the slopes, taking out trees as they went.

Aubrey wiped rain out of his eyes to see it better—it was really raining heavily now—and then appreciation struck him. He'd been hit with blinding powder, but now his vision was entirely back to normal—better than normal, even.

Healing properties.

He took an experimental deep breath and enjoyed how, for the first time in weeks, there was no pain, no cough. He took another one and could have laughed again, it felt so good, although something did feel tight somewhere. It took him a moment to remember that he'd been stabbed.

Heavens, what a day he'd had.

Was it one day? he thought, as he pulled at his clothing to check precisely how stabbed he had been. There certainly was a hole where the knife had passed through his waistcoat and another tear through his shirt, but there was no sign of blood and no pain. He pulled the wet fabric away completely to stare at his side. There was a scar, narrow and white; barely anything at all, like the wound had been inflicted years ago.

The water had healed everything.

Even his muscles felt good; all the aches and pains of months of battle and training had been loosened. He felt like he had had a wonderful sleep and was ready for anything.

Now, to get back into Saben.

CHAPTER 25

Edmund was . . . busy, with something.

He couldn't have told you what he was doing; it was very confusing. There were a lot of parts to it, and he had to keep them all in balance; this was vitally important. Except that someone had touched him—had they kissed him?—and he'd had a whiff of a citrusy scent that was important for a better reason, and everything else could wait.

He opened his eyes. The familiar sight of canvas greeted him, and the smells of an army hospital, all boiled bandages and medical supplies. Movement on his left caught his attention, and then he was presented with another familiar sight: Aubrey, absorbed in reading. His mouth was pursed slightly, and the lamplight was gilding his hair; shorter than it used to be but growing back.

Edmund reached for words, but his throat closed as tears started forming in his eyes.

"Darling!" Aubrey said, dropping his book. "You're awake! Are you all right?"

"You woke me up," Edmund said, not meaning only that, but still taking the opportunity to cling to Aubrey's proffered hand with one of his own. He couldn't move the other; he glanced down to see that his arm was in a sling. "I thought you were killed. I was told—"

"I'm alive, I'm right here. Yes, for a few hours there, everyone thought the Third Battalion had been wiped out. It wasn't true, and I wasn't even with them. There was some confusion because—well, Wilson was there. He took one look at how many monsters there were and how quickly everyone was dying, and managed to get over his love of rules for long enough to go against orders and lead a retreat into the city."

Edmund was still groggy, but something didn't sound right with that.

"*Wilson* led—"

"Yes, no one should have listened to a mere lieutenant, but it was all such chaos, and the colonel and half the captains were already dead, so the chain of command was unclear, and everyone just went along with him. He is *very* bossy. He even got them to close the gates. It saved a lot of lives. The army can't decide if they want to bring him before the Martial Court or give him a chest of medals. I'll tell you all the details later. Now, would you like me to fetch the nurse? How does your arm feel?"

Edmund tried to move it and then hissed through his teeth.

"I was shot."

"Yes," Alicia's voice said as a white-clad arm pushed aside a privacy panel, and then he was being hugged by his sister. "You gave me quite the fright."

Aubrey laughed, but Edmund was still trying to piece together what had happened. "They shot at you, too," he said. "Are you all right?"

"I am," she said. "Me, they missed."

He looked at her closely, but nothing in her face contradicted her breezy tone.

"And Papa?"

"Past the danger point and recovering well."

The relief hit Edmund like a physical thing. His vision blurred suddenly as the tears came again. Alicia handed him a handkerchief.

"Thank you," he said. "For following me, I mean. I was being foolish, not wanting you to see me. I was worried, I . . . I don't even know what I was worried about. That you would be afraid of me."

"Yes, you were very fearsome out there, asking their soldiers to please stop all their nasty violence. Anyway, has Aubrey told you? You did it. The Honals have lost their magic water. The war is over."

He closed his eyes.

Over.

The war was over.

He had a thousand questions—it couldn't have been that simple—but he gave himself a moment to let those words sink in. He let himself feel them in his bones.

His bones hurt.

Something must have shown in his face, because Alicia said, "The surgeon says you can have anything you want for the pain, you know. All the laudanum you can drink."

He gave her a look. She waggled her eyebrows at him.

"I don't think so," Edmund said, but could hear the smile in his own voice. "That sounds like a very good way for me to accidentally . . . I don't know. Grow us a meadow in the middle of the tent."

"I said something similar to her, when she dosed you two days ago.

She said she didn't want to see what you do when you're in a great deal of pain. I'm going to go tell her you're awake."

She dropped a kiss on his forehead and disappeared behind the same panel she had sprung from. Edmund tried to sit up, to see more of where he was, and was rewarded with a stab of pain up his shoulder. Aubrey made a concerned noise, moving to the edge of the wooden chair he was sitting on. Edmund waved him back.

"It seems wrong for the war to not be over in my body, when it is outside," Edmund said. "Are *you* all right? You seem to be, but . . . why were you not with your company when they were attacked?"

"I was off on an adventure," Aubrey said airily. "I got stuck on the wrong side of the Honal border on an intelligence mission, and I couldn't go back through the Helm because bits of it kept on falling down, and I didn't know where I was anyway, so I had to go around it via the coast. I walked for three days," he said, and laughed at the expression on Edmund's face. "Then I had to convince Sabresian soldiers at the border that I was Lieutenant Aubrey Ainsley. I didn't have anything identifiable on me, since—you know—*intelligence mission*, but luckily, Mother's old captain was there and it turns out she's a general now, and she handed me a horse and told me that your father had issued an edict from his sickbed that if I turned up, I was to be sent straight to you because he had 'had enough of this nonsense.' So here I am. And now," he added, smoothing Edmund's hair off his forehead, "I think we have just fulfilled the very first vision-dream I had about us."

Edmund gazed around in wonder and squeezed Aubrey's hand, which was here and warm and real.

"I wish you would have a thousand more visions of us together."

"About that . . ."

As much as Edmund enjoyed hearing that Queen Helen the First had Seen that he and Aubrey were going to achieve great things together, he was more distracted by the bit of the tale that involved the Penitent stabbing Aubrey and them ending up in the Honals' water. He was demanding details when the surgeon came in to check on him, moving aside all the privacy screens.

He complied with her examination, and meanwhile, something at the entrance to the tent had caught Aubrey's attention. Edmund looked as well. Canvas and more canvas—he was never going to want to go inside a tent ever again—and ten or so other patients in camp beds, most of their inhabitants either sleeping or staring at him. But none of that was what Aubrey was looking at.

Sir Jenson had come in and was walking toward them arm-in-arm with his wife. She was a handsome woman with very dark skin and was currently wearing some sort of theatrical costume—an old-fashioned gown that showed quite a bit of décolletage—and an elaborate curled white wig pinned with decorative fruit and flowers.

"Who is *that*?" Aubrey asked.

"It's Lady Frenric," Edmund said. "Did you never happen to meet her?"

Aubrey stared at him, his hand floating out to grip Edmund's leg. "That's Sir Jenson's *wife*?"

"Yes, she must be putting on entertainments for the troops while she's here. She used to be quite a famous actress, in Hasprenna. Julia . . . something."

Aubrey's eyes were getting so wide, Edmund was worried he was in pain, but then he said very urgently, "Sir Jenson's wife is *Julia Huppert*?"

". . . If you say so? Is that all right?"

Aubrey looked at him. "Julia Huppert. Who all the news sheets couldn't get enough of when we were younger. Who had a series of affairs with nobility all across the continent but then ran off with an obscure Sabresian baronet. That Julia Huppert. You're telling me that baronet was Sir *Jenson*?"

Edmund winced. "Maybe?"

Aubrey made an impatient noise at him and threw up his hands.

Edmund went to say something else—apologize for not keeping up with the news sheets, perhaps—but Aubrey was busily straightening his clothing, his eyes back on the approaching couple, muttering something that sounded like "this is the best day of my life" over and over in a singsong sort of way. The surgeon rolled her eyes and left.

"Sir Jenson," Edmund said, nodding his head in greeting now that they were here. Aubrey stood up. "Lady Frenric, I do not think you have met Lord Ainsley. Aubrey, this is Lady Frenric."

The lady appeared just as enthusiastic to meet Aubrey as he was to meet her, her painted eyes wide as he bowed. The two peeled off in animated conversation while Sir J and Edmund watched, forsaken. Then Sir J said, "I am glad you're awake, sir."

"I'm glad to be awake. Especially since I hear the war is done."

"Well, it will be once you get them to agree to terms. They won't even talk about what they are willing to accept; they just withdrew all troops and wiped out all the runes they'd left behind. Places we didn't even know, sir. Their new leaders are being very obliging. After you—well, they don't have their magical water anymore, and it would appear that once you start taking it, you can't stop."

"*Can't* stop? What do you mean?"

"The Honal sorcerers are . . . well, they are all dead, sir. Or nearly all. There are only a handful left and they're unwell; they are not expected to live much longer."

Edmund didn't know how he felt about this. It was unexpected. He supposed he should feel relieved they were gone, or horrified to have caused the deaths of who knew how many people. Mostly, hearing the news just made him feel tired. He reached for his water goblet as Sir J went on.

"The prime minister wants the last of the sorcerers handed over for trial, but their new leaders say they are being imprisoned in their own country for treason. They say that a lot of their soldiers were magically coerced into fighting. Well, we saw that at Downfall Cove. But it is not only that. A lot of their water sources were rerouted or polluted for magical purposes; there are whole areas without safe drinking water. They are facing food shortages as well. I expect that's partly what they want to talk to you about."

"And I'm to help them?" Edmund said, hearing the weariness in his voice. "I'm to go around fixing the farmland of the people who made war on mine?"

There was a pause, and then Sir J said, "I know that Your Highness will do what you feel is right."

Edmund regarded him for a long moment and then gave a defeated nod. He glanced over at Aubrey and Lady Frenric, who were now tête-à-tête, as Aubrey pointed to a passage in his book. Lady Frenric threw her head back, her hand over her mouth to muffle a great peal of laughter. The ornamental fruit attached to her wig was dancing. He reminded himself that the fruit trees of Honal were innocent in all this and felt a little better.

"Well, sir," Sir J said in a different tone, and Edmund glanced at him to see him smiling at his wife. "I shall take my leave. I will tell the prime minister that you're awake. He wants the meeting as soon as possible, you understand."

Edmund bowed his head, feeling grumpy with the man again—

could he not just have a few more days to heal his *gunshot wound*—and then the couple was gone and Aubrey was settling back down next to him, book in hand.

"Wait, what is that? Your bookmark?" Edmund asked him sharply.

Aubrey held up the pale scrap of fabric. It had a bird embroidered on it. Edmund felt a pang of loss, like it had just been torn from his body.

"They had to cut my shirt off you before they operated on your shoulder. The nurse who was given the pieces to use for bandages realized just in time what she had and saved the tail; and then when I arrived, she gave it to me, since the whole point is that sweethearts return them to each other once they're safely together again."

Aubrey grinned and added, "I suppose that was presumptive. What if you'd been wearing a shirt from some other sweetheart?"

Edmund let out a surprised laugh and then winced at the pain.

"Not possible," he said. "Not ever. But does that mean you have to give me mine back now?"

"I already gave it to Mattheson. It needed to be repaired; it was *stabbed* after all." He took Edmund's hand. "Goodness, what a pair we make."

"Yes," Edmund said, and brought Aubrey's hand to his mouth.

Edmund made the Honals wait another full week before he would meet with them. His father was not recovered enough to walk yet and so would not be joining him, since he refused to appear in a chair before "those bastards."

Contemplating his father's decision, Edmund did the opposite, refusing to take off his sling or hide his injury.

"They shot me," he said flatly; and while he was being political, he insisted on Aubrey coming as well.

CHAPTER 26

The newly appointed Sabresian ambassador to Honal, Lady Hastings, and the newly appointed Honal ambassador to Saben, a Mr. Horst, had agreed that Adurnmouth, the northern seaport that had been one of the first sites of attack at the beginning of the war, would be an appropriate location for the peace talks. They would be using Customs House, one of the only administration buildings still standing in the city.

Edmund was nervous before the meeting. He did not like that the Honals had insisted on his presence, given their history.

He reminded himself that their sorcerers had been neutralized. He also reminded himself that Aubrey would be with him, and Sir J. The prime minister, Lord Dell, would be in the party too, as well as the minister for foreign affairs, Dame Edwina, and both their secretaries. Lawyers and historians and military officials and messengers would be on hand to help as well.

His arm hurt.

"They're ready for you now," some sort of diplomatic clerk said.

The meeting room was like hundreds he had been in before: mullioned windows parenthesized with rich drapes, a timber floor covered with a fine carpet, furniture polished to a high shine. He scrutinized the party waiting to see him and found himself wondering how the room appeared to them.

They looked wrong in it, even though their dress and general appearance were not so dissimilar from his own group. The differences were slight, as though deliberate mistakes had been added. The embroidery on their clothing was exquisitely done, but the fabric was more roughly woven, the colors more muted. The women's hairstyles were severe, and the men all had long sideburns, which had not been in fashion in Saben for many years.

"Your Highness," Lady Hastings said. "May I introduce the representatives from Honal's newly created high council."

The Honals dropped to their knees. Edmund, mortified, quickly motioned for them to rise. Was this normal for them? He supposed their previous leaders had wanted the entire continent to obey them mindlessly, so perhaps it was.

There were seven of them—three councillors and four attendants—and he wondered if their number had been negotiated in advance to match the Sabresian party. He was sure Sir J had told him that Honal's new high council had an administrator—a mayor or other official—from all six of their counties, so that meant only half of them were here. He was so busy wondering if the rest had been left behind to run Honal, or were lurking around somewhere, he missed taking note of everybody's names, except for the tall man in the center who had been introduced first, as Chief Councillor Whit.

Lady Hastings, knowing nothing of Edmund's plight, went on with, "Councillors, Ambassador, may I present the rest of His Highness's party."

The Honals merely bowed at the others—until Lady Hastings got to Aubrey.

All of them dropped to their knees again.

Time seemed to slow down as Edmund watched them. The Sabresians stared, first at the Honals and then at Aubrey. The prime minister's face was getting redder and redder as it cycled through emotions, none positive. Aubrey, his eyes wide, shrugged elaborately to indicate that he had no idea what was going on and certainly wasn't to blame for this.

"The Lord of the Waters," Councillor Whit said, without raising his face. "It is an honor."

Aubrey cleared his throat. "You may rise," he said, his voice going up at the end of his sentence, as though showing them how it was done.

"Is the party familiar with Lord Ainsley?" Ambassador Hastings asked, as they all got to their feet.

"His lordship was cherished by the old water," one of the councillors said fervently, still bowing his head, "while the Penitent was found wanting."

A ripe, full silence followed these words.

The councillor, who was a younger man, looked up and then said a little defensively, "It was witnessed by the Penitent's guards. It was widely Seen. I Saw it myself. She had thought to stop the Prince of Fortune from cracking open the mountain. You helped him fulfill his destiny. Honal knows what happened that day, my lord, and it thanks you for liberating us all from her tyranny."

"Well, you're very welcome," Aubrey said after a moment. "Lady Hastings, I believe we should be getting on with introducing the rest of the party?"

Edmund tuned out the niceties that followed, his mind racing with everything they had said. He and Aubrey had not worked out the timing between them of when precisely he and the Penitent had gone into the Honal water, but she had told Aubrey she was "stopping" Edmund. The Pater had said something similar that day on Downfall Cove.

He remembered the way that the air had felt different on the morning he had found out that Aubrey was missing, how he had been able to feel the Helm again. Had he really only been able to cause that earthquake because the Penitent had been killed?

Someone touched his hand. It was Aubrey, indicating to him that he needed to be seated.

He sat.

"We asked to meet with His Highness," Ambassador Horst finally said, "not only to discuss the terms of our surrender, but to discuss the future."

"Yes," Edmund said slowly. "But these are things for you to discuss with my father's government. Not with me."

"No, it must be you, sir," Councillor Whit said. "We want you to take Honal back into Saben when you are king. Make us all one country again."

The entire Sabresian party had gone very, very still. Edmund cleared his throat.

"Take Honal into Saben?" he repeated.

"I am sorry," the councillor went on. "I think I have spoken more bluntly than a more experienced diplomat would have. We were until recently just regional officials; none of us ever thought to find ourselves in this position. But a new path has been Seen, and this way, Honal will never again go to war with Saben."

Edmund glanced around. Everyone in his party, at least, looked as startled as he himself felt; except for Aubrey, whose eyes were sparkling and who had his lips pressed together in that way he did when he was trying to stop himself from speaking.

It was Dame Edwina who recovered first. "Is there a reason you wish to delay this . . . merger you propose? Why will you not allow King Theodore the honor of reuniting us?"

This time the female councillor spoke, a small older woman with gray hair and a stronger Honal accent than either of her cohorts.

"We thought that a longer transition period would give us time to organize things like taxes and currency and government representation," she said. "Time to move everything across to the common alphabet. We know that you lost all of your records when Saben moved scripts. You destroyed everything with runes on it, and this was not . . . convenient for you. If you give us time, we can translate everything so that nothing will be lost. We have annals of our shared past that you might be interested in," she added, focusing on Aubrey, since he had leaned forward upon hearing all this. "Historical documents. Old stories and plays, all kinds of things."

Councillor Whit was nodding. "A delay will also give your country time to heal somewhat first. It will give us all a chance to get used to the idea."

Edmund studied the faces around him; even in the last minute, his party appeared to have gotten over their shock at the proposal. Lord Dell's expression, in particular, had turned calculating.

"All very practical," the prime minister said. "Very reasonable. And the Honal people? How do they feel about all this?"

"They do not want to starve," the younger councillor said baldly. "And they did not enjoy the way their previous rulers used them. They will accept this."

"And yet they do not want our king to be their king. They want the

Prince of Fortune. Is His Majesty so much weaker, in their eyes, than His Highness?"

Edmund's breath was trapped in his throat. He watched the councillors exchange looks.

"We would not put it that way," Whit said finally. "Not even behind these closed doors. But . . . this way will make everything go more smoothly, and . . . His Highness is the one who vanquished us, after all."

"What we really want to know," the younger councillor said, "is whether we will be able to claim the Prince of Fortune's protection up until the point when he *can* be our king?"

Another silence. The two ambassadors gave each other tense glances; the councillors' eyes skittered over the group. Then, to Edmund's right, a helpful voice spoke up.

"A principality, perhaps? Or a protectorate?" Edmund could only stare at Aubrey, as he continued speaking. "Several of the island nations to the north have a history with such things. I believe one of the Frithan isles is technically a separate dukedom, with slightly different laws from the rest; Dame Edwina, that is right, is it not?"

Dame Edwina just stared at Aubrey in alarm.

"Principality," Councillor Whit said, as though trying the shape of the word in his mouth. "Yes, that sounds well. Could your scholars and lawmakers draw up some draft proposals and acts and so on, so we may begin the negotiation?"

"Wait, wait," Dame Edwina said, her expression very worried now. "We must slow down. We are still processing the theoretical, and you have already moved onto practicalities. Taking you into our borders may be in violation of Helen's Treaty. It clearly states that none of the signatory countries' borders may change—"

"Yes," the gray-haired councillor said, waving one of the Honal assistants forward, "except that provision was always included for us to join."

The assistant was handling a scroll reverently. Edmund could feel Aubrey containing himself, merely leaning forward slightly rather than jumping up from his seat and running over for a closer look.

"This is Honal's original, unsigned copy of Helen's Treaty," she said. "It has been kept on display in the old palace as a reminder of why our country was formed, of what we objected to. It should be identical to your own. Addendum four is the relevant one, as you will see . . ."

She put on a pair of old-fashioned spectacles and read aloud:

> Honal, encompassing the Helm and all land to the north of this mountain unto the sea, has been recognized as a separate nation, and one that refuses to be a signatory of this treaty. If, in the future, Honal chooses to join with Saben, all signed nations agree that this will reflect the original intention of the treaty, which still stands.

She took off her glasses again and gave Edmund a small smile. "This was planned for."

"Queen Helen Saw this," Aubrey said, breathing out the words. The Honal party all looked at him sharply, but his focus was on Edmund. "She left you a way—"

"No," the prime minister said, shaking his head. "That—that clause was in case Honal agreed to sign later—"

"That's not what it says," Whit said.

"Well, tell that to the Hasprennans or the Folbrans or the Arnicians when they take umbrage!"

Lord Dell's voice had risen to a shout; Dame Edwina's tone was suppressive when she pitched in with, "They won't do that. If I were

Hasprenna or Folbrage or Arnici, I would not worry about Saben extending its territory into Honal. I'd be glad Honal had been finally brought to heel. I would be more concerned about Prince Edmund's intentions for the rest of the continent now that the magnitude of his powers is clear. I would not do anything to suggest that the treaty should be declared invalid."

Edmund glanced at Aubrey, who was now watching the Honals closely. He had a faraway look on his face that wasn't quite like any expression Edmund had seen on him before. It made him look older, but it also reminded Edmund somehow of his own brief vision of Queen Helen, where she had seemed to see through him to some deeper knowledge.

And then Aubrey asked, "If I might inquire, how many of you on the high council are Seers?"

The councillors all exchanged glances.

"All of us, sir," Whit said.

The rest of the Sabresian party exchanged glances at this, but Aubrey seemed completely unsurprised.

"And *will* the other countries raise a fuss?" Aubrey asked.

The Honals eyed each other again, and then they all shook their heads as though they were sharing a secret, and Edmund had a burst of gratitude that Aubrey was here.

Aubrey nodded again. "What else have you Seen coming out of this alliance, if Edmund agrees?"

Edmund felt sweat prickle his palms inside his gloves as they all focused on him.

"The Prince of Fortune will use his gifts to renew the land in Saben, now that the war is done. We beg for you to help us in the same way," the young councillor said.

"Helping restore your farmland and waterways . . . is within my power," Edmund said, trying to avoid explicitly agreeing to anything. "But that is not all you are asking for, is it?"

More glances.

Finally: "Queen Helen laid the curse on our sea," the female councillor said. "You could choose to make it safe again, sir. Calm our waters—"

"No," the prime minister said. "I'm sorry, Your Highness, but I can't just sit here and be expected to swallow any more of this. We've never seen these people before—this could be a traveling troupe of actors for all we know—and all of this could be a plot to pit you against your father, to weaken King Theodore's position."

"I agree, Lord Dell," Dame Edwina said, though she sounded more measured than her party leader. "Before we go any further, I would like their copy of the treaty checked against ours. I would prefer to hear any of these claims backed up by Seers from our own country. And I would also like to see proof that their days of handling dark magic are over. Are all of their sorcerers really gone?"

"You will have all of the proof you want," the female councillor said. "You will send troops to occupy us. Send them now, if you wish. We will not resist."

"Don't you dare paint us as the aggressive party here!" Lord Dell's face was a deep red now. "You people—"

Edmund tuned the man's rant out, studying the Honals instead. They were exchanging glances, bewilderment and dismay clear on their faces. They also looked completely exhausted. He did not think they were lying, and he did believe that they were who they claimed to be: regional administrators thrust into the highest level of leadership after their previous rulers left them in disarray.

They were Seers, just like Aubrey, except that nobody knew them here. Nobody trusted their word.

He could assist these people, or he could send them away, and their trees and crops would die from drought. That would probably lead to a famine, he thought. Their poorest and most vulnerable citizens would starve.

He didn't have to help these people. He could let the bad blood between the two countries go on and on, with or without any magic water, or he could put a stop to it all.

His arm hurt.

He stretched out his other one and reached for Aubrey's hand—protocol be damned—and closed his eyes. He took a deep breath and let it out. They were not far from the shoreline; he could sense it now, the salt water lapping at the rocks. He reached out to the border, feeling his way along the sand under the sea and—*there*. There was a section where the seabed changed, feeling organic and calm one moment, then all jagged and manufactured the next, almost like the storms created by the Pater or the Penitent or whichever one of them it had been.

He knew how to fix that, make everything balanced. Slowly he breathed in and out again.

He wasn't sure if the tremor underneath him was perceptible to anyone else until he heard Lord Dell's voice falter in the middle of saying something about treachery and tradition. There was the sound of clinking in a cabinet.

"Edmund?" Aubrey asked, squeezing his fingers. Edmund focused on that touch to pull himself back into this tiny room and his tiny body, where he was supposed to be. He opened his eyes to see everyone watching him.

"It is done," he said. "As a show of good faith, I have calmed the waters around Honal. There will be no more war between us. I am willing to take Honal into Saben when I am king, and until then, the country will be under my protection—unless the parliament has legal reason to object," he added, because Lord Dell looked like he might be ill.

"Your father—" he started, but Edmund was having none of it.

"No action I take will ever be a threat to my father, who trusted me to come without him today and with whom I have no quarrel. A calm sea around Honal helps everybody. The Nordans will be happy. And Frithay. Oh . . . your privateers," he added, turning back to the councillors. "You will take immediate action to remove them from your waters. Your navy will act with respect to other ships."

"*Your* navy, sir," the young male councillor said.

Edmund sat back in his chair. This was going to take some getting used to.

"I will expect . . . law and order on land as well," he added, not sure how else to put it.

"Yes, sir." This time the answer came very quickly.

"I will not be," he said, feeling even more out of his depth and wanting to be understood, "your new sorcerer tyrant, if that is what you are hoping for."

"No, sir."

Edmund groped for something else to say, because everyone was staring at him.

"And the last of your sorcerers," he said a little desperately. "They will be brought here for their trial, for crimes against both our countries."

He risked a glance at the prime minister, whose expression of outrage changed as he took in what Edmund said. "They absolutely will!" the man burst out. "They will see no preferentialism here! Those . . . *monsters* kidnapped his uncle, and yet you feel entitled to the prince's mercy? They chopped a member of our royal family into pieces and then used those against his own people!"

"Yes," Councillor Whit said. "We understand that talks between our former leaders and Prince Willard did not go as planned."

Edmund's rib cage tried to shrink into his stomach.

"Talks?" Dame Edwina asked. She glanced at the prime minister for guidance; the man appeared stumped.

The Honal leaders exchanged looks among themselves. Edmund did not know what to do and threw a panicked glance to Aubrey, only to find him wide-eyed himself. Edmund opened his mouth to say something—anything—to shut down the topic, but Whit was already talking again.

"Prince Willard was approached by our previous . . . ruling class, demanding he betray your royal family. We brought the correspondence that we found with us for His Highness, since we thought . . ."

"We thought His Highness might want to destroy it all," the young male councillor said with all the bluntness he'd shown so far. He waved, and one of the attendants came forward, this time with a bundle of letters tied in a black ribbon. "We would not have him embarrassed."

"Why would—" the prime minister began, but he was cut off by Aubrey.

"His Highness will indeed take them, thank you," he said in the sharp voice Edmund so rarely heard, reminding him how many battles Aubrey had fought in recently. "And we would prefer the matter not be discussed any further until he has made himself acquainted with their contents."

Edmund would never have dared say such a thing. He was so glad that Aubrey had come. He glanced over at Lord Dell; his expression made it clear that this was not his own preference at all.

The new way that the prime minister was looking at Aubrey, though, was what worried Edmund the most.

—

Edmund curled into Aubrey's side in the carriage as they left Customs House and dozed off almost immediately. The day had been exhausting, and the pain in his arm was a dull throb that made everything worse. He awoke when the horses stopped in front of Burside, the royal residence they were using. It took him a moment to remember where he was.

He had never thought much about it before, but it was a slightly odd building. It had started its life as a fort, just after the civil war, so it was all crenellations and holes for archers to shoot through. The interiors had been updated at various points over the years, but never all at once or by anyone with much enthusiasm for the job, so it was a bit of a mishmash of styles. Edmund had promised Aubrey that he could explore the residence's every nook and cranny, but they would not be doing that this evening: there was a carriage parked at the front steps. They had a visitor.

There were footmen stationed outside the first drawing room. Inside, there was a large box waiting for them—and Lady Ainsley.

She was sitting very neatly on a sofa upholstered in a leafy sort of shade that matched the watered silk that lined the walls. Her dress was purple, and she looked, somehow, like a flower among all that green. Edmund felt calmer than he had for hours.

She stood up to curtsy.

"I am sent from the Support Office, Your Highness, to answer whatever questions I can for you about Honal," she said around Aubrey's shoulder as his arms went about her, "and to report that Seers all over the country have spent the day sending reports into the War Office of a future in which Honal becomes part of Saben, and somehow it all goes well. Heavens, dearest, you are *firm* these days," she said to Aubrey as he pulled back. She squeezed his arms. "You get that from my side of the family."

Aubrey ignored this. "Any word of John?"

The satisfaction and relief radiated from her face. "He is healing a few small wounds in an officers' rest home not far from here. They aren't bad. The rest of the team you were with . . ." She patted Aubrey on the arm, and Edmund's breath hitched. "Well, there were a lot of injuries. I'll tell you the details later. But firstly, Your Highness," she said, turning back to Edmund, "I am sorry to arrive without warning, but Queen Margaret insisted that I stay here and not at the barracks with the rest of the officials. I hope it doesn't inconvenience you."

"Of course not, my lady," Edmund said, but before he could say anything further, Aubrey interjected.

"It's so good that you're here. The Honals gave us the letters they found from Prince Willard, in front of *everyone*. We'll all need to get our stories straight—"

"Not tonight," Edmund said, all but collapsing into a chair. "I can't."

The words just came out. They were too blunt. He felt his face move into rueful lines. "I am very grateful that you are here to help, ma'am, but today has been quite disturbing enough, and I want tea and rest, and to reflect on what happened. Aubrey, did I really just become Honal's leader? Did that happen? Am I their—their monarch now?"

"Yes, but I'm sure it will all be fine. The ministers will be sitting down with the legal experts at this very moment, working out how to set it up so that the Sabresian parliament makes all the decisions. But is that what you want?"

Edmund stopped short. His immediate answer was a desperate yes, until the realization quickly followed that he didn't necessarily trust them to be fair. Not after everything that had happened between the two countries. The confusion must have shown in his face, because Lady Ainsley said, "I think you're right to want to think about it all after a good night's rest, sir. Ah, here." The door had opened; two maids arrived with trays. "I took the liberty of ordering food for your arrival."

Aubrey made interested noises. There were two sorts of fruitcake, fragrant with spirits and spices. Aubrey moaned as he bit into a piece of the darker one, his eyes fluttering closed, and Lady Ainsley caught Edmund's eye, her mouth twitching.

"What's in this enormous box, Mother?" Aubrey asked finally, sitting back with his teacup and gesturing to the thing. "Is it a man? After today, I don't think I would be surprised by anything."

"It isn't mine. It arrived just as I did, for His Highness. I believe it's a goodwill gift from the Honal delegation."

Aubrey looked at him expectantly. Edmund shrugged. "If you want to open it, by all means, feel free. But please close it again if it's upsetting or . . . complicated."

Aubrey was already moving forward and undoing the latch. "It's beautifully crafted," he said, pushing up the lid. He peered in at the contents and then stopped dead. After a moment, he pulled out a sword.

"That doesn't bode well," Edmund said.

"No," Aubrey said, laughing. "It's mine. The one I lost in Honal. Look!"

Edmund leaned forward; there was a label attached to the hilt. "'For the Lord of the Waters. We hope that he will never need to use it again.' Is everything labeled?"

"Some things are, and some aren't," Aubrey said, reaching in. "Furs—oh, these are nice and soft. Those look like spirits. Preserves, jam—ooh, there are books! Wait," he added, flicking through one of them. "These are just . . . normal. It's printed in the common script. No runes."

"Yes, they do print some things in the common script," Lady Ainsley said. "Something to discuss tomorrow."

Aubrey nodded and put the books on the table next to the tea tray.

"There are textiles—no, they're wrappings," he said, pulling them off something like a jewelry box, inlaid with tortoise shell. "'Samples for our reparation payment proposal,'" he read aloud, and handed the box to Edmund.

It was full of rocks. Edmund spent a second thinking wildly of automatons until he saw the note slipped into the lid.

> *His Highness's earthquake diverted a particular waterway not far from our border with Folbrage, where an old gold mine had been abandoned. A new vein of the metal was exposed. There is also evidence of tin, which we had not previously known was there. We hope that mining rights for these new sites will smooth the way for Honal's reintegration into Saben.*

Gold. The rocks were gold, raw from the ground. Edmund picked one up. It felt like the Helm.

"'Reintegration,'" Lady Ainsley said, reading the note herself. "That is a very good way to put it. If it can be put to the public in that way—that the sorcerer class broke Honal away from Saben in the reign of Queen Helen, and now that they are gone, we are reuniting—that will ease things almost as much as the gold."

"Why did they not mention the gold today?" Aubrey asked while he worked out how to open the next item: another box, in wood this time, and bigger.

"Did you discuss reparations?" Lady Ainsley asked.

"No, we didn't get that far—seeds!" Aubrey exclaimed, thrusting the box at Edmund. "They really are trying to please you."

The case was stacked with envelopes, each labeled in a spidery hand. Herbs, flowers, vegetables. Grains. Edmund did not recognize some of the names, which was intriguing. He wanted to open the packets but restricted himself to merely putting his hand over them, feeling their calm, dry, dormant potential.

He looked up after a while to see Aubrey and his mother both smiling at him.

"If you don't mind me saying so, sir, you look as tired as I feel," Lady Ainsley said. "I might take my leave and go and rest before dinner."

Edmund leaned back so that she could kiss her son. As soon as she was gone, Aubrey held the books up. "Bedtime reading?"

When they hopped into bed, however, and opened the first book, Aubrey froze.

"There are runes in this one after all," he said after a moment, "penned in on all the verso pages. Oh, there's a note."

> *Your Highness, we hoped that you might enjoy this book of old stories, which is used in our schools to teach Thasbian script, and that it might demonstrate that our writing does not need to be feared in ordinary circumstances.*
>
> *We will, of course, understand if you decide otherwise.*

Aubrey slipped the note back into the front of the book and closed it. Edmund didn't like the way Aubrey was looking at him, as if he was bracing for something. Edmund stopped himself from saying what he had been about to: that he couldn't feel anything bad coming from those runes. Instead, he took the volume from Aubrey's hand and put it down very deliberately on the table on his side of the bed, and then wrapped his good arm around him.

"We can throw it into the fire, if you want," he said into Aubrey's temple. "Or I can send all the books back to the Honal delegation right now."

Aubrey was still for a moment before sinking into him. "You saw what they were used for," he said. "You know that Saben destroyed all our own records to get rid of them, so they wouldn't hurt anyone else. There might be good, honest uses for them, but . . . they have done so much harm. And we don't know the difference. We apparently didn't know the difference even when we used them."

"I'll get someone to pack them up and return them to the Honals tonight. They said they would understand. I believe them. They've been hurt as well. And—runes are illegal here, after all."

Aubrey examined him for a moment and then pressed a kiss to his mouth.

"Let's just check the other books first," Aubrey said, extracting himself to reach for one, and Edmund suppressed a smile. Then he remembered what he had wanted to ask.

"How did you know? That they were all Seers, in the meeting, and they were holding something back?"

Aubrey held the book to his chest as he searched for words. Eventually his expression turned rueful.

"I don't even know if it's real, to tell the truth, but . . . you know how sometimes in a vision, the Seer knows things? The context of what they're Seeing? So, you might know where you are, even if you've never been there, that sort of thing?"

Edmund nodded.

"Well, now I sometimes . . . seem to know that sort of thing even when I'm awake. I knew that walking to the coast would be the best way to get back into Saben after the earthquake. It wasn't just that it seemed logical; I *knew*, like I knew to look around for someone I recognized when I got to Downfall Cove. Or perhaps it's nothing. Instinct or lucky guesses."

"You did go into Honal's water, though," Edmund said. "You said it healed you. Perhaps that wasn't all it did."

"We could ask the councillors about it," Aubrey said, covering a yawn with the little volume in his hand. "Although I'm worried they might give me another name. Dub me Lord of the Hunches as well as the Waters."

"At least you are a lord of *something* now," Edmund said.

Delight flitted over Aubrey's face for a moment, before being replaced with mock indignation.

"A something you hid *forever* under a *mountain*," he said, and whacked Edmund in his good shoulder with the book.

CHAPTER 27

It was past ten o'clock when Edmund and Aubrey woke up from their nap. They were informed that Lady Ainsley had eaten dinner and retired for the night. They called for supper in their room and went straight back to bed afterward. It had been a long, strange day.

After breakfast, they went downstairs in their morning robes to find Lady Ainsley embroidering in the drawing room where they had sat the previous afternoon. The space looked different in the morning light; or perhaps they were, after a few good meals and a decent night's sleep—together again, finally.

"We're going to read Prince Willard's letters now," Aubrey said.

Lady Ainsley put down her work. "If you would prefer me to leave—"

"No, ma'am," Edmund said. "We hoped you would help us."

He called for some tea, and the three of them sat at a card table staring at the bundle of letters. Edmund found himself reluctant to put his hand out, didn't want the feel of that paper against his skin. He glanced at Aubrey.

"I'll open it, shall I?" Aubrey said, and soon the ribbon was slithering off the package, and the first letter was open in his hand. "This first one is from your uncle to—oh," he said, sitting up a little. "It's to the Pater."

This was all so unsettling. Edmund had *killed* the Pater. Aubrey started to read aloud, but Edmund could not take the words in properly at first. Then Aubrey laughed.

"Goodness, listen to this bit:

> *It seems peculiar to me that you will not speak to our government but still thought fit to write me such a letter. You say that my position marks me as a figure of interest to you, and yet you took the opportunity to insult both my family and my own gifts. I do not tolerate insolence from anyone, let alone from a mere elected official from a place nobody cares about except to hate it. Do not write to me in such a manner again.*"

"No wonder talks between them failed!"

"Yes, well," Lady Ainsley said. "I've seen some of the letters the Pater sent him, and he wasn't wrong to be offended. You'll see that he liked the ones from the Penitent better, and his replies to her are much more polite."

Edmund shifted uncomfortably. Was his own correspondence picked through and copied? That of his parents? Alicia? Were none of them to have any privacy?

And yet, this was the reason.

Aubrey read out the next letter, and the next. A pattern started appearing. Prince Willard would insist the letter he had received was offensive nonsense, and yet he still replied. He started alluding to offers he was being made in exchange for his cooperation. A deal. Several were disturbing: his uncle agreeing that "starting" by destroying the ports would be a wise tactic and replying that yes, munitions were indeed manufactured at Manogate. Aubrey would not read out some parts, which Edmund assumed contained hurtful statements about himself or the rest of the family.

The last one, dated just before his uncle's disappearance, finished very bluntly:

> *I cannot take any of this seriously when surely you must know every Seer in the country says that my weakling nephew is destined to have a long reign over Saben after his father expires. Your offers to increase my magic and put me on the throne can therefore be nothing more than puffery. I do not have anything else to say to you until I see results.*

They all three looked at each other.

"It was a good thing of the council, to think to give these to you," Aubrey said, surprising Edmund yet again. "Like you said, Mother; if these were made public, it would destroy some of the trust that the people have in the royal family. Especially Charlotte, even though you did say nobody believes her to have been involved. Has she been told, though?"

Edmund held his breath as Lady Ainsley spoke. "She was not at any risk that we could see, and it was decided she couldn't have known. There was no benefit to the nation's security in us telling her."

Edmund was shaking his head now. "When she goes to . . . sort through her late father's things, she will find the replies. Or she will ask someone for help and they will find them, which will be worse."

Lady Ainsley cleared her throat delicately. "That has all been taken care of already, Your Highness."

Edmund flushed. Of course the security service had thought of that. Of course they would have snuck in and removed the evidence of his uncle's treason before it could be stumbled upon.

"Well," he said, "I think she ought to be told anyway. It isn't right that I should know this about her father without her knowing it as well."

Aubrey took his hand. Lady Ainsley looked thoughtful.

"It will hurt her," she said. "And that will also be one more person who knows the truth. But . . . it might help your cousin to have more of the picture. If you would like me to take those"—she gestured with an elegant hand at the letters—"we can cross-reference them with the ones we have to make sure that none are missing. We can brief you after that, and you can choose to invite her, if you will."

Edmund nodded.

"Thank you," he said. "For your diligence in service of our country, my lady. I am glad to know that we have people like you working to keep everything . . . right."

"I have four soldier-aged children, Your Highness, and I lost a brother in the last conflict. I could not have stayed at home embroidering while others do their duty. It's not in my nature."

Her brother.

"Aubrey was deliberately given tinctures to bring on visions at the garrison," Edmund said. "Despite the law decreeing that such things must be voluntary. Was my uncle . . . involved in that, as well?"

Lady Ainsley did not quite wince; Edmund tightened his grip on Aubrey's hand.

"Not that we are aware of. That appears to have been unofficial military policy, sir. I'm sorry," she added as he flinched. "John contacted me after he saw it happening at his own camp. It is being investigated. I expect to have news soon, in fact."

Aubrey squeezed his hand.

"Well, then," Edmund said. "There's nothing else to do now but go to Customs House."

They arrived to a greeting party: a small group of journalists camped outside the building, hoping for interviews or at least some information of what was being deliberated between Saben and Honal. They did not receive either. Day two of negotiations with the Honal delegation mostly consisted of discussions of reparations and mining rights, but since nobody would tell the press that, the papers and news sheets chose to focus upon Aubrey's presence instead.

A cartoon of the two young men entering the building together appeared in one of the news sheets the next afternoon, entitled "As They Mean to Continue." Edmund's sling was visible, his white jacket hanging loose over that side, the sleeve with its dragon badge empty. Aubrey was offering Edmund his arm to help him up the stairs. The caption said something about them being a matched pair in their braid and boots, and how everyone could only wish to be as lucky as their prince, to have such an attentive lieutenant at their side. The prime minister was shown off to the side, his arms crossed.

Mattheson handed over the paper silently while helping Edmund change. Lord Dell had been illustrated with an exaggerated sour expression, but neither he nor Aubrey had been caricatured or lampooned in any way that he could see.

"These flowers," Edmund said, pointing to where they had been drawn, climbing up Customs House. "Those aren't actually there."

Mattheson's mouth twitched as he started inspecting Edmund's jacket. "Yes, of course you would notice the plant life, sir," he said.

"Can I see?" Aubrey asked. "Oh, I daresay those are supposed to be peonies and carnations," he said, and when Edmund just looked confused, he added, "They're associated with marriage, darling. The hydrangeas are for perseverance. I expect they're calling us stubborn, there."

"Or the prime minister," Mattheson said. They both stared at him, startled. "Oh, sirs. I think you are the only people in the country to not think the government is being absurd, holding out on their decision about the two of you. You should hear the talk in the kitchens. Lord Dell is not making himself popular."

Edmund let this sink in as he and Aubrey went down to dinner. They took the paper with them to show Lady Ainsley and Sir J, but they were busy with their heads together poring over another news sheet. Edmund couldn't make out their expressions.

"Mother?" Aubrey asked.

Lady Ainsley closed the paper and held it up to them.

The entire front page was devoted to three large words, like an old-fashioned notice. It said LET THEM WED.

Aubrey and Edmund stared at her in confusion.

Lady Ainsley opened the paper to a particular page and handed it to her son.

"Read the editor's letter," she said.

SERIES OF REVELATIONS LEAVES ONE QUESTION

In the weeks since the war ended, the Sabresian public has been startled by revelation after revelation, not the least of which was that our beloved Prince of Fortune was responsible for the earthquake that ended the war, and that Seers all over the nation are reporting that Honal will, during his reign, reunite with Saben.

The government has not revealed any of the details of the peace talks they are currently conducting with Honal's new leaders, but this paper is able to at least report one thing: His Highness is being supported through the negotiations by his long-term companion Lord Aubrey Ainsley. Does this mean that the parliament has decided to allow His Highness and his lordship to marry? And if not, why not? We know that Prince Edmund submitted his petition months ago, and that the prime minister said that the parliament has had more pressing matters to worry about; and yet in the last month alone it has voted on all manner of trivial matters, including an increase in salary for its own members, so we will give that excuse all the respect that it deserves: none.

To have some certainty in this matter would have been such a comfort to them during the last months of the war; a comfort they were denied. Both risked life and limb in service of our country. It seems the least that the members of parliament could do was give them an answer—and yet they did not. I cannot help but feel that their prevarication can have been motivated by nothing more than cruelty and cowardice. But what are they so afraid of? Of setting a precedent they will regret? Or of losing the only thing they have to hold over the head of our crown prince?

Such plays seem unwise. This paper printed, before

the war, an impression of His Highness and his lordship, as they had been spied embracing at the ball held in honor of Princess Alicia's fifteenth birthday. We published such an image with no other goals in mind than to please our readers and to tease a competing publication; but that issue and subsequent pressings of the image have sold more copies than we could ever have imagined. I mention this not to boast, but to point to the funds we raised from their sale as a cold, quantifiable fact that I can use in evidence of this statement: the relationship between Prince Edmund and Lord Ainsley has the support of the people.

I urge the parliament to remember this when they debate the issue, but I primarily urge them to *debate the issue*, rather than leaving these two young people to wait any longer.

This paper plans to print the same cover page every day, until they do.

Aubrey was a teeny bit apprehensive when he got dressed the next day. His mother and Sir J had agreed on one thing last night: the prime minister was going to be very, very annoyed by the previous days' news sheets.

"The man does not like to be surprised, or embarrassed, or criticized in public," Lady Ainsley had said. "It isn't going to help your cause. Prepare for him to be stiff or even rude to you, dearest; and, sir, you should prepare for him to be inflexible in negotiations, since he may very well take it out on the Honals."

As it turned out, however, Lord Dell had no opportunity to be discourteous to Aubrey during their work that day. Two express messengers appeared just as Edmund and Aubrey were leaving for Customs House. Aubrey assumed they would be carrying something for Edmund, or one of the other officials, but one letter was for him and the other, his mother. Furthermore, he needed to sign a receipt for his.

Intrigued, he inspected the message. The seal was from the War Office, and it was not the usual red wax, but green: important official mail. He cracked it open.

> *To Lt. A. Ainsley,*
>
> *This letter is to inform you that you are relieved from duty, effective immediately, pending the results of an investigation into the treatment of Seers by military medical staff. You are to be considered on compulsory leave with full pay, effective from your receipt of this letter. Should you wish to resign your commission, your request will be given priority.*
>
> *If you have any information that might be pertinent to the investigation, please contact the War Office. All communication on this matter will be treated with absolute discretion.*

Aubrey skimmed the rest and looked up, expecting that his mother had received something related, but saw that she was standing stock-still, her face pale, staring at her own message. He went to her instinctively and was shocked when she collapsed into his chest, her hands still around the letter.

She was normally impeccably controlled. He put his arms around her, his brain supplying him with a dozen horrible scenarios—John or Wilson killed in action, Hemcott raided by Honal soldiers and his father murdered, Aunt Dorothea's town house blown up with her asleep in her bed—before reminding himself that the war was over.

"Cedric is in the military hospital in the capital," his mother said into his shoulder. "He's badly injured. A stray explosive device."

She leaned back, handing him her letter. He gave her his own in exchange.

Aubrey scanned hers quickly. Cedric had been inspecting a town that had been attacked by Honal soldiers the day the war had ended. The site had already been given the all clear by the military as safe; Cedric's party was only there as a formality to ensure everything was in order, except that they had come across a concealed explosive that the army had missed.

Cedric and two other clerks had been wounded. Their superior had died at the scene.

"I will leave at once, go back to the capital," Lady Ainsley said, standing up straighter and extricating herself from Aubrey. His immediate feeling was that he should pull her back—she was deathly pale and seemed unsteady on her feet—and he was about to say that he would go with her, but then he recalled where he was. He could not leave Edmund now, not while he was in the middle of doing something so important.

It hit him that his mother must be taking this blow extra hard because it would be bringing back what had happened with her brother after the border conflict: the war should have been over, and yet it hadn't been. He pressed his lips together unhappily as he watched her eyes flit between him and Edmund. He dragged his own eyes over to Edmund as well.

"Aubrey should go with you, my lady," Edmund said. He looked like the words came at a price, but he still said them. Aubrey took his hand.

"It's all right," Edmund said, squeezing his fingers and then letting them go. "You helped me so much. I can see how to manage. Your family needs you now."

The Ainsleys left within the hour.

CHAPTER 28

They arrived at the capital by the late afternoon. Aubrey had been gazing out of the carriage window idly, but his curiosity turned into a relief that became happiness when he saw how changed the capital was.

The last time he had been here, passing through on his way to the garrison, Elmiddan had been a city braced for attack, with most of the shops closed, and the faces too. Now banners and pennants flew with Sabresian dragons and trees everywhere, and everyone looked lighter, as though a burden had been taken from them. The street trees and parks were also putting on a show, not as neat as they used to be but the flowers colorful, enjoying the summer weather.

It took Aubrey a while to recognize what else was new, but he could hardly miss it when they passed an entire city wall covered with LET THEM WED notices. He sprang back, as though he had seen something he oughtn't, but then peeked out again. People had them showing in windows, on doorways, on the sides of vendors' street carts.

His mother was not quite hiding a smile. He wondered how long she'd been waiting for him to react.

"You could have warned me!" Aubrey said.

Her apologetic shrug was as sincere as his own outrage. "We shouldn't be surprised. The people are grateful to their prince. The war could have gone on for a very long time. The border conflict between Hasprenna and Folbrage wasn't resolved for two years, dearest. The civil war in Arnici went on for nearly ten. Edmund saved a lot of lives, hastening its conclusion. The Prince of Fortune smiled on us all, and now the public want to smile back."

Aubrey was spared having to reply by the carriage slowing down. They had arrived at Aunt Dorothea's town house. The sun was just starting to set, and the sky was reflected in the windows in cloudy lines of pink and orange and blue and gray. The front door did *not* have a LET THEM WED notice on it, for which Aubrey was grateful. It was, however, painted such a bright, fashionable red that it made his military coat look a little shabby. He was very much going to enjoy taking the damned thing off and never wearing it again.

"The man of the hour!" his aunt cried when he came inside, grabbing his face with both hands and pulling it down to be kissed. "The entire town is talking of you."

"Oh, forget about that," Aubrey said. "Cedric. Have you seen him? Is there news?"

"I left your brother not one hour ago. It is only his foot they are worried for now; they say he will almost certainly keep his leg."

Aubrey sagged with relief. A foot was much easier to carry on without than an entire leg, he thought, and then caught himself. A year and a half ago, to be grateful for such a thing would not even have occurred to him, but then a year and a half ago, he had never seen someone lose a foot. Or a leg.

He felt his mother move closer to him. He put his arm around her.

"Can we go now?" she asked.

"Visiting hours are over," Dorothea said. "They're very strict about them. And anyway, they had given him poppy for the pain. He fell asleep as I left, mumbling a bit of poetry that did not sound like something he should have repeated in front of an aunt."

Lady Ainsley let herself laugh at that, even though her eyes were still pinched with worry, and Aubrey had a rush of feeling for the two women. Aunt Dorothea took Aubrey's other arm, guiding them farther inside.

"Come and get settled," she said. "Then let's have a nice supper—I have wine—and read the evening papers and play cards, and then we can all go to the hospital in the morning."

The evening papers proved very distracting, as it turned out:

STRATINGFORD TO HAVE NEW MARCHIONESS AS WELL AS NEW MARQUESS

In a move that is sure to break the hearts of many young women up and down the country—and some older ones as well—the most honorable Marquess of Stratingford, James Malmsbury, has submitted banns of marriage to the Stratingford courthouse.

His intended, one Rosalie Tsung, is currently serving as an ensign in the Sabresian army. Before her military service, Miss Tsung is believed to have worked in the Craywick branch of her family's importing business.

> One can only speculate on what the late Lord Stratingford would have said about his heir marrying a merchant's daughter, although given that his first wife was the daughter of a viscountess and his second, of an earl, he might have questioned whether such an unequal match is respectful to the marquessate. One can also imagine that he would be shocked at his eldest son taking such action so quickly after his own death without observing a proper mourning period. Perhaps, in his grief, Stratingford is making an error he might regret.
>
> Or perhaps impatience to marry far beneath oneself has simply come into vogue with the younger set.

Lady Ainsley, seeing Aubrey's face, read the article as well.

"The papers getting through can be a mixed blessing," she said, folding the thing up.

Aubrey shook his head.

"Ensign Tsung," he said, and then forced his teeth to ungrit, "is a very fine woman, and if anyone ever disrespected the Stratingford marquessate, it was Malmy's father, no matter how suitable anyone might consider his marriages."

"And anyone acquainted with the family knows that," Lady Ainsley said. "Do not let this upset you. Please pass on my best wishes to Malmy when you next write to him, dearest."

Aunt Dorothea's maid came in at that point with bread and cheese and wine, and Aubrey allowed himself to be distracted. They did exactly as his aunt had proposed and had a nice supper, played cards, and generally forced themselves to enjoy a respite. Aubrey was grateful for it the next day, because the military hospital was a shock, in more ways than one.

The large, modern building hosted hundreds of patients, all displaying the reality of what the nation had been through. Burns. Limbs ending in bandages instead of feet or hands, or no limbs at all. Fevered voices, crying out incoherently. There were also a lot of bandaged eyes. Aubrey wondered if seeing those would always make him feel an uneasy combination of guilt and gratitude, or if that would fade.

It was the smell that hit Aubrey the hardest, though: sickness and blood and the sharp scent of apothecary supplies. He suddenly couldn't see what was in front of him at all, just the field hospital he had sat in not two weeks ago, holding Edmund's hand, worried; then the medical tents attached to his garrison.

Now that he had no immediate need to buck up and be brave, he found himself frozen on the spot, his mind gone completely blank.

Then someone in a nearby bed called out for their mother, and Aubrey became aware of another smell: the floral notes of his own mother's perfume. He made himself breathe in again, to think about what else was different now, compared with then. There was no smell of gunpowder here, no churned mud.

Aubrey focused on the way that his boots felt on the clean-scrubbed floor as he stepped forward, and the three of them moved on.

It was easier not to think about himself when they reached Cedric's bed. His brother appeared drawn and febrile. His leg was covered in bandages from mid-thigh down to his foot, which was elevated on a cushion as he lay on the bed, a gray blanket arranged around his leg. His eyes were half-closed, not quite focused on the ceiling; they flicked over to his visitors as they got closer, and his brow relaxed, one corner of his mouth tilting up.

for a man who had set up an entire village school so that he wouldn't have to send his sons away, and then had had to watch them all leave him anyway to go and get stabbed and bashed and shot at and exploded.

"It'll grow back," Aubrey said into the side of his father's head, trying to will him to understand everything he meant by that. He felt his mother come around to embrace her husband as well. Aubrey extracted himself and moved out of the way, because Cedric had put his hand out to his father.

"My boy," he murmured, as he took it, but then there was a sudden commotion on the other side of the privacy paneling.

A nurselike voice said, "Sir, I'm afraid I can't let you disturb the family—"

"A family nurturing a *serpent*," someone else replied. "That boy needs to be told that what he's doing is wrong, that he has no right to prevent the Prince of Fortune from making a proper marriage, that—"

The voice was shouting self-righteously now, but also fading. Aubrey peeked out in between two of the panels; two large nurses were forcibly dragging an older man out. There was a chorus of cheers and heckles from the other patients, but Aubrey did catch one voice saying, "Quite right, quite right! Little upstart!"

"I told you," Aunt Dorothea said to him again, but she seemed less happy about it now.

Cedric glanced at her, then at their father, and then at Aubrey.

"You shouldn't be here," Cedric said.

Aubrey swallowed and then managed, "You do not . . . want me?"

Cedric put out the hand that their father was not already holding. Aubrey took it. "I am glad you are here, but, no, I do not. Not while I'm like a bear with a sore head, and while your future is causing so much . . . discussion. Why don't you go home, get some peace while you can. There will be none for you here, I assure you. Anyway, don't you have to go to Marisetown to resign your commission? You are going to, are you not?"

Aubrey was torn. If he wasn't to be in the capital, he really should go back to Edmund. Edmund needed him. But he did want to be out of the army as soon as he could, and the idea of going home felt like stopping for a cool drink on a warm day when there was still work to be done outside.

Aubrey looked around. His mother and his aunt's expressions appeared neutral, but it was the hope on his father's tired, thin face that settled it for him.

"All right," he said.

CHAPTER 29

Edmund arrived back at the residence after another day of discussing details with officials about how the temporary Principality of Honal would work. Very little had been accomplished. Everything had dissolved into squabbling over details, and Edmund felt as though his brain had been poured into a clock, each cog turning around and around to no purpose other than to process time. The prime minister had been very stiff, while Dame Edwina had seemed impatient with everybody present except for himself, which had made him uncomfortable in a different way.

He was sure that if Aubrey had been there, he would have said something to diffuse the tension or help Edmund explain himself. Edmund felt like all his failings were suddenly on display, and everyone would be able to see how spectacularly he would let Saben's next province down.

"Are you all right, sir?" Mattheson asked, and Edmund started. His valet was holding a banyan out for him. His posture suggested that he had been doing so for a while.

"No," Edmund said, letting the man put the robe onto him. He then sat down to pen notes to the ambassadors informing them that he required a day of recess; and then he wrote to his parents for help.

The queen arrived the next evening with a retinue of ladies in tow—even more than usual. Edmund was not familiar with any of them. They were not in uniform, instead wearing austere dresses with cropped jackets in military colors and braid detailing. These designs had come into civilian fashion, Aubrey had said, as a show of support for the troops.

The queen waved everyone inside.

"Sweetheart," she said, putting her arms out. He returned the hug with his good arm and managed to get his buttons tangled in the rope of her aiguillettes.

"I'm going to bathe," she said, extracting herself, "and then I want you to tell me everything. Also, have you been out into the town at all?"

Edmund shook his head.

"Well," she said, her expression complicated, "you should know that every single shopfront in the main street has one of those notices up in the window, saying that you and Aubrey should be allowed to wed."

Edmund felt his face heat up.

"Oh" was all that he managed to reply.

When she called for him an hour later, his mother was swathed in a soft embroidered dressing robe in shades of dark pink and yellow, but she was still all business. She presented him with a series of letters she'd had drafted before she came, and then a pile of documents. Every sheaf that he read made him feel a little better—he was not alone in this; all he'd had to do was ask for help and his mother had given him a plan of action complete with legal paperwork—as did learning that her entourage was not noble, idle ladies-in-waiting at all, but clerks, attorneys, and bureaucratical experts.

He was so grateful that she had agreed to come. It was, however, impossible for him not to feel at least somewhat nervous the next day, when they got to Customs House.

"I was surprised," Queen Margaret said as she sat down at the table next to Lord Dell, "to learn that this group has not yet approved a single preliminary document. Only this morning, Edmund wrote to Nordan and Frithay to launch trade discussions, now that the waters around Honal are safe, and I could not help but think that it would be quite embarrassing if those nations are quicker to establish these agreements with Honal than Saben is."

The silence that followed was so profound, it sat like something physically in the room with them. After a few moments, Edmund glanced over at the Honal delegation. They were so still, they seemed almost frozen in place. Chief Councillor Whit, in particular, put Edmund to mind of someone who had unexpectedly found themselves in the presence of a wild animal they were attempting to befriend and was being careful not to make any sharp or sudden movements.

The Sabresians found their tongues as quickly as they had lost them. There was a confusion of protest before Lord Dell's voice won out. He spluttered something about political action by the royal family being unconstitutional without the approval of parliament, and the queen's eyes flickered over to Edmund. She had warned him that Lord Dell might say something like this. His stomach was in knots, but he straightened his shoulders.

"Saben's constitution is not relevant here, since I was acting as the monarch of Honal." He had practiced the words in front of a mirror in his bedchamber earlier that morning. "Honal is vulnerable right now, and I have made it more so by calming the waters around it and thus removing one of its defenses against attack from its northern neighbors. Those neighbors needed to know that the country is now under my protection."

Lord Dell was blotchy now and wide-eyed. "Sir, you cannot threaten Nordan and Frithay!"

This, Edmund had not prepared for. He blinked at his father's prime minister. "Why would I threaten them? I informed them of the situation and invited their ambassadors to come and meet with me and the Honal high council, to discuss opening diplomatic and trade channels. Given our recent . . . miscommunication with the Nordans, I even offered to visit them instead, and suggested I would not be averse to touring farmland while there. Hopefully that will help ease the path a little."

"You—" Lord Dell was staring at him, the blotchiness receding, leaving white patches. "You cannot do that! You can't use your gift so—so casually in other countries—our Thasbian allies—"

"I also thought to offer to visit them, Lord Dell, to show our gratitude for their assistance during this war. Especially since, as we have discussed"—Edmund took a deep breath—"my plans for marriage do not include any of their royal houses."

Resentment flickered over the man's features. Not the indignation or outrage he had expressed so often in this room, but the less helpful sort of anger you saw on the faces of people used to getting their own way, who had nevertheless been thwarted. It was gone as quickly as it had come, but Edmund's heart still sank. He straightened his shoulders again and forced his voice to be steady and gentle. "This way, I can give of myself to them freely—to *all* of them—to everyone's benefit."

It was Dame Edwina who found her tongue next.

"That is a good thought," she said, "although—and with all due respect, Your Highness—you are not Honal's head of state yet. The lawyers have still not been able to work out if it is within our law for you to hold a title in another country, even one that is to be joined with our own when you become king, and the government has not signed off on any of this. There is no precedent for it."

"I do not see why that should matter," Edmund said. "Your government passes new laws all the time. As it is, the delays in this room ran the risk of hurting the people of Honal, and I could not have that. I *will* do my duty to them as they have asked me to."

He let his eyes shift to his mother. She gave him a satisfied nod—as well she might, since she was the one who had suggested that phrasing—and sat back in her chair, as though nothing more need be said on the matter.

"Thank you, Your Highness," Councillor Whit said into the silence. The Sabresian party watched as the councillor glanced to his colleagues on his left and right and then bowed his head low. The rest of the Honals followed suit, and Edmund felt his face heat up. He turned back to Lord Dell.

"If the government requires me to consult with Saben's parliament before I take such actions, then you need to organize that with me. Until you do, I have to act as I see fit."

He worried he was sounding defensive and forced his voice to be softer. "You know firsthand that I have always been willing to work for and with my country, Prime Minister. I have never shirked my harness. There's work to be done now. Let's get on with it."

He looked back to the queen, and he was the one who nodded this time, to signal to his mother to go ahead. She glanced over her shoulder and waved a gloved hand, and then the room was invaded by her legal army, all holding draft documents waiting for approval and signatures.

There were no surprises in any of the papers, nothing that had not already been discussed and agreed upon in principle. The drafts were read over, debated, improved, and signed by sunset.

Aubrey read about the signings in the newspapers the next day. The day after that, he read that the parliament planned to discuss the crown prince's marriage over the coming weeks.

His father upped his subscriptions so that they covered every major publication, delivered express from the agent in Marisetown.

"They are going to be talking about my son," he said. "I resent it, but I can't do anything about it, and at least this way I will know what they're saying."

"Do not worry," Aubrey said, worrying a great deal. "You know that it's not even really about me. Everyone just wants something nice to talk about. Love, not war."

His father held up the cartoon from the most popular news sheet from that morning, showing the prime minister depicted as a snail. An ugly one. It was titled "Lord Delaying Continues to Delay Lucky Prince's Happiness."

"Yes, very nice," Lord John Ainsley said.

He turned the page and held that up as well. "'The MPs expected to oppose the match include Lord Fallset, who has been heard around the capital saying that he believes in tradition and wants to support the spirit of the Royal Marriages Act. One wonders how all of the other women rumored to be involved in his own marriage feel about this, given that traditionally there should only be one.'"

Aubrey snorted with laughter.

"It's getting *personal*," his father said with his eyebrows raised. "I want you to understand how much more personal this could get."

His father was proved right the very next day. The newspapers reported that Lord Fallset was booed on his way to parliament. The news sheets printed more scathing reports of the other MPs thought to be opposed, and while Aubrey felt that he should be grateful to be supported, he found himself wishing it were not like this, especially since the day after that, one of the newspapers ran a piece, for the sake of "balance," from "a loyal Sabresian" who was against the match.

There were a lot of statements about convention and custom that didn't really hold water when Aubrey thought about them later, and a swath of others that were simply irrelevant. Aubrey was most offended, though, by the attacks made on Edmund and by extension the entire royal family. The article concluded by saying that any prince who would divide the country like this was clearly more interested in getting his own way than in doing his duty and that they would all be better off without him, and perhaps he should just go off to Honal, since he seemed to like the place so much now.

A flurry of angry letters to the editor from readers were printed in response to this, which heartened Aubrey greatly, but then the paper produced a follow-up piece, this time from a "patriot" saying that while they did not agree with every sentiment expressed by the previous author, they had made some relevant points, including that a king must think of his country first.

Most irritating for Aubrey, though, was when the writer concluded by quoting "the embroidered love letter" as an example of unselfish devotion, compared to "the carryings on we are seeing right now":

> What its many enthusiasts miss so often is that, despite being full of passion, its writer manages to also

be modest; and though clearly facing some obstacle, perhaps the same sort of withholding of approbation from their lover's family as Lord Ainsley faces from the parliament, their writing suggests that they would be happy with whatever arrangement can be managed. It is a shame neither His Highness nor his lordship can manage this humility.

Aubrey flung the paper across the room after reading this, causing pages to fly everywhere, and stomped out.

The full humor hit him when he was about halfway up the stairs, and by the time he'd reached his bedchamber, he was no longer interested in sulking. Instead, he reached for paper and ink, considering what to write to make the absolute most of the drama of the situation.

He then proceeded to walk at a smart pace to the post office in the village to send the letter before he could talk himself out of it.

CHAPTER 30

Aubrey's letter was published two days later. He had not expected to see it in print so quickly and was therefore surprised when he went down to breakfast to find his father with his most sardonic face on. The man picked up the newspaper in a very deliberate fashion and read aloud:

To the Editor,

I write to you in response to an opinion piece that you recently published from a "patriot" suggesting that I emulate the example of the writer of the "embroidered love letter," as it is being called.

I was quite dumbfounded by this proposal, given that the pen responsible for that particular missive was my own. Up until that point in the column, I had been willing to forgive this unnamed patriotic person's didactic tone and apparent dislike of me, personally, but when they suggested that I should try to be more like my own self and take notice of my own modesty, their argument reached such heights of absurdity that I felt I could not, as a gentleman, allow the situation to continue.

It will no doubt be a surprise to you to learn the identity of the letter's writer—not to mention a scoop for your publication to be able to reveal it—but you can understand how my humility would have made me disinclined to come forward before now.

Should you have any doubts about my claim, I would recommend, given that your office still carries what is left of said letter (and are making quite a profit selling copies of it), that you compare its hand with the one I am conveniently providing you with, via this document.

Once you are satisfied, I would appreciate either the letter's return to me, or for you to pass it on to its intended recipient, whose identity you can perhaps deduce.

Most humbly yours,
A. Ainsley

His father handed him the paper. The letter was followed by an N.B. from the editor, confirming that Aubrey's handwriting did indeed match the letter they had on file and that they had sent the original on to "the appropriate person."

"A quiet life," his father said. "All I wanted for you boys was a quiet life, where you could live freely, away from the pressures of the court and the capital. But you've done it now. There'll be rioting in the streets if the parliament doesn't let you marry him, you mark my words."

Aubrey had assumed his father was being overdramatic, but when John arrived home two days later on rest leave, the first thing he said to his baby brother was "Well played, Aubrey."

"The letter to the editor, you mean?"

"The streets of Elmiddan are now lined with demands that the government let you and Edmund wed."

"Yes, but they were already—I saw that with Mother—all those newspaper covers."

"Oh no," John said. "No, now it's in giant letters drawn with chalk down all the main roads. People have been chanting 'Lord Delaying' at the prime minister's carriage when it goes past in the street. And you should know that a section of your letter was graffitied along the walls around parliament house. 'The colors of you are painted over my soul' made it onto the gate."

Aubrey sank his face into his hands.

"I possibly forgot how intimate that letter was," he said, his voice muffled by his own palms, and John laughed.

"They'll vote soon. The minister for defense, of all people, put forth a special motion yesterday to speed things up, and it was supported by other MPs. They have agreed to debate it on Wednesday."

Aubrey's head twitched back up. "But that is tomorrow!"

John smiled. "So it is."

Edmund felt like he couldn't breathe.

He was riding in the carriage back to Elmiddan with Sir J. He had not returned at the same time as his mother and the rest of the Sabresian officials, instead staying for an extra day to discuss practical matters with the Honal high council. They'd required his authorization to set up royal residences for him, to mint new coins with his profile on them, to rename governmental departments to reflect the change in leadership. The list went on and on.

He'd refused some things, because there was so much politics involved, and he needed more time to think, to get it right. He had outright rejected their offer to fit him for traditional Honal robes or a Honal military uniform, even though he was now theoretically their commander. He had also refused to name a date when he would come to Honal in person, since he knew he would have to be seen putting Saben first when it came to touring farmland. Every refusal was easier than the last, but the day had still been exhausting; and then, just as he had hoped to be allowed to leave Customs House, a coach had arrived carrying the last three surviving Honal sorcerers. He had not expected to have them literally delivered to him.

Two of them had died on the trip.

Edmund felt his stomach sink when the last one was presented, strapped into the sort of chair invalids used. His posture was even more stooped than it had been the last time Edmund had seen him, but he recognized the man's strangely wide eyes and long, thin form immediately.

"This is the Cultivator, sir," Chief Councillor Whit murmured to him.

"No," Edmund found himself saying. "That is the title he was given when he held office. He is not to be called that now."

The councillor looked at him in surprise and approval and then bowed his head in agreement. Edmund wondered how ignorant Whit thought him about Honal customs and felt guilt prickle at him, since he *was* woefully uninformed on the country he had agreed to protect; but that was a problem for another day.

"You," the man said from his chair, his voice weak but still vicious. "If there was any justice in the world, I would have strength enough to stand right now and kill you with my bare hands."

"Is that how you killed my uncle?"

The words were too unguarded. He had not planned to say them, but he was overwhelmed. The horrible man started to laugh.

"We didn't kill your uncle. It was the water. It did not want him. But we still found a use for him . . ."

His voice cracked with fluid on the final words, and he started to cough. The man made no effort to cover his mouth; spittle went flying. A long string of phlegm, red with blood, landed around his chin.

"See to the prisoner's care while he is in our custody," Edmund said to the attendants before turning away. "I will inform the prime minister that he is here."

The man tried to call out after him. Edmund heard something about the "natural order" that sounded like a threat, but he wasn't particularly interested. This was all just so wretched.

He received word the next morning that the Cultivator had died overnight.

So that was it. The last of the Honal sorcerers was dead.

His death did not have Edmund struggling to breathe in the carriage, however. No, that was because even now, as he traveled, the parliament was debating his petition to marry. The anticipation had him tapping his feet and hands nervously against the door as they trundled along, his mood causing the wind outside to blow chaotically. He'd tried to control it after he'd seen a group of young men's top hats go flying, but he kept forgetting. All he could think of was the vote.

It felt so foolish to be anxious now after all the events of the last week; of the last *year*. But he was so worn out, and the decision was being made today. He reminded himself of his plan to just petition again if the parliament voted no. Aubrey would be patient, and the entire country now knew it, after that letter Aubrey had written to the newspaper.

Edmund felt his mouth twitch upward in something that might have been a smile, another day. Heavens, that letter.

The carriage rattled on for another minute or two, and then Sir J, who was clearly aware of Edmund's nerves, finally said, "You could always just get married in Honal."

Edmund looked at him.

"If the parliament votes against the match, I mean," Sir J added.

Edmund looked at him for a little longer.

"No," he said, and that was the last conversation they had for a while.

They were nearly at Talstam Palace when the carriage stopped. Edmund could hear a commotion ahead.

"Now what?" Sir J muttered, banging on the roof of the carriage.

"I'm sorry, sirs," the coachman called out. "There are people in the street. Some sort of celebration. We might need to take a different way."

"What are they doing? Can they not do it off the road, or at least make way for a royal coach?" Sir J was grumbling when Edmund was struck with a thought. He opened the flap and stuck his head out the window.

The crowd was cheering and waving papers in the air. It took him a moment to make out that they were LET THEM WED notices. He watched a young man writing the words "my soul" in chalk on the footpath before Edmund quickly ducked his head back inside.

"I think it's for me. The parliament must have voted. Oh heaven," he said, feeling suddenly like insects were crawling all over him, but Sir J was already sticking his own head out of the window with an uncharacteristic lack of dignity.

"What is it?" he yelled to the crowd. "Is the prince to be a husband?"

"Yes!" a nearby woman replied, running over to tuck a flower behind his ear. "They voted yes!"

Sir Jenson peered at Edmund, and whatever he saw in his expression made him yell at the coachman to "Just go, man!" Somehow, the crowd must have parted for a royal coach after all, because they were back at the palace quicker than Edmund would have imagined.

The coachman stopped at the main entrance, and Edmund all but flew out. He ran up the five front steps. Someone opened the door for him, and then Alicia came out of a door down the corridor, motioning at him frantically to come in. He spared a look behind him; Sir Jenson waved him on. He ran to his sister, who dragged him into the king and queen's favorite drawing room.

His parents were sitting on a sofa listening to a string quartet, his father's leg bandaged and elevated on a footstool. The king waved at them to stop playing.

"His Highness's mail from today, his mail," the queen was calling over her shoulder to the servants, but one of the footmen was already coming forward with a silver salver, slightly wild-eyed.

There were two letters. The bigger one was from Lord Dell, the seal official. The thick wax cracked loudly, as Edmund broke it open. His eyes skimmed over the words, catching *officially approve your request* and *my private compliments.* He threw the thing in disgust at Alicia, who was dancing next to him, and snatched up the other one, which was from the minister for defense.

Your Highness,

My warmest congratulations for your future felicity.

Your humble servant,
Prestan

"Can we send for Aubrey now?" Alicia asked, and Edmund glanced up in time to see her thrusting the prime minister's letter in turn at their mother. "Edmund, write to him at once!"

"No," he said, trying to wipe his eyes discreetly. He glanced over at the musicians, who looked enraptured. The servants were all watching him too. He decided he didn't care. "No, I want to go and get him. I want to go now. Papa, can I go now?"

"You have only just arrived here!" his father said, but he was spoken over by Alicia crying, "Go on horseback immediately! It's more romantic!"

"Yes, arrive stinking of horse and tired from the ride. Very romantic," the queen said. "You will do no such thing. You will use one of the finer carriages and take a route through every single city and town you can along the way, so that everyone can see what you're doing and feel like they are all a part of it."

Edmund turned to his father for his input. The king only shrugged.

"I've just finished a book John loaned me," he said. "Can you take that with you as well?"

His wife hit him with a cushion.

Edmund's meandering route from Elmiddan took so long, he arrived not the following lunchtime, but the day after that. Aubrey was practically expiring from anticipation.

A messenger came from the palace ahead of Edmund to let Aubrey know that the vote had passed, and that the prince was on his way. Aubrey contemplated and dismissed several scenarios for the moment of Edmund's arrival and decided in the end to set himself up with tea and a novel at a little table under a tree in the garden with a view of the road, close to the entrance of the house where the carriage would stop. He meant to paint a picture of a simple country gentleman lounging in pleasant idleness, taken unawares with his coat undone; but when Edmund arrived with his procession, surrounded by guards and with the carriage hood down, Aubrey could see how wild his prince's eyes were. He immediately dropped his book and stood up, locking eyes with Edmund. The prince called out for the coachman to stop and practically leapt from the carriage while it was still moving, so Aubrey strode forward to meet him. He took Edmund's head in his hands and kissed him.

Edmund was trembling, but Aubrey held him tight, and he felt the moment when his poor, worried prince believed it and surrendered, his body relaxing.

Edmund pulled back to touch their foreheads together. "I am yours. I get to be yours."

"Yes, but whatever took you so long?"

There was the crunch of gravel behind them; both John Ainsleys had come out of the house, along with the housekeeper. They all bowed. Edmund bowed back.

"Father," Aubrey called out, "a prince has come. He wants to take me away and marry me. Is that all right?"

"Well, Cook is expecting four for dinner, so he'll have to wait until tomorrow to carry you off," Lord Ainsley said, getting out of the way as the housekeeper started motioning the driver around to the stables.

"Wait, my lord," Edmund said, walking toward them. "We would not inconvenience you; we can stay at—"

"You can stay here," Aubrey's father said. "Your Highness," he added, a twinkle in his eye. Aubrey knew that twinkle.

Edmund shook his head.

"I would . . . that is, please will you call me Edmund from now on, sir?"

His father regarded him for a long moment. "We'll see, son," he said finally. "Come on, let's get you settled before dinner."

And then he turned and walked away up the corridor. Edmund, his face reddening, followed him.

"What's that look?" Aubrey asked.

"I've never been inside your house," Edmund said a little helplessly, and Aubrey took his hand and pulled him over the threshold.

EPILOGUE

The morning of the wedding arrived, clear and bright. It was late autumn, the earliest auspicious date that could be arranged. Edmund had wanted sooner but had been more or less laughed at for vastly underestimating both how long it took to plan a wedding, and how grand his own would have to be. Everything was a bit rushed as it was—the palace had wanted to wait until the following spring—but Edmund would not hear of it.

As was traditional, two separate breakfasts were held that day in the palace. Alicia had threatened to attend Aubrey's instead of her brother's, but since she was part of Edmund's attendant party, he had known she was only teasing. Mostly.

Edmund could barely eat. He half wanted to run off to Aubrey's breakfast himself. There were so many people at his event: dignitaries and distant relatives whom he hadn't seen in years. He knew he had to act in a manner that befitted his station, but he knocked over his water goblet and accidentally made several of the nearest potted plants grow to twice their size. When a Hasprennan cousin tried to make a joke about how nervous he looked, all his knowledge of the man's language flew out of his head.

Edmund would not be comfortable until the ceremony was over. He just wanted everything set in stone.

As for Aubrey, he was thoroughly enjoying his own breakfast. They had little cakes and cinnamon buns and oats topped with fruit compote—sweet foods for a sweet marriage—and the most wonderful hot chocolate, topped with cream.

It was a much smaller affair than Edmund's but was notable as the first society appearance from the new Lord and Lady Stratingford. They had married a month earlier in a quiet ceremony at the Stratingford courthouse with only their families and the celebrant present. Malmy had used his newly inherited clout to have both himself and Rosalie discharged from the army as quickly as possible, so they were free to go wherever they pleased. Rosalie had quietly told Aubrey that had mostly meant their marital bed.

The dowager marchioness was not invited to Aubrey's breakfast, but Malmy's aunt Harriet came. Aubrey took the opportunity to make sure that she knew how highly he esteemed his friend's bride, and what a fine woman he thought that she was.

"Oh, you don't need to tell me," she said, patting him on the arm. "Look at how happy James is. But what about this prince of yours? It's not too late to run, you know. A little bird like you, letting yourself be caged so soon. Are you sure?"

Aubrey just gave her a big smile.

The wedding itself was, of course, glorious.

Edmund stood in front of the master of ceremonies, smothered in a vast green cloak trimmed with some sort of very soft white fur, with a heavy crown on his head, and waited for Aubrey.

A loud instrument blasted.

He saw Aubrey's brothers in the procession first; as his groomsmen, they went ahead of him. They were in age order, with Wilson pushing Cedric in a wheeled chair, since his amputation was still healing.

One of the organizers had tried to protest Cedric's inclusion, saying something vague about setting the right tone for the day. When Edmund had asked what she had meant, she had looked uncomfortable and said something about unsightliness and delays to the ceremony's rhythm and spoiling the mood.

"It just isn't fitting," she had concluded, and Edmund had finally understood.

"We have just been at *war*," he had replied, feeling annoyed beyond belief. "It is *perfectly* fitting. The king himself now needs a cane. The doctors tell me my own arm will never be the same."

He had been about to start listing the numbers of dead, of injured, of the requests he was receiving to open memorials, like the park that was being planned at the farming village at Mester, where the garrison of soldiers had been killed near the start of the war. Then Aubrey had put his hand on his leg, and Edmund had known that he did not need to argue with these people.

Instead, Edmund informed them that all three of Aubrey's brothers would be attending him. Now here they were. He nodded at them—shortly to be his own brothers—and then there was Aubrey, dressed in a huge cloak that matched Edmund's own. They were both completely dwarfed by them, but it was traditional. Aubrey had seemed a bit startled by the idea of wearing something that looked like it belonged on a wall, but that wasn't visible on his face now. He was smiling his biggest, most dazzling smile, and Edmund felt as struck in the chest by it as the first time he had seen it.

The event mostly went as planned. All the papers reported that, halfway through the ceremony, every plant within a mile started to bloom and grow, the Crown Prince clearly overset. Only the news sheets, however, were bold enough to make mention of his composure breaking down right at the end, when the two young men were pronounced married, and how he grabbed the newly created Prince Aubrey into his arms, nearly knocking Aubrey's new crown off his head.

They could not, however, report what Edmund said to him when he pulled back, since no one but Aubrey heard.

"They can't take me away from you, after this," he said. "They can't separate us."

"You really are *my* prince now," Aubrey replied, and Edmund laughed.

"And now you're my prince too."

The news sheets knew from experience, however, what would sell best. One of them printed an illustration showing the two princes in this moment, wide smiles lighting their faces; another, a few days later, showed them leaning into each other as they settled into the carriage to leave afterward. Just as last time, they managed to avoid a fine from the censor by just a hair's breadth.

A rumor circulated that the two papers had colluded to make sure that their pictures were suitably different and would not eat into each other's sales. Each denied this. Aubrey told Edmund about it with gossipy relish, in the dressing chamber at the residence they were honeymooning in: a half-crumbling castle picked for its location, which was as close to the middle of nowhere that Saben had to offer. Wilderness, no press, and no associations with the war for either of them.

"I bet they did," Edmund said. "Plan it, I mean."

Aubrey nodded. "That is very possible, husband," he said, and then laughed immoderately when this made said husband launch himself at him.

"Say it again," Edmund demanded, his face buried in his neck.

"Husban—" Aubrey said, lingering on every letter, making each one a syllable in its own right, the last muffled by Edmund kissing him. After an interval, Aubrey added, "Though I shall say it differently when I am cross with you." He affected a haughty, unimpressed tone. "What do you think you are doing, husband? You're killing the lawn, husband. Do you think you could stop freezing the room, husband? You'll damage the paneling."

He would have gone on, but Edmund was kissing him again.

This is what the rest of our lives will look like, he promised himself, and held Aubrey tighter.

ACKNOWLEDGMENTS

It is such a privilege to be writing this final page. So many people helped to get this story into its ultimate shape, and I have many thanks to give.

To my wonderful agent, Jim McCarthy, for his seemingly endless patience and professionalism.

To the team at Simon & Schuster: most especially my editor, Kristie Choi, whose enthusiasm for the project has meant the world to me; Reka Simonsen for putting the story into her hands in the first place; and Jeannie Ng, Kaitlyn San Miguel, and Tatyana Rosalia for all their care with the book's production.

To Serena Archetti for her absolutely dreamy cover artwork; Feyta for our map, which almost made me cry; and Rebecca Syracuse and Lisa Vega for all their work in making this such a beautiful book.

To Writers Victoria, not just for community but for offering such an amazing program of courses for members over the years. The opportunity to learn from so many wonderful Australian writers was immensely helpful. Speaking of community: I don't think I could have survived without the Submission Slog Comrades and the LGP Discord servers, for being there for sharing info and emotional support, as well as the 2025 Debuts Discord server, who did not kick me out when my publication date was moved, and the 2024 debuts Slack group, for taking me in.

To everyone who read various early forms of this story, especially my critique partners C. D. Hunt and Erin Schultz, who gave me such helpful feedback and encouragement with the first drafts; Xine Rose, for more generalized help; Vicki and Vanessa, for somehow managing to deliver the advice "you should delete most of the first half" in the most delightful way possible; R. Lee Fryar, for casting fresh eyes over a much later version and loving Edmund; and to Felicity, who read every incarnation and loved each one.

Lastly, to Katie, for lending both moral support and her dining table, when I needed to write somewhere I wouldn't be distracted; to Jason, for being right by my side through some of the hardest experiences of my life, while the book was in its infancy; and to Abby, for the story's very first fanart, even though she knew she wasn't supposed to be drawing in my notebook.

I am grateful for you all.